Healed

Jennifer Lanzilotti

Published by Mirror Publishing
Fort Payne, AL 35967
www.pagesofwonder.com

Printed in the USA

Preface
Central Pacific Ocean

The pain ripped across her abdomen as Lily McCallister focused on her breathing. The aircraft dipped, sending her hand scrambling for the support of the armrest beside her.

"Hang in there, baby. I'll speak to the pilot." Patrick gently rubbed her shoulder. "We've got this, Lil. It's going to be alright."

"I can't believe the baby's choosing now!" She gritted her teeth against another wave of pain.

Patrick surveyed the small cabin. If only one more soul had boarded, he wouldn't be in the position to deliver his own child. Though he had read some books in anticipation of this scenario, the reality of the situation caused a sense of panic. Another turbulence-induced jolt sent him stumbling.

"Go!" She suppressed a scream. "Find out what's happening with this plane!" As he hurried towards the cockpit, she frantically rummaged through her suitcase, casting aside clothing as water trickled down her legs. She was going to give birth on the grimy cabin floor. Removing her wet undergarments beneath her skirt, she almost fell over, but Patrick's arms wrapped around her, guiding her gently to the floor.

"I've got good and bad news... which do you want first?" He spread t-shirts to create a makeshift birthing space.

She could barely speak; the intensity of the contraction overwhelming. "Just tell me something! Our baby is coming!" She reached for his hand.

"The good news is the pilot believes we can stay airborne for another twenty minutes." Another contraction wracked her body. "And the bad news… we're down to one engine, the landing gear won't deploy, and the fuel is nearly gone." He lifted her skirt, his hands trembling. "I can see the head, Lil! This is it, baby. Let's welcome our little one into the world."

The contraction surged through her as she pushed against the pain. So many emotions flooding her mind. How would they protect their child when they were constantly on the run? She'd had three different identities in a short time, traveling from Australia to Canada to Jamaica, and their last escape had been from Hawaii. Regret gnawed at her for boarding the old plane, unused for a decade. She should have listened to her instincts and refused to fly.

"That's it, Lil! Just one more push!" His heart pounded. He couldn't bear leaving this world without seeing their child. His love for Lily was fierce. Every decision he made, every action he took, revolved around her safety. She was his anchor, his reason for being, and as long as he had her, he felt complete.

The pilot's voice crackled through the static, a warning to prepare for impact. The plane bounced up and down as their newborn slid into Patrick's trembling hands.

"I love you, Lily!" His voice caught in his throat, tears of emotion welling in his eyes. "We have a…"

The plane hit the ground.

Chapter 1

2068
Jacksonville, Florida

Over a hundred teenagers gathered in the courtyard of the Saving Souls Orphanage, anticipation thick in the air as they awaited the administrator's address. Mr. Jamerson, a short, balding man with a neatly trimmed beard and mustache, seldom held assemblies, reserving them typically to introduce new arrivals.

"How much longer does he plan to keep us waiting?" Julie grumbled, squinting against the harsh sunlight that beat down from the glass dome above. She glanced at her warm arm, resenting the lack of shade inside the courtyard.

"I told you to stand in the shade." Caleb glanced to his right, where a cluster of students stood crammed together, each holding their precious spot under the shade of palm trees that lined only one side of the glass wall. Through narrowed eyes, the uniformed figures blended into a cream-colored blob.

"It's too crowded over there," Julie retorted, gathering her curtain of blond hair into a ponytail.

The orphanage was an edifice surrounded by an all-glass dome. Seen from a distance, it looked like an enormous greenhouse with clear glass panels. Large leafy shrubs grew wild around the glass as a wall, blocking the view of the white brick building within. The courtyard was attached to the school, offering the sense of being outdoors, except the glass walls and ceiling kept the children from feeling the wind. Tall palms lined half the glass wall, providing shade from the rising sun. If the kids felt like they were in a glass cage, they didn't voice it. Perhaps it was because they believed what they'd been taught. The glass was there for protection.

"Oh my gosh, is that the new O?" Amy asked, leaning around Julie to look at her best friend, Cassie. "He isn't wearing the uniform yet."

"Wow," Julie smiled. "He's a definite ten."

Caleb crossed his arms in annoyance and muttered under his breath. His irritation at Julie's shallow comment went unnoticed as she fixed her attention on the newcomer.

Cassie remained absorbed in her book, paying little attention to her friends. She was more interested in the history book Mrs. Reynolds had given her after class— a cherished subject. The orphanage's limitations on historical knowledge made each book a treasure. She eagerly accepted any information her teachers offered. She'd heard Julie's comment but hadn't cared enough to glance up.

"Hey, check him out!" Amy nudged Cassie, breaking her concentration from the book she had been engrossed in. "Seriously, Cass, put the book down for a sec and look at the new guy. Doesn't he look older than seventeen to you?"

With three hundred and sixty kids living in the orphanage, Cassie limited her interactions to her own age group. While she recognized the faces of many of the other residents, she maintained a reserved demeanor and wasn't particularly social. The arrival of yet another orphan, aka new O, didn't excite her the way it did Julie and her closest friend, Amy.

"I've been made aware of certain... activities occurring after lights out," Mr. Jamerson's stern voice cut through the murmurs of the gathered students. "It's important to remind you all that mingling between boys and girls is strictly prohibited once curfew has been enforced."

Cassie snapped her paperback shut, casting a wary glance at the administrator. Though Mr. Jamerson made her uneasy, he had her attention now. She exchanged a nervous look with Amy, who brushed her brown bangs aside to see better. She had recently cut her hair, convinced her forehead was too prominent, and now struggled with her bangs. Cassie tried to warn her bangs would be a mistake.

"I will not repeat myself," Jamerson continued, his tone stern. "Anyone found breaking curfew or engaging in unauthorized contact will face severe consequences." His gaze swept over Cassie's friends—Julie, Amy, Caleb, and Andrew—before settling on her. "Now, onto more pleasant matters. Allow me to introduce our newest addition to the orphanage." With a sweeping gesture, he indicated the young man beside him. "This is Shane Webster. He has recently experienced a tragic loss, and I trust you all will extend him the compassion and understanding he deserves."

"I'll be sure to give him a warm welcome," Julie whispered with a sly grin, prompting Cassie to roll her eyes.

"I hope you all will make Shane feel welcome during his time here. Show him the ropes, make him feel at home. Although his stay will be brief, I'm confident you'll make it memorable." Mr. Jamerson addressed the assembled students, extending a handshake to Shane before passing him the neatly folded standard uniform.

"It's a shame he'll have to change." Julie's gaze lingered on Shane's rugged appearance—tight, torn jeans, a black t-shirt, and combat boots offering an air of toughness. She couldn't help but notice Cassie's discreet observation and frowned slightly.

Caleb thrust his face into Julie's line of sight. "Aren't you more concerned that the administrator seems aware of our activities than what Shane's wearing? He looked right at us during the warning."

"They don't have any evidence." She dismissed Caleb's concerns with a wave of her hand. "If they did, they'd be making a bigger fuss. Besides, they're clueless about the tunnel we found. They'll never suspect we're planning an escape from this glass prison."

Amy crossed her arms. "I'm not doing it again," she inclined her head towards Cassie. "We're done. It's too risky. Sneaking out of our rooms was one thing, but venturing beyond the school walls into

9

the unknown? It's reckless. The glass dome is there for our protection, and we should respect that."

Andrew, who always listened to his friends but often remained more silent, chuckled. "And you believe that?" He glanced at his roommate Caleb, who was still frowning intensely at Julie.

Surprise flickered in Amy's brown eyes. "Don't you?" They had all been warned about the dangers beyond the glass dome's safety—the orphanage's rules and regulations designed to shield them from harm.

"Maybe." Andrew folded his arms. He had doubts, unwilling to accept everything they were told.

"Why else would they encase our school in glass and keep all the doors locked?" Caleb's voice was a whisper of suspicion. "I've seen people entering the building in hazmat suits."

Julie refused to remain silent as her friends talked themselves out of leaving. "It doesn't matter. We've discussed this countless times. We all agreed that we wanted to explore what was out there and had every right. No one has expressly forbidden us from leaving."

"They've imposed rules, though. We're not permitted to leave our rooms after lights out," Caleb countered. "If they suspect we're sneaking out, it would be foolish to attempt an escape." He felt satisfied as Cassie and Amy nodded in agreement.

Julie narrowed her eyes at Caleb. "Don't tell me you're suddenly scared. We found a tunnel that leads out of here, and I intend to use it, with or without you guys." She tipped her nose down at Caleb, who was at least a foot shorter than her. "We'll wait a week or two, or even a month if necessary. I'm sure they'll start checking rooms, and I've got to find out if my roommate blabbed her big mouth." She wiped sweat from her neck. "Eventually, the staff will think no one is leaving their rooms, and they'll stop worrying about it. But I *am* going to see what's out there." She glanced at Amy with a half grin. "Besides...I intend to bring the new O, and won't that be exciting?" She thought the new orphan looked like a young man who'd welcome a little danger. "I think—"

Andrew nudged Julie in the elbow, and she quickly stopped talking as Mr. Jamerson approached the group with the new O.

"Cassie..." Mr. Jamerson halted before her, his gaze peering over his glasses as he often did. "Shane Webster, I'd like to introduce you to Cassie Cameron. She's one of our brightest students." He extended a hand towards Cassie, but she instinctively stepped back, holding her book tightly against her chest like a shield. Jamerson chuckled softly. "I understand you're shy, but I'd appreciate it if you'd give Shane a tour. Show him how our system operates." He handed her a sleek glass computer tablet. "Here's his schedule. I've already arranged for someone else to cover your afternoon shift in the garden house."

The garden house held a special place in Cassie's heart, and she couldn't help but feel disappointment at the thought of missing her favorite job. Tomorrow's assignment in the cleaning sector didn't excite her either; it ranked only slightly higher than food prep on her list of least favorite tasks.

"I'd be happy to show Shane around, Mr. Jamerson," Julie offered cheerfully, positioning herself next to Cassie. "Cassie mentioned she wasn't feeling well and needed to rest."

"Actually, you misunderstood," Amy interjected, stepping up beside Cassie on the other side. "I'm the one feeling under the weather, but it's just a minor headache. I'll manage just fine." She flashed a reassuring smile at Julie. "I'm sure Cassie would love to introduce Shane to the school."

"Cassie, you can start by showing Shane the classrooms and then the workstations," Jamerson instructed briskly, guiding them towards the double glass doors. "And Julie, since you're so eager to assist, you can take on a double shift in the food sector. They're short-staffed today."

Chapter 2

As Cassie strolled alongside Shane in the deserted hallway, a loud ten-second bell echoed through the empty space. With classes canceled for the assembly, they had an hour of unexpected free time. She wanted to kick off her shoes, sink into the green grass, and lose herself in her book beneath the palm trees. Rare leisure moments were precious, and the thought of spending them giving a tour was the last thing she wanted.

Shane recognized her reluctance and paused in the hallway. "I'm sorry you got stuck with me."

She glanced up at him, a pang of guilt tugging at her for not being more welcoming. "It's okay." She continued explaining the structured system the orphans followed. "The bells always ring on schedule, but since there's an assembly, classes are canceled for now." Sensing his intense gaze on her rather than the surroundings, she felt a slight unease. He stood out from the other students, as he was not yet wearing the school uniform. Sidestepping to add distance from him, she shifted the focus back to the school environment.

"This wing houses all your classes," she gestured towards the surrounding area. "The other wings cater to different age groups, so we don't interact much with younger kids. Adjacent to the next building is the dormitory, which is divided into separate wings by gender and age. The complex might initially seem overwhelming, but you'll soon get the hang of navigating it."

As they paused by a glass wall, her gaze was drawn to a mesmerizing digital image of a cascading waterfall displayed on an enormous, quarter-inch-thick screen. The sight captivated her, evoking a sense of wonder. "It's my favorite visual." She imagined what it would be like to witness such a spectacle in person.

"You like waterfalls?" His eyes fixed on her as she admired the moving image.

"It's beautiful."

"Hawaii has a waterfall just like this one. They're great for jumping off."

She stared up at him in surprise. "You've seen a real one?"

He would have laughed if it weren't for her true look of astonishment. With her anxiously waiting for his reply, it gave him a chance to study her unique eyes. They were reddish brown, with specks of gold in them. He'd seen eyes like hers before. And the way her hair color matched the red in her irises was no surprise. "I lived in Kauai for a while with my dad. It's the most beautiful place on earth and the most lush and green island of the Hawaiian chain."

"Wow, you're incredibly lucky." She observed Shane's smile and upbeat demeanor. Despite having recently lost his parents, there was no trace of sorrow in his expression. His cheerful mood remained unchanged even when mentioning his father. She couldn't help but wonder about his circumstances—if he had any family left, he wouldn't be attending the orphanage. Calling him lucky may not have been the most appropriate choice of words.

Turning towards the glass digital display, she pulled her long hair self-consciously over her shoulders and averted her gaze. "After classes, we have meals, followed by work detail. You'll be assigned to a different work location each day, and your station is displayed on the screen with your name." With a wave of her hand, she activated the digital display, causing a hologram to materialize featuring a building diagram. "You simply touch the screen here," she continued, reaching up to demonstrate as the screen scanned her thumbprint. "I'm not sure if you're in the system yet."

He brushed her arm as he reached up the same way she had.

13

His name and assignment for tomorrow appeared. "So tomorrow I'm working in the garden house."

"Garden house is my favorite." She stepped away. "I love pulling the plants and washing the leaves. I like the smell of the earth and the way the sun shines through the glass. We have birds that live in there, and they chirp."

"It's the job of just picking and planting the food, right?"

Her eyebrows knitted together as she noticed his smirk. Was he teasing her? "It's a good job." She assumed that Shane's physical labor had contributed to the corded muscles on his arms. Her friends Caleb and Andrew had developed their muscles over the past two years from working in the mines, carrying heavy stones and equipment, yet their physique was only half the size of Shane's.

Turning towards the doors, she began walking. "It's better than dish duty or food prep. Sometimes you'll have to wash the cafeteria dishes and plan meals for the next day. Everyone learns to cook here. You'll be a skilled culinary chef when you leave the orphanage." Though the food industry appealed little to her, she recognized the value of acquiring skills for potential employment outside the orphanage. "We grow and eat our vegetables and drink a lot of green smoothies. I suppose the taste is suitable."

"Huh."

"You must have done heavy labor jobs."

His smile stretched wide as a pink blush flushed her cheeks. "I've done my fair share of lifting." He used to lift weights regularly with his father, and hard training was part of his childhood, but he wouldn't share that with her.

Shane already knew everything there was to know about Saving Souls Orphanage. He knew it was a fine place for orphans to live, providing them with education, nutritious meals, and meaningful work opportunities that instilled responsibility. Overall, everyone seemed to get along well together. It was arguably better than traditional boarding schools, but the residents were prohibited from leaving the grounds or venturing beyond the glass dome. Their existence was more secluded and sheltered than even the Amish community. With no access to televisions, cell phones, or the internet, and lacking even a newspaper to keep them informed about the outside world, they were cut off from external information. The expansive building, spanning 181,000 square feet and constructed from brick and cement, was enclosed by a towering glass ceiling that reached a height of 110 feet, covering the entire campus area. The glass enclosure not only housed the building itself but also enclosed outdoor gardens and wheat fields. Connected by a tunnel, a separate dome enclosed acres of garden fields. Some individuals believed it was unjust for orphans to be confined to working and living indoors, never experiencing the realities of the world beyond. And Shane knew the outside world remained oblivious to the enormous secret harbored within Saving Souls.

"How long have you lived here?"

They continued down a hall lined with moving digital display panels rather than cement walls, and new scenes and writing appeared. The 3-D screens gave a fully immersive experience of walking through a forest. Cassie loved the motion effects and the beauty of what she hoped the world truly looked like. "I was five when someone brought me here."

"Who? Who brought you here?"

Her head snapped up. His eyes were wide with interest, and the demand in his tone was unusual. Why should he care who brought her here? She drew her brows together in confusion. "We aren't informed about our pasts until we turn eighteen. Then they'll give us a file supposedly telling us our parents' names and other important facts. So I don't know." Glass doors of classrooms opened automatically, sliding up into the ceiling, but she wasn't sure if he'd care to see inside the rooms. "This is the math room." She motioned for him to enter.

He extended his hand, setting it on her shoulder to stop her. "Have you been happy living here all this time?"

It startled her to feel his hand on her shoulder. She wasn't used to being touched, and wondered what made him ask such a question. "Have I been happy?" No one had ever bothered to ask her that before. Why would anyone care? She never really thought about happiness. Saving Souls was a way of life. She had friends, liked school, and the work wasn't terrible. Some jobs she enjoyed while others not so much, but it didn't matter because each day was different. She liked the structure and schedule.

"Are you happy?" He wondered why she was giving so much thought to his question.

"This is a good place to live. I've heard from other orphans that the world can be scary and dangerous." She'd also heard stories that made the world seem wonderful. Most of the orphans at Saving Souls came from very wealthy families. Some had lived exciting, rich lives and would share their stories. She didn't like to think about what she could be missing. "Here you can live a decent life, because people are basically kind to one another, the days are structured, and needs are well met."

He folded his arms across his chest. "Are you always this hard to get an answer from? I don't care how great the place is, I'm asking if you're happy with your life."

"I... Yes," she hesitated, feeling irritated at his probing interest. His intense green eyes seemed to bore into her, making her uncomfortable. She wasn't accustomed to discussing her feelings. Her best friend Amy had never asked such questions; perhaps because they shared the same life, neither felt the need to scrutinize it. They simply accepted it.

But as she reflected on his question, Cassie admitted, "I'm content living here because it's all I've ever known." Observing the furrow of his brows and the contemplative set of his lips, she realized he might be asking out of concern for his own potential happiness.

"I'm not sure if you'll find contentment here, given your different background. But I can assure you, it's not a terrible place to be." She shrugged casually. "Besides, you won't be here for long."

Her response wasn't satisfying. He wanted to hear that she loved her life and was truly happy, but he gathered that her answer was truthful, and "content" was the word she'd used.

"Hi, Cassie!" A slender teenage boy, covered in freckles, stopped in front of her. "Will I see you later in the garden house?"

"No, Owen. Mr. Jamerson asked me to show Shane around." She realized her voice held the tone of disappointment and tried to cover it with a smile.

"Hi." Owen offered his hand to Shane. "Welcome to Saving Souls." His eyes flew right back to Cassie's face. "Cassie loves the garden house. It's her favorite job. Will I see you at dinner tonight? I'll save your favorite yogurt if they start to run out."

"Yeah, I'll be there. Thanks, Owen." She stepped back.

It didn't take a genius to see that Owen had a crush on Cassie, making her uncomfortable. Shane observed as the kid walked away, glancing over his shoulder. "He really likes you."

"He's just overly friendly." She thought Owen was nice, but he had poor hygiene. He rarely smelled clean, making her suspect he often skipped showers. There was no excuse not to bathe. Saving Souls encouraged cleanliness with nightly or morning showering, and after doing some jobs, the sectors would allow students to shower. The Orphanage ensured the dorms had plenty of homemade lavender soap, shampoo, and deodorant with Tea Tree. The sanitation station was broken into three sectors: one for water purification, another for proper garbage disposal, which included composts and recycling, and the other sector for making soaps and various cleansers from the lavender fields.

Shane wondered if Cassie was aware of her beauty. Jamerson had called her shy, which seemed fitting, as he studied how she allowed her thick veil of dark red hair to hide her face as she stared at the floor. "I can show myself around if you want to work in the garden house. I'm sure there isn't anything here I can't figure out on my own."

"I don't mind showing you around." She just wished he'd stop

17

staring at her. The truth was, he made her nervous. He wasn't like her fellow students. His size and demeanor were unnerving.

"After you, Cass." He stepped to the side, raising his hand for her to lead the way.

He had called her "Cass," as if they were already close friends. His smile seemed oddly placed, and his green eyes sparkled with either mischief or a curiosity unfamiliar to her. His striking eyes were complemented by well-defined black brows and thick, dark lashes, making his appearance notable. His dark hair, which seemed effortlessly styled, exceeded the length permitted by the school's policy.

She took a deep breath and focused on the tour. "As you know, the orphanage isn't just a home for parentless children. It's also a school and business all in one. We're referred to as students. I guess it sounds better than orphans." She never liked to think of herself as an orphan.

"Do you remember anything from your past? Your parents?"

"No. I don't remember anything before ending up here." Another personal question she wanted to ignore. "Everyone wakes at six A.M." They stepped into the enormous cafeteria. "This is where meals are served. We stand in line over there." She pointed to a long orange counter. "We receive our food and have half an hour to eat breakfast. We're given an hour for dinner. Class begins at seven." She glanced at his schedule, noticing he had the exact five class times as her.

"What's wrong?"

"Nothing." She swiped the tablet, turning it to sleep mode. "You're in all my classes. I guess that's why Mr. Jamerson asked me to show you around."

"Great." He took the tablet from her. "Do you remember who brought you here? Was it a man or a woman?"

"What?" Why did he care who brought her to the orphanage? "I told you, I don't know." She couldn't find anything out until she turned eighteen, so there was no point in wondering about it.

"You don't remember the day you came here at all? Who

18

brought you... a man or a woman?"

She lifted her gaze to his, trying to hide her annoyance, wondering why he was so adamant. "Why do you care? I'm not here to talk about me. I'm here to show you around." She walked to the digital screen, swallowing the nervous lump in her throat. If she wanted to be rude, she could ask him how his parents died, and why he doesn't appear sad, the way many new orphans do.

"Cassie." His eyes conveyed warmth as they met hers, his smile genuine. "I'm simply curious because I'd like to get to know you better. You might be the only friend I make here."

She felt her cheeks warm at her own ineptitude. Shane was new, and of course, he'd want to make friends. She knew she was somewhat socially inept, with limited social experience. She felt foolish for not recognizing he was trying to make a friend. "I'm sorry, I'm not very good with people. I honestly don't remember anything before coming here. I was too young, and what little memory I have is faint, like the fragments of a dream. I do think you'll be happy here, Shane. My friends will become your friends, and I know you'll fit right in." She offered sincerity and decided to overcome her timidity around him.

Chapter 3

The cafeteria filled rapidly with kids pouring in for breakfast. Cassie arrived at her table early and finished a piece of French bread and celery soup. She glanced up as Julie took the seat beside her.

"You're here early this morning," Julie noted, removing the green juice from her tray.

"So are you." Julie had braided her hair the night before so she could have a full head of waves this morning, and Cassie knew exactly why she wanted her hair to look pretty. "You look very lovely, Jules."

"Thanks." She made a face at her green drink. She hated the juice but drank it because she knew the nutrients made her hair shine, skin smooth, and nails firm. She quickly set down her drink and smiled. "Here he comes!"

Shane set his tray on the table across from Cassie before plopping down. "Good morning."

"Good morning, Shane."

Amy silently laughed at the eagerness in Julie's voice as she nudged her on the shoulder. "Scoot down so I can sit."

"No." Julie shoved her. "Sit at the end. I want to ask Shane some questions."

Cassie watched Shane sit with ease, as if he were joining friends he'd known for years. He displayed a confidence she admired, and Julie obviously admired everything about him. Cassie glanced at her as she took a bite of her applesauce. Leave it to Queen Bee to dig up the most personal information she could get from him. She'd probably come right out and ask him what tragedy brought him here.

20

"So, Shane, how did your parents die? Not just anyone gets to come here. Your parents must have been wealthy or prominent figures."

Amy gasped at Julie's blatant question. Everyone knew how crass and forward she could be, but sometimes hearing her talk was still surprising. "Gosh Jules…"

Caleb and Andrew took their seats beside Shane. Caleb, as always, set his eyes directly on Julie, and any moment, he'd offer her a compliment. Andrew dug right into his food, as if the boy woke up starving every morning.

"Your hair looks beautiful, Jules. I like it when you wear it like that." Caleb's praise was delivered in his typical chipper suck-up voice, and Cassie wasn't the only one who rolled her eyes as she caught a glimpse of Amy and Andrew doing the same.

Cassie knew her friends all too well. She waited a moment for Julie's standard response to Caleb. She'd comment with a toss of her head, barely audible thanks, and proceed to ignore him.

"So Shane," Julie continued, "What's your story?"

"His story isn't anything special, Jules," Caleb replied firmly. He shared the adjoining dorm room with Shane and Andrew and had already heard Shane's tall tale. Last night, he sat up and listened to Shane talk about the world. Caleb figured he was a bit full of himself, and no doubt Julie would eat it up.

Julie tossed a glare at Caleb before turning her smile back to Shane. "You're our new friend now, Shane. You'll eat breakfast, lunch, and dinner with us, so I'd like to know more about you."

After quickly downing his green drink, Shane set the glass down, anticipating only a few minutes left to eat and avoid the annoying blonde.

Cassie finished breakfast, noticing Shane's dark five o'clock shadow along his jawline. Caleb and Andrew never wore facial hair, and she found herself intrigued by the appeal of facial hair on a man.

Amy leaned forward from the end of the table. "He can't possibly tell us his life story in ten minutes. There's not enough time."

She enjoyed Julie's irritation at the lack of answers. "Shane, I noticed you'll work in the tunnels tomorrow."

Glancing up from her tray, Cassie caught Shane's gaze. She'd listened intently to the conversation but had kept her eyes fixed on her food to seem disinterested. When their eyes met, a slight blush warmed her cheeks. It annoyed her how his emerald eyes twinkled with amusement, as if he found her shy demeanor amusing.

"Did you live underground?" Julie's tone was filled with more excitement than was necessary.

"No." Shane's eyes held Cassie's. "My family and I moved around a lot growing up. We never stayed in one place too long. I've slept in underground houses. The underground tunnels of shopping, food courts, and parks are pretty amazing." He glanced down at his plate and made a face. "What did you say these things are?"

"Kale chips." Andrew grabbed a handful off Shane's tray. "Not everyone likes them, but I think they're amazing."

Amy laughed. "You think all food is amazing."

"I'd like to know if everyone in the world eats like us or if there are other things out there," Andrew replied with a full mouth. "I'm so tired of vegetable this and vegetable that."

Shane nodded. "Many fast-food chains selling hamburgers and other meats have gone out of business due to too many animals suffering from radiation poisoning and viruses. As a result, meat became very expensive. People are now afraid to eat anything they didn't grow themselves or that didn't come from mechanical greenhouses."

"Yeah, the last newbie to come here said everyone is health conscious. Everyone wants to eat healthy since there's so much cancer and pollution."

Shane met Amy's brown eyes. "It's true." Many years ago, nuclear plants in the United States were blown up. Terrorists attempted to devastate the country with dirty bombs and radiation. Much of the land was contaminated, and the world went through a horrific depression. However, progress was made over time. Artificial ventilation systems with advanced air purifiers were developed, allowing people to live underground. Robotic machinery cleared the contaminated land above, removing and burying the toxic soil deep underground before the land was reclaimed.

It was a frequent fantasy to imagine how the outside world lived. Cassie caught herself staring at Shane, with a million questions running through her mind. She enjoyed hearing him speak. He spoke smoothly and confidently, so she decided he must have already had a lot of education.

"It's time to go." Andrew stood, taking his tray to the recycling station.

Julie stood up. "Will you walk me to class, Shane?"

"Sure, sweetheart." He offered her a charming grin before casting a glance at Cassie. She appeared uninterested and unfazed by his response. "How long have you lived here?" He took Julie's tray for her.

"Since I was two. I have no idea who my family was or how I ended up here." She slipped her hands into her pockets. "The administrator says we get to have our files when we turn 18. Some kids have information on their families and where they come from, and others don't. I hate that they make us wait." She longed for answers about her past, eagerly counting the days until she'd turn 18, receive her file, and finally leave Saving Souls. "Watch out!" Julie pushed Cassie away as Julie bumped into her. "Gosh, can't you walk in a straight line?" She wished Cassie weren't in her first-hour class with her and Shane.

Cassie almost lost her balance, but Shane reached out, pulling her to his side. She caught Julie's look of disappointment. Shane's strong arm draped securely over her shoulder was a small reward for Julie's rude behavior.

"Don't let her get to you," he whispered in her ear. He'd been at the school two days and already knew Julie wasn't the sweetheart she pretended to be.

"I'm used to her." She considered Julie her friend because

23

they shared a joint dorm room and bathroom. She'd known Julie for twelve years and remembered a time when she hadn't always been this way. Her attitude changed during the last two years when she suddenly became interested in boys and wanted their attention. Julie admitted once that she liked being the prettiest girl in the school, but Amy quickly corrected her, stating Cassie was the most beautiful.

Shane opened the door for Cassie, but Julie breezed in first, rolling her shoulders back. Cassie mouthed the words "thank you" to Shane. She sat in the middle of class, aware that Shane had chosen the seat directly behind her.

Glancing around the classroom at the students settling into their seats, everything seemed like a typical class. Most students appeared perfectly normal, especially those who had entered the orphanage later in life after experiencing the outside world. Their worldly experience often influenced the other kids who had only known the structured routine of Saving Souls. Without them, those orphans might seem more robotic. However, kids like Shane brought a bit of personality and current slang words into the mix. "I forgot my pencil." He gently tugged on Cassie's long hair.

She turned in her seat to face him. "We don't use pencils."

Placing his hand on the desk, a thin tablet popped up from the glass surface. Running his finger over it, he watched the computer come to life, displaying a greeting and the day's assignments. "How come you're the only one I see that reads paperback?" He'd seen the library, which was mostly digital with only a small section of paperback books.

She shrugged her shoulders. "I prefer books rather than tablets. I like the paper and the way books feel in my hand. I enjoy turning a page rather than swiping a screen." She also enjoyed how some books smelled old and musty, but she'd keep that to herself. "Do you like to read?"

He nodded. "I do. I didn't always have time to read, but I loved visiting the library. You'd love some of the libraries I've been to."

"I'm sure I would." Her curiosity piqued. She imagined what it

24

would be like to walk down rows and rows lined with books.

"I think I'm like you. I prefer books more than tablets. I like the way they smell."

She turned more in her seat, studying his wide smile, straight white teeth, and the slight dimples beside his full lips. "You don't seem like someone who's recently suffered a tragedy. Are you at all sad?" He didn't talk about his family, and when he'd mentioned moving around a lot, the memory didn't appear to trigger pain.

Shane suddenly felt like Cassie was looking straight into his mind. She was intuitive and observant. She wasn't talkative, didn't flirt, and wasn't interested in his charm, but the way her eyes held his put a slight knot in his stomach. "How do I seem?"

The math teacher, Mr. Mazer, stood at the front of the room, demanding everyone's attention. Cassie was spared from having to answer him as she slowly turned to face her teacher. With a tap of his computer, a hologram sprang to life in front of the class—a giant 3-D mathematics equation. He launched into an explanation of algorithms, his hands moving over the hologram, manipulating numbers as more digital images appeared.

Cassie sensed that Shane had secrets he wasn't willing to share. He was unlike her friends Caleb and Andrew, who wore their hearts on their sleeves. There was a mystery to Shane and something very different about him, evident in the way he studied her and spoke. Normally disinterested in people, Cassie was intrigued by him and curious about what he was concealing.

Chapter 4

The tunnels ran deep under the western periphery of the campus. Shane, wearing a set of brown coveralls, a cloth mask, hard hat and gloves, made his way through the echoing sounds of machinery and shouted commands until he reached the stairs leading to a horizontal passageway. Much of the tunnel's construction relied on manual labor rather than explosives or heavy machinery, which prolonged the process but made it safer for workers.

"Ready?" Andrew's hand landed reassuringly on Shane's shoulder.

"I suppose." He followed his roommate.

"After every hour, we're granted a fifteen-minute water break." Andrew gestured toward a table holding barrels of water. "Today, we're assembling steel for support beams rather than excavation. Your task is to acquaint yourself with the disk cutters. I'll introduce you to Brian; he's our go-to expert here." Andrew had a fondness for the tunnels. Though fifteen rooms had already been built with reinforced steel and concrete, their interiors were impressive with their contemporary décor, a far cry from the plain dormitories the orphans called home. Artificial skylights gave an illusion of natural daylight. The rooms would be an exquisite step up for resident staff members, including the rumored extravagant suite for the Administrator.

An hour into their labor, Shane removed his mask and met Andrew at the water station, accepting a paper cup from him.

"How's it going?" Andrew took his helmet off and ran a hand through his sandy brown hair. He'd just gotten his hair buzzed on the sides, but kept the top and back longer, because that's how Amy said she liked it.

Shane swiped perspiration from his neck. "Not bad. I'm learning some intriguing skills."

"By the time you leave Saving Souls, you'll be proficient in tunnel-building, carpentry, masonry, culinary arts, and more. We receive comprehensive training here." Andrew's aspirations leaned toward carpentry and construction.

"That's cool." Shane took a sip of water.

"It's not quite as lively as working alongside the girls in the greenhouse or kitchen, but time seems to fly down here. You seem to have taken a liking to Cassie, eh?" He had observed Shane's subtle glances toward her. Andrew wouldn't share his thoughts about Cassie's personality. She was his friend, but their energies didn't mesh well, unlike his and Amy's. Amy was so easy to connect with, and he felt a strong rapport with her.

"Yeah, she's alright." Shane didn't want to let on that he was too interested.

"Be cautious around Julie; Caleb's been keen on her for ages." Andrew didn't want Shane to step on his buddy's toes.

"I gathered that." Shane moved over as a few older men approached the water barrels.

"Hey, I've meant to tell you something, but not in the dorm." Andrew lowered his voice. He didn't trust the rooms weren't monitored. Unsure of how the administrator found out about their nightly excursions, he didn't want to risk discussing it openly. Though Saving Souls presented as anything but a prison, Andrew believed otherwise. He felt safe enough to speak freely in the tunnels with noise and activity. He leaned closer to Shane as they reached the wall and continued, "I found a hidden tunnel in the science lab."

Shane raised an eyebrow, "Oh yeah?"

"I was messing around with some marbles during science class." He lowered his voice. "Accidentally dropped them, and they all rolled under this big cabinet by the teacher's desk. So, I slid the cabinet out to reach them. The teacher yelled at me not to touch it, but before he caught me, I saw that it was blocking a door." He scratched his head, leaning in closer. "Thing is, that door didn't lead to another classroom. It was the outside wall on the other side. I wondered what was behind it and why the cabinet was covering it."

"Go on." Shane leaned against the wall, folding his arms, listening intently.

"So, you know the square vent door in our ceiling, where the cold air comes out? If you open it, you'll find ventilation shafts that run throughout the building, narrow and dark but spacious enough for the average person to crawl through."

It didn't surprise Shane that the students discovered the ventilation system. "Are there no alarms or infrared sensors to detect when someone's accessing it?" He suspected that Andrew couldn't be the only student to have discovered the shafts.

"I was concerned about that, but no, there isn't. They might have other methods of knowing when we're not in our rooms. Anyway, I familiarized myself with the vents and shared the information with the girls and Caleb. We all gathered in the science class a week ago after lights out."

"So Amy, Cassie and Julie are the only ones who know?"

Andrew nodded, his gaze shifting subtly away from Shane to maintain the appearance of casual conversation. "And Caleb. I moved that cabinet out of the way and opened the door. It led directly down steep steps, and at the bottom was a tunnel. We walked about half a mile through the tunnel until it ended at a gate." He paused momentarily as some workers passed by, their shovels slung over their shoulders. "The girls were too afraid to go past the gate, but we know it ended outside the glass walls. I never told the others, but the next night I went back. I wanted to see what was beyond the gate."

"What did you see?"

"A lake and a road."

Shane knew Andrew had never stepped foot outside the orphanage before. Like many others, he arrived young and grew up within its confines. Shane wondered how seeing a lake for the first time or walking along a road would feel. The image of Cassie admiring the digital waterfall came to his mind.

"We're planning to sneak out again soon. Julie and I both want you to come."

A few more men walked by, and Shane shifted his stance to appear as if he was stretching. "Is Cassie going?"

"Amy will only go if Cass goes, so I'm kinda hoping you'll talk Cassie into it."

"Got a little thing for Amy, huh?"

"A little." Andrew chortled. She'd been his friend for years, but now that they were turning eighteen soon and would be leaving, he'd given more thought to their future.

A man with an orange hard hat announced, "Your water break is up."

Andrew stepped back. "I'll talk to you at the next break." He walked away, securing his helmet back on.

Shane was carrying a steel beam when the man before him stumbled. Shane took a step backwards to avoid hitting him, lowering the beam. He felt a sharp pain stab the back of his shoulder as he heard the words, 'watch out!' Then his body was shoved to the wall.

"Geez, buddy, are you okay? Damn, I could have sliced you in half!"

Shane's shoulder throbbed as he examined the torn material on his suit. The man had been carrying a long saw with razor-sharp teeth, and he had nearly stumbled into it.

The man, Steve, whom Shane had been working with, shook his head. "Come on, I'll show you where the first aid clinic is." He tugged at the torn material of Shane's suit. "They'll give you a pass to go back to your room. They're real good about taking care of kids around here."

The last thing Shane wanted was to return to his tiny, depressing room with nothing to do. He followed Steve out of the tunnel as

29

his throbbing shoulder became more painful. The clinic was a long walk from the tunnels, and Shane couldn't help but worry about the difficulty of getting help quickly if someone was ever badly hurt down there. Nevertheless, he was impressed with the supervision and the professionals demonstrating proper techniques to the kids. So far, all the staff—and even the students—at Saving Souls were proving to be both friendly and patient.

Steve waved his hand for the clinic door to open and smiled reassuringly at Shane. "They'll take good care of you, Shane. Take it easy."

As Shane thanked Steve, he immediately spotted Cassie sitting in a corner chair. "What's wrong? Are you hurt?" He was at her side in three long strides.

"Shane," Cassie stood. "What happened? Are you okay?" She wanted to laugh when she realized he seemed just as concerned for her as she was for him, his gaze scanning her as he waited for her reply. "I'm fine. I'm working here today." Students were in and out all day, needing various medical attention. Just before his arrival, she had administered a pain pill to a young girl for a migraine. She was inputting the student's name and treatment in the log when he walked in.

"They have students playing doctor here?"

"No. There's a full-time doctor on call, but he had to leave. I was told he'd be back in less than an hour. We receive medical training, and every student is taught basic first aid. Some of the advanced classes teach nursing."

"So you get to bandage me up?" He angled his body so she could see the cut across his shoulder.

She smelled the blood first. "Oh gosh!" She pulled the material down and stared at the dark redness seeping from his shoulder. "That looks bad." Her head spun a little, and she suddenly felt weak. She turned from it abruptly, trying to breathe through her mouth. The smell of blood was too strong and made her want to gag. She opened a cabinet to take out gauze pads and antiseptics.

"Nah. Looks worse than it is. I don't think you'll need to prac-

30

tice stitches on me today." She looked pretty, he thought. Her tan pants and white blouse looked neat and clean, whereas he was covered in dirt, his hands were filthy, and his work suit was a mess.

She cut a few strips of gauze. "Can you take your shirt off?"

"Sure." He pulled down the one-piece coverall they'd made him wear over his clothes. He was lucky the extra material offered protection; otherwise, the saw blade might have gone deeper.

"I'll just..." Her words trailed off as she focused on Shane's muscular body, the tattoo catching her attention. She struggled to sound casual. "That's an interesting tattoo." For the first time, she understood Julie's interest in guys. Her gaze shifted as she noticed the seepage of blood. She quickly looked away.

"You look flushed, Cass. Are you okay?"

"I'm fine." She reached for bigger cloths. "The doctor should be here for this. I think you need stitches."

He took the white cloth from her hand and pressed it against the wound. "Just clean it and cover it. It's not that deep."

She tried not to stare at the lean muscles rippling down his abdomen. "What does your tattoo mean? It's an interesting pattern." It was solid black with two half stars and a wave in the middle.

"It's the symbol for evolution." He handed the bloody cloth back to her and watched as the color drained from her face and her eyes fluttered shut. "Hey," he took her by the shoulders. "Does the sight of blood bother you?"

She was about to faint. Her head was spinning, and her entire body felt limp. Her knees were giving way.

"Easy, I've got you." He helped her ease into the chair, holding her tight in case she collapsed. "Don't pass out on me, Cass. Do you want some water?"

"No, thank you. I'm okay," she lied. Sitting there with her eyes closed, she felt foolish, trying to catch her breath. Maybe if she didn't look at the blood. Oh, who was she kidding? She wanted to tell him to put his shirt back on. "There's a blue gown in the drawer over there." She pointed to a metal cabinet below the sink. "Maybe if you

31

put that on, I won't have to see your cut, and I'll feel better."

"Sure." He put the gown on.

"Why do you have an evolution tattoo on your back?" It filled about four inches between his shoulder blades in the middle of his back.

He wanted to tell her the tattoo represented her. He wanted to tell her she was the reason he'd grown up differently from other kids, and she was the reason he was here. But he had to be sure first. He needed proof that she was the person he believed her to be. The fact she was dizzy from the sight of blood wasn't the proof he was looking for. He set his hand over hers. "Are you okay now, Cass?"

She nodded, opening her eyes. "Blood has a strong scent, and it makes me nauseous. I guess I won't become a doctor when I leave here."

Shane looked at her intently, offering a smile at her humor. With their eyes locked on each other, Shane decided to try something. "Cassie, do you want to heal me? Do you feel anything in you that could heal me?" That's not quite how he wanted to word it, but he didn't know how else to say it. From the confused and suddenly freaked out look on her face, he figured his question did sound odd.

It took a moment for his words to register, but then warning bells went off in her head. "What?" The administrator had asked her similar things. He'd make her touch his hand or arm, asking her if she felt anything or had any desire to heal him. When she responded with confusion and fear at such odd behavior, he'd tell her he wasn't feeling well and hoped she'd make him feel better. It was creepy. He'd done it to her a few times, and finally, last year, she asked him why he was asking her those things. His response was, "Because you're special." She glanced down at Shane's hand over hers. "Why did you say that?" She stood up, feeling a surge of anxiousness. Why would Shane ask the same thing Mr. Jamerson had asked her? "I'm not a doctor. You need to wait for the doctor."

He regretted his words when he heard her alarmed voice. His words would have sounded strange if he had been wrong about her.

32

Clearly, she wasn't aware of anything special about herself. "I mean, can you help me with a bandage? Since you're filling in for the doctor today, right?" He tried to sound casual and make light of the situation.

She breathed deeply through her mouth to avoid the smell of blood. He was right; she was supposed to take care of him. Just because Mr. Jamerson was weird didn't mean Shane should be, too. He had a reason to ask if she could help him. Still, she shook her head at her own reasoning. The wording confused her. 'Anything in you that could heal me,' he had said, as if she had some personal ability to heal. It was all strange, and she felt she had embarrassed herself enough. Glancing at the blood seeping through his gown, she felt her head spin. "I'm sorry, Shane. I can't help you." She plopped back down in the chair, covering her face with her hands.

The door suddenly opened, and a man in a white lab coat carrying a stethoscope around his neck walked in. It was apparent he was the doctor, and he was totally old-school.

"Great timing, doc." Shane turned his shoulder toward the man, lowering his gown. "I've got a little cut."

"I can see that." The doctor promptly retrieved some sutures from a drawer. "Sit down, young man, and take off that gown." He glanced at Cassie and chuckled. "Cassie will never make a good doctor's assistant or nurse." As he began cleaning and examining Shane's wound, he added, "You didn't pass out, did you?" with a smile directed at her.

"No." She had never been so relieved to see the doctor. She'd worked with him many times and was grateful he knew her well.

"Cassie, you can go back to reception now. I know you can't stand the sight or smell of blood."

Shane watched as she slowly walked past him to the door. "Cass…" he waited till her eyes met his. "I'll see you at dinner tonight. Thanks for your help."

"I wasn't any help, but I hope the doctor here can *heal you*." She emphasized the words before leaving the room.

Chapter 5

Amy folded her shirt, placing it carefully in her dresser. "Don't you think life's more exciting since Shane arrived?" She turned toward Cassie with a cheerful grin. "Dinner was so much fun tonight."

"Why do you say that?" Cassie climbed into bed feeling drained. She didn't want to talk about Shane.

"Oh, come on, he was just playing when he teased you for being weak at the sight of blood. You know he was joking. I think he likes getting a rise from you."

"I know. I feel foolish. He was bleeding, and he expected me to heal him." She nibbled on her bottom lip, recalling the intense gaze he had fixed on her. It felt like he was searching for something. She couldn't shake off the discomfort of his behavior, similar to Mr. Jamerson's. The whole idea of 'healing' unsettled her.

"I thought he was amusing and kind. He was trying to cheer you up. You realize that don't you?" She wondered whether Cassie's reserved nature prevented her from recognizing Shane's affection.

"Yes, I know." She wished she could be more outgoing and flirtatious like Julie. "What did you think of how Julie acted tonight?"

Amy swiped her hand over the nightstand. A built-in computer screen displayed an alarm clock. "I think she's ridiculous and phony. I don't think Shane is impressed with her." She glanced at the screen. "Are we getting up at normal time, or do you want more time for breakfast?"

Reaching out, Cassie touched the alarm to ON. "I'm going to arrive at the last minute. I think I'll let Shane have some quality time alone with Jules."

Amy flipped onto her back. "You're funny." She suspected Shane was flirting with Julie to elicit jealousy from Cassie. She didn't comprehend male behavior entirely, but she was certain Shane had no genuine interest in Julie. He just needed more time with Cassie to realize that. Julie's overt approach was too obvious to everyone. "Yeah, poor Caleb," she mused aloud, knowing Caleb for some reason worshiped Julie.

"Yeah." The room plunged into darkness as the lights automatically shut off. Having read about it before, she understood the importance of melatonin for rest and body repair. The darkness didn't bother her like it did Amy. If they needed light, they could swipe a hand over the nightstand. "I don't know what Caleb sees in her either."

"He's just always liked her."

As silence filled the room, Cassie thought about the mysteries of Shane. "Did you know that Shane has a tattoo on his back?"

"Huh?" Amy was already almost asleep. "What is it?"

"It's a symbol. He says it represents evolution."

"That's odd. Did he tell you why?"

"No."

Cassie closed her eyes, wondering about his life. He'd avoided answering Julie's questions during dinner, and she never seemed able to get much information from him either. She figured if she got to know Shane Webster better, she'd need to overcome her shyness.

***

The house smelled musty. The curtains were yellow with faded stains, and voices murmured in the next room. "She's just a little girl. Special. We must protect her."

The shattering glass startled the child. Crouching by the window, she clutched the yellow curtain tightly.

"We will keep her and raise her. If we get sick, we can use her. Or we

can sell her! She's worth a fortune!"

"No! She's a human being! She's a sweet little girl!"

"She's not human. You've grown attached to it. I told you not to!"

"I'm taking her some place safe. Somewhere she can be protected from the world, and no one will find her."

"No, you're not."

More glass shattered with the sounds of struggling. Suddenly, a woman grabbed her arm. "Come with me." She was placed on a horse. She was trying to hold the reins. "You're special, sweetheart. Always remember that you're special."

She was falling off the horse. It was galloping too fast, and she was slipping. The ground below looked very far down. "I'm falling!" Fear tore through the child.

Cassie jerked up in bed, her heart racing. She felt oddly weightless. She opened her eyes and ran a hand through her tangled hair. Amy was breathing softly in the bed beside hers. It had been a long time since Cassie had a dream she could remember. She closed her eyes, wondering if it was a dream or a memory. She could still hear the woman's voice. "You're special."

Light appeared under the bathroom door, and Julie or Kelly turned the water on. She waved her hand over the nightstand to see the screen read 5:20 a.m. As her head sank back to the pillow, she smiled at the thought of Julie waking up early to fix her hair. All so that she could look her best for Shane.

The dream was unsettling, but that's what it was—a dream. Cassie couldn't see any faces, but she remembered the house. She remembered the curtains and the horse. She closed her eyes again and wondered where she came from for the first time in a long time.

Chapter 6

Mrs. Reynolds asked the class to take out their tablets and swipe to yesterday's assignment. "Did everyone finish reading about Madame Therese Peltier?"

Cassie held her tablet, swiping until an image of an old plane appeared. Madame Peltier, the first woman to pilot an aircraft in 1908. Feeling a tug on her hair, she turned her head.

"I've seen a real airplane," Shane whispered from behind her. "They don't look anything like this."

"It costs too much to operate them, so aren't they just sitting around taking up space?" It was hard for her to imagine, since she'd never seen one in real life. She turned to the front of the room when Mrs. Reynolds projected the text from the tablet with a laser, turning it into a hologram. The three-dimensional image of the plane appeared almost life-size in front of the class. The window blinds were down, making the image shimmer in the darkened room.

Cassie envied Shane. He'd seen much of the world, and she wanted to hear about it. But she wouldn't talk during Mrs. Reynolds' lecture.

After half an hour, Mrs. Reynolds opened the blinds and distributed a blank sheet of paper. "Now, I'll demonstrate how to make a paper airplane for fun," she announced. "Once I'm finished, you can pair up and create your own. Then, we'll see whose plane flies the farthest." Mrs. Reynolds loved to do fun and silly things with her class. It was one of the qualities Cassie liked most about her.

"Shane…." Julie glanced over from her seat, three down from Shane's.

"Sorry, Jules. Cassie already asked me." He shrugged his shoulders and felt a slight pain from his healing cut.

"Nice." Cassie rolled her eyes but suppressed her smile when she saw the frown on Julie's face.

During the project, partners moved their desks to face each other. Shane turned Cassie's desk around to face his. "Watch the cords." The desks were plugged into the floor with charging cords.

"Are you okay today?" He'd wanted to speak with her, but she'd been late for breakfast and seemed distracted during their first class.

"Yes, I'm fine. Why?" Had it been a dream or a memory? She kept thinking about it since it was still fresh in her mind.

He set his hand on hers. "Cassie." When she looked up, he studied her a moment. "Something is bothering you. What is it?" He hoped he hadn't said or done anything to upset her. He only flirted with Julie to see if she would respond. A flicker of jealousy, a flush in her cheeks, anything. She was usually quiet, but he knew she was observant and always paying attention. Today, her focus seemed off.

His eyes were sincere. He seemed genuinely concerned, and the fact that he knew something was bothering her surprised her. "How do you know?"

He held her hand in his. "Am I right? What's wrong?"

His hand felt warm and slightly rough, and she appreciated the comfort. "I had a weird dream, and I've been thinking about it. That's all."

"What was it about?"

She wasn't ready to talk about the details. "I'm wondering if it could be a memory rather than a dream. Sometimes I wish I could remember my life before I came here. I don't often remember my dreams, but this one feels strong... like a memory." And if it really happened, what did it mean?

Mrs. Reynolds began moving around the class, gently reminding students to stay focused on their assignments. She noticed some were getting distracted by other conversations. While she encouraged them to have fun and chat, she also expected them to work on their planes.

"That's not how you fold it," Cassie laughed at his attempt. "Look." She took the paper from him and folded it in half lengthwise. "Remember, you have to crease it really well so you can tear it. It has to be.... *ouch*," she immediately brought her finger to her lips.

"Paper cut?" He reached for her finger to examine the slice. "Oh, this is a good one." There was already a red line of blood. As he studied the cut, the skin suddenly filled in and the wound disappeared before his eyes.

"It's gone. I'm fine." She pulled her hand back.

"Let me see your finger, Cass."

"No." She laughed when he took her hand and wouldn't let her pull away. "Stop trying to squeeze my finger and make it bleed. I'm fine. It doesn't even hurt now." She pulled her hand away and wondered why he was so interested. "It's not a big deal, Shane. I heal fast." She'd never thought anything of it.

"Have you had other injuries that have healed that fast?"

She looked at him quizzically. "I guess so. One time, I sliced my finger on a knife while working in the kitchen. It seemed deep and bled at first, but..." She turned as Mrs. Reynolds approached their desks.

"You haven't gotten very far with your planes. Do you need help?"

"We're okay, Mrs. Reynolds." Shane began to fold the paper. He didn't speak again until they were both standing at the front of the class. "I'm going to make mine fly over Julie's head. How many points will you give me?"

"Lots. Fly it."

His plane flew over the first desk before landing on the floor. She pulled her hand back and sent her plane flying. Hers glided through the air and landed behind the desk at the back of the room.

"Wow, we have a winner!" Mrs. Reynolds shouted, clapping her hands enthusiastically. "Looks like Cassie Cameron knows how to make a plane that can fly."

Julie frowned, disappointed as she glanced at her plane, which had landed on a desk right in front of her. Under her breath, she muttered, "Cassie's probably read about how to make a great plane in a book. She had an advantage."

Shane tipped his head at the apparent display of jealousy. "Actually, Jules, I've made plenty of paper airplanes in practice, and it was obvious Cassie hadn't. Yet her plane still beat mine. So, I guess it's either luck or skill she has. I'm going with skill." He turned and winked at Cassie.

Cassie appreciated his defense; more than anything, she enjoyed the look on Julie's face as the bell sounded. She brushed against Shane and whispered in his ear, "You just earned a lot more points."

Shane stared at her back. Did she just flirt? Was that humor? He shook his head with a smile. Progress.

Chapter 7

The ceiling fan rattled. It was on high to help relieve the extreme heat. Florida was too warm in the summer. Saving Souls was built with state-of-the-art solar-powered technology, but the dorm's air-conditioning only ran at night because students were typically not in their rooms during the day. Today was different, though. Cassie lay on her bed, staring at the whirling blades. She wondered if she'd become sick like the rest of her classmates. There was a possible viral outbreak, and the administrator ordered all the kids to stay in their rooms to prevent the spread. Amy was currently moaning in the bed beside her. "Can I get you anything?" Cassie offered.

"No. I need to throw up again to relieve this horrible nausea." Amy flipped to her side. "How come you're never sick? You never catch anything."

"I guess I'm lucky. But it's strange they would keep me with you while you're sick. I could easily catch it."

"I think we were poisoned. I bet someone put the wrong spice in our soup this morning. Maybe Shane. He was working in the kitchen yesterday." Amy wanted to smile at her jest but was in too much agony to move a muscle.

It'd been two weeks since Shane arrived. He seemed to be adjusting well, Cassie thought. "Julie told me he's not sick. Looks suspicious if you ask me," she smiled playing along.

Their room was a cramped ten-by-ten square, with crisp white walls and bedspreads. A small closet barely left space for the wooden dresser. Two twin beds faced the door. They shared a tiny connecting bathroom with Julie and her roommate, Kelly, who harbored a clear dislike for Julie. Cassie went to the bathroom and opened the door to find Kelly kneeling over the toilet. "I just need to use the sink. I'm sorry you're so sick, Kelly."

She turned the water on and ran a washcloth under the faucet. Kelly was too busy vomiting to respond. Her black hair was pulled back in a ponytail, and she'd changed out of her uniform into the orphanage's black lounge clothes. They were only required to wear the three different uniforms during school hours.

"This is horrible," Julie complained from the connecting doorway. "I'm feeling sick now, too."

Cassie held her breath while she wrung out the washcloth. The scent of Kelly's vomit was stomach-turning. "Maybe you could put a cold washcloth on Kelly's forehead. Seems to help."

"I've got my own problems right now." Julie wrinkled her face in disgust. "I heard the administrator is going to allow outside doctors to examine us and determine what's wrong."

Cassie raised an eyebrow. Julie always seemed to have the inside scoop. If there was any gossip going around, she somehow knew. Kelly made a loud retching noise, and Julie quickly shut the door. Cassie grabbed another washcloth, ran it under cold water and laid it on her neck. That was all she could do for her. She had to leave the stinky bathroom quickly.

"Thanks," Amy whispered as Cassie placed the cool cloth on her forehead. "You're such a good friend, Cass. I feel sorry for Kelly. Julie would never do this for her."

"I know. I want to help her but can't stay in the bathroom. The smell's too strong." Cassie felt anxious at the thought of special doctors coming in. What would they do? She'd never needed a doctor before, but she'd read about them. She hoped she'd never have to be medicated or be stuck with a needle. She'd read negative portrayals of pharmaceutical companies making billions off drugs that supposedly healed every ailment known to the human body. Still, it sounded as if doctors were in the business of pushing medication. She'd read that people were forced to take a vaccine to cure a virus causing a pandemic. Cassie feared the thought of being forced to put something in her body, even if it was supposed to help. Being forced to trust something didn't seem right. She inhaled a deep, calming breath through her mouth and hoped she wouldn't be called to the clinic or the administrator's office.

Mr. Jamerson would ask her to do strange things, saying she was different, but he'd never tell her how or why. He made her uncomfortable, asking her to put her hands on him. He'd say, "Do you feel anything? Does your body tell you anything?" What was she supposed to feel? Once, a very sick woman was in his office, and Cassie was asked to hold the woman's hand. Mr. Jamerson encouraged her to think about healing the woman. It was disturbing and bizarre.

Amy struggled to sit up. "I wonder if Shane will get sick." She studied her friend's face. It was obvious Cassie liked him but was trying to ignore it.

Amy's question interrupted Cassie's thoughts. She shrugged her shoulders. "Julie says he's fine." She couldn't imagine Shane sick. He seemed too strong… too commanding. He'd tell the virus to go away, and it would. She smiled at the thought.

"That's good, because he told me he needs your help with math."

"He doesn't need my help with anything." Shane was more knowledgeable than he let on. "He just wants to be part of our group." She rolled over to her stomach, resting her head on her hands. "He likes Jules."

"Ha, you know that's not true." Amy felt another wave of nausea and closed her eyes. "You know darn well he barely tolerates her. He likes you, Cass, so you must come with us when we sneak out."

"You promised you wouldn't go!" Cassie sat up, crossing her legs in Indian style. "You told Jules we were out. I can't believe you're suddenly changing your mind. I don't want to see you get in trouble. You're only going because Andrew asked you." Andrew started flirting with Amy a few days after Shane arrived. She didn't understand

43

the sudden interest, but it didn't matter. Amy had her head in an 'Andrew cloud' and was not getting it out.

"I know, but I'm curious what's out there. Andrew says most of the facility is off for some religious holiday, so we won't get caught. Besides," she took the washcloth off her head and handed it to Cassie. "Shane is going, and I don't want him to go with Jules and not you. She'd get way too much satisfaction from it."

"Jules can have him!" What was the point of trying to 'be with' a guy? It's not like they could go on dates, have time alone, or do anything people in the world do. The orphanage forbade it and ran a tightly structured unit that prevented it. Their days were planned entirely, and everyone was too exhausted to do anything at night. Boys and girls were allowed to be friends, but no intimate relations or physical contact were ever permitted.

"She can't have him." Amy released a loud sigh. "We aren't letting Jules get her way this time. Besides, Andrew is right about us not living a free and fun life. We're almost adults now and will be leaving soon anyway. We can risk seeing what's out there first." She planned to follow Andrew when they left the orphanage, but she didn't have the heart to tell Cassie yet. It was always assumed she and Cassie would enter the world together.

As a bell rang, Cassie stood intending to refresh the washcloth. "You need to rest. We can talk about this more when you're well."

A sudden knock on the door startled both girls. "Who could that be?" Amy watched as Cassie hesitantly opened the door.

Surprised, Cassie dropped the washcloth, and Shane picked it up. She stared at Shane and Andrew before she peered out the door, checking for anyone else. "What are you doing here?" She pulled them inside. "You're not allowed on the girls' wing!"

Shane handed Cassie the cloth and shut the door. "We were careful." He walked to her bed and sat down. "Dang, your room is even smaller than ours."

"No, it's not," Andrew corrected Shane while looking at Amy with concern. "It's just because they have a dresser and two night-

44

stands 'cause they're chicks and chicks need more stuff than guys."
He placed his hand on Amy's forehead. "You feel warm."

Amy scooted over, making room for Andrew to sit. "You shouldn't be here. We'll all be in big trouble if you're caught, and you'll catch whatever I have."

"Nah." He tucked a piece of Amy's brown hair behind her ear. "Everyone's doing it. The Administrator called a meeting with all the teachers and staff. We've got about an hour before anyone will be around. The students who aren't sick are concerned for those who are. They'll be lenient if we get caught."

Shane leaned back on the bed, studying her closely. "You're not feeling symptoms at all, Cass?"

"No." She stood by the door, squeezing the washcloth, not noticing the water dripping.

"Come sit down." He patted the bed beside him. "I'm not sick either."

"Cassie never gets sick. She never even gets headaches or a sniffle. Like *ever*," Amy said.

Cassie felt the weight of everyone's stare, especially Shane's. "I'm going to get this wet for Amy. The cold cloth seems to help."

Shane stood, taking the cloth from her and handing it to Andrew. He pulled her to sit with him on the bed. "Have you thought about next Saturday?"

She watched Andrew head toward the bathroom before turning hesitantly toward Shane. "I'm not going."

"Yes, we are." Amy met Cassie's gaze with determination. "She's just being cautious, but I'm confident we'll be fine. It's been nearly four weeks since our last try. I think Julie might be onto something... I think they've forgotten about us."

"I won't let anything happen to you." He took Cassie's hand.

Her stomach fluttered nervously. "We've confirmed the tunnel leads to an unlocked gate, and who knows what's beyond that. We're stepping into the unknown, without knowing what lies ahead."

"Maybe there's a lake with a waterfall." He knew she loved

waterfalls. "I could teach you how to swim."

Her cheeks warmed at the thought. He'd seen far more of the world than she. What if a waterfall was close by and they found it? To hide her interest, she shrugged her shoulders. "I've read it's unnecessary to learn to swim unless you live near water. When I leave here, I'm not planning to live by water. She wasn't sure what her plan was, but she longed to see the world and experience things she'd read about in books. The possibilities seemed endless.

"Everyone should learn to swim, sweetheart. And I can tell you this place is close to the ocean." He could only imagine what it'd be like for the orphans to enter the world for the first time. There was much she didn't know. It was almost cruel for the orphanage to send the kids out into the world, never having been exposed to it. Granted, they had skills and knowledge that would be useful in obtaining a job, but it was like releasing a domesticated zoo animal into the wild. Cassie's sheltered life would soon change drastically, and he wasn't sure how she'd handle it.

"Oh gosh, I think I'm going to puke." Amy sat up, placing her hand over her stomach. Andrew was coming back in the room and quickly helped her to the toilet.

It was good he helped, because Cassie didn't think she could handle the smell. She moved closer to Shane to breathe in his fresh, clean scent. "Don't you think it's odd that the healthy kids are being forced to stay with the sick kids?"

Shane nodded in agreement. He wanted to touch her, but he feared she'd pull away. "Sneak out of here with me on Saturday."

"Shane…"

He set his hand on her face and stared into her eyes. "I won't go without you. I promise if you go, you won't regret it."

She wasn't sure how she found herself nodding and would kick herself later for agreeing. But in that moment, the way his magnetic eyes searched hers, she would probably agree to anything he asked. It was his knowledge of the world that intrigued her. She had many questions to ask him—about his life, where he lived, who his parents were, and whether the world was good or bad. She had read that America was a great nation that had risen above destruction and chaos. Though land had been lost to nuclear fallout, the country had survived. She was eager to see and learn for herself. "I'll go on one condition."

"What's that?"

"You have to promise to answer my questions. You don't have to talk about the tragedy that brought you here, but you must tell me some things. Like how you know there's an ocean nearby."

"Cass," he smiled into her eyes. "I promise that someday I'll tell you everything."

There seemed to be more behind his words than she understood.

"We should go now." Andrew opened the bathroom door with his arm securely around Amy's waist. "Amy needs to rest."

\

Chapter 8

All students were required to eat dinner in their rooms, while younger children, on a separate wing, were permitted to dine in the courtyard. They had not fallen ill—only the teens had.

Those who weren't sick stood in line to receive food trays for the ill kids. Cassie didn't mind the task. She wondered who would have taken care of her had she gotten sick.

Shane walked up behind Cassie, placing his hand on Harold's shoulder to cut in front of him. "Excuse me, Harry." He slid into line. "I need a private word with Cass."

"Don't touch me, bro." Harold rolled his shoulders away from Shane. "I'm not touching any of you. My roommate is puking his guts out, and I don't want to catch whatever's making everyone sick."

Cassie turned to face Shane, pleased to see him again. "It must not be contagious," she assured Harold.

"Listen, Cass." Shane moved closer and whispered in her ear. "There are doctors here. They're taking blood samples from all the kids. Have you ever had your blood drawn?"

"No."

"Don't let them take your blood. You must ignore the order to go down to the clinic. Just stay in your room."

"Why? What's going on?" She glanced nervously around the cafeteria, which held only about thirty healthy teens, while the rest of the orphans were sick.

"Just trust me." He set his hand on her arm. "Do you trust me?" He had been trying to befriend her and earn her trust. She wasn't easy to get close to—reserved, quiet, and kept to herself. He didn't know if she liked him because she never cared when he flirted with other girls. At times, she appeared annoyed with him, which baffled him. She was hard to read.

"Tell me what's going on, Shane."

"I can't tell you yet." He dropped his hand when he noticed a teacher watching him and getting ready to walk over. "Calm down, Cass." He sighed at her obvious distress. "Look, you're special. Just trust me."

There it was again. Those words! Those words she'd heard in her dream, the exact words Mr. Jamerson used, now coming from Shane. A surge of panic ran through her. "Why do people tell me that? I don't understand! I've been told that for years! Why? Why am I special?"

"Shh." Shane turned to see Harold watching them. "Keep your voice down, Cass." He angled his body to block Harold's view.

"No!" She gripped his arm. "Tell me right now why you just said that. Tell me what that means!"

"I promise I'll tell you what I know, but I can't right now." He glanced at the teacher again. "We're being watched, and that teacher is about to come over if you don't calm down."

The line moved up, and the kid standing before Cassie glanced at Shane. He was probably trying to figure out what they were arguing about. Cassie didn't care. "I'm not going to stay calm. I've been told I'm special before. I've been asked to do weird things, and now you're telling me to–"

"Who? Who told you that, and asked you to do what weird things?"

"Get your tray, please," yelled a tall, lanky kid behind the counter. "Don't forget plastic forks are being used today."

Shane stepped around Cassie, picking up a green tray with various food bowls—green soup, fruit, and pureed items he couldn't recognize. Among them were three warm, soft yeast rolls. "Take it and go." He handed her the tray. "I'll come to see you later." He wanted an explanation from her, but not in the presence of nosy kids and watchful staff. Harold stepped beside Cassie, grumbling for her to hurry up. She took the tray reluctantly, knowing their conversation would have to wait.

She walked toward the cafeteria doors and spotted Mrs. Reynolds in the hallway.

"Is everything all right?" Mrs. Reynolds noticed the look of distress on Cassie's face.

"I'm fine, just concerned for the sick. Shane was telling me about the doctors." She tried not to let her hands shake as she held the food tray. "Do you know why they're taking our blood?"

Mrs. Reynolds paused for a long moment before answering her. "I think it's just to see who may need antibiotics."

"Oh." Cassie knew she didn't need antibiotics, so perhaps not having her blood drawn was fine. And the way Shane warned her had raised the hairs on her neck. "Stay well, Mrs. Reynolds." She forced a smile before walking away.

"Cassie!" Mrs. Reynolds called out as if there was something more she needed to say. She hesitated a moment. "Be careful, okay? Don't... well... just." She sighed and smiled. "You stay well too."

Clearly, Mrs. Reynolds had more to share. What was happening? Why the secrecy? Cassie wanted answers. She returned the food to her room and paused momentarily as a few sick girls wearing black t-shirts and lounge pants walked down the hall. Two of them carried wash buckets in case they got sick. They had Band-Aids over white cotton balls on the inside of their elbows. Their faces were pale, their lips dry, and all three walked like they'd collapse any moment.

When she arrived at her room, the air conditioning blasting from the vents made it feel nice and cool.

"I can't eat," Amy groaned from the bed.

"Do you feel worse?" Setting the tray down on the nightstand, she touched Amy's forehead. She was clammy but not too warm. A knock sounded at the door. What if it was someone coming to take her blood? "Don't try to get up, Amy."

Cassie swiftly opened the bathroom door and stepped into

the adjoining room shared by Julie and Kelly. Both girls were sound asleep in their beds. Quietly, Cassie opened their door and peeked into the hallway to see the person at her door. It was a woman she recognized from the sanitation station, though she didn't know her name. The woman looked around thirty years old with her long brown hair pulled into a tight ponytail. Holding a tablet and no sign of any needles, she rapped a little harder on Cassie and Amy's door. Placing her hand over her stomach, Cassie slowly opened the door wider. "Everyone is sleeping." She tried to sound unwell. "They're all too sick to get out of bed."

"You all need to go to the clinic. If you can't walk, I'll need your names to send a nurse to your room."

That was perfect, Cassie thought. "I'll give them to you." She waited while the woman approached her, picking up a Stylus pen. She held the tablet ready to write.

"You know my name, right?" Cassie knew the woman would recognize her.

"No, I'm sorry, I don't. I know I've seen you, but we've never been formally introduced." She appeared impatient at having to go through the pleasantries.

"It's okay. I'm Amy Drift. I share room 301 with Cassie. I was just checking on my friends." Cassie tipped her head toward the other door to indicate that it was her room. "I'm well enough to walk, so I'll leave after I use the bathroom." She leaned over and tried to appear as though her stomach was upset. "My roommate is Cassie Cameron."

The woman nodded as she found Cassie and Amy's names on the tablet with their room numbers. "And Julie Ashcon and Kelly Reader are in this room?" She glided the Stylus across the screen. "And they're too sick to walk as well?"

"Yes."

"Someone will come shortly to take their blood and provide medicine."

"Thank you." As the woman walked away, Cassie turned to

Julie, who was softly moaning from her bed.

"Who was that?" Julie asked. "What were you talking about?"

"That was someone letting us know that a nurse will soon come to take our blood. She should have medicine." Cassie offered her a glass of water from the nightstand before returning to her room. Julie seemed to drift back to sleep quickly. "Amy, are you awake?" She called out softly.

"Yes. I feel horrible."

"A nurse is coming to take your blood. If they ask you your name, you need to give them mine."

"What?" Amy opened her eyes. "Why?"

"I need you to say you're me. Can you do that for me?" She knew Amy would demand answers. "I won't be here because they'll think I'm you at the clinic, getting my blood drawn. But I'm going to see Shane. So if you say you're me, you'll get the help and medicine you need."

Amy's lips twitched in a small smile. "I'll cover for you."

"Be sure you say you're me, and that Amy went to the clinic, okay?" Cassie hated having to make her friend lie.

"Don't worry." It was nice that Cassie and Shane were getting close. "You're turning into a rebel, and we haven't even left the facility yet."

It was time to start getting answers. Perhaps breaking the rules was the only way to get them. "Yeah, wish me luck."

Chapter 9

Grabbing the first aid kit from under her sink, Cassie breathed a sigh of relief when she saw the Band-Aid. She didn't have a cotton ball, but she carefully folded a small piece of toilet paper in half and placed it under the Band-Aid, inside her arm. If anyone saw her, it would appear she'd already had her blood drawn.

She tied her hair into a bun and carefully placed Amy's ball cap on her head. Thankfully, her baggy pants and black t-shirt resembled the boys' lounge clothes. Grabbing a wash bucket, she took a deep breath, feeling anxious. Sick kids were walking down the hallways, so blending in wouldn't be difficult. If she got caught on the boys' wing, she could feign delusion and disorientation due to a high fever. She'd read in a book that it was very possible.

She passed the school hallways to the boys' wing, managing to slip by two teachers engaged in deep conversation. Each hallway was color-coded with cheerful paint. The classroom hallways were bright yellow. The girls' hall was teal, and the boys' wing a bright sherbet orange. As she passed boys in the hall, she kept her face down, almost in the bucket, and the hat helped her go unnoticed. Shane's room was number 412, which she knew because he was Andrew's roommate. She knocked on the door, and a firm hand pulled her inside as soon as it opened.

"Cassie, I can't believe you're here."

When she raised her head, his surprised look turned to humor as his eyes lit with mischief.

"Nice disguise." He took the bucket and set it on the floor.

"I need answers, Shane. I had to make Amy lie for me." She

glanced around the room. "Where's Andrew?" It was good they were alone.

"Getting his blood drawn. You look cute in a baseball cap."

She ignored his comment. "I'm sick with worry. Why couldn't I get my blood drawn? Why did you say I'm special? What do you know, Shane?"

He could see she was determined to find answers. He'd have to give her something, but he wasn't sure how much to tell her. He took her hand and led her to the bed, since it was the only place to sit. "What do you know about yourself, Cass?"

"What do you mean? Don't talk in riddles." Frustration turned to anger. "I'm just an orphan. I don't know my family history. I don't know anything, other than I'm just a normal girl."

"Are you?" He noted the distress in her eyes but wasn't sure where to begin. He'd thought they'd have more time to bond before he had to tell her who she is. "Be honest with me, Cassie. Is there anything about you that makes you feel… different?"

She didn't believe he was trying to upset her with evasive answers. Instead, she sensed he was trying to approach her delicately, as if unsure where to begin. "I'm not a violent person, Shane, but if you don't just come right out and tell me what you know, I'm going to start hitting you. Just tell me!"

"Have you ever heard of a woman named Lily McCallister?"

"No. Who is she?" Saving Souls did not share worldly news with students. They were completely shut off from society. Their only information was what they'd found in books and the lessons their teachers taught.

"She's the most famous woman on earth." He took her by the shoulders and thought, *tell her.* "Her body heals itself, and she can heal other people. Cancer, radiation poisoning, wounds, cuts, you name it, she can heal it. She can take a dying person and make them perfectly well."

"What does this have to do with me?"

"She's your mother."

The air left Cassie's lungs, and she forgot to breathe.

Shane watched closely. "You're special because you might be able to heal people, too." He hadn't seen any signs of unnatural abilities, but there was no question that she was Lily's daughter. The same eyes and identical hair, but what hid her identity was she looked more like her father. "I know your parents, Cassie. I was sent here to find you."

"You were sent to find me?" She shook her head, the blood suddenly pumping behind her ears. She hadn't expected anything like this. Part of her couldn't believe what he said, yet her every instinct trusted him. She rose on shaky legs and dropped back down. "My parents are alive? They know I'm here?" Feeling lightheaded, she squeezed his arm. "Where are they? Why am I here?"

He took hold of her shoulders. "I had to be sure you were her. I had to know before I could tell you."

Her eyes filled with tears as she tried to speak, trying to comprehend the incredible news. "Who? Who am I?"

"Your birth name is Faith Alexis Reeves. You're the daughter of Lily and Patrick. Lily McCallister married your father secretly, so you have his last name, but the world still recognizes your mom as Lily McCallister. She's the most famous woman on earth…the only person who can heal."

She was overwhelmed as she processed the possibility her parents were alive. "How do you know?"

"Your parents didn't abandon you, Cass. They've been searching for you since the day you were stolen from them. Few people know this orphanage exists. Only kids of wealthy parents come here. This was a safe place for you to be raised." He couldn't help but feel pride in how she calmly listened. "This facility was built near formerly radioactive ground. It's in a long-secluded area."

"I read something about this." She tried to absorb what he was telling her.

"This orphanage is a test site to see if people can survive here. The dome shields and protects us from exposure to long-term radiation. The orphanage is proving that the land was successfully cleared and cultivated and is, in fact, viable."

"Tell me about my parents. I have a mom and dad who are both alive and looking for me?"

"Yes." He smiled. Her face was so close to his that he could feel her breath and smell her soft lavender scent. Her face was flushed from emotion, her eyes welling slightly and searching his.

The door opened, and Andrew walked in. "Man, that nurse had to stick me three times before she could find a vein." He glanced at his arm, missing Cassie's startled, distraught look. "More medical personnel are coming."

"Cassie, you have to leave now." Shane stood, pulling her up with him.

"Oh hey, Cass." Andrew noticed her face and frowned at Shane in concern. "What's going on? Is Amy okay?"

"Amy's fine. Can you do me a favor, Andrew? Stand outside the door and knock twice if you see anyone coming. I need a moment alone with Cassie before she leaves." He handed her the wash bucket from the floor.

Andrew nodded, sensing the guy's code of why Shane might want a private goodbye. "Are you okay?" he asked one more time, still concerned.

"I'm fine," she forced a smile. "This is all just a bit overwhelming, having all my friends sick."

As Andrew closed the door, he muttered, "Yeah, I get it."

Cassie turned toward Shane, her heart suddenly racing again. "I can't go yet. I still have questions. I need to know what happened to me. Why did it take 17 years to find me? What happens now?"

"19."

"What?"

"You're 19 years old, Cassie. I'm almost 20."

She felt the blood rush to her head again. "I can't believe this. I need to talk about it." She tried to run her hand through her hair and bumped the baseball cap. He reached out to fix it.

"We'll speak again soon. Saturday, we'll meet at the tunnel and talk all night. But for now, please hold it together. You can't tell anyone who you are, not even Amy. Give me time to explain more to you. There's still so much you don't know, but no one can know about us. Do you understand?" He could see her mind racing, hoping she could handle it.

"I'm 19?"

He nodded. "Wait till you meet your mother. She hasn't aged a bit and still looks almost as young as you. Cassie, do you understand about not telling anyone? I'll give you many more answers, but for now, you must act normal. And don't let them take your blood." He rested his fingers over the Band-Aid on her arm. "You're quite clever, you know that?" He leaned down and brushed his lips along her cheek. "Go."

"No!" Her eyes pleaded. "Please, Shane. I can't wait until Saturday. I can't keep this in and act normal." She couldn't breathe. "I can't—"

"Okay, okay." He pulled her to his chest and rubbed her back. "Just take it easy." He regretted telling her everything at once. His father had warned him. There had been a plan, and he'd deviated from it. Now she was having a panic attack and practically hyperventilating. "Meet me in the science room tonight. Sneak out the way you did before, and I'll meet you there after lights out."

She nodded, trying to calm her racing heart. "I want to leave tonight, Shane. I want to see my parents."

He tipped her chin up so he could look in her eyes. "Not yet, Cass. I know this is a lot, but I need you to trust me. I need you to stay calm and act normal. It's too soon to leave."

"Why?"

"Meet me tonight, and I'll explain." He glanced at the clock on the wall. "You have to go now."

Chapter 10

The ventilation shafts ran above the buildings' ceilings. Each room had a large vent screen built into the ceiling. Cold air blasted through the shafts, which were big enough to crawl through. Cassie wrapped a sweater around her waist before climbing into bed.

At night, guards walked the halls to ensure kids stayed in their rooms. It wasn't like daytime, when students were allowed to roam freely. Caleb had discovered the shafts and learned his way around them. He wasn't the only kid to use them to sneak out, but no one had gotten caught…yet.

Amy had received antibiotics from the doctors. They seemed to be helping.

"What are you doing?" She watched as Cassie climbed into bed in her clothes.

It was a relief to see some color back in Amy's face, and her voice sounded stronger. "I'm meeting Shane tonight."

Amy's grin stretched wide as she tried to sit up. "That's great. Is Andrew going too?"

"No." Cassie ached to tell her what she'd learned. "Shane wants to see me alone."

"I knew you two were in love."

"We aren't in love. You can't fall in love in a matter of weeks, and I barely know him."

"Yes, you can." Amy pulled her pillow behind her head. "I think people can fall in love in a day." She believed in love at first sight. "When it happens, you just know." She thought about Andrew but then frowned at the look on Cassie's face. "What's wrong? Is there something else you're not telling me?"

It was no surprise Amy could tell. Feeling torn, she forced a smile she wasn't feeling. "I guess we like each other." She leaned back in bed, her stomach tight with anticipation. "I don't know what to do about it. I don't know how to be with a guy." She couldn't reveal anything else, but that was true.

"Just tell him how you feel. I think I'm in love with Andrew." She remembered the young boy who was too skinny, his nose a bit too big for his narrow face, and the acne that plagued him for a short time. But he'd grown more handsome; weight had changed the contours of his face, especially his jawline and cheekbones, creating a more chiseled look. His arms went from lanky and narrow to muscular and toned. When Shane came along with his handsome features and powerful muscle tone, it made her realize she'd been falling for Andrew for years. Their friendship had also deepened, and she admired more than just his appearance. "I'm going to tell him how I feel on Saturday when we sneak out."

Her friend's voice carried a wistful tone. "I'm happy for you." Cassie wanted to respond normally, even though her insides were turning. Her mind was consumed with the plan: moving the dresser, climbing through the vent, and navigating the shafts to reach the science room. Usually, she'd be fully engaged in Amy's excitement. After all, her best friend was experiencing love for the first time. But tonight, she couldn't focus on boys. Her thoughts were on her parents and her unanswered questions for Shane.

"Well, are you?" Amy asked.

"What?" She hadn't been listening.

"Are you going to kiss Shane? You're not even paying attention. You must have it bad."

"I don't know." The lights were about to go out. It was time. "Are you well enough to help move the dresser?"

Amy stood up from her bed, grateful she was feeling better. She was excited for her friend. "Shane is a good guy. I know he hasn't said much about himself, but Andrew said Shane is the friend he's always wanted. That means a lot."

With a little effort, they were able to move the dresser over. Cassie got on the bed first, then climbed on the dresser. "I'm a little scared to go alone."

"You remember which way to go? You count four shafts on the right, turn left, then count two, then go right."

"I know." She swallowed, feeling the anxiety building. She hated the narrow, tunnel-like shafts. A person could easily panic, feeling that they are closed in. She felt her heart jump and tried not to think about it. There was enough space to crawl, and she'd done it before. The darkness probably bothered her most. She'd need to keep turning her tablet on to see. She'd felt better last time with Amy right behind her.

"You'll be okay." Amy gave her a quick hug. "I want full details in the morning."

The journey through the cold shafts was seventy excruciating yards. She had to stop frequently to rest her knees and hands. She was thankful for the cool air; otherwise, she'd probably pass out from exertion and heat exhaustion. Fortunately, vented heat was rarely needed in their warm location.

As she moved forward, Shane's words kept playing through her mind. The orphanage was constructed on radioactive ground. Years ago, another orphan had tried to warn Amy and Cassie about this, mentioning that people were still afraid to go near former nuclear plants. She felt like a fish in a bowl, surrounded by a world she knew nothing about.

The crawl was torture on her hands and knees. She was enormously relieved when she finally made the turn leading to the science room. The vent screen was already open. As she dangled her feet down, two hands wrapped around her waist.

"I've got you." Shane gripped her, lowering her to the floor.

"You scared me." She was glad to be through the shafts and in his arms.

"Are you okay?" He brushed her hair aside to see her eyes.

Her nerves were jumping again, and she realized her hands shook slightly. "I'll feel better when I know more." There was a sound by the hidden door, and she quickly looked past Shane. She jumped back, startled to see a man standing there.

"Don't be scared." Shane draped his arm over her shoulders.

"Faith?" The man said and stepped closer. He placed his hand over his heart. "I mean, Cassie. I'm sorry, I know you have another name." He was nervous. "God, you look like your father but have my sister's eyes."

"Cassie, this is your uncle Alex." Shane gave Alex a warning look when she leaned into him, her hand tightening on his waist. "Dude, don't freak her out." He knew Alex would feel emotional meeting her for the first time, but thought he'd play it cool. Instead, feelings were written all over his face.

"I go by Brian Reed now, but you can call me Uncle Al." He smiled, taking her hand in his. "I've waited a long time to meet you. I can see so much of my sister in you." He used his other hand to touch her hair. "Same eyes and almost the same hair color."

"I... your..." A lump grew in her throat as she struggled to find her words. She had seen the emotion on her uncle's face. Standing at six feet tall with broad shoulders, he possessed a nicely groomed white beard and mustache that matched his short white hair. Though his hair color and a few deep wrinkles around his eyes hinted at his age, perhaps late fifties or early sixties, he didn't otherwise appear to be an older man. Despite this, he was quite handsome, with kind eyes. "Are my parents with you?"

"No." Alex glanced at the door. "I can only stay here a minute, because I can't risk getting caught. But I had to see you. I've waited 19 years for this, and Shane was worried he might need some help convincing you to stay awhile longer."

"Why can't I go with you?" Her voice trembled with a mix of anxiety and desperation. Sensing her weakness, Shane gently guided her to a nearby chair. Leaning against the desk beside her, he rested his hand on her shoulder, which helped to ease some of her tension.

"We have a plan to get you and your friends out. If they think you're missing, they'll search for you. We don't want them looking and can't let anyone know who you are."

"I don't want my friends involved. Why can't I go now?" She glanced at Shane. "Amy is my best friend, and I trust her not to tell anyone. I can go back and explain what's going on. I'll say goodbye, and she'll understand." Her other friends were leaving soon anyway, once they turned 18. She could see them again when they got out, but didn't want to leave without saying goodbye to Amy. "Where are my parents?"

"Look," Alex leaned forward, gently touching her arm. "I know this is a lot to absorb, but I've spent my life rescuing the people I love. I know how to get you away safely. It needs to be done a certain way, and I don't want the administrator to know that you know who you are. I need him to think that you and your friends just chose to run away."

"But…"

"Cass," Shane interrupted her. "Trust your uncle. We have a plan for Saturday. There'll be a Windmobile waiting for us." He could see the confused look on her face. "It's fast transportation. We're going to tell your friends we're running away together. If they choose to come with us, fine. If not, they will stay behind and tell others what we did. It looks innocent enough. They will believe it's the truth, which will help keep them safe. We stay for one more week, playing the role of lovesick fools. Then we run away together."

Alex knelt in front of the desk. "There's more. Cassie, once you leave, we'll be going far away. You'll be given a new identity, and you'll have to be protected. The administrator knows who you are. He's kept your identity a secret so far but may not once you disappear. Your friends might not be safe here, but we can't stop them if they choose to stay. For their safety, they can't know the truth."

Alex's words sent blood rushing to her head. "Where are my parents? Why didn't they come?" If her uncle were here, why couldn't they be?

"I can't tell them I've found you until you're in my care. They have to stay safe until I can bring you to them." He wouldn't get Lily's hopes up until he could deliver Faith in person. For nineteen years, his sister and Patrick suffered the loss of their firstborn child. "You have a fifteen-year-old brother, Cassie. He must be kept safe and hidden from the world." He glanced at the hallway, placing his finger to his lips, as someone walked by. The lights were off in the room, except for the glow of the computer screens. Someone paused outside the door, and Shane and Cassie quickly moved against the wall.

Shane squeezed Cassie's hand in reassurance. The door was locked. Whoever was outside the door did not try to unlock it.

"I think they left," Alex whispered. "I need to go." He took her by the shoulders and hugged her tightly. "You'll never know what it means to find you finally." He glanced at Shane. "Keep her safe and stick to the plan." He kissed the top of her head. "It's going to be okay, and soon you'll be where you belong."

After Alex left, Shane moved the cabinet back in front of the secret door. He turned to Cassie. "You have to act normal. Tell Amy we're in love. When we go out on Saturday, we'll tell your friends we aren't returning. I'll make up a story about having a place to go."

"I have a brother." She felt her eyes pool, recalling the look on her uncle's face. His words, 'where you belong,' echoed in her mind. She had a family that loved her. "I don't think I can act normal, Shane." She'd never feel the same again. "I can't believe this."

"Cass," he whispered, pulling her to his chest. "I know." He kissed the top of her head and rubbed her back softly. She'd handled things well so far, and it was understandable that she'd be emotional. Soon, there would be even more tears when she finally met her parents. He had spent his life preparing for this.

"Shane." She moved away from him and ran a shaky hand through her hair. "I have so many questions."

"I know you do." He leaned against the desk with a tender smile. "I'm not going anywhere. We've got all week to be together.

I'll answer all your questions soon. But right now you need to get back to your room. We can't afford to take any chances, and someone was just outside the door. They might come back."

Taking a deep breath, she knew he was right. She stared at him a moment, remembering what his body looked like with his shirt off. He stood tall and broad-shouldered, muscles carved like stone, and the rugged shadow of facial hair squaring his jawline, with his quiet confidence. She didn't want to leave him. She needed the way he made her feel safe. There was strength in every line of him, and a great deal of trust, though she still had so many questions. "How do you fit into all this? How do you know my family? Who are you?"

"My dad is a good friend of your mom. Before I was born, he helped rescue your aunt Kate. I should probably tell you your mom is a twin. You have an aunt who looks identical to your mother." He smiled when her eyes grew wide. "I guess the reveals just keep getting better." He could only imagine what it was like for her to hear all this. "Anyway, a year after the rescue, your parents asked for his help again. And for the past 19 years, my dad hasn't stopped looking for you."

"What about your mom?"

Shane crossed his arms and sighed. "It's a long story, Cass. Basically, my mom split because she didn't want to live her life that way. My dad was always moving, always helping your parents. When my mom left, she left me too." He wanted to tell her he'd never lived an everyday life, because his father was so obsessed with finding her. As a result, his childhood was far from normal.

Now that she was found, he wondered how his life would change. Would he and his father finally settle down? Would he get a job or maybe go to college? Would he know how to live a life that didn't center around searching for a missing girl? Three years ago, he attended a school he genuinely liked, where he was starting to make friends and develop feelings for a girl. But then his father uprooted them again upon hearing about a strange redhead who allegedly healed children in Alaska. Naturally, his father chased the lead, dragging Shane along. As always, it was a dead end, just another false hope. Alaska hadn't been too bad, and he had enjoyed the natural beauty, but he knew better than to get attached.

"So, your life has revolved around finding me?" She wasn't sure how to feel about that. She thought about the question he'd asked the day they met. He had wanted to know if she was happy. Now she wondered the same about him. "Have you been happy, Shane?"

He rested his hands on her waist. "It wasn't a bad life, Cassie. I learned a lot, and I got to see some great parts of the world."

"Are you always this difficult in answering a question? I asked you a simple question, Shane. I don't care if it was a good life. I want to know, are you happy?" She tried remembering the words he'd used the day they met. She gave him the same raised eyebrow look that he'd given her, and repeated. "Are you happy?"

"You're funny." He smiled. "Yes, Cassie, I've been happy." And he realized it was the truth. His life may have differed from other kids', but he was close to his dad. He felt a sense of pride and accomplishment in finding her. He knew how important it was. How important *she* was. He loved Lily and Kate like they were his second moms and felt part of a family. Lily is truly the most important person on earth, and being part of her life felt like a privilege. It was meaningful, and he understood why his father had chosen to commit to keeping the family safe.

"I have an Aunt? My mom's an identical twin?"

"I love your delayed responses. I can practically see wheels spinning in your head. I actually can't wait for you to meet your aunt. I know Kate well. She's a fun, straight-forward lady."

"Tell me about my family."

He shook his head. "We can't stay here. We've got to get back to our rooms. You're going to meet your family soon enough."

She reached for his hand when he started to move away. "Wait! How did you contact my uncle? How did he know to come here tonight?" She didn't want to leave with so many unanswered questions.

"I have a hidden wire in my belt. My dad and Alex can hear me when I press the button."

"Oh my gosh." She tried to think of all their shared conversations. "They've been listening to everything we talk about?"

"No. I don't keep the feed on. Only when I need to reach them."

She glanced down at Shane's belt. "Can they hear us now?" It felt strange to think her family was listening in.

"It's off right now." He planned to turn it on in the tunnel, so they knew everything was okay. He guessed what was going through her mind. "It's fine, Cassie, don't worry. They only hear what I want them to. We were worried about the blood draw. We don't want anyone knowing your blood is different."

Her mind was racing again. "I have different blood?" She hadn't thought of that. "Why is my blood different?"

More footsteps sounded outside the door. Shane put his finger to his lips. Then he whispered in her ear, "No more talking tonight. We've got to get back to our rooms."

His breath was soft on her cheek, and her pulse quickened from the gentle way he stroked her arm. She knew her mind would be swimming with a million questions soon, but at the moment, those thoughts vanished, and she hugged him tightly. She felt a pull toward him, an unspoken thread tying her to him from deep in her core. Something she couldn't explain, only that being near him felt effortless, like gravity. She glanced up at him, trying to ignore the force that pulled tighter when she tried to move away. "I dread crawling back. I can't stand those vents."

"I know." He wasn't claustrophobic, but the coffin-like passages were enough to bother anyone. "I'll go with you, so you're not alone. But it'll take me longer to backtrack to the boy's wing, so we'd better leave now."

Chapter 11

It wasn't like Cassie had difficulty waking to her alarm, but she felt as if she'd just fallen asleep, which she had. She dragged herself out of bed and watched Amy take her medication. She was still sick, but the antibiotics were helping her and the others. A bacterial infection caused the illness, infecting only those who drank a particular batch of juice.

Everyone in Cassie's age group was given another day off from school. The 'free day' was fun for those who hadn't been sick. Students used the opportunity to hang out in the courtyard and play games such as frisbee, croquet, and soccer. Those still recovering got another day of bed rest. Cassie would have preferred checking out new books in the library, but no new shipments had arrived. She'd already read every book they currently had.

Julie chose to lie under the palm trees and watch the shirt-less guys play soccer. She was feeling better, but still too weak to do anything beyond lying on the grass and drooling over boys. Amy stayed in bed for a while, then walked down to the art room where she could sit and paint. For the past few weeks, she wanted to paint a portrait of Andrew. Her palms itched to mix the paint colors to create the hazel of his eyes. It sucked that she wasn't allowed to keep her paintings in her room, but she was proud that the art teacher hung them in the hallway.

Cassie sat on the grass and watched Shane kick a soccer ball toward the net. He only wore black shorts, again revealing his mus-cled upper body. Cassie found her eyes wandering to his chest a lot. They needed to keep up appearances while conveying an obvious interest in each other. That part wasn't hard to fake.

It was a relief that her friends were recovering, but she still had a sick feeling in her stomach—anxiety from the new knowledge she was keeping inside. She ached with anticipation of her future and couldn't stop thinking about meeting her parents. Knowing she belonged somewhere, knowing she had a mother and father who had been searching for her all her life, was mind-blowing.

What would they think of her? She hadn't experienced anything in life, so there was very little she could say about herself. More than anything, she wanted to know about their life. What kind of people were they? She was anxious to learn about her mother's ability. How and why was she able to heal? Shane had said that Lily Mc-Callister could heal wounds, radiation and cancer. Would her blood be different, like her mother's? Her mother was famous, known by everyone, except her.

I have a brother. She supposed Amy was the closest thing she'd had to a sibling. Her friendship with Amy was all she'd ever had in the way of family. Could she have that kind of bond with her brother someday? She pulled her knees to her chest to rest her weary head.

Feeling his heart wrench at the despair on Cassie's face, Shane kicked the ball to where she sat. She was so beautiful, he thought. He'd enjoyed the way their friendship had changed since he'd been able to share the truth with her. He could be his authentic self, and for the first time, he felt a deep connection with someone without secrets and pretenses standing in the way. He'd shared more of his vulnerabilities with her and hadn't felt judged. She seemed to understand his moods, reactions, and playful humor. He was pleased she was letting her guard down, but with it, he became aware of the strain she was under. It was good they were leaving soon, because he could see her drowning from all the secrets. He ran to her little spot in the shade, then kicked the ball back to his friends, before sitting beside her.

"Will you give me a smile?" He lifted her hand gently, kissing the inside of her wrist.

"Shane, you can't do that when staff can see. It's not allowed."

"I want them to see how much I like you." He glanced at one of the administrative assistants. He knew which people had the job of monitoring teens. "It's part of our plan."

"Has all this been an act?" She couldn't help but wonder if his attention and affection had just been part of his mission. She hoped it wasn't all strictly for show, since she believed their unspoken understandings.

He knew what she meant. The uncertainty in her voice made him reach his hand up to her face. "Hey," he rubbed his thumb along her cheek. "You know nothing I feel for you is fake. I care about you, Cassie. You didn't make it easy for me to get to know you. I like that. I like that you challenge me."

"You need to move away now," a voice behind Shane urged. "You're too close."

Shane sighed and looked up at the man standing over him with arms crossed. "We're just friends. I'm asking if she's feeling better."

"No intimate contact allowed." The man didn't emphasize the command; instead, he sounded somewhat bored with his job.

"Got it." Shane winked at her. "I'll see you again soon, Cass."

***

The walk to the greenhouse always brought a sense of tranquility, especially at the entrance where a transparent glass bridge provided a view of the sky. Cassie never failed to pause and admire its beauty, if only for a moment. However, dark storm clouds blocked the sun today, and raindrops pelted the glass. Despite the storm, Amy, Andrew, Julie, and Caleb still planned to sneak out that night. It was Cassie's last day at the orphanage. The time had flown by faster than she anticipated. While part of her was excited to explore the world and meet her family, leaving the only home she'd ever known also weighed heavily on her heart. She gazed at the sky and wondered whether she'd ever see her teachers or classmates again. Who among her friends would choose to join her or stay behind? The uncertainty gnawed at her, leaving an ache in her chest.

"Are you going to stare at the sky all day?"

Cassie forced back the urge to cry as she met Amy's eyes.

"What's wrong with you? You haven't been yourself." She moved to Cassie's side as classmates passed them to the greenhouse. "You've been distracted and quiet for days. Did you and Shane fight?"

"No."

"You're supposed to be happy and walking around with a stupid grin when you're in love. You and Shane clearly like each other, but you seem sad or worried." She placed her hands on her hips. "What's going on?"

"Nothing." It was too mentally draining to discuss this with her. The past few days had been the hardest of her life. Trying to act normal when she felt her mind would explode. Her heart was heavy with anxiety and uncertainty. She knew she'd leave the orphanage someday, but not like this. She thought she'd have Amy. She thought she'd get a job working in a greenhouse somewhere, live in an apartment with her best friend. Maybe travel someday.

Stepping to the side so students could pass, Amy shifted closer. "Are you worried about tonight?"

"I guess."

Owen walked by, waving to Cassie before jumping in front of her. "Hi, Cass!" He spoke with his typical excitement. "I'm working in Greenhouse today but won't be in your section."

"You're in my section, Owen." Amy nudged him gently away from Cassie. "I'll see you in a few minutes."

Owen's smile dropped. Amy's tone had told him to get lost. "Is everything okay?" he asked Cassie.

"I'm fine."

"She's in love with Shane, Owen. Deal with it."

"Oh." Owen couldn't have appeared more crushed if he tried.

"Bye!" Amy waved her hand at him.

Cassie's heart sank as he walked away, his gaze fixed downward, shoulders slumped. Would she miss seeing his freckled face and brown eyes every day? Would she miss his overly cheerful grin and that high-pitched voice? She returned her gaze to Amy's stoic face. "You didn't have to be mean to him."

Shane's plan to make everyone believe they were in love had worked. Amy was convinced, and so was everyone else. If they ran off, no one would suspect anything other than two lovesick teenagers seeking freedom.

Amy sighed, feeling guilty for hurting Owen's feelings, even though she found his crush on Cassie annoying. "You're not thinking of backing out, are you?"

"No." Cassie stood up straight and squared her shoulders. "I'm fine, let's get to work." Their time to report to the greenhouse was almost up.

Chapter 12

The greenhouse was kept at eighty-five degrees. The air was thick with humidity, but the giant fans used to keep bugs away from the vegetation made it easier for Cassie to breathe. She lined trays with pebbles and covered them with water. The idea was to allow the water to evaporate, adding humidity to the greenhouse. Next, she started seeds in trays. Some of the seedlings already emerging would be transplanted to the soil line.

The black soil felt warm. The smell of earth filled Cassie's senses, but she was elsewhere. Thoughts clouded her mind, again creating the urge to cry. She held the dirt in her hand. She'd seen pictures of forests and trees lining the earth for miles. She loved nature and imagined sitting in a quiet forest, listening to the sounds of animals. Feeling the wind caress her skin, the sun warm on her face. She'd never seen a live animal except for the seeing-eye dog her teacher brought into the classroom when she was ten. Or had she been twelve? Once in science lab, Cassie had helped dissect a bird. She hadn't gotten very far because as soon as her partner had cut into it, she passed out. She'd awoken in the hallway with an ice pack on her head.

"Umm… I think you've dug that hole deep enough."

She looked up to find Julie standing over her, then glanced down to see the hole was in fact deeper than needed for the seeds. "Why are you here, Jules?"

"I was asked to switch jobs with Michelle because she wasn't feeling well." Julie pulled her hair back and knelt beside Cassie. "I hate this hot box, but I guess it's better than folding laundry." There weren't any jobs Julie liked. She found most of them unpleasant and tedious. She couldn't wait to leave the orphanage and never have to work sections again.

"You hate digging in the ground, too." Cassie handed her a tray of seeds. "You can place them in the holes if you want." It meant less dirt under her nails.

"Thanks." Julie held her hand out, admiring her long, clean nails. "So... you and Shane have been pretty tight this week." She had noticed how they huddled together every chance they got. Shane was always looking for excuses to touch Cassie now, and Julie resented that he no longer paid attention to anyone but her. His charming flirtations with other girls were gone. "Have you kissed him yet?"

A seed fell from Cassie's hand, and she carefully picked it back up. "It's none of your business, Julie."

"Don't get all bent out of shape. Tonight, I'm going to kiss Caleb. I might even do other things with him." She waited for Cassie to reply, but when she didn't, she continued. "We're almost eighteen and practically adults. I want to know what I'm missing. I want to know what it's like to touch a man. Don't you?"

A bead of sweat dripped from Cassie's forehead, and she wiped it with the back of her hand. "I'm not having this conversation. I know how you feel about guys. I think everyone in this school knows how you feel about them."

Julie set her tray down. "Gosh, Cass, you're such a prude. You act so cool and read so many books, but you don't really know anything, do you? You're no fun to talk to. You like living in your little inexperienced bubble." She brushed a piece of black soil off her knee. "I'm going to wash veggies with Amy. At least *she* can talk about guys." She stood up straight and squared her shoulders. "I'll see you tonight at dinner."

Out of everyone and everything Cassie would miss, Julie wasn't one. Usually, she would ignore her rudeness, as her words usually meant nothing. However, at the moment, Julie's words were sinking in. Of course, she thought about kissing Shane. He and the secrets he'd shared were all she thought about. She was aware of how naive she was. In a few short hours, she'd be leaving the only safe, structured life she'd ever known and entering a world she knew nothing about.

Chapter 13

"Why are you staring at your clothes?" Amy laughed, checking the clock on the nightstand.

Cassie pondered what belongings she should take. Should she bring extra shoes, just in case? She and Amy wore the standard work uniform, black pants and a beige t-shirt. Her shoes were plain black with jagged rubber soles. Shoes that Julie hated. She closed her drawer. "I just wondered if we should change. We don't know what the weather will be like outside the dome."

"It'll be warm, I'm sure."

There were no knick-knacks or mementoes that Cassie would miss or need, except for a necklace Amy had made for her in art class. It had small glass beads strung on a thin, black string. It was the only gift Cassie had ever received, and it meant a great deal to her. Amy called it a birthday present, though no one at Saving Souls celebrated birthdays. Most kids had no idea when their birthday even was. Christmas was celebrated with games and songs, but never gifts. When Amy turned her back, Cassie slipped the necklace into her pocket.

"Help me move the dresser." Amy turned around and gathered her hair into a ponytail at her neck. "I'll go first if you want me to."

In that moment, Cassie desperately wanted to tell her the truth. She wanted to tell her who Shane was and that her parents were alive and waiting for her. She wanted her to know she was leaving the orphanage and would never again share this room with her. Her life was about to change drastically. She wanted…needed her best friend to be with her.

"Hey, Cassie... seriously, what's wrong? You've got this look like you're about to cry. Are you scared?" Amy's hand rested gently on her shoulder, her eyes drawn with concern. "Don't worry. I don't think we'll get caught. Remember what Andrew said? We're leaving in nine months anyway, so why does it matter? We need to find out what's out there."

Swallowing the lump in her throat, Cassie hugged her tightly. "You're the best friend anyone could ever ask for. I'm just glad we're doing this together."

"Me too. Stop worrying so much."

***

The journey through the ventilation shafts felt never-ending, maybe because Amy, who was in front, kept stopping to rest her hands and knees. She paused to shine the tablet's light down the tunnel. "Did we pass the shaft?"

"Not yet. We'll be turning left just ahead."

"I can't breathe, and I'm feeling dizzy." Amy stretched out on her belly and closed her eyes. "I need a minute to rest." If she closed her eyes, she could pretend she was in her bed, not a confined tunnel.

"We have to keep moving." Cassie also hated the shafts, but it was worse when you stopped. The tablet went to sleep mode, shutting off the light. The darkness was so complete, Cassie couldn't see a thing. "Amy?" Panic sent a rush through her. She banged her head on the shaft, feeling trapped in the tiny space. "Amy!"

"Be quiet!" Amy turned the light back on. "They'll hear us." She got to her forearms and began to slither again. When they finally reached the end, they were relieved to find it open. Amy dropped down first. Cassie followed and landed in Shane's strong arms.

"What took you so long?"

"Have you waited long?"

"Long enough," Andrew replied, gently pulling Amy by the arm. "Let's go!"

Shane tipped Cassie's face back so he could look in her eyes. "You okay?"

"I'm glad I'll never have to crawl through those shafts again."

"Hey, let's close the vent," Caleb said, trying to reach it. He wasn't tall enough, so Shane shut it.

Andrew had opened the door to the tunnel, and Julie and Amy followed behind him. They walked down a few flights of cement stairs before entering a narrow passage. The cement tunnel walls felt cool, and the dirt beneath their feet was hard and lumpy. The only light they had was from their tablets.

No one said anything until Amy tripped. Andrew caught her around the waist. Everyone laughed. They continued walking slower, watching the ground until Julie let out a yelp and stumbled back. Suddenly, the tunnel was bright with light.

"Mr. Jamerson!" Julie couldn't have sounded more surprised. "I…we…" She moved aside as the administrator raised his lantern.

"I knew you kids were coming this way. I thought I'd wait and catch you in the act." His eyes roamed past the kids and landed on Cassie. "Everyone can go back to their rooms, except for Cassie. You need to come with me."

Shane stepped in front of her, reaching back for her hand. "She's not going anywhere with you."

"Why me?" Cassie asked at the same time Andrew did.

"You'll all be dealt with tomorrow. Cassie, do as you're told and come with me now," Mr. Jamerson demanded, stepping forward.

"What do you want with her?" Amy glanced nervously at her friends. Andrew stood beside her, with Julie slightly behind him. Caleb had his hand on Julie's shoulder, and behind them stood Shane and Cassie. "Why do you always want to see her?" Amy knew about all the times the administrator would ask to see Cassie and make her uncomfortable with his odd questions. She felt it was bizarre the way he'd touch her and hold her hand. Now, something about him being in the tunnel and only wanting to take Cassie didn't sit well with her. She moved protectively in front of her friend.

"Let them all go, Jamerson." Mrs. Reynolds appeared behind him. "You can't do this."

Caleb asked, "Do what?"

"What are you doing here, Mrs. Reynolds?" Julie asked, sounding more shocked.

"What's going on?" Andrew glanced sideways at Shane.

Jamerson turned to Laura Reynolds and pulled a gun from behind his back. "I knew you couldn't be trusted, Laura. I should have fired you years ago."

"Let them go." Laura held her hands up. "You're not a violent man. You don't want to hurt these kids. You know this is wrong."

"Is that a gun?" Amy asked softly, turning to Andrew and squeezing his arm tightly.

"She's worth too much money," Jamerson replied. "I can retire and never work again. My entire family will be set for life. I can't turn it down."

"What's he talking about?" Andrew asked, looking around.

Jamerson turned the gun on Shane and, at the same time, pushed Laura back. "Cassie, if you come with me, no one will be hurt. But I'll shoot anyone who gets in my way. I'm warning you kids. Do as you're told!" His voice had a tone of harsh command the kids had never heard before.

Shane stepped forward and pulled Amy and Andrew behind him. "Jamerson, we are leaving—all of us. You need to put the gun down. If you're after money, I can get that for you."

"I had a feeling you weren't who you claimed to be. Are you even a teenager?"

As soon as Jamerson glanced away, Shane quickly removed the gun from his hand. In a matter of seconds, Shane had it, and Jamerson was on the floor unconscious.

"That was amazing!" Andrew stated in a high pitch, setting his hands on top of his head. "I can't believe you did that."

"Who are you?" Julie whispered in awe.

"You can't go out that way." Laura grabbed Shane's arm.

"There's a group of men with guns waiting for you just outside the tunnel."

Shane pointed to his belt and showed her the wire tucked inside. "I've got friends who can hear us. They're outside waiting to help." He reached for Cassie's hand again. "We're going this way." He stepped around his teacher.

"No wait!" Amy pulled Cassie's arm. "What's going on?" She didn't feel right going against Mrs. Reynolds. The whole situation was wrong. Her heart was slamming in her chest. "Don't go out there!"

"Kids, you can follow me, and I'll take you back to your rooms." Laura stepped over Jamerson's body. "There are tons of tunnels leading out of this compound. It's how they built the dome. The tunnels were made first."

"We have a plan." Shane glanced down at Cassie. "I've got help waiting for us. This is the way we need to go. Your uncle's out there. You need to trust me."

"It's a trap." Laura put her hands on Julie and Caleb's arms. "You need to trust me. I can keep you safe."

"Why? Why are you helping us?" Cassie wondered.

"I know who you are, Cassie. I've known for years. I knew you were brought here for safekeeping. I provided the anonymous tip to your family that you were here. I discovered that Jamerson also knew the truth about you, and I no longer trusted him. You're not safe here anymore."

Shane narrowed his eyes at her. "You posted the link to our website?"

"Yes." Laura looked at Cassie. "I knew you were Lily McCallister's daughter because of your eyes. And then, when Jamerson started asking you to heal people, I knew he'd also discovered you. Do you have the ability, Cassie?"

"No."

"What ability? Who are you?" Caleb ran a frustrated hand through his hair.

"What is she talking about?" Amy wondered why Cassie appeared to understand what was happening.

"We need to go. We don't have time for this." Shane wanted to leave before Jamerson became conscious. He began to pull Cassie.

She pulled back hesitantly. "Maybe we should go with her."

"I'll go with you," Julie told her teacher.

"No." Shane squeezed Cassie's hand, staring into her eyes. "You have to trust me, Cass. I need you to trust me."

She felt torn. Her heart was pounding as she glanced from Mrs. Reynolds to Amy. She knew she had to make a quick decision. "Amy," she took her friend's hand. "I trust Shane. We need to go with him, and I'll explain what's going on as soon as we're safe. Please come with us."

Amy shook her head and took a step back. "I'm scared. I'm going with Mrs. Reynolds."

"No." Andrew wrapped his arm around Amy's waist. "We're going to follow Shane." He didn't have a clue what was happening, but he'd gotten to know Shane and trusted him. Clearly, Shane was someone who could take care of himself.

"Be careful," Laura told her students. "If you return this way, I'll wait for you in the science room. If I'm not there, you can find another tunnel in the east wing of the greenhouse. The water cooler covers the opening. Just push hard on the seam line for the door to open." She pulled Cassie into a hug. "I hope you find your family, sweetheart. You were always my favorite."

Julie watched as her teacher walked away. "Who the hell are you?" She asked, turning back to Cassie.

"We'll explain later. We need to move." Shane tucked Jamerson's gun behind his back and pulled Cassie along. He was relieved to see everyone following at a fast pace. He had Andrew to thank for that. They had another few yards to go, and then he saw the gate at the end of the tunnel.

"Stay behind me," he told the group. "If we get separated, head for the Lake. My group belongs to an organization called FAITH. If you get taken by anyone, ask for the password. If they respond with

FAITH, you can trust them. They're here to help."

"What happens if they don't know the password?" Julie's mind raced with uncertainty and fear.

"Then they aren't with me, and you need to get away." Shane carefully pushed the gate open and glanced around at the dark. As his eyes adjusted, he saw an open field with rolling sand hills and a few large oak trees. The orphanage was about one hundred and twenty yards behind them. He wasn't sure how far away the road was.

"Oh my gosh." Cool wind blew against Amy's face for the first time, and she glanced at the sky. "Look at the moon!" It was a solid white face against a black, endless expanse. The glow was brilliant.

"Come on." Shane pointed. "Head for the trees." He didn't like that it was dark, and no one was there to greet him. Alex was supposed to be waiting at the gate.

As they sprinted from the tunnel, shots rang out. The noise pierced the quiet night, and Caleb fell to the ground groaning. Cassie glanced back as Julie called out and dropped beside him to see what was wrong—three more shots. Amy screamed before Andrew dove on top of her. Before Cassie could turn, Shane grabbed her around the waist, pulling her to the ground, his body shielding hers. More gunshots sounded, and she tried to look at her friends. "Amy!" she called out. Her heart was racing, blood pounding in her ears.

"Stay down!" Shane yelled to everyone, shifting so his weight wouldn't crush Cassie. He glanced at Caleb, lying next to Julie, holding his leg. Shane saw the red light flicker behind the trees and cursed under his breath. It was the danger signal. His team was warning him to clear out. "We have to get back to the tunnel!" He shouted at Andrew, who was a few feet from Caleb, holding Amy in his arms. "Oh no." He rolled off Cassie. "Follow me, Cass, and do exactly what I do." He crawled over to Andrew, his hands sinking into the thick, damp sand, and stared down at Amy's blood-stained shirt. "Can you get her back to the tunnel?"

Andrew nodded and quickly reached his feet, holding Amy in his arms. More gunshots sounded, and Andrew ran as fast as he could.

"Run!" A voice sounded from behind the trees.

Shane grabbed Cassie's hand, pulling her up. Then he helped Caleb stand and ordered Julie and Cassie to run fast, back to the tunnel. Andrew returned first, followed by Cassie and Julie stumbling into the gate. Shane wasn't far behind, struggling to pull Caleb along. The shots coming from behind the trees had been Shane's men providing cover. The initial plan had been compromised.

"Shane!" Cassie yelled, slowing her pace to wait for him.

"They aren't following us." He caught up to her and took her hand. "Yet."

**

Andrew stopped to catch his breath, his chest heaving from carrying Amy. "Amy, can you hear me?"

Julie leaned over her. "Guys, I think she's dying! There's a lot of blood."

"We need to get her to the clinic and wake the Doctor!" Shane took Amy from Andrew. "I'll take her from here. You help Caleb."

Cassie's heart raced as they stumbled back to the science room, relieved to escape the dark, lengthy tunnel. Mrs. Reynolds's absence only added to her panic. Shane gently set Amy down and searched for towels to try to stop the bleeding, while Andrew leaned over her, tenderly stroking her cheek. Concern and fear were swimming in his wide eyes.

"There's so much blood." Julie glanced around, feeling helpless.

"Amy!" Cassie pushed Andrew aside to kneel beside her friend. Tears streamed down her face as she struggled to avoid the scent of blood. Shane knelt and lifted Amy's shirt.

"Apply pressure," he told Andrew, as he pressed the towel to the oozing hole in her side. Shane suspected she passed out either from too much blood loss, pain or shock, dropping her blood pressure dangerously low. Either way, her wound was severe. He glanced at Cassie. "She's losing too much blood." They could get help from the night staff wandering the halls, and there was a call button used for emergencies, but getting medical help would still probably take more time than they had.

Hearing the strain in Shane's voice, Cassie stared transfixed at Amy's pale face. Fear swamped her. She couldn't lose Amy. She was everything to her—the one person in the world she loved dearly, her most cherished friend, and the only family she'd ever known.

Cassie gripped Amy's hand tightly with a surge of panic and fear. She wanted to make the wound go away, to stem the flow of blood from Amy's still body. A massive heat rose inside her, causing her arms and legs to tingle. Placing her hands on Amy's arm, she felt a surge of energy—something inexplicable and entirely new.

"I'll heal you," she whispered, her voice barely audible amid the chaos. She felt something powerful building inside her, every fiber of her being focused on stopping the bleeding. Her body responded in a way she knew wasn't normal; the intense heat practically took her breath away. In that moment, she realized she held the power to heal, feeling something coursing through her veins and flowing past her fingertips.

"What the heck?" Julie leaned back as a blue light emanated from Cassie's hands.

"Holy…" Andrew's eyes grew wide as he slowly exhaled. "What's happening?"

Shane's gaze shifted from Cassie's hands to her face. Her usually pale skin was now bright red, and he observed with astonishment as a blue glow hovered like fog from her hands. He had witnessed Cassie's mother, Lily, heal people before, but never in such a spectacular manner. He could practically feel the heat and electric waves radiating from her body.

Shane removed the towel from Amy's bullet wound, his eyes fixed on the miraculous scene unfolding before him. As he watched, the skin slowly closed over the wound, leaving not a trace of the gunshot injury behind, not even a scar.

Cassie opened her eyes, no longer in control of her body. The flow of energy felt like all her nerves were being pulled from her flesh. She couldn't catch her breath.

"Stop now, Cass. She's healed." Shane touched her arm, feeling intense heat and a slight vibration.

"I can't." She gasped, staring down at her hands and the blue halo beneath her palms. Overwhelmed with the knowledge of what her body was doing, panic surged through her, and she gasped for air.

"Cassie, look at me." Shane gently framed her face in his hands. As her eyes met his, he calmly instructed, "Slow your breathing." She was panting, hyperventilating through her mouth. "That's it," he encouraged softly, guiding her to take slower, deeper breaths.

The sensation began to fade, and tears welled in her eyes as she grasped the magnitude of what had just occurred. It felt surreal, completely overwhelming. Her entire body felt charged.

"Why are you crying?" Amy asked, staring at her friend. "What happened?"

"Unbelievable." Julie covered her mouth in astonishment as she watched Amy sit up and wipe away the blood from where a wound had been moments ago. "Did you all see what just happened?" She stared at Caleb and then glanced at Andrew. "That's not possible." She took a step back in disbelief. "It can't be possible."

"Um... Can you do that for me?" Caleb held up his bloody hands to her.

Shane swiftly moved to Caleb and pressed a towel to his right thigh where he'd been shot. "How bad is it?"

"How should I know? I've never been shot before."

"This is insane." Julie couldn't grasp it. "You're a freak with some superpower. I'm... this isn't real... this can't be happening."

"Get a grip, Jules." Andrew knelt beside Amy and chuckled with relief. He was immensely relieved and overjoyed to see she was okay. Feeling a bit in shock, he helped her to her feet, and Cassie grabbed her tightly.

"I thought you were dying. I was so afraid of losing you." She glanced down at her hands, relieved to see they looked normal again. The heat in her body was subsiding. Overwhelmed with emotion and out of breath, she held on to Amy.

Amy glanced down. "I was shot. How am I okay now?"

"Cassie, a little blue glow over here would be nice," Caleb said, holding a towel to his wound.

"I don't know if I can do it again. I'm not even sure how it happened." Cassie let go of Amy, feeling a sense of urgency for water. She licked her lips. Her mouth felt parched, and she was incredibly thirsty.

Shane tied a rag tightly around Caleb's leg. "We need to get out of here." He was afraid that whoever had shot at them would soon come storming through the tunnel. Mr. Jamerson was gone, and so was Mrs. Reynolds. Who knew when or if they'd be back and where they went. "Can you walk, Caleb?"

"I think so."

"Can we talk about what just happened?" Andrew placed his hands on his head in disbelief. "Cassie, you just made Amy's bullet hole completely disappear."

Moving over to Caleb, Cassie set her hand on his arm. "Let me see if I can do it again." She wanted to heal his leg, but nothing was happening. She tried to build that strange energy again, but it wasn't there. Instead, she felt incredible thirst and couldn't focus on anything except her need for water.

Shane noted the blank look on her face. "We don't have time for this. Caleb's wound isn't life-threatening. It appears to be more of a graze along his thigh muscle." He flipped his belt over to reveal a small silver microphone. "I've got people out there waiting for us, and we need to get to the tunnel in the greenhouse." He'd turned the transmitter on. He hoped his father or Alex could hear him now.

"No way," Caleb complained. "I need the doctor, and I'm not walking all the way to the greenhouse. You're not a doctor, Shane."

Irritation lined his voice. "I need medical help now." He glanced at the emergency call light.

Andrew stepped forward, holding a dolly that the science teacher had left by the desk after using it to transport large boxes filled with the lab's new equipment. "Get on this, and I'll wheel you to the greenhouse." He felt uneasy about their prolonged stay in the science lab and the lack of pursuit from anyone. Like Shane, he was eager to leave the orphanage. "We need to get out of here, Caleb."

Chapter 14

At 2:00 a.m., the hallways were deserted, with everyone mandated to be in their beds. Security guards continued their patrols, so Shane knew to keep the group quiet. The corridors were dark, except for intermittent illumination provided by digital flat-screen art displays. The displays alternated between scenes of tropical waterfalls and tranquil fields and forests. Andrew pushed the dolly with Caleb aboard, moving rapidly, causing everyone to jog to keep up.

"I know I'm not the only one whose mind is blown." Andrew tried to keep his voice low, but he was obsessing over what happened and needed to talk about it. "How did you do that, Cassie?"

"Where did the blue light come from? What was that?" Julie moved closer to Cassie's side.

Caleb groaned as he held on to the dolly.

"You guys need to keep it down," Shane whispered, glancing around. "We can't risk anyone hearing us. We have to get out of here." Just as he warned them, they caught sight of a flashlight beam up ahead. He cursed softly under his breath. "You guys stay put. I'll handle this."

"You're not supposed to be out," the security guard stated, shining his light directly at Shane's face. "I'll need your name and—"

Before he could finish his sentence, Shane quickly delivered a right hook to the guard's jaw, rendering him unconscious.

"How does he do that?" Julie whispered in amazement, scanning the area for more guards. "We didn't even need to use the vents when Shane could just knock people out."

Shane returned to the group. "We've got to run and keep

quiet!" He took the lead, and the others followed closely behind, running to keep pace. Focused on what Cassie had just done, they forgot that just recently they'd been shot at and were still potentially in danger. When they arrived at the greenhouse, they were all gasping for breath.

"I don't like this. It seems too easy." Andrew nervously glanced around.

Shane nodded. "I don't either." He slowly opened the door to the greenhouse and peered inside. The lights were off, but the dome had track lighting along the ceiling, providing enough light for them to see. "Cassie, wait!"

She ran to the water cooler, snatching a paper cup. "I'm so thirsty! I need water." She took the cup and gulped it down. Unsatisfied, she refilled the cup again.

All eyes were fixed on her as she continued to gulp down cup after cup of water. Shane's eyebrows furrowed with concern as he observed her. "We need to move this cabinet." He gestured to Andrew, and together, they pushed the heavy water cabinet aside, revealing a large seam running down the wall. With a little effort, they pushed until the door swung open. He glanced back at Cassie refilling her cup yet again. "Take it easy, Cass. You're going to make yourself sick."

"I'm so thirsty it's torture. I've never felt this thirsty before." She continued to drink, relishing the way the cold water soothed her parched throat and mouth.

"We need to run through this tunnel. That security guard is probably awake now and calling for help. There could be more people looking for us now." Shane glanced at the ceiling, where small holes were spaced along the metal beams. "And I think there are cameras in here."

"I always suspected they were watching us." Andrew scanned the walls. "I bet this place is full of hidden cameras. I bet that's how they knew we snuck out." He pushed the door open wider. "Let's go."

"Wait!" Julie called out in a strained voice as she reached for Caleb. "I'm not going!" She had had time to process everything that had happened. "Mr. Jamerson isn't interested in us. We should have just gone back to our rooms. Cassie is the one he wants." And now she knew why. She still couldn't believe what she had seen. She was relieved that Amy was alive, but the entire ordeal terrified her. "What could he do to us? I don't think anything will happen." She shifted nervously. "Doc sleeps in the medical wing. I will wake him up and have him tend to Caleb's leg." She liked the doctor and trusted he would keep her safe.

"Julie, you've been so eager to leave here. Now we finally have the chance to go, and you want to stay?" Amy said, feeling confused and concerned.

"Not like this." She put her arms out in a helpless manner. "I'd like to have my file and know who my family is and their information on me. I want to feel safe, and I don't feel safe with you." She glanced at Shane with trepidation in her eyes. "You're... I don't know who you are, Shane, but you're..."

"Trouble." Caleb finished her sentence for her. "I agree with Jules, I'm staying."

"We need to stay together," Andrew replied.

"Cassie's the reason we were almost killed! She's why we're in this mess. I'm not leaving with her." Tears welled in Julie's eyes as the weight of their ordeal overwhelmed her. "I'm sorry, Cass, but my gut says to stay far away from you." She turned her gaze to Amy. "You should stay with us."

Feeling anxious to keep moving, Shane stepped forward. "I get you're scared, Jules, but you're not safe here. My people can keep you safe."

Caleb hobbled to Julie's side and leaned on her shoulder. "Julie is right, Shane. You told us to trust you and follow you outside. Look what happened!" He spoke with disbelief, still processing being shot. "I'm not going through another tunnel to end up shot again or worse. At least inside here, we know we're safe."

Cassie cast a nervous glance at Amy, wondering if it was safer for all of them to stay behind. Despite her trust in Shane, Caleb was right—his initial plan to get her out hadn't succeeded. She didn't want to be the reason her friends were in danger. "I think you should all stay here."

"What?" Shane stared at her, his expression incredulous. "No."

"Julie's right, Shane." She felt torn with concern. "Here, they might be safe. But out there, it could easily be another trap or worse." Her stomach twisted with unease, the night's events casting a shadow of doubt over their escape plan. She couldn't shake the feeling that more trouble awaited them outside. She looked at her friends, her mind racing with questions about Mrs. Reynolds and Mr. Jamerson. "I don't think Jamerson will hurt them. I'm the one he wants."

There wasn't time to debate. Shane wanted to get Cassie out of the orphanage and meet up with his father and Alex. Too much time had already been wasted.

"I'm going with you." Amy took Cassie's hand. "You're my best friend, and I won't stay here and worry about you." There was also a part of her that needed answers. She needed to know how Cassie healed her and who she was. She couldn't return to her room alone, nor could she go back to the orphanage's everyday life.

With a sigh of relief, Shane turned to Julie. "Take Caleb to the clinic. Don't tell anyone what you saw tonight." He glanced at Andrew. "Coming?"

"I go where Amy goes."

Amy turned and quickly hurried to Julie and hugged her. "You've been a pain in my butt for years, but I'm still going to miss you. Please take care." She reached for Caleb next. "I hope you'll be okay." She kissed his cheek.

It was suddenly awkward watching Amy and Caleb say their goodbyes. Cassie felt a lump in her throat, unsure whether Caleb and Julie would welcome a hug from her. But then Julie walked up to her and wrapped her arms around Cassie's shoulders.

"I always knew you were strange, but I love you." Even though she'd always been jealous of Cassie, she didn't want any harm to come to her. She'd shared every day of her life with her, and Cassie was her friend no matter what. Julie felt tightness in her throat at the thought of never seeing her again. "Take care of yourself." She turned to Shane. "How will we find you one day?"

"I'll find you," He promised, his tone softening as he observed the emotional farewell between Caleb, Andrew, Julie, and Cassie. Shane knew it had to be hard to say goodbye to someone you spent your entire life with. They were more than friends—they were family. As he wrapped his arm around Cassie in a gesture of comfort, Shane couldn't help but feel a sense of responsibility to ensure her safety. He hoped he could get her someplace safe, and Julie and Caleb would be okay. The traumatic experience they had—being shot at and witnessing Cassie's extraordinary ability—had left its mark on each of them. Yet, Shane admired how they managed to stay strong and keep a level head. Even Julie, who was shaken, managed to maintain her composure. One thing he could say about the orphanage: the bond between the kids was as strong as their character.

Chapter 15

The east tunnel was surprisingly large. Bulldozers and machinery would have no problem traversing it to make the dome above. Motion sensors were set into the cement walls, lighting up as Shane, Cassie, Amy, and Andrew walked in front of them. The lights stayed on briefly before shutting off automatically and casting the tunnel into darkness.

Andrew glanced down at Amy, who was walking briskly behind Cassie. He could see she was struggling with her thoughts. "It's going to be okay, Amy." His own emotions were close to surfacing. There was no way to know what would happen next or where they would end up. All he knew was that he trusted Shane and was ready to leave the orphanage.

Cassie turned, and seeing Amy's distress only added to her own. She'd been trying to keep her emotions in check. "I'm sorry, Amy. I'm sorry you got shot, and that I couldn't tell you who I am or about Shane's plan." She still couldn't believe she had the power to heal. Part of her felt as though she was walking through a dream. This wasn't real.

"Tell me now." Amy loved Cassie, but now she seemed like a stranger. "Tell me who you are and how you healed me."

"It starts with Cassie's grandma." Shane angled toward Amy and Andrew while walking. He knew Cassie needed to hear the story as well. "Cassie's grandma needed money when she was younger, and raising a son alone. Her boyfriend had left, leaving a pile of bills, no car or money." He looked at Cassie. "Your uncle Alex never knew his father." The tunnel ahead was still dark, making it difficult to judge the distance. "Anyway, to get money, your grandma signed up to be a test subject for experimental drugs. However, the doctor lied about the nature and purpose of the experiment. The female volunteers were instead made pregnant by embryo implantation. This lead scientist had created genetically modified DNA. He'd used all sorts of reptile, mammal and amphibian DNA to construct a new strain, mostly from species that could regenerate or grow body parts, or had extremely long natural lives. A computer then mixed and manufactured this man-made DNA, replicating a synthetic regenerative species' chromosomes. It was a technology that never should've existed." Shane sighed at the confused look on all their faces. He knew they had no idea what he was talking about.

"The mothers were brainwashed into thinking something else had happened to them, to explain their sudden pregnancies," he continued. "Your grandma was told she was raped. The result of the experiments was that all the babies died, except for two. A set of twins." Shane stopped so he could gauge how Cassie was handling the information. "The twins were your mom, Lily, and her identical sister, Kate."

"That's crazy," Andrew mumbled quietly.

"Go on." Cassie needed to hear more. During the few days she'd had with Shane, there was never enough time to share lengthy stories. She'd been disappointed that Shane's normal response to her many questions was often, 'it's too long a story, Cass, I'll tell you later.' Always adhering to schedules, people watching them closely, friends around, she'd been desperate for information she couldn't get.

"Your mom discovered she could heal when she was about ten. She's the only person in the world with the ability. Kate doesn't have it. It's a miracle that they both lived when all the other test subjects died. Lily's ability to heal is an accident of nature. But her DNA cocktail and ability were somehow passed to you." Shane rubbed his fingers down Cassie's soft, warm cheek. Her face showed no emotion, but her breathing was steady.

93

Information and answers were what Cassie needed. Discovering who she was and where she came from was surreal, but it was helping to calm the rolling of her stomach. "Keep talking." She could see that Shane was trying to read her, and surprisingly, she felt a bit calmer. "I'm okay, Shane. I want to hear more. I want to hear everything."

"I do too, but can we keep moving?" Amy peered down the dark tunnel. The knot in her stomach wouldn't leave until they were safe.

Shane held Cassie's hand firmly as they walked. "When the government discovered that your mom was the real deal, capable of healing cancer, radiation poisoning, and wounds, they took both your mom and Kate hostage." He debated how much to share, but he had their attention in the long, silent tunnel and just kept talking. "They tortured them both, trying to learn the secrets of how your mom can heal. Eventually, your mom and Alex were led to believe that Kate had died from the procedures she was forced to endure. But Kate wasn't dead. Instead, they held her captive for a year. It was my dad who helped your parents and Alex rescue Kate." Shane had heard the story many times and felt a swell of pride toward his father each time. "It was a big deal at the time because the entire world had been fooled. The government had told everyone Lily was an alien."

"Your Mom's an alien?"

"No, Andrew." Shane didn't mean to sound frustrated. "Her mom's not an alien. However, the government thinks she is because her DNA is unique. They don't know the truth of how she was created."

"Created?" Andrew was perplexed. He didn't understand much of what Shane had said.

"Cassie, do you understand all this?" Amy thought it all sounded strange and beyond crazy, and she was starting to wonder if anything was the truth and if they could trust Shane.

It was too much for Cassie to absorb. Fatigue, thirst, and fear clouded her thoughts. "Some," was all she could manage in response.

The faint light ahead indicated they were nearing the end of the tunnel, prompting Shane to slow his pace. "It's a long story. I'm going to let your mom tell the rest. She'll want to explain a lot to you. How you were taken, and why." He placed his hands gently on Cassie's shoulders, locking eyes with her. "Your mom was told by the scientist who created her that she was the next step in evolution. If she could have children who could heal, then the human race would never die." That was the most essential piece of information he could give her.

"Oh... my... gosh," Amy's voice was filled with awe as she stared at Cassie. "You have the power to heal. You saved me." She'd learned about the theory of evolution in science class, so that aspect she comprehended. The magnitude of what happened was starting to sink in.

"So, is she man-made because her mom was?" Andrew was still trying to understand how Lily had been made from modified DNA. All he could think about was the science experiments he participated in that used fruit flies to teach the students about genetics. They'd learned a little about DNA codes by experimenting with fruit flies in class.

"Is that why you have an evolution tattoo?"

Shane locked eyes with her, his gaze unwavering. "I believe in preserving the human race. And yes, Cassie, I believe you're the key to evolution, to saving humanity."

It was a powerful statement. Everyone took a moment to absorb Shane's words, while Cassie breathed in his clean scent mingled with the cool night air coming from the tunnel's opening. Freedom was only feet away, and Shane forced himself to break their stare. He took a deep breath to calm his racing heart. He'd told her a lot, and it felt amazing to share it. To voice the reason he spent his entire life looking for her. The reason he'd give his own life to protect her.

He turned to Andrew. "You three stay here. I'll go out first and make sure it's safe. If anything happens to me, you get them back inside the school. Find the doctor and ask him to help you." Shane believed the doctor was a good man who genuinely liked Cassie. "Once I get help, I'll come right back."

"No!" Cassie grabbed his arm. "I'm coming with you."

"Me too," Amy said firmly.

"So am I." Andrew nodded his head.

Shane rolled his eyes. "Let's not all be so eager to meet danger. I need to ensure none of you end up in the wrong hands. Please." He gently pulled his arm free. "No one else is getting shot tonight. Just wait here until I know it's all clear."

Opening the gate, Shane saw the large sand hills. It had rained that evening, so the sand was still damp and smooth. The bright moon was high enough to reflect off the sand, offering enough light to see. Shane's footsteps sank into the soft grains as he walked out, surveying all directions. There were few trees, creating the feeling of a dark desert. He figured the road was to his left, possibly less than a mile away. He glanced down at the transmitter secured to his belt. Something had gone wrong, but if Alex or his father had been listening, they'd have known to meet here.

Since there was no shooting or signs of life, Shane decided he'd take the others to the main road. He frowned when he saw them already headed toward him. "You guys take direction well."

"We saw it was safe." Andrew leaned back to look at the night sky. The stars were incredible. He could get used to seeing a sky like that for the rest of his life, but preferably without the nervousness he was currently feeling.

Amy stared down at her feet. "Why is there so much sand?"

There was no cover where they stood. Shane knew he had to get them to a safe place, especially since his father and Alex weren't there. "I'll explain as we run. We need to reach the road and put some distance between us and the orphanage."

The kids were given an hour to run on the indoor gym track every Wednesday and Friday. Amy loved to run, but this was so much better. She'd never felt the cool breeze blowing against her skin or her feet sinking in soft sand. She smiled at Shane as she realized freedom meant more than leaving the rules behind. Freedom was also breathing fresh air. "Start explaining." She still wanted to know the reason for the sand.

"The sand is for protection. I'll explain more later, Amy." Shane led the way to the road.

When they finally reached pavement, all four were exhausted. Shane was more fit, so he explained to Amy why there was so much sand without sounding out of breath. He told her the sand was dumped by drone machinery and constituted a barrier from potential ground radiation.

"And makes it hard to run on." Andrew shook his foot, feeling the sand in his shoes.

Amy wasn't sure what to think of yet another strange and confusing explanation from Shane. She looked at Cassie, wondering if she was truly more knowledgeable of the world, having read so many books.

"I'm thirsty." Cassie wiped her forehead with the back of her hand. "I need water."

"There's a town twelve miles from here. We have no choice but to walk."

Andrew shook his head at Shane. "Twelve miles is a long walk, bro."

A strange sound caught their attention, drawing them toward the winding road ahead. They stood still with nowhere to hide and no cover in the open sandy terrain, waiting and watching as a peculiar silver machine approached. It hovered just above the ground, its loud, whirling blade at the back spinning like a fan. The roof and front were clear glass, revealing the occupant inside.

The machine's door swung open, and Alex yelled, "Hurry up and get in!"

Cassie didn't hesitate. The round interior had soft white leather seats that formed a circle. There was no steering wheel or pedals, just a hologram touch screen in the center. Andrew immediately stared at the center console, while Amy quickly sat beside Cassie.

The door shut automatically, and the craft spun around, flying back down the road. Shane noticed the wonder on his friends' faces. "This is called a Windmobile. They just came out five years ago. Pretty much everyone on the planet wants one." He turned to Alex, "What happened?"

The screen turned into a GPS map, and Alex quickly typed their coordinates. "I'll tell you when we get to base." He swallowed the dread he felt and stared at his niece. "Are you okay? I'm sorry things didn't go as planned." They rarely did. He was even sorrier for the bad news he'd eventually deliver to Shane. But first, he needed to reach the safe house.

"She can heal," Shane stated firmly. Sharing this information was essential. Though uncertain if Alex knew, Shane felt compelled to tell him. Despite his desire to celebrate, he detected unease in Alex's demeanor. Something felt wrong, whether it was his avoidance of eye contact or subdued reaction to the news. "Where's my dad?"

Alex smiled at Cassie. "I didn't think you had the ability. It's incredible that you do. It changes everything." Lily's son didn't have it, and everyone wondered if the ability would die with Lily. "Evolution." Shane gripped his arm. He looked up into the kid's eyes and knew he'd have to tell him something. "I'll tell you at the base."

"Tell me now."

"Your dad was taken."

Shane swore under his breath and leaned forward, his head in his hands. "Which group?"

"A.S.A."

"What's A.S.A.?" Cassie placed her hand on Shane's back and gently rubbed his shoulder. Usually, she felt awkward offering comfort, but since he had given her so much support, it was easier to do the same in return.

"The name stands for Alien Surveillance Association." Alex leaned back on the seat, feeling exhausted. "It's a group of fanatics who believe aliens have invaded our nation. It all started when the government tried to convince the world that your mom is an alien.

98

They knew she didn't have normal DNA and believed she wasn't human. It was the only explanation they could think of for her ability to cure."

Andrew's eyes grew wide. "So, Cassie's an alien?" He still didn't understand the whole experimental DNA thing.

"No!" Shane sighed at Andrew's confused look. "No, Lily isn't an alien. Cassie's father is human, so Cassie has more human DNA than anything else. But the point is, people think aliens are here. A.S.A. looks for anyone they believe is different." There had been an increase in missing people, and often, the secret organization was blamed for unexplained disappearances.

Alex rubbed the stubble on his chin. "They're radical, basically just shoot first and ask questions later," he muttered, anger evident in his voice at the thought of the kids being shot at. "They're reckless, and I'm convinced most are just psychopaths." Alex regretted his words when he noticed the fallen look on Shane's face. "We'll get your dad back, Shane."

Shane nodded and pushed back the trepidation he felt. He knew Cassie was watching him closely, and he didn't want to add to her fear by showing his own.

Alex pulled a water bottle from under the seat and offered it to Shane, who immediately gave it to Cassie. "A lot of groups still look for Lily," Alex watched Cassie drink the water. "Most of the world believes we all died many years ago in a military battle in the Upper Peninsula. But not everyone was fooled. Some still want to capture your mom, to use her to heal their loved ones. Others want to experiment on her, and some want to rid the planet of anything they deem non-human."

Shane scanned the terrain outside, looking for any signs of trouble, but he turned slightly to say, "There's also a group called the Twin Seekers. They spend their time trying to find Lily and Kate. They aren't as harmful as the Alien Surveillance Association and don't cause as much trouble. They're far less radical. A.S.A. uses guns and acts like we are living in an apocalyptic world.

Alex nodded in agreement, anger tightening his mouth. "Hence the reason they shot at a bunch of damn kids. They'd followed us and ambushed us." He was still berating himself for the way the plan failed.

Shane quickly read Andrew's thoughts. "We're not," he assured him. "Granted, things have never been the same since the nuclear explosions, but the world is still far from wildly unrestrained, unlike A.S.A." The fact that Shane's father, Ian, had been taken by the group meant he was not safe. Shane turned toward Alex. "How'd they get my dad?"

"We were outnumbered, taken at gunpoint. I was able to break free because your dad started a fight. He knew one of us needed to escape to call for backup and retrieve you kids. He diverted their attention so I could get away." Alex felt a headache coming on and rubbed at his temples. "It's been a long night."

Shane saw that Andrew was about to speak, probably to ask a million questions. This all had to be so confusing for the orphans. He glanced at his weary friends and noted how they appeared exhausted and defeated. He set his hand on Andrew's shoulder. "I feel bad you guys have had a ton of information thrown at you tonight. This must all seem so crazy."

"Like I'm in a dream." Amy sighed as Andrew nodded his head. "I'm confused about a lot of things, but honestly, I don't know where to begin and what to say." She touched Cassie's hand. "How are you handling all this?"

Cassie looked wearily at Amy and took a deep breath. "I'm scared." More than that, she was exhausted. It was well past the time she'd usually be sleeping. The adrenaline that had kept her going earlier was crashing.

Shane knew the situation was bad, and he wasn't sure how to reassure his friends. He sensed a lot more to the story that Alex wasn't sharing. "What aren't you telling me, Alex? How were we compromised?"

Alex offered a faint smile, he wasn't feeling. Shane was too smart and intuitive. "One of our team members is a rat. The A.S.A. knows everything about Cassie. They had made a deal with the school's administrator to deliver Cassie to them. Since that didn't work, they will trade your father for her."

"I'll do it," Cassie replied quickly. "Whatever it takes to get Shane's dad back, I'll do it."

Shane was surprised by the passion in her voice and the fact that she didn't hesitate to respond. Usually, she'd take a minute to think her response through, but this was fast and genuine. "Never." He shook his head at Alex, knowing he felt the same way. He knew his father would also never allow it. Finding Cassie had been their life goal. They'd put their lives in danger many times helping Lily and Kate. Now that Cassie was finally found, they'd never trade her, and Shane would protect her at any cost.

"But…"

"It's not even an option, sweetheart." Alex stared at her momentarily, thinking that's just what his sister would have said. "We'll get Ian back while safely returning you to your parents. It's not your concern."

The Windmobile stopped at an intersection. The dirt road merged into a solar road with plastic diamond-shaped designs instead of cement. Instead of traffic lights, the street itself was lit red. Cassie stared out the window as an oval-shaped car pulled up in the far-right lane. There were more cars on the road than Windmobiles. When the street color turned green, the Windmobile flew forward.

"I've never seen a road like this," Andrew commented. "I've seen roads in picture books, but they weren't like this."

"A lot of damaged roads have been replaced with solar sheets." Alex hadn't properly introduced himself to Cassie's friends but was aware of who they were. He even knew their backgrounds. Andrew Hayzel's parents had both died from cancer. His father had been a U.S. senator for many years, and his wealth and connections allowed Andrew to be raised at Saving Souls when he was three. Amy Drift's mother was the teenage daughter of a wealthy movie pro-

101

ducer. Amy's young mother had not survived her complicated labor, and Amy was sent to a foster care family for one year before being secretly placed in the orphanage by her grandfather.

As he read the concern on all their faces, he offered a reassuring smile to them. "It's going to be okay. It's not like we've never met these challenges before."

Amy leaned across the seat and placed her hand on Cassie's thigh. "I'm feeling a little sick to my stomach."

"It's motion sickness from the Windmobile." Alex studied the computer GPS. "We'll arrive at the safe house in just a few minutes. Look out the window and not inside. That'll help."

Chapter 16

The sun was beginning to rise above the white brick house Alex had brought them to, turning the stretched clouds a soft pink hue. Palm trees provided shade along the side of the house, and Yellowhead Geckos scurried along the flower beds as they walked to the front door.

Alex punched numbers into the digital keypad on the door while everyone stood anxiously waiting to enter. They all felt exhausted, and Cassie was still thirsty. Considering what they'd been through, Andrew was holding up well. Cassie studied Shane, who hadn't lost his troubled look since leaving the orphanage. The wind rustled the leaves, and that's when she smelled it.

"Wait!" She placed her hand on Alex's arm when he opened the front door. He turned to stare at her. She took a deep breath through her nose. "That scent." She'd smelled it before, and it was familiar and overwhelming. Goosebumps crept up her arms. "Something's wrong." She glanced around the yard. The scent was nearby, and she knew something bad accompanied it.

Both Alex and Shane sniffed the air. Amy gave a puzzled look and began to speak.

"I don't smell anything." Alex pulled his gun out from behind his back.

Cassie tried to remember where she'd smelled the scent, when suddenly it hit her. "Mr. Jamerson!" She'd smelled his powerful cologne when they were in the tunnels.

Shane pulled Cassie's arm. "Quick! Get back in the craft."

As they turned, numerous armed men appeared around the

house and quickly surrounded them.

"Dad!" Shane yelled out as Alex grabbed him hard by the arm to hold him in place.

Ian's hands were bound behind his back as he was dragged into the front yard, just feet from the front door where everyone stood. From the horrific beating Ian received, it was obvious they tortured him into giving up the safe house location. He'd never have done so unless he was in unbearable pain. Alex felt sick seeing his friend's bloody face and his torn, blood-soaked shirt.

Mr. Jamerson emerged from the side of the house with an apprehensive look. "You said you'd only take the girl. You promised to let the other kids go." He turned to the man with long black hair slicked back in a ponytail.

"I lied," the man said, a smile spreading across his face, revealing a missing front tooth.

"I'm sorry," Jamerson expressed sincerely, as he looked at Amy and Andrew. He'd known them since they were little, and they were good kids. He didn't want anything to happen to them and regretted his involvement. Initially, he had only intended to assist A.S.A. in locating Cassie, providing information about the tunnels for a large sum of money. However, the violence he witnessed shocked him. When the kids didn't emerge as expected, the leader resorted to torturing their prisoner for more information.

"No!" Cassie cried out as the ponytail man kicked Shane's father. She tried to squirm out of Shane's grip. "I'll go with you if you let them go! Please don't hurt these people." She'd never seen anything so horrible. What had they done to Shane's father? He was a bloody mess, and she couldn't help but feel that she was somehow responsible.

Shane locked eyes with his father, and his gut clenched. He'd known immediately what had happened. He glanced to his left at the four men holding guns, then his eyes moved right to observe the other three men aiming their weapons. The leader stood in the middle beside Jamerson.

Only eight men in total, and Jamerson and the leader weren't an issue. Shane caught the slight nod from his father. He'd been beaten but not broken. If Shane made a move, his father would be able to help. Alex would follow suit. Shane glanced at Alex and caught him eyeing the gun behind Shane's back that he'd taken from Jamerson in the tunnel.

"Take the right," Alex whispered.

Shane whispered to Andrew, "When we move, get down."

Shane pulled the gun from his back and began shooting the men on his right—Alex dove on Cassie while shooting the men on the left.

Cassie felt the weight of her uncle as Amy screamed. Gunshots continued, and she squeezed her eyes shut, fearing for her friends' lives. Then someone pulled her to her feet, dragging her into the house.

The wood on the front door splintered as bullets splayed and wood fragments went flying. Someone yelled to stay down, but Cassie's ears rang too loudly to know who was speaking. She caught sight of Amy and Andrew crawling toward her, with the look of fear and sweat on their faces. Cassie shifted and saw Shane slump under the window, with Ian applying pressure to his chest. Alex managed to secure the door, telling everyone to go downstairs.

Shane groaned when his father helped him up. Everything seemed to be happening in slow motion. She barely noticed the green marble floor, the black furniture that filled the gloomy rooms, or the grandfather clock that chimed as she stumbled past it. Her heart was racing so fast that she felt dizzy. She glanced over her shoulder as Alex dragged her downstairs.

"How bad is it?" Alex asked, as Ian helped lean his son against the wall. They were in an underground tunnel leading to another underground house less than a mile away. The home was built as a fallout shelter years ago.

"He's losing a lot of blood." Ian tore open Shane's shirt and examined the bullet wound. "It went clean through but might have hit an artery." Ian turned to Cassie, as she slumped against the wall to sit on the cold floor. "Are you Faith?" He knew she was. She looked like Patrick and had her mother's hair and eyes. "You'll never know how thrilled I am to finally meet you. I'm Shane's father, Ian." There was no thrill in his voice when he spoke. He sounded calm, but his anxiety was obvious.

Alex rummaged through the backpack for medical supplies, not noticing the look on Cassie's face. "She goes by Cassie," he reminded Ian. He turned to his niece, and his eyebrows drew together in concern. "I think she's in shock." He rested his hand on her cheek and wiped away a small smudge of dirt. "Sweetheart?" Her eyes were wide and unblinking. "Cassie, we're okay, honey." He stuck his hand in front of her face and snapped his fingers.

Cassie didn't blink. Nothing was okay. Shane was wounded, blood soaking his shirt. Ian's appearance was equally alarming—his eyes were encircled with ugly bruises, with the left eye swollen shut, a deep, bloody gash marred his cheekbone, and his lips were split and bloody. There was a jagged cut below his chin. His jaw was black and blue, with blood trickling from his ears. The metallic scent of blood filled her senses, causing her stomach to churn in revulsion.

"Son, don't you dare die on me!" Ian cried frantically, feeling for Shane's pulse.

The alarm and terror in Ian's voice drew Cassie's attention. She noted Shane's pale face, heard the shallowness of his breaths, and tried to ignore the scent of his blood. Her head spun, but she crawled over to Shane's side and touched his arm. The waves of energy were already moving through her, and she was surprised that she didn't have to do anything. She just knew that every part of her wanted to stop his bleeding and heal him. She closed her eyes, focusing on the change happening in her body. It was building faster than it had last time with Amy. She could feel every cell in her body moving with incredible force, sending heat through her like a wave.

"My God." Ian watched as a blue light radiated from her hands.

Alex reached out to touch Ian's shoulder and lowered himself to the ground in awe. "This is unbelievable."

When she opened her eyes, she turned to Ian, hating the wounds she saw on his face. Without thinking, she set her hand on top of his. He flinched from the heat, but she curled her fingers around his. She closed her eyes again, wanting to take all his pain away. The energy wasn't fading, as she felt her mouth dry. She squeezed his hand, unable to stop the flow. Her nerves felt like they were being pulled from her body, but it didn't hurt. It felt powerful.

"She's too hot." Ian's hand wasn't burning yet, but it was getting there. He scooted back slightly as if he'd been sitting too close to a space heater. He glanced in awe from Cassie to Alex. Lily never omitted heat the way Cassie did. He'd never seen her hands glow blue. "This is incredible." He was unsure of what to do.

"Cassie, you can stop now." Alex couldn't believe how fast Ian's wounds disappeared. He'd watched the skin close in a matter of seconds. Bruises disappeared. Shane's chest bore no sign of damage. The blue light was some energy he'd never seen before. Her hair was raised, full of static. He'd seen his sister heal people, but never that quickly. Cassie's ability was different. Stronger.

Amy reached her hand out and felt Cassie's shoulder. "You're burning up. Cassie, make it stop."

Beads of sweat rolled down everyone's skin as the heat in the tunnel rose. The track lighting built into the ceiling flickered, and Andrew decided he hated tunnels. If he ever had the chance to buy a home, it wouldn't be underground. The cement walls were over six feet apart, but still, he felt closed in, and the heat wasn't helping. "What's wrong with her?" She wasn't stopping, although both Shane and Ian were completely healed. He'd never understand it and had to force his mind to accept it.

"Stop now, Cass." Shane put his fingers under Cassie's chin and lifted her face to his. He leaned in closer and kissed her cheek when she stared into his eyes. "You saved me." Glancing at his dad, he laughed. "You're amazing." It blew his mind that moments ago

107

he'd almost died, and yet now he felt better than ever. In fact, he could probably run a marathon.

"Cass." Amy felt the heat diminish from her friend's body. "What you did…" She didn't think it was possible, and yet she witnessed it. This power you have…it's…" She was at a loss for words as Cassie leaned against the wall. Amy glanced at Alex and Ian, and they offered her an understanding grin.

Overwhelmed with thirst, Cassie felt weak. "I need water."

"Here." Alex retrieved a water bottle from his supply pack and handed it to her. "Let's keep moving." The tunnel would lead to an underground bunker. More like a home than a mere hideout, complete with a kitchen, shower, and bedrooms. Once they arrived at the house, he planned to activate a mechanism to seal off the tunnel, designed to protect them once they reached the bunker. With the threat of danger still following them, he was determined to ensure their safety and keep them moving. Ian helped Cassie to her feet, and although everyone was exhausted and emotionally drained from the night's events, Alex was relieved to see everyone move.

Chapter 17

The horse was galloping, tossing her small body up and down on the hard leather saddle. Her little hands gripped the reins desperately, trying to hold on. "You'll be okay. They'll take good care of you. No one will hurt you there," a voice said from behind her.

"I want to get off!" The little girl cried. "Please, I want down!" The trees were on fire, and smoke surrounded her. She couldn't breathe. A black cloud blanketed the child, and she began to cough. "I can't breathe!" She gasped for air and closed her eyes as the smoke surrounded her.

"Wake up, Cassie!"

"No, stop!" Cassie shouted, pushing Shane away and bolting upright. "I can't breathe." She clutched her throat as her eyes slowly adjusted to the room.

"You're safe. It's just a dream." Shane stroked her arm. She'd been talking in her sleep, then gasping and breathing hard. He'd slept beside her on the floor and turned the light on when she began speaking. He wasn't sure if he should wake her until she appeared distressed.

"I was on a horse." She leaned her head into the crook of his shoulder and felt the warmth of his body. He wasn't wearing a shirt, and he smelled clean—no trace of blood or sweat. "There was a fire, and I couldn't breathe. The smoke…"

He rubbed the back of her neck and held her a moment. "It's okay, you're safe now."

She shook her head. She'd had the dream before and believed it was a memory. "I think it happened to me." She leaned back to look into his eyes. "When I was little, I was placed on a horse. I was scared and falling off. I…" Her tongue was heavy, and her mouth was dry, making it difficult to speak. "I need water."

Shane reached for the water bottle he had beside his sleeping bag. "Drink slow, you're still breathing heavy."

The warm water filled her mouth and felt soothing. Soon she was gulping it and wondered if she'd ever quench her thirst.

"Easy." Shane held out his hand. "You'll get sick if you drink too much. You haven't eaten anything."

The room felt warm and cozy as a fan rotated above her head. Two walls were a pretty grey stone, and the others were painted a pleasant orange, reminding her of the boy's wing at the orphanage. In the corner stood an old rocking chair beside a small mahogany desk. No windows, like the small white room she'd shared with Amy. "Where are we? Where's Amy and Andrew?"

"Everyone's here and safe. This is an underground home. It belonged to one of our organization members. The house above is used as a decoy. If A.S.A. returns, they'll find the house empty, and they won't be able to access the tunnel." He bent down and retrieved his shirt from the floor.

She remembered when she felt too exhausted to keep walking. Shane had picked her up and carried her. She must have fallen asleep immediately because she didn't remember climbing into bed. "You belong to an organization?"

"Yeah. It used to be called the 'Save Lily' organization, but now we just call it 'Faith.' It's dedicated to keeping you and your family safe. Your uncle Danny always points out that your mom and her kids could be the next step in evolution. You could create a race to survive all the disease and devastation in the world."

The weight of his words sank in—a group named after and dedicated to her. A few days ago, she was just an ordinary orphan; now she was the key to humanity's survival. Her ability to heal was shocking, and her mind could barely process all the events. "What happened to Mr. Jamerson? Did all those men die?"

"Try not to think about it." He brushed a piece of her hair

110

behind her ear.

She pulled her knees up to her head and rested her chin on them. "I'd like to know, Shane. I know you think I probably can't handle it. I shouldn't have freaked out so much, but…"

"Hey…" he interrupted her. "You've been courageous. You handle yourself better than most people would." He stood, feeling a restless urge to comfort her, but aware he needed to put more space between them. "The leader of A.S.A. got away. I'm unsure if Jamerson was hurt, but I saw him running. Everyone else…." He didn't want to tell her they were probably dead. He glanced at the door. "We should get moving."

"You should have let them take me. It wasn't right to put others in danger because of me. What if I hadn't been able to heal you?"

"Cass." He opened the door. "Those men would have taken you and killed us anyway. We had no choice but to do what we did. And you need to know that nothing is more important to me than keeping you safe and alive." He offered her a small smile. "Come join us when you're ready. There's a bathroom right here." He pointed just outside the door to his left.

"Shane," She called out before he started to leave. "Why did you stay with me, and not Amy?"

His lips curled in amusement. "Amy was as exhausted as you were, so Andrew carried her and wanted to stay with her. They're in the room next to us. My dad crashed out on the couch, and I don't think Alex ever sleeps. " He dropped his smile as she stood from the bed and approached him.

"Thank you." She wrapped her arms around his waist and pressed her cheek to his chest. "For everything."

"You're the one who healed me and my dad. We should be thanking you." He'd never get over how fast his father's wounds closed. Whatever DNA she carried that caused blood vessels to repair rapidly and new skin cells to multiply at accelerated rates was truly miraculous. His feelings for her were starting to make him nervous. He gently moved her out of his arms and walked away.

The blue-tiled shower was much larger than the dorm's. It had a neat shower head that sprayed her body from all angles. The shampoo smelled like grapefruit and had a wonderful, rich lather. She would have enjoyed more time under the warm water but was starving and could smell the food. Quickly drying herself off, she was about to wear her uniform when Alex's knock interrupted her. She grabbed the white bathrobe hanging on a hook by the shower door and wrapped it around her, with the towel still underneath. She cracked open the door to find Alex standing there, holding out clothes. "This was all I could find for you. I hope they fit."

"Thanks." She took the clothes with a pleasant, clean scent and shut the door. Standing in front of a long mirror, she held up the dress. She'd never worn a dress before. It was light pink and made of soft material with a band around the waist and short sleeves. Until now, she had only worn the five alternative outfits provided by the orphanage, all consisting of slacks or lounge pants and button-down shirts in four conservative colors.

Alex knocked on the door again. "I've got something else for you." When she opened the door, he took her wrist and draped a bracelet over it. "You won't be able to remove this, and it's water-proof." He carefully placed it over her wrist and secured the special clasp. "You remind me so much of your mom when she was your age." He could always tell what Lily was thinking from her expressive face. "You have her innocence and honesty, Cassie." He couldn't wait to reunite her with his sister and brother-in-law.

When Alex left, a small thrill rushed through her. She held the dress to her waist, admiring the bracelet and the clothes. She realized she must have seemed silly, grinning so happily at his gift. But she'd never had jewelry before, except for the necklace Amy made. Remembering the necklace, she dug it out of the pocket of her uniform that she'd folded and left on the bathroom counter. The small glass beads Amy had strung in art class would look pretty with her pink dress.

With her hair still wet, she hastily braided it back, though she wasn't as skilled at braiding as Julie was. Thinking of Julie, her concerns weighed heavily on her mind. Was Caleb's leg okay? What had happened to Mrs. Reynolds? Would Mr. Jamerson let her keep teaching? Was Mr. Jamerson safe? Would they meet more danger today?

Today was the start of her new life. Today, anything could happen. There would be no schedule to follow, no classes to attend, or work shifts to be done. She could see part of the world, meet new people, hopefully her parents, and finally experience life outside the institution she'd grown up in.

Part of her felt afraid, and part of her was highly excited. She stared at her eyes in the mirror. She'd never thought there was anything unusual about them. Now she knew they were the same color as her mom's. Her stomach flipped at the thought of meeting her. Glancing down at her hands, she observed their normalcy—dainty fingers with medium-length nails. How could she possess such power without ever knowing it? "I never needed it," she spoke softly, thinking of her life. She'd rarely ever been scared. She couldn't remember ever being hurt, other than the time she cut herself during food prep. And she'd never had to worry about anyone she cared for being injured.

"Cassie, are you okay in there?"

She startled at the sound of Shane's voice. Opening the door, she nervously ran her hand down her dress. It stopped at her knees and made her feel very feminine. "It fits."

"Wow." The dress hugged her in all the right places and was extremely flattering, much more feminine and attractive than her baggy school clothes. He touched her beaded necklace with a questioning look.

"Amy made it for me years ago. It's the only gift I've ever received."

"I like it. You look gorgeous, Cassie."

She felt heat rise to her cheeks at his sincere compliment and look of approval. She touched her French braid and suddenly felt very self-conscious. "I normally don't wear my hair up, but it's still wet."

Sensing her unease, Shane took her hand. "It's perfect. Come on, everyone is waiting for you." He led her down a short hallway covered in brown, shaggy carpet. Black-and-white photos of people lined the walls. Cassie wondered if they were family members of the people who owned the house.

"There she is." Ian stood up from a tan couch to approach her. "With all the chaos last night, I never really had the chance to thank you. I feel amazing today, thanks to you."

"Don't crush her, Dad," Shane laughed. He caught the surprise on Cassie's face when his father hugged her tightly.

"I can't wait till Lily and Patrick meet you. They'll be so happy." Ian held her out and stared at her flushed face. "You look so much like your dad, but there's no mistaking the eyes." He glanced at Shane. "You were right, son. One look at her and you'd know she's Faith. Her eyes have the same gold." He smiled back at Cassie. "Over the years, we found a lot of girls we thought were you, but none of them had such an obvious resemblance. If you weren't able to heal, I was going to have you take a paternity test, but we obviously have confirmation now." He was thrilled to find her finally, and almost giddy with excitement that she could heal.

Cassie also found herself smiling and felt less awkward. Ian was an inch shorter than his son, and his short black hair was turning gray at his temples. He wasn't unattractive but lacked Shane's strong, rugged features. Shane had fuller lips, but their smile was similar, and she saw the resemblance.

"I love your dress!" Amy had waited for a chance to join the conversation. She'd sat with Andrew at the kitchen table, observing how everyone seemed to dote on Cassie. Despite a slight jealousy, she genuinely felt happy for her friend. As Cassie walked toward her, she stood up and reached out to touch the fabric of her dress. "It's so soft and looks comfortable." Then her eyes settled on the necklace. "You thought to bring it." She was touched.

"Of course." Cassie set her fingers over the beads. "I love your clothes too." Amy was wearing a blue knee-length skirt with a white tank top. She reached out to feel the light material. She had also showered, and her hair was still slightly damp as it hung straight down like a black curtain, her bangs still too long over her eyes.

"Are you hungry?" Alex held up a plate of food from the kitchen counter.

"Yes." She sat across from her friends, chuckling at the sight of Andrew hastily devouring pancakes.

"These are fabulous," he mumbled through a mouthful of food. "They're nothing like the pancakes at the orphanage."

"That's because they aren't made from almond flour and co-conut." Shane settled beside Cassie. "I can tell you they aren't as healthy."

Andrew shrugged, feeling satisfied enough to decide that it was worth the indulgence if all unhealthy food tasted that good.

The kitchen was modern, with built-in appliances. The re-frigerator had clear glass doors that showed the inner shelves. One would never know the house was underground, except there were no windows. The home was filled with artificial daylight, giving it a warm, cozy feeling. The counters were a pearl color that matched the white cabinets.

A glass water pitcher rested on the kitchen table. Shane poured some into Cassie's glass, and she immediately drank it all. Then she took a bite of her pancakes and sighed with pleasure. "Where are we going today?" She smiled when Shane winked at her.

He turned to share a look with his father, and she caught the unspoken gesture. "What? What's going on?" She heard Amy's sigh and watched her smile vanish.

"Cassie, we've got something important to tell you." Amy set her hand on Andrew's arm and looked at him as if she wanted him to break the news. When he set his fork down, she met Cassie's worried eyes. "We can't go with you. You have to meet your parents, and they live in another state. Your uncle said the trip could be dangerous, and he doesn't want to worry about our safety."

"What? No!"

Amy struggled to speak past the lump in her throat. "I'm so happy for you, Cass. You have parents, a brother, an aunt, and an uncle who love you so much. You have a whole family now, and you... you don't need me." Tears welled up in her eyes.

"That's not true!" Cassie rose from her chair and crouched down beside her. "I'll always need you. You're my best friend. You're my family too, and I don't want to be without you." Her tears were falling as she glanced up at her uncle. "She has to come with us. We have to stay together. I can't do this without you." Her words choked as Amy bent over to hug her.

Andrew cleared his throat. "Cassie, Alex is giving us a great opportunity, and we want to take it." His voice sounded sad, but he offered Alex a slight smile. "There's a giant greenhouse in the state of Colorado. It's bigger than Saving Souls, and they need experienced workers. They have apartments nearby for workers to rent. Alex and Ian said they can get us jobs there. They said it's a great place to live and safe. And Amy and I want to be together."

Cassie leaned back and wiped her tears. It boiled down to Andrew and Amy wanting to live their lives together, and it couldn't include Cassie. Part of her understood, but being separated from Amy was too painful. She didn't know what to say.

Amy squeezed Cassie's hands tightly. "Alex said you can visit us soon. This won't be a long goodbye."

Shane leaned over. "The most important part is that they'll be safe. If they stay with us, we can't guarantee they won't come across more incidents like the one that happened last night. The leader of A.S.A. is still alive, and he won't stop looking for you." He paused a moment to let his words sink in. "Your life is going to be very different now, Cass. You won't be able to stay in one place for long. You won't work for a while, at least until your parents find a place.

116

You'll—"

"That's enough explanation for now." Alex walked over to his niece. He didn't want to overwhelm her, and from the look on her face, he figured she was close to breaking down.

He knew how hard the changes would be for her. Saying good-bye to Amy and Andrew would be painful enough. "Cassie, you'll be able to visit Amy and Andrew. We'll make sure you guys talk regularly on the phone. Eventually, in time, your life will become more stable." While he and Lily could sometimes settle down and enjoy living for a while, it was never normal. They could never let their guard down or ignore precautions.

Amy sniffed and wiped the tears from her eyes. "They said I can paint, and there's an art studio nearby. I'll be able to hang my paintings in my bedroom."

"That's great." Cassie knew how much she loved to paint. The orphanage never allowed her to keep her artwork in their small white room. It would have made it more cheerful and pleasant, but it was forbidden. Amy and Andrew could live the kind of life she would want for them. "I will miss you so much."

Alex handed Amy a box of tissues. "We can't stay here any longer. It's time to go." He was worried the A.S.A. would be back with more men, and they might find their underground location. He moved to Cassie's side, wrapping his arm over her shoulder. "I've got good friends who will drive Amy and Andrew to Colorado. They'll set them up there and watch over them. And you, my sweet niece, are coming with me to meet your parents." He checked his watch and saw that it was already four o'clock.

Chapter 18

Cassie, Amy and Andrew sat in the back seat of an oval-shaped electric car. Amy sat in the middle holding Andrew's hand. Ian drove while Shane played with his phone in the front passenger seat. They'd been driving for hours, and it was still light at eight o'clock. They were going to meet the people who would take Amy and Andrew.

"The sky looks amazing." Andrew leaned against the window. Brilliant orange, yellow, and lavender clouds swirled like oil paintings. After years of rarely glimpsing the sky at the orphanage, he'd never take it for granted. He'd catch the sunset each day for the rest of his life.

Amy stared out the window. "I'm going to paint a sky just like this, next time I get the chance."

With so many thoughts on everyone's mind, the ride had been quiet with little conversation. It was the first time Amy had felt at ease since they'd left the orphanage. The thought of painting lifted her spirits.

Ian suddenly yelled, "Hold on and keep your heads down!"

The car accelerated. Shane turned to look out the rear window. He grabbed his gun from under the seat and checked the chamber.

"They found us!" Ian weaved in and out of traffic. They were on an old cement highway riddled with potholes. The car bounced wildly when he hit them. Someone honked a horn, and a Windmobile flew past them from the far-left lane.

"What are we going to do?" Andrew felt his heart race as he laced his fingers tightly with Amy's.

"We've got a plan. Just hold on!" Ian glanced in the rear-view mirror, watching Alex's car speed up behind him. Alex drove separately so that he could intervene should they encounter trouble.

A Windmobile illegally veered into another lane, edging alongside Ian's car. Windmobiles, constructed with shatterproof plastic, were virtually indestructible machines. While designed to maintain speeds of ninety miles per hour, they were capable of much faster. The far left lane was the only lane designated for low-flying crafts unless they were exiting the highway. Surveillance cameras along the highway snapped photos of any vehicles breaking the rules. Ian knew that once the Windmobile was detected breaking the law, Windchoppers—police-operated Windmobiles—would be alerted and could show up at any moment. Amy yelled out when the car swerved again. "Get us out of here!"

Shane glanced back at Alex's car and smiled. "He's got it."

Cassie turned in time to see her uncle half hanging out his window holding a weapon. A missile shot out, followed by a large blast. The Windmobile's back blades exploded. Ian swerved to avoid a piece of metal blade as it flew out and whacked the side of the car. The glass window beside Andrew cracked as he leaned down over Amy. The Windmobile spun out of control. Cassie's seat belt tightened across her chest as cars swerved and honked. The car jolted forward as someone hit it from behind.

"It's okay!" Ian shouted, watching the plastic bubble of the Windmobile disconnect from the bottom base and roll down the highway like a ball. It hit a car, bouncing to the left, and crashed into the median. The two men inside were still fastened to their chairs and were safe.

Alex honked his horn to gain Ian's attention and pointed toward the exit ramp. Ian followed, knowing patrol choppers would soon be everywhere. They needed to ditch the cars and hide.

"I feel sick." Amy held her stomach.

"Please don't barf on me." Andrew kissed her cheek.

Ian pulled into a shopping mall parking lot. A large glass building with two large wind turbines on the roof held a giant neon sign reading "Mega Plaza." They needed to abandon the car and find a hiding place before the cops found them. Sirens were already wailing on the freeway.

Everyone quickly exited the car. Shane and Ian grabbed backpacks from the trunk. Shane clasped Cassie's hand as they followed Ian across the lot. Cassie glanced back to see her uncle hurrying toward them, throwing his black bag over his shoulders.

Alex opened the mall door. "When we get inside, act like casual shoppers. Don't draw attention to yourselves." Scanning the area for safety, he pulled a silver phone from his pocket and began making calls to arrange new transportation and a safe exit from the mall.

Shane leaned close to Cassie's ear. "Are you okay?" He knew her expressions and was concerned.

She nodded, forcing her shaky legs to keep pace with his long stride. Her heart pounded, and her hand felt warm and sweaty in his, but she was grateful he didn't let go.

"Thanks, Danny." Alex ended his call and caught everyone's attention. "Danny already has people here to help." He kissed his cell phone before stowing it away.

"Who's Danny?"

"Your other uncle." Alex smiled, but then caught the look on Cassie's face, and his brows drew together in concern. "He's your Aunt Kate's husband, and probably why we're all still walking around today."

"How many family members does Cassie have?" Amy wondered as she took in the bustling shopping mall.

"Enough." Alex pulled a cap from his backpack and adjusted it on his head. He then retrieved a pair of black-rimmed glasses from the side pouch and put them on. Disguises were his standard protocol.

"What's our plan?" Shane was scanning the area anxiously. The approaching sirens outside only heightened his unease. It wouldn't be long before the mall was overrun with police, their faces likely captured by the road cameras.

Alex pointed to the escalator. "We go down, find the east lower exit and meet a man who looks like Santa Claus and calls himself Fred. He's on his way to help." His eyes fell on Cassie. "Hey." He set his hand on her cheek. "Keep it together, sweetheart. It's going to be okay."

Amy was in awe. She followed everyone down the moving steps, staring at all the massive stores. She touched a dress hanging from a rack as they hit the bottom. "It's all so pretty." She picked up her pace to walk beside Cassie. "This is our first trip to the mall." Her voice might have sounded more cheerful if she hadn't been dazed. She and Cassie decided long ago to head to the nearest mall after leaving the orphanage. They couldn't wait to see the clothes and accessories. "Hey." Amy noticed the look on Cassie's face.

Cassie was holding back a wave of emotion she couldn't begin to process. She was glad Amy seemed to be handling things well, because she wasn't. They'd almost been run off the road. She witnessed a Windmobile get blown apart and roll down the road, causing cars to crash. They were on the run from the police, and it was finally sinking in that people were truly after her. What had she gotten herself involved in? She was desperate to meet her parents, but at what cost?

It didn't matter that the shopping mall was marvelous, with so many never-before-seen wonders for sale. Under normal circumstances, she'd love to stop and watch the computerized mannequins made of computer screens that changed clothing. She barely glanced at the video displays of fashion shows playing on the wall. The bright-colored clothing seemed to blur together, as tears filled her eyes. Part of her wanted to slow her pace and enjoy her first time in a mall, but she could only focus on the back of her uncle's silver head of hair. Moving quickly meant reaching safety sooner. She wanted the security of walls. To know they weren't being followed. What kind of life was she entering? Shane, Alex, and Ian seemed at ease with everything. Were they so accustomed to this way of life that it no longer fazed them? A woman wearing a yellow dress and holding her child's hand walked by and directed a concerned glance at Cassie. People lived everyday lives and enjoyed shopping. That was the life she'd wanted. It was the life she realized she might never have.

"Stop, Cass." Shane pulled her to his chest. He glanced at his father, his eyebrows drawn in concern. He understood why she was upset. He knew she was struggling not to break.

"She may be in shock again." Alex wished they'd been able to retrieve Cassie under less dangerous circumstances. Having A.S.A. hot on their trail was a real problem. He glanced at the GPS on his watch. They were close to meeting Danny's contact, who'd have the car and a safe exit strategy.

When Cassie felt the warmth of Shane's arms around her, she released the sob she'd been stifling. Her body shook as all the stress she felt poured out. This wasn't how she had imagined her life. Constantly running from danger, being chased by people who formed strange groups she didn't understand. What if Amy and Andrew didn't make it to Colorado? Who were the men in the Windmobile? She couldn't stop hearing Ian's voice in her mind, *they found us*!

"Shane, take her outside." Alex pointed to a revolving door. "I'll meet our contact, get what we need, and come get you." He turned to Amy and Andrew. "You two go with Ian."

"But…"Amy wanted to protest. She was worried about Cassie and wasn't ready to leave her yet.

Ian set his hand on her shoulder. "She'll be okay. Let Shane take care of her." If anyone was watching, it might look like a lovers' quarrel. People would be less apt to stop and question them.

Shane felt her tremble, but he knew she needed to say good-bye to Amy and Andrew. Time was running out. "Cassie, give your friends a hug goodbye." Andrew and Amy enveloped Shane and Cassie in a tight embrace.

Andrew was eager to part ways once Ian and Alex had explained their plan. "Call us as soon as you're safe. Alex gave me a phone, so I'll always keep it on me." He squeezed Shane's shoulder. He'd miss Shane as much as he'd miss Cassie.

122

Shane offered Amy and Andrew a bittersweet smile. "This isn't goodbye. We'll see you again." Though he knew it could be a while, this wasn't the farewell he'd hoped for. The sound of approaching sirens reminded them to hurry. Ian and Alex wore their "let's get out of here" expressions.

"Amy..." Cassie turned her head, her heart breaking. She held Amy tightly, trying to handle her own emotions. "What if I can't do this? I'm not sure I can handle this. I don't want to leave you."

Amy pulled back, staring at her best friend with her heart in her eyes. "You're not an orphan anymore. You're special."

Chapter 19

Cassie awoke with a start. With her head resting on Shane's lap, it took her a moment to realize she wasn't in her orphanage bed. She was in the back seat of a small car with Alex driving. They'd escaped from the mall, and she'd been emotionally drained. She sat up and wiped her eyes. She wasn't used to feeling such fatigue and being off her regular sleep schedule.

"How do you feel?" Shane shifted his body. He'd been sitting uncomfortably for hours, too afraid to move, because he didn't want to wake her. He knew she needed sleep.

"I'm okay." She inhaled deeply, recalling the most recent events. When they'd gotten in the car, Ian had called Alex to report that a much older gentleman named Fred Brown was driving Amy and Andrew to Colorado. Lily had cured Fred many years ago, and after his wife died, he'd dedicated his life to helping Lily any way he could. Alex assured Cassie that Fred would ensure her friends arrived safely in Colorado and settled in. She was glad Ian's father had gone along for extra protection. She owed Shane for that, because he'd asked him to see to their safety personally. Looking out the window, she stared at the night sky with a clear view of the Big Dipper. She leaned against Shane, who put his arm around her. She was content in his arms and slightly light-headed from exhaustion.

"I think you were having a bad dream." He'd felt her twitching and mumbling in her sleep. He caught Alex's eyes in the rearview mirror. They shared a silent understanding, both aware of her fitful sleep and concerned about her mental state. Stress, fear, sorrow... It was a lot for a young, sheltered woman to face suddenly.

She thought for a moment. She only remembered a small part of her dream, but knew she'd been back in the tunnels, terrified and alone. With concerns and fears weighing on her mind, she took a moment before speaking. "Shane?" She smoothed down her dress and felt her braid, wondering how disheveled she must look. When their eyes met, she let out a soft sigh. "In the tunnel, you mentioned my mother being captured and tortured. What exactly did they do to her?"

"Is that what's bothering you?" He wanted to kick himself. He shouldn't have told her. He was careless in sharing her family's history. "You shouldn't think about that." Her eyes were wide with concern as he gently stroked a strand of hair from her cheek.

Alex remained silent while listening to the conversation. He didn't know all the details Shane had given her, but he wouldn't hold Shane liable for anything. Shane had done a fantastic job of befriending and delivering her from the orphanage. He knew Cassie was in good hands. Shane would always keep her best interests at heart.

Cassie continued her thought. "The men that want me… the men Mr. Jamerson tried to give me to…will they torture me?"

His heart ached at the fear in her eyes. He had no idea she was suffering from such worry. "Cassie, no one is ever going to torture you. We'll never let anyone take you."

Alex's heart squeezed. "That bracelet I gave you… It's a GPS. I'll always be able to locate you, and nobody will ever know that's more than a bracelet. I need you to trust us, Cassie. Trust that we will always keep you safe."

"It's just… I can't stop seeing your dad's bloody face. I don't know what torture is. My mind is coming up with strange and ugly things."

Alex glanced in the rearview mirror as he slowed the car to make a turn. "The world seems pretty scary right now, because we've had some unfortunate encounters with A.S.A. I regret that's all you've seen since leaving the orphanage, but I can promise you the world's not all bad. Once we get you to your mom and dad, you'll see there will be a lot of good." Alex wanted to cheer her up. See that worry on her face go away.

"But did they hurt my mom's face, the way they did your dad's?"

"No." Both Alex and Shane replied at the same time.

Shane could see she wasn't going to let it go. "Cassie, your mom was never hurt like my dad was. I shouldn't have used those words. Your mom was apprehended by a government agency that wanted to study her, but she came out okay. They didn't do to her what they did to my dad. Don't let your mind dwell on terrible thoughts; it wasn't what you think." He noticed Alex's gaze shift, both of them aware that Lily had endured a much different form of torture, but for now, he needed to steer Cassie's thoughts away from fear. If Cassie ever learned the truth about her mom's ordeal, it would be Lily's story to tell.

She felt a minor release of tension at his words. "What will happen when I meet my family? Will you stay with us?" Would he always be around to protect her?

Shane honestly didn't know how to answer that. He had no idea what would happen after she was reunited with her parents. His entire life had been focused on finding her, and now that goal was met. He honestly didn't know what his future held. He'd be turning twenty-one in a few months. There was a chance Lily and Patrick would want to leave the country again, and of course, Cassie would go with them. He'd thought about attending college, but now that seemed silly. He couldn't imagine living a normal, everyday life.

"For now, I'm staying with you. We'll figure the rest out later. Tell me what other concerns you have."

She gazed intently into his green eyes, almost seeing her reflection. She found them kind in contrast to his rugged, strong features. Her eyes drifted to his full lips, a warmth flooding through her. "What?" She hadn't heard his question over the pounding of her heartbeat.

"What else is worrying you?"

126

She turned to stare out the window, feeling breathless, trying to ignore the steady pull she felt toward him. "Everything worries me. So much has happened."

"Do you miss the orphanage?" Alex asked as he glanced at the rearview.

"Not really." She could answer that without hesitation. The only thing she missed was peace of mind. She'd felt protected and content there before Shane came along. "I can't wait to meet my parents and feel safe." She looked at Shane again. "Did you like being there?" It seemed strange to think he was only in the orphanage to find her.

He smiled. "Yeah, I didn't mind it." He'd enjoyed the few weeks of getting to know her and her friends. "It's not too bad there, but..."

"But what?" Alex wanted to hear Shane's thoughts.

Shane had to be careful. He didn't want to hurt Alex. He was going to say that although he thought the place wasn't bad, it wasn't where he'd have wanted to grow up. Alex might feel sad knowing his niece had been in a place Shane wouldn't have wanted to live. He smiled at Cassie, "But Cassie sure made it hard for me," he teased, trying to make her laugh.

She smiled.

Chapter 20

The long drive lasted through the night, but Cassie enjoyed getting to know her uncle and Shane more. The sun was rising when Alex pulled into a small restaurant. She had enjoyed the views from the window; everything she saw was new. They had driven past vast open spaces with trees and forests. She'd never seen so many different types of trees and foliage. The highways were interesting, and she was surprised by the variety of vehicles traveling on them. They'd arrived in a small town, which she had read about in books, but seeing the small stores, restaurants, and a park was a thrill. She was going to experience a restaurant for the first time, and hoped she'd never forget the name: Twenty Four Hour Health Stop.

Alex opened Cassie's door and smiled as she stood on her toes, stretching her arms overhead. She sighed slightly before rolling her shoulders to loosen her stiff muscles. "You remind me of your Aunt Kate." Kate always stretched the same way after long road trips. Glancing around at the tall trees lining the brown brick building, he noted the closed hardware store next to the restaurant. Across the street, rows of shops were closed. It was five in the morning, and the small town was still sleeping. It was a habit for him to assess the surroundings. Mentally mapping out possible escape strategies.

When Shane opened the restaurant door, Cassie paused, feeling a tight squeeze on her heart. "Amy should be here. We always thought we'd eat our first restaurant meal together."

"You get to have your uncle and Shane instead, kiddo." Alex casually patted her shoulder, hoping she wouldn't cry. He appreciated that Shane had managed to lift her mood. Ten hours ago, when she'd been sobbing at the mall, he'd been worried she wouldn't bounce back. "You'll have something to tell her when you talk to her next."

"Thank you for coming to Health Stop. Would you like to try our new black-bean veggie burger?"

Cassie glanced from the friendly hologram to Shane. "You can order for me." She walked over to a machine on the wall with levers and silver cones. She listened as Shane and Alex placed an order, wondering what she was looking at.

"It's a beverage station. You can pick which type of smoothie you want." Alex handed her a cup. He still preferred to drink pop, even though they were at a health stop that wouldn't serve Coke or Pepsi. He had nothing against healthier choices but could use some carbonated caffeine.

Shane stepped up to the machine, placed his cup under the silver cone and pulled the lever. "They all taste pretty good. What's your favorite fruit, Cass?"

"I like grapes."

"Then try the power punch, because it tastes like grape juice. It's made with little sugar and real grapes." He helped Cassie pull the lever down. He took the cup from her when she eyed the restroom sign. "Go ahead and use the bathroom. I'll wait for you here."

A hologram figure appeared before Shane and said, "Please be seated. Your order will be served in just a moment." Cassie walked around the hologram, heading toward the restroom.

When she returned to her seat at the table, beside Shane and across from her uncle, Cassie glanced down at the blue plate of food. She lifted the round bun and stared at the oddly colored black piece of meat. Her eyes darted up at Alex when he took an enormous bite of his burger and moaned in satisfaction.

"Try it." Shane took a bite of his own, and noted the man who'd walked in. "It's made with beans, hummus, and breadcrumbs."

Alex ate fast. He wasn't a fan of lingering in public places. "We aren't too far from the person who is loaning us a Windmobile, which will get us to the helicopter faster."

The food tasted different from anything Cassie had ever eaten at the orphanage. It wasn't bad, but didn't warrant a moan. "How do you keep getting these people to help us?"

Alex's grin widened, deepening the creases at the corners of his eyes. "Because your uncle Danny is a genius. Years ago, when your mom was your age, she held healing conventions. People came from all over the country to be healed by her. She wanted to help as many as possible, but she was only one person, and thousands were in need. However, those she healed were so grateful that they pledged their loyalty to her. Danny recognized the value of these connections, knowing we might need help one day. So, he started making a list, keeping track of contacts and forming a secret society from all over the country, ready to assist Lily when the time came." After a long draw on the straw, he set his cup down. "Danny has incredible networking skills."

Shane hurried with his meal. "Danny tracks us with GPS. Wherever we go, he can locate someone nearby willing to help us. Usually, it's just borrowing a car or finding a place to stay for the night. He's almost always one step ahead of us."

"Sometimes, we've had people hide us." Alex carefully watched the stranger who sat at a table in the far corner of the restaurant. "The best part is knowing we always have access to money. Lily healed some very wealthy people, people willing to pay anything to have their loved ones cured. We take what we need and leave the rest as future assistance. It leaves people happy and grateful."

Leaning back, Cassie finished her burger, thinking Andrew would probably love it. "Wow." She couldn't imagine healing hundreds of people.

"Nine o'clock." Shane met Alex's eyes.

"Yup, been watching."

"What?" Cassie shifted her gaze from Shane back to her uncle.

The man sitting alone at his table had been paying too much attention to Cassie. "We can continue this conversation in the car." Alex stood, noting the disappointment on Cassie's face. Leaning forward, he lowered his voice. "Your mom isn't able to heal anymore without getting very weak and sometimes passing out. We try not to use her ability unless it's absolutely necessary." He knew Cassie enjoyed hearing all the stories and information he could give, but they needed to leave. Shane was already clearing the table, his guard up. "Your mom is going to want to explain a lot of things to you. She'll be upset if you already know everything about her. Mind if we hold off on more of this conversation?"

"Sure." Cassie rose, sensing Shane's unease.

"Keep your eyes down, Cass," he told her.

The man in the corner rose, and Alex stepped in front of his niece. "Get her to the car, Shane." He knew better than to talk in public, even though the stranger sat far enough away to hear their conversation. But now the man was texting on his phone. Alex had a bad feeling.

As Cassie approached the door, she heard a grunt and turned to witness her uncle blocking a swing from the stranger. A startled yelp escaped her as Shane grabbed her arm, urging her to move. "Get her out!" Alex's voice rang out, avoiding another strike.

"Come on!" Shane pulled her toward the car. She looked back, seeing her uncle duck and punch the stranger.

"Shane, we should help him!" She tried to pull free, to see if her uncle was okay. Alex was close to sixty years old and in great physical shape, but the stranger was much younger and just as large. What if he needed help? How could Shane abandon him? She jerked her arm away. "We need to help him."

Tires screeched on the cement as a car pulled up directly in front of them, with another vehicle halting behind, effectively boxing them in.

"Run!" Shane grabbed her hand, pulling her toward the back of the restaurant.

Glancing back, she saw four men emerging from the cars and chasing them. Shane's backpack bounced with each stride as he urged her to run faster. Suddenly, the men shouted at them to stop. Shane pulled her toward a cluster of trees, tightening his grip on her hand.

"You have to run faster!" The men were closing in. Without hesitation, he yanked off his backpack and threw it at a man wielding a gun. The firearm went flying through the air as Shane drew his own weapon and took aim. "We just want to see her eyes," one of the men said, holding his hands up and stepping closer.

"Are you part of the Twin Seekers?" Shane hoped they were, because that group wasn't as violent and deadly as the A.S.A.

The shorter man nodded. "We know she's Lily's daughter."

Shane's heart sank. How did they find out? He knew most Twin Seekers didn't carry guns. They were ordinary civilians who got their strength from numbers. More men could easily appear in a matter of minutes. If they didn't get away soon, they'd be outnumbered.

Seeing that the other three men had no weapons, Shane felt confident they could get away, but he wanted to avoid Cassie having to witness more violence. "Just let us go, and nobody needs to get hurt."

"We're taking the girl," the larger man replied.

Shane could see he was about to make a move, and hesitated, not wanting to take a life. The Twin Seekers were merely individuals seeking Lily for her healing abilities. They probably had loved ones desperate for a cure. Shane knew he couldn't afford to waste time with the larger man. Taking careful aim, he shot the man's leg, intending to disable rather than kill. The shorter assailant lunged toward him as the man fell to the ground. Swiftly sidestepping, Shane drove his knee into the man's chest, knocking him out with an upper cut. Cassie yelped in shock as she jumped behind a nearby tree while the third assailant closed in on her. Shane swiftly acted, using the butt of his gun to knock one of the men unconscious before restraining another in a headlock until he passed out. The man he shot writhed on the ground in agony, prompting Shane to approach and deliver a single punch, rendering him unconscious. With all four assailants now unconscious, Shane quickly checked their pockets.

"What are you doing?" Cassie glanced around at the men lying on the grass.

Another man was trying to get up. Shane kicked him unconscious. Then he pulled out a silver phone from the pocket of the man's shirt. He swiped the screen and opened the phone with the man's face ID. "Damn it!" He held the phone out to Cassie so she could see her photo. "Where was this picture taken?"

"At the orphanage. It's last year's school picture."

"Jamerson." Shane spat the word out like profanity. "He probably gave your picture to A.S.A., and then A.S.A. notified the Twin Seekers." If more people knew about her, A.S.A. would have a better chance of finding her.

"How is my photo on their phone?" She barely understood how cell phones worked and couldn't believe her picture was on a stranger's phone. As her mind processed that, her heart pounded.

There was a shout from the front of the building. Shane turned to see three more men rounding the corner. He swiftly picked up his pack and grasped Cassie's hand. "You need to run a lot faster, Cass."

They dashed towards a cluster of trees, branches whipping against her face as she pushed her legs to move as quickly as possible through the small woods. She ignored the sudden sting and the heavy ache in her chest, driven by the fear of capture and the desire to avoid Shane having to fight more men.

Almost stumbling over some roots, Shane caught her around the waist as they entered the backyard of a nearby house. Clothes hung on a line; blue jeans flapped in the wind alongside pink and white striped sheets. A purple tricycle lay tipped on its side, with pink and yellow ribbons on the handlebars fluttering in the wind. They hurried towards the side of the house, Cassie stepping over a doll lying face down on the cracked sidewalk. Tall weeds grew between the cracks; loose bricks lay scattered nearby.

Shane paused when they reached the street of a small neighborhood with run-down homes. He searched for a direction to run. Cassie had done well keeping up with him. Turns out she could be quite the runner when prompted.

The sound of a Windmobile down the street drew their attention, followed by a man's shout from behind, "Don't run or I'll shoot!"

They turned to find a man with thick eyebrows aiming his gun at them.

"Put your hands up." The man glanced nervously at his companion, who stood next to him.

Shane swore under his breath, positioning himself in front of Cassie. Though he could have fought if they were unarmed, facing a nervous man with a Glock left him with fewer options. Reluctantly, he put his hands up, watching another man, dressed in business attire, step out of the Windmobile. This was the problem with Twin Seekers—there were too many of them, and they were everywhere.

"Get in the Windmobile." The armed man waved his gun at them.

Shane felt a twinge of panic. "You're taking both of us!"

The gunman nodded at the man who drove the Windomobile. Shane was able to assess what he'd be dealing with. Civilians with no combat training always made his job easier. Cassie was holding up well. She wasn't crying or freaking out, but Shane noticed that her eyes hadn't left the gun. He figured she was also concerned with the way his hands shook. Shane turned toward the driver, who had probably been on his way to work, when he received the info about Cassie. He had no weapon and stared at his phone as if looking for guidance. The nervous, armed, bushy eyebrows guy wore a wedding band and was probably a family man. Shane entered the Windmobile and sat beside Cassie.

The Windmobile smelled like nicotine, and Cassie felt her stomach turn. The businessman worked the computer, placing GPS coordinates, while the nervous eyebrows guy kept the gun aimed at her.

"Would you mind taking your finger off the trigger? I don't care if you aim the gun, but your finger doesn't need to be on the trigger." Shane could see the guy accidentally firing because he had

134

no clue what he was doing.

The Windmobile took off. Cassie leaned back, taking a deep breath. She still wasn't used to the speed. Shane placed his hand on her leg, giving it a gentle squeeze. "It's going to be okay." Now there were only two men across from him, and nervous guy took his finger off the trigger. Their predicament had significantly improved.

"Where are you taking us?" Cassie tried to maintain her composure.

"I'll be asking the questions," Nervous Guy replied, his tone tense as he aimed his gun at the young girl. "How old are you?" He lowered his weapon.

"Seventeen." Cassie glanced at Shane recognizing she'd forgotten she was nineteen. A fact that would take some getting used to.

"We've been searching for Lily for years. Initially, we didn't believe the rumors about her having a long-lost daughter. But the man who sent us your photo is willing to pay over a million dollars for you, promising to heal whoever needs it." Nervous Guy nodded towards his companion. "Dom needs the money."

Shane noticed that the businessman, Dom, also wore a wedding ring, indicating a connection between the two. "So, you're Dom." He glanced at Nervous Guy. "What's your name?" He liked that the gun lowered more.

"I'm Tom."

"Tom and Dom? That's funny." Shane smiled. He sat back and angled his feet, placing them more in front of Tom. "You have the wrong girl. She's not Lily's daughter, and you'll see you're making a mistake."

"My ten-year-old daughter has Cancer. I joined T.S. when I learned she might die. My wife has always believed Lily is alive. If we can find her, there could be a chance to cure my daughter."

"If I cure your daughter, will you let me go?"

"Cassie." Shane's tone held a warning as he looked sharply at her.

Tom scooted forward. "You have the power?" He searched her up and down. "You have her eyes and hair color. You *are* Lily's daughter."

"I always knew the government was right when they said the twins weren't human." Dom reached his hand out to touch Cassie. "You're not human either, are you?" He spoke the words with contempt, and a look of disgust crossed his face.

When Dom extended his arm, Shane seized the opportunity. He grabbed Dom's arm, pulling him forward while simultaneously kicking the gun out of Tom's hand. With a swift motion, he jabbed Dom's neck with his right elbow and delivered a solid punch to Tom's face with his left fist. Rolling to his side, Shane quickly incapacitated Tom with another kick before pressing his knee into Dom's back to restrain him. He then retrieved the gun from the floor and used it to knock Dom unconscious.

"You didn't have to do that!" Cassie was dismayed by the turn of events. "I could have just healed his daughter."

"It doesn't work that way." Shane felt a surge of anger at how Dom had accused Lily and Cassie of not being human. He hated that so many civilians had believed the government's lies, making people hostile. "I couldn't risk them handing you over to A.S.A." He tried to keep his anger in check, knowing the consequences could be dire. "A.S.A. would likely want the money and you. They believe the world is overrun by aliens and their sole objective is to eradicate them from our planet." Shane brought the Windmobile to a stop on the side of the road by swiping his hand across the computer screen. He was frustrated that Cassie let the men know she could heal. She didn't understand the circumstances, and he couldn't explain things without scaring her. "Listen… if this happens again, I'd like you to stay quiet." He spoke harsher than he'd intended, but keeping Cassie's secret was crucial to her safety.

Cassie felt a lump in her throat as she felt reprimanded. She hadn't seen this side of Shane. He was angry.

Once the Windmobile came to a stop, Shane wasted no time

dragging Tom's body out and dumping it on the side of the road, followed by Dom's. As a passing car honked, he hoped no one was videoing his actions, but there wasn't anything he could do about it. Quickly returning to the vehicle, he took his seat and entered new coordinates into the computer. As the craft took off, he purposely avoided Cassie's gaze. He retrieved a cell from his backpack, intending to inform Danny of their situation. They needed a new vehicle and a place to lay low. He hoped Alex was okay.

Chapter 21

It was time to switch vehicles again. After ditching the Windmobile, they had walked long, winding back roads, evading police and passing cars. Exhausted from the walk, Cassie found little comfort in the flimsy shoes she had worn from the orphanage, especially when they had to hide in forest brush to avoid being seen.

Finally, Danny had sent Nora to pick them up. Nora, a middle-aged woman with soft creases at the corners of her eyes and silver just beginning to lace her dark hair, revealed to them that Lily had healed her cancer years ago. She explained that she would have reached them sooner but didn't have a car when Danny contacted her. Now, Nora passed them on to Kelly, the next person to take them further to Texas.

The sun's rays shot through a small hole in the clouds, touching over a low green hill dotted with mature trees and brush.

"You look pretty tired, Cass. I think you should try to sleep when we switch vehicles." Shane glanced at Kelly's parked car, ensuring the surroundings were safe. Her windows were rolled down, and he hoped she wouldn't mind using air conditioning, because the van's AC was broken and the heat had been miserable.

Cassie nodded, breathing in a scent that permeated the air. "Where are we now?"

"We're in the state of Mississippi. There's a woman here named Kelly. She brought us lunch and coffee." He wished he could have an ice-cold beverage instead of warm coffee. He'd been texting Kelly and Danny but wouldn't ask for anything. He was grateful that things were working out so far.

That's what Cassie smelled. She glanced out the open van window. They were parked on a dirt road. She was relieved it was desolate with no other cars in sight. A woman with shoulder-length blond hair, wearing a yellow sundress, exited her car holding a box. "Smells good." Cassie took Shane's hand as he helped her out of the van.

"What smells good?" He couldn't smell anything.

"The food."

"You can smell the lunch from here?"

"Yes, it smells sweet, with a hint of vanilla and sugar." She stretched her legs and arms, surveying the area. She had only ever seen Mississippi on a map of the United States. Her view only offered a secluded dirt road surrounded by lowland plains and green hills. She caught a few outdoor scents mixed with the food.

Kelly waved in a friendly greeting and smiled. Kelly's clean, attractive appearance made Cassie feel self-conscious as she stared down at her ugly black, dirty shoes, which clashed horribly with her pretty new dress, which was full of wrinkles. But since the ground was damp and muddy, she knew she was lucky to have shoes at least. An insect buzzed around her head, and she swatted it away.

"Thanks again, Nora!" Shane raised his voice and waved goodbye to her, and Cassie turned to do the same. Although Cassie had said very little to her on the drive, she had listened to Nora and Shane's lengthy small talk. Nora was caring for her ailing father when Danny called and asked for her help. Nora was likely eager to leave now and return to her family.

Shane shook Kelly's hand in greeting. He watched as Nora drove away, and then he opened the box of doughnuts.

"Here, sweetie, put your hands out." Kelly poured a few clear drops of hand sanitizer onto Cassie's open hands. "Rub your hands together."

"It's hand sanitizer." Shane waited for her hands to dry before handing her a donut. "Wait till you try this. You're going to love it." He thought of Andrew.

"I would've brought something healthier if I'd had more time

139

to prepare. It's so nice to meet you." Kelly's cheerful voice had a southern accent. "Go ahead and get in the car. I'm sorry it's messy. I do a lot of traveling for work." She was a traveling nurse, driving from house to house, bringing medications, and caring for sick individuals in their homes.

The car had leather cream-colored seats, and the floor was littered with papers, crumpled bags, clothes, and a pink backpack. Shane tossed his pack on top of hers.

The donut melted in Cassie's mouth. She licked the glaze from her fingers as Shane pulled the seat belt over her waist. Her dress had ridden up to her thigh, and she felt her cheeks warm as she pulled it back down.

"It's good, isn't it?" He handed her a cup of coffee. "This doesn't taste the same as the orphanage, but you might like it."

She could smell the sweet scent of vanilla. She took a sip and sighed contentedly. "It's wonderful." She thought of having another doughnut, but didn't ask. So far, the donut and coffee were the best things she had tasted. Memories of the burger at the Health Stop and the image of her uncle fighting the stranger flashed through her mind. Shane had been texting with Danny and assumed there was still no word. "Do you think Alex will be okay?"

Shane nodded his head. "Alex can take care of himself, and I'm sure he'll contact Danny soon. Don't worry." He grabbed the donuts from the front seat and handed her another. He sat in the back to be near her.

Kelly started the car and drove slowly down the rough, potholed road. She glanced in the rearview mirror. "We have about a 10-hour drive now." She turned right when they hit another road and headed for an expressway sign. "My mom was so excited when Danny called her. She gave him my number, knowing I could help. I've prepared for this day for a long time. I was starting to think he would never need our help." She increased her speed as she turned onto a two-lane highway. "Both my momma and grandma are alive today because Lily cured them. My momma had radiation poisoning.

She was just a young girl then, but she'd lived through the aftermath of those nuclear explosions. She told me how ill she was and that she was about to die from all the bleeding and sickness. My grandma had severe melanoma, and back then, it was hard to get treatment." She explained that was why she became a nurse—to help people. "Lily cured my grandma and my mother. Because of her, my mom's alive today, and I was born. Lily's an angel."

"What did Danny tell you about us?" Shane wondered if she knew who they were. Kelly might work a lot, and she might not have seen Cassie's photo if she hadn't spent time on social media.

"He said a young couple Lily cared about was in trouble." Kelly glanced from the rear-view mirror back to the road. "He told me where to find you and said that Lily would be grateful if I gave you a ride to Texas. I'd help in any way I can. I'd do anything for her."

That answered Shane's question. Kelly had no idea Cassie was Lily's daughter. Danny wisely wasn't sharing that information. "We appreciate your help."

"My grandma gave Danny our contact information years ago and begged him to let us repay the favor we all owed Lily. We'd do anything for that woman. I'm the grateful one."

It warmed Cassie's heart to know there were people in the world who loved her mother and wanted to help her in any way possible. It was only the third day in the outside world, and she had to admit, the world wasn't offering much hope. There didn't seem to be an end to the organizations that wanted to harm her or find her mother. Fear, anxiety, and exhaustion had been her primary emotions until now. "Thank you for sharing this story. It's nice to hear."

"I like to see you smile," Shane whispered, resting his hand on hers. "Drink your coffee before it gets cold." The air conditioning in the car was nice, so finally he felt more comfortable. He glanced out the window at the busy highway, where cars and trucks filled the road. Occasionally, a Windmobile would whiz by in the far lane. He wished they were traveling faster, but at least they were safe. Danny was monitoring the police radios and internet. No one had yet reported Shane and Cassie to the police. The man he'd shot must not have gone to the hospital. If they had, there would be questions. A.S.A. probably helped them, along with Dom and Tom. They likely wouldn't say anything because Twin Seekers liked to remain anonymous. The TS organization was secretive, which was one reason they had so many members. Ordinary people could belong, and no one would know.

"So you're not mad at me anymore?" Cassie said quietly, hoping Kelly wouldn't hear their conversation.

"What?" Shane stared at her for a moment. His eyes drew together with concern. "Is that why you've been so quiet?" He figured she spoke very little during their ride together out of fear and trying to process things mentally. She'd been silent in the van ride with Nora, but he figured the heat was to blame for her crestfallen appearance. He didn't perceive that she thought he was angry with her.

"I'm sorry I told those men…"

Shane squeezed her to stop her from finishing the sentence he wouldn't want Kelly to hear. "Nope," he interrupted. "I'm sorry if my anger felt directed at you." He had been angry then, but got over it quickly and knew she'd unintentionally made a mistake.

Kelly turned the radio on, filling the car with pop music. The beat sounded pleasant. Cassie was pleased it was low enough to still speak with Shane, but it would limit Kelly's hearing ability. The appreciative look on Shane's face told her he was thinking the same thing.

"I don't like it when you're angry. I know you were mad at me." She scooted closer to his ear and kept her voice low enough for him to hear.

Shane thought for a moment. "I was mad more at the situation and wished you hadn't said anything. No one can know you exist. Don't admit your ability or who you are ever." It occurred to him she'd felt hurt and yet remained silent. "Cassie, if ever you've got something on your mind, don't hesitate to talk to me. You can tell me if I say or do anything that hurts you. I want you to know you

142

can tell me anything."

Cassie thought about that for a moment. "Okay… well, I thought you were…" What word could she use?

"A Prick?" Shane supplied.

Cassie laughed. "Yeah." She hadn't heard that terminology before, but the word seemed to fit. "I didn't like how you spoke to me."

He smiled and kissed her forehead. "I'm sorry."

A weight lifted. Was that their first quarrel, so easily fixed? She had little experience with confrontation. She and Amy occasionally had disagreements or arguments but usually moved past them without issue. Cassie had time to think about Shane's words. "Shane…" she began and sat up a little straighter to look in his eyes. "I understand what you mean about keeping me a secret, but this is my life now. You're keeping me safe, and I'm grateful, but don't I have a say in anything? What if I want to help? What if I don't want to go along with a plan or need more understanding?" She didn't want to be helpless, following every command with no voice of her own.

Shane smiled. "I'll try to keep you better informed." He understood what she was asking. The truth was she might not have a say regarding her safety. Her mom, Lily, always took a stance, but in the end, her safety came first. Shane figured the sooner Cassie could be reunited with her family, the sooner others would share this with her. She would learn how everything works. But he also knew how important it was for Lily to feel in control of her life. "You will always have a say."

Cassie caught a glimpse of a large cemetery out her window. The old tombstones lay in a field of green grass. American flags blew softly, and a variety of flowers blanketed the graves. The car seemed to wiz by fast, but Cassie caught enough of the landscape to understand. "Was that a cemetery?" She'd seen photos of them in books.

Shane nodded. "This must be exciting for you to see everything for the first time?"

"It is. I've only ever seen things in books and movies." Cassie loved movie night at the orphanage, which usually fell on holidays like Christmas or Easter. The students were allowed to watch a chosen movie during these special occasions. Usually, they were funny and straightforward, but Cassie loved catching a glimpse of the world outside. Thinking about the world, she wondered, "Did Danny hear from your father? Is there any news on Amy and Andrew? What about Julie and Caleb?"

He nodded empathetically. "My dad checked in with Danny last night, and everything was fine. Amy and Andrew are both safe. I'm not sure about Julie and Andrew yet, but I'll find out next time I speak with Danny. Tomorrow, you're going to meet your parents, Cass." He kept his voice low, so Kelly couldn't hear them over the music. "You'll meet your aunt Kate, Uncle Danny and your brother." He pressed his lips to her forehead. "Come here." He pulled her closer as she angled her body to the side and cradled her head in his arm. The way he'd held her when Alex was driving the previous night.

"What's my brother's name?"

"PJ."

"PJ?"

He chuckled. "There's a funny story behind his name. I'm sure your aunt will want to tell you. It sounds funnier when she explains it."

"I'd rather you told me."

He stared down at her. Sometimes she made it extremely difficult to stay focused. With the sun shining on her hair, he could see the shimmer of dark red highlights. He could smell the faint trace of coffee on her breath and noticed all the flecks of gold in her dark reddish copper eyes. He cleared his throat. "Well, the way your aunt tells it… your parents hadn't been able to decide on a name. Your mom wanted to name him after your father, Patrick. But your dad had this horrible nickname, and was worried his son would inherit it."

"What was the nickname?"

"Prick. It's Patrick with the 'at' taken out."

144

Cassie smiled. "Oh, and it means unpleasant or not nice."

Shane laughed. "Yeah. Anyway, your aunt started calling your brother Junior before he was born. Then, a few days after his birth, Danny said that Junior had Patrick's smile. So, he started calling him Patrick Junior. That's when your mom told them his name would probably be Jason. Your Aunt Kate is a smart ass, so she started calling him Probably Jason, which eventually got shortened to PJ. Since he was just born and both Kate and Danny continued to call him PJ, that's what your parents went with."

"So his name is Probably Jason?"

Shane laughed at the confused look on her face. "No, it's Patrick Jason. Or Patrick Junior, or Probably Jason, according to whatever Kate calls him on any given day. Your aunt tells the story better."

"Oh." Cassie smiled. "And he's 15?"

Shane nodded. "She had him four years after you were taken."

"How was I taken?"

Shane sighed. "Remember when Alex asked you to wait on your questions? I don't feel right telling you everything, Cass. Your parents will want to share these things with you."

"Fine." She understood his reluctance. "Then tell me about yourself." Her hands were folded in, resting across her heart, but if she turned them, she could touch his chest. She was lying sideways across his lap, enjoying how he used his arm as a pillow. She wondered if his arm was getting tired.

"Don't move. I like holding you like this."

She smiled and thought there wasn't anywhere else in the world she'd rather be. "Tell me about your childhood. Where'd you go to school?"

Kelly was swaying her head and singing softly along with the music while driving. Traffic was moving steadily, and no one driving by could see Cassie. Shane felt pleased they'd have all this time in the car to get to know each other better. He'd wanted moments like this at the orphanage, where they could be uninterrupted for more than ten minutes, but life at the school never allowed for much reminiscence. "I went to public school when I was little. Then, at age nine, my dad began homeschooling me because I missed school too much. My mom left us when I was three, and Dad had a hard time working, helping Lily, and getting me to school."

"Your mom left you." She remembered he'd mentioned it briefly and tried to imagine how a young boy would handle such a tough thing.

"She and my dad had a one-night stand. After she got pregnant, my dad married her. She never really wanted to be married or have a kid. After a few years of trying, she decided she didn't like how my dad lived his life. She didn't want anything to do with him." He shrugged. "My dad and I were a package, and he wasn't willing to let me go. So, she moved away, and I stayed with my dad. It didn't take her long to disappear from our lives."

"I'm sorry." She absentmindedly stroked his arm. "Do you miss her? Do you want to find her?" Cassie knew how it felt not having a mother, but to have known one and then lost her, she imagined would be harder.

"Maybe one day, but it doesn't bother me much. My childhood wasn't typical. We were always on the move. While most kids my age were in school, I was taking fighting lessons and learning about guns. I didn't mind it, though." However, as he entered his teen years and became interested in girls, he started to resent his lifestyle. Dating or having a girlfriend was out of the question, and even making friends was challenging due to the constant movement. "Moving to Hawaii was great, as was being close to your mom and dad and living near the ocean. Alex had a house on the cliff overlooking the sea, where he lived with his girlfriend, Sarah. My dad and I spent much time there, and I learned to surf." A slow grin spread across his face. "Those were good years."

"I didn't know Uncle Alex has a girlfriend."

"Not anymore." Shane's smile faded, and he glanced sadly out the window. "She died."

Her breath caught, and her eyes widened as she sat up slightly.

146

"How?"

"Five years ago, Alex rushed home to pack. Lily and Patrick had been discovered and needed to leave the island immediately." He could still feel the fear he'd experienced for the family he'd grown to love. "The A.S.A. had found their homes and was coming for them. Alex had already put Lily and Patrick on a plane." He gently touched the side of her cheek. "He went back to get Sarah, and the two took off on his motorcycle. But the A.S.A. was chasing after them. My Dad and I couldn't reach them in time. A Windmobile hit the motorcycle, and Sarah was thrown from the bike. She died instantly. My Dad and I found Alex alive, but in terrible shape. He had tons of broken bones, his skin was torn half off, and he almost died. We got him to the hospital and then to a safe place, where he spent three months recovering, until your mom was able to get to him and heal him finally."

A heavy weight settled on Cassie's chest as she realized the extent of his sacrifices for her family throughout his life. She imagined there were countless untold stories he could share. The sorrow on his face mirrored the emotion she felt. "Poor Alex."

"Yeah." His eyes met hers. "He never got over her." Alex didn't keep long-term relationships. While he occasionally went out with women, they never seemed to stay around for too long. "In the last five years, he became more obsessed with searching for you." As if finding Cassie could somehow bring peace and meaning back to Alex's life. "I think it helped to give him purpose and a reason to continue."

She pictured her uncle's warm, handsome smile. She imagined him in love and tried to picture him torn and broken, lying helpless in a hospital bed.

Shane's face lifted slightly. "Anyway, I liked the years I spent on that gorgeous island and hanging out with your family. You wouldn't believe how beautiful the waterfalls are. I hope to go back someday." He didn't want her to feel sad. "You have an amazing family, Cass. You're going to love them."

"I already do." Her throat felt tight with emotion. She could sit and listen to stories of her family forever.

"I didn't mean to upset you." He tenderly stroked her arm and pulled her closer.

"I've missed so much with them. I have no good stories to share about life in the orphanage. It was so dull and uneventful." What could she tell her parents? There was nothing special about her. "Will you tell me about PJ?"

"We've got some trouble." Kelly slowed the car. Her cell phone rang, and she turned the radio down to answer it.

Cassie sat up, and Shane leaned forward to hear what Kelly said. He noticed the highway was backed up with cars. Everyone was stopping. "What's going on?" He took the phone from her when she offered it to him.

"Okay, listen up." Danny's voice sounded urgent and concerned. "I need you and Cassie to get out of the car. See the big open field to the left on the other side of the highway?"

Shane stared out the window. "Yup."

"That field leads to some back roads and property. Keep heading that way, and you'll come to a small river." Danny zoomed in on his GPS. "It looks like a decent-sized river. Hang on." He studied the computer, trying to place the coordinates. "I've got a safe house nearby, where you should be able to stay. How much battery life is on your phone?"

Shane pulled his cell phone from his backpack pocket. Most phones had weeks' worth of solar battery life. "It's good."

"Okay, just start walking. I'll call you when I have more information."

"Has Alex spoken with you yet?" Shane wanted to ask about Julie and Caleb, but now wasn't the time. He knew it was time to hustle when Danny needed them to move.

"Not yet. Keep her safe, kid."

"Will do." He swiped the screen, handing Kelley's phone back to her. "Thank you for getting us this far." He reached into the backpack and pulled out a pair of sunglasses and a baseball cap. "Put these on, Cass. See if you can get your hair under it."

Kelly looked at both with concern. "It was nice meeting you, and I wish you luck. Give Lily my best when you see her."

Here we go again. Cassie felt her stomach flutter as she tied her hair up in a bun and pulled the baseball cap over it. "Thank you so much for everything."

The cars were all stopped in a gridlock. A Windmobile in the left lane hovered loudly in place. He took her hand. "Just smile and stroll." He weaved them around the cars, waving at the drivers, as if nothing was wrong. He reached the median and saw the roadblock was far enough ahead that no one would see them crossing. It was good she had practical shoes, because the field was damp and uneven, and filled with tall blades of grass. "Watch your step." He kept his eyes peeled for danger.

Chapter 22

The Mississippi sun was at its warmest at five in the afternoon. Shane was feeling hungry, and the heat started getting to him. He looked at Cassie's pale skin, knowing the sun had to be burning her. However, her arms didn't look pink. He wondered if her body was healing from sunburn. "How are you holding up, Cass?" He was impressed that she'd kept a decent pace with no complaint.

"I'm hot and thirsty." They'd both drunk the only water he had in his pack. The ball cap was too big, making her scalp itch. The glasses kept falling down her sweaty nose, so she took them off and handed them to him. "I don't need this anymore."

He put the hat and her sunglasses in his pack. They had walked eight miles, and he had taken three calls from Danny trying to guide them. "Do you want to stop?" He glanced around at the trees for a good place to pause.

"I'm not sure we're getting anywhere." She kept hoping Danny would work his magic, which usually involved a stranger coming to their rescue. But in the middle of nowhere, it felt like they were the only two people left on the planet, with no one coming to help.

"Hang on." He stopped and glanced around. They hadn't seen a car in over an hour, and the dirt road seemed to stretch forever. Along the way, they had passed a few houses, more like shacks. Thankfully, trees now lined the road, providing some relief from the scorching sun.

Beads of sweat clung to his brow, and a V-shaped sweat patch darkened his shirt-front. Their water bottles and energy bars were now gone. Danny had told them to look for a big red barn next to an old farmhouse, but so far, all he could see were trees. Mississippi was known for its dense forests outside of the Mississippi Delta.

Danny was doing his best to help but having to detour from the road complicated things. They were in the middle of nowhere, on a narrow road flanked by forests, supposedly heading west toward Texas. Cassie was right—they needed to find a place to stop walking soon.

She bent down to remove a pebble from her shoe. As she did, she spotted something red through the trees and pointed. "Could that be it?"

He bent and followed her line of sight. "It's a big red barn." Supposedly, it would be safe to spend the night there. "Let's go."

As they approached the barn, he felt uneasy. It was eerily quiet and desolate, and the barn itself appeared ancient. He doubted whether it would even be safe to enter. The roof sagged on one side, and the door hung from a single hinge, with many of the boards rotted and crumbling.

Turning his attention to the nearby farmhouse, he found little reassurance. The porch was visibly sunken on one side, with the steps deteriorating beneath a tangle of weeds. Layers of dirt blocked the two front windows. Sections of the roof were missing shingles. The white paint on the siding was so faded and chipped that the original wood was showing.

He voiced his concerns as he swiped the phone to call Danny. "Doesn't look like anyone lives here." He noted the concern in Cassie's eyes, the exhausted stance of her body. "I think we found it. The place looks abandoned." Just as he said the words, Cassie yelped. Then he felt a sudden sharp pain in his shoulder.

Danny answered the phone immediately. "Get out of there! It's not safe!"

Hearing Danny's frantic words, he quickly spun around. A man aiming a dart gun at them shot again. He felt another sting in his leg and saw the red dart sticking out. He turned to Cassie, who was pulling a dart from her arm. "Darts!" he yelled into the phone, pulling Cassie behind him. His vision was already blurring; his legs were getting weak. "We've been darted." He dropped the phone as he collapsed to the ground. He knew Danny would know that meant they were shot with tranquilizers. He hated dart guns. Years ago, when the government made it illegal to own handguns, people began using a new model of tranquilizer darts that would render a person unconscious in a matter of seconds. The new dart guns were so popular almost everyone had one. He knew there was nothing he could do before the darkness overcame him.

Chapter 23

A foul stench permeated the air. Cassie felt her stomach turn and opened her eyes. She felt light-headed, and her eyes were blurry. It took her a moment to notice her hands were bound behind her, and she was leaning against a metal pole. "Shane?" A single lamp lighted the room. A window was near her, but dirty pink curtains kept out the daylight.

She glanced around, trying to determine her surroundings. She was in a bedroom, and her hands were tied to a metal bed frame. The carpet was stained. It might've been pink once but was now a faded mauve brown color. Pink flowered wallpaper peeled from the wall, and the dresser in the corner was stacked with piles of newspapers.

The stench made her gag, and when she struggled, the ties around her wrist got tighter and bit into her soft flesh. Her mouth was dry. Panic made her heart slam inside her chest. The room was musty, but the odor came from somewhere else.

The door flew open, and the man she saw earlier walked in. He was wearing a red tank top that fit snug over fat rolls, sagging over the waistband of his dirty jean shorts. He wore white tube socks and an old pair of heavily stained tennis shoes. Duct tape was wrapped around the front of his left shoe.

"Well, hello there. I see the dart gun didn't work long on ya's. I guess you's body already removed the poison." The man tipped his head to the bed. "Your boyfriend's still out, though." He crouched down low in front of Cassie. She leaned back at the smell of his atrocious breath. "My name's Jackson. Not a bad name for living right outside of Jackson, Mississippi, don't ya think?" He lifted Cassie's chin with his fat finger. "You look at me when I'm talkin to ya."

"What do you want with us? Why did you tie me up?" Her voice trembled, and she prayed Shane would wake up.

Jackson leaned closer, staring into Cassie's eyes. His eyes were dark, the lids and corners swollen from his extra girth. His face was round and chubby, and he had three rolls under his chin. "You're way prettier in person than you are in the picture they got's of you on TV. The news says you's another one of them aliens. We ain't heard 'bout no aliens in a long time. I guess you got that um there power to heal, like they been sayin." He moved his hand down her arm. "I zip-tied your wrists together. Do it hurt?"

"Yes." She couldn't feel anything, so she figured that wasn't good.

"You're beautiful." He sat beside her, placing his large legs on either side of her body. "I ain't been with a woman in a long, long time."

Bile shot up her throat, and she swallowed hard. "Please, don't touch me." She leaned back away from the odor that seemed to pour from every crevice of his body. His teeth were rotten, and she wondered if he ever bathed. Tears stung her eyes, and her body shook with fear.

"If you's an alien, you sure do look human. Where'd you come from?" He picked up a strand of her hair that had come loose from her braid and brought it to his nose, rubbing it across his cheek.

There was something wrong with the man's mental state. Maybe she could reason with him. "I'm not an alien, Jackson. I'm a human being just like you." She tried to breathe through her mouth so she wouldn't gag. She hoped by using his name and talking to him, she could appeal to his sympathy if he had any. "I have some experimental DNA in my body that came from an experiment done on my grandmother. I just recently found out that I can heal people. If you let me go, I can heal you or someone you love." She had his attention, and she hoped that if she kept talking to him, kept him distracted, that he'd stop touching her.

"You got no hair on you's arms." He trailed his hand down her legs, which were crossed in front of her. "You got soft skin, and no hair on your legs, eezer."

"I'm not sure why I have no hair. It's just the way I was born." She realized she'd said something wrong when his eyes lit up and he stared down at her waist. Her dress was pulled up to her thighs, and she wished she could pull it down. "Look, isn't there someone you love who might be sick? Do you have a family?"

He shrugged. "I lived with my Ma, but she died a few years ago. She's still sittin' in her rocking chair." When he found his mother dead, he decided to leave her in the chair. He didn't have money to pay for a funeral, and he was afraid that someone might try to take him away from his home. He had tried to dig a hole in the backyard for her, but it was too much work, and he was sure she wouldn't fit. "Ma liked her rocking chair best."

The man was clearly mentally unstable, and she was about to throw up. "I'm sorry you lost her. I know it's never easy to lose a parent."

"No. No, it ain't." He sat back a little and sighed. "You seem like a nice alien."

"I'm human."

Jackson glanced around the room. "I'm going to do things with ya. I want to see what parts of you are alien."

"Oh God." She leaned to the side and gagged, waiting for vomit to come up, but nothing did. "I'm so thirsty. Can I please have some water?" Her heart was beating so fast, she expected it to jump from her chest.

"It's warm in here. I'll get you's somtin' to drink, in a minute." He licked his lips as his eyes roamed over her.

She tried to think of something that might make him sympathetic. "My family is looking for me. Imagine how your mom would have felt if you were missing and she couldn't find you." She pulled her legs up, keeping them closed tight and on the floor. "You seem like a nice man, and I think you could do something good, and let me

155

go, so I can find my family."

He reached his hand out and began rubbing her leg, then lifted the hem of her dress. "It gets lonely out here. When I looked out my window and seen you standing in my driveway, I got excited, cuz I knew you looked like that alien girl they been showing on the news. I got my darts ready, 'cuz I knew I was going to keep ya." He smiled wide, revealing many missing teeth in the back of this mouth. "I could call the number they put on the screen, and I can get money for you's. They's got a reward for finding ya's. But I ain't interested in no money. I ain't wantin' a reward. I'm going to keeps ya."

Chapter 24

Shane had woken to the fear in Cassie's voice and Jackson's dim-witted, illiterate slur. The odor almost made him gag out loud, but he forced himself to remain quiet as he studied their predicament. Cassie was doing a great job of talking to him. She was saying everything right and begging him for water was perfect. When Jackson left to retrieve her water, Shane pulled himself up enough to study the plastic zip ties. He knew how to pull zip ties apart with momentum but being bound to the wrought-iron bed spindle, he wouldn't be able to. Luckily, the base of the spindle was highly rusted. Shane sat up, turning his body. Using his foot, he kicked the spindle as hard as he could.

Cassie heard the noise and let out a startled gasp. "Shane? Are you awake?" She twisted, trying to see over the bed. She heard another loud noise before Jackson walked into the room.

"Oh, look who's awake!"

Shane pushed the pillow up to hide the broken spindle, pushing his back against the frame. "Let us go."

Jackson stormed over to Shane and punched him across the jaw. "You be quiet or I'll stab you's with my darts." He turned his back, and with a wobbly gait, he walked to the foot of the bed and plopped down beside Cassie. "Here." He held a glass of cloudy water up to her mouth. She took a swallow, but it tasted funny, so she spit it out.

"Please…" She gasped as he tried to force more water on her. "Untie me."

"Your dress is wet." He rubbed his hands over her chest, smiling when she tried to turn away. "I'll just take this off." He looked at her, puzzled. It was one piece and would need to be slipped over her head, which he couldn't do with her hands behind her back. Maybe he could untie her and take her to the other room. He wanted to be alone with her anyway. "I'll get some scissors to untie you's." He grabbed her chin. "You's won't run from me?"

She shook her head, waiting for him to leave again. "Shane? Are you okay?"

"No worries, Cass." Just like that, he was crouched down in front of her. "I'm getting us out of here." He examined the zip ties biting into her flesh. "I need something to cut these with. I'll be right back." He kissed her head and was out the door before she could respond.

"What?" The word came out too late. She wanted to call him, but didn't dare make a noise that could alert Jackson. She couldn't believe he'd just left her. The relief she felt a second ago when he kneeled before her was gone. She was swamped with panic, her stomach twisting violently with fear. Sweat dripped down her back and temples. Her arms ached from being held in the same position for so long. Suddenly, there was a loud clatter, and it sounded like a door was slammed shut. She could hear grunts and lots of scuffling.

Minutes ticked by, the silence was killing her. She began to think the worst. What if he were hurt or lying dead on the floor? The thought of losing him was worse than what Jackson could do to her. She could not hold back the sob that tore from her throat. What if both men were dead? She'd die a long, slow death of dehydration, and no one would ever find her. She closed her eyes, tears streaming down her face. Just then, Shane came barreling back into the room.

"Sorry it took me so long." He reached behind and cut her zip ties with a pair of scissors. "Jackson was a big boy. I had to finish him out back."

She threw her arms around his neck, releasing a ragged breath.

He cupped the sides of her face. Fear, relief, and worry were all in her beautiful eyes. "Let's get out of here." He helped her to her feet, wrapping an arm around her waist, sensing her instability.

"What happened? Is he dead? Are you hurt?" She noticed the splash of blood along his neck and shoulder.

The rage Shane had felt at the sick bastard for touching and terrifying her had helped pump his adrenaline, giving him the strength and wrath he needed to stop Jackson. At first, he hadn't intended to end his life. He'd wanted to tie him up and send the police in after they were gone. The police would find the corpse of Jackson's mother rotting away in a rocking chair, see the man was clearly disturbed, and lock him up. But Jackson was out for blood. Shane knew it was kill or be killed. Looking at the tears on her cheeks, the weariness in her eyes, he felt sick imagining all the horrible things Jackson would have done to her. "He's not our problem anymore."

She squeezed his arm in relief. Her throat ached from trying not to cry. "I thought... I've never been so scared."

"I know." This could potentially be the most traumatic thing to happen to them so far, and she'd already experienced enough. The sun was setting, with little light left. He felt how weak and shaky she was. He wanted to escape the foul-smelling house and breathe fresh air, but he knew they both needed water, especially her. When he reached the gravel driveway, he carefully let her go. "Stay right here. I will go back inside and get some water." He'd spotted his pack on the porch and needed to check the contents.

He pulled his T-shirt over his nose to diffuse the sickening stench. It was hard to believe Jackson dealt with that stench daily; clearly, the man was deranged. Standing in the kitchen, he grabbed the dart gun he spotted on the old wooden table. It still had three darts in the chamber and was small enough to tuck into the waistband of his jeans. The refrigerator contained a case of new water bottles. Searching the cupboards, he found a box of crackers and a small, unopened jar of peanut butter. He wouldn't take anything open that the slob may have touched.

When Shane returned, slinging his heavy pack over his shoulder, she quickly took the water bottle and paper towel he handed her. She wiped her face and drank the water down. "What are you doing?"

"I'm looking for the cell I dropped." He walked over to where they were hit with the darts. "Here it is." He picked it up, dusting off the dirt. When he swiped the screen, he saw it was still powered. Thank God for solar batteries. Lying in the sun all afternoon had recharged the phone. "I'm going to call Danny." He'd already hit redial and was holding the phone to his ear. When Danny answered, he began to explain what happened.

"I'm so sorry I messed up." Danny had been worried sick and hadn't been able to send help. He'd directed them to the house of a woman who had promised to help years ago. But he learned too late that the woman had died, leaving only her dysfunctional son in the home. Danny was in touch with Ian, but he was fourteen hours away. "I'm so proud of you, Shane. I couldn't have asked for a better man to care for Cassie."

"Thanks." Usually, Shane would appreciate the praise, but he was aching, bone tired, and swarmed by mosquitoes. Cassie was smacking them, and it would soon be dark. He needed to get her someplace safe. "We need shelter. Tell me where to go. It looks like the psycho didn't have a car, and there's no damn way we're going back in that house."

"You can't walk along the road. Her face is all over the news and social media. You have to stay hidden now." Danny ran a hand through his formerly blond hair, now mostly white with age. He sat back in his chair, his gaze fixed on the picture of his beautiful wife on his desk. Kate was cooking dinner and had been extremely anxious, worrying over her family.

"We still haven't heard from Alex, and the A.S.A. is pursuing Cassie with every means they have. They took a big chance exposing her like this. She'll never be safe now." Danny felt bad about adding to Shane's stress, but the information was important to share.

"I know." Shane sighed. It was definitely going to be harder now to get her home.

"According to the GPS, there's a river close by. It's probably not the kind you can follow." Danny was thinking of Gators and marshes. Traveling at night was dangerous when they couldn't see where they were going. "I don't think you've got a choice, Shane. I just don't have any contacts close enough to help out. You've got to hang tight until your Dad arrives." Ian was on his way.

"I'll figure something out." He ended the call and turned the phone flashlight on. Cassie looked barely held together with days of dirt and fear, clothes wrinkled and disheveled like she'd been in a storm. Her red-rimmed eyes held exhaustion, and her hair was half falling from the messy braid. "Let's check out the barn." He took her hand, leading the way with the light. As they walked toward the barn, they could hear the river. "Watch out!" He pulled her close, and they ducked as a cluster of bats flew out the door. Moving to the side of the barn, something to his left caught his eye. He aimed his light towards the river and saw a dock with an old fishing boat attached. "Psycho didn't own a car, but he does have a boat. It's even got a cabin." He glanced at her as she swatted another mosquito. They were both being eaten alive. "Come on."

The boat was a seventeen-foot watercraft designed for inland navigation. He helped her onto the bow. He pulled the dart gun from behind his back and squeezed her hand in reassurance. "Just let me make sure the cabin is empty. Stay here." He didn't trust Jackson at all. He wouldn't be surprised to find another corpse or rabid animal in the cabin, although it had no foul smell.

Frogs croaked, and crickets chirped. The scent of Jackson's house lingered distantly but was masked by the nearby wildflowers and muddy water. Cassie kept smelling blood and wondered if she'd ever get that scent out of her mind. A loud splash sounded nearby, and she felt her heart jump as Shane stepped out of the cabin.

Glancing at the river, his eyebrows drew together. Whatever had splashed in the water was big. He figured an alligator, but didn't share that with her. At least they had a safe place to stay for the night, and the door would keep the mosquitoes out. "It's fine. I don't think he used it very often. It seems clean." He had pulled the blankets

161

off the bed and pushed them in a corner, but the white fitted sheet appeared clean.

The cabin smelled musty, but considering the previous odors, Cassie welcomed it. Two steps led down into the cabin. A small sink and counter were to the right, and a little bench and table were in the middle. A grey curtain covered the entrance to the bedroom, where a full-sized bed fit snugly between dark-stained plank walls. "I keep smelling blood." She turned to him and leaned wearily against the doorframe.

"It's me." He examined his clothes. He felt that stitch in his side and realized his shirt was soaked. "Damn."

As he pulled his shirt off, her heart sank. He had severe injuries. His shoulder was badly bruised, and his wrists were red and bloody from the zip ties. The worst wound was a cut along the side of his torso, which was slowly oozing blood that pooled above his jeans. "What happened?" No wonder the scent was so strong. "Shane, this is bad!" She walked over to the little sink and grabbed a paper towel. Her hands shook as she folded it over his wound.

"I'm actually…" He swayed a little and stumbled over to the edge of the bed. He'd been running on adrenaline and hadn't noticed the wound. Now that he could see it, he realized he felt off-kilter.

"This is deep." Panic was making her heart race, the sight of the blood made her light-headed. "You're losing a lot of blood."

"I'm okay." He hadn't meant for his voice to sound strained. He was trying to stay strong for her. But his vision was beginning to blur.

"No, you're not!" The paper towel was already soaked. Between the sight and smell of his blood, she was beginning to think she might pass out. She knew what she had to do, but she felt weak. Closing her eyes, she focused on trying to build the energy. But she kept seeing Jackson's round, swollen face in her mind. She kept hearing his words: "I'm going to do things to you." Nothing was happening. Her heart was slamming inside her chest, and her hands were shaking.

162

He was growing weaker by the moment. He stared at her, knowing she was trying to heal him. Instead, tears began to stream down her face. She was shaking. "Cassie, it's okay." He leaned up, moaning from the pain that suddenly throbbed in his side, setting his hand on her cheek. "Don't cry."

"I can't make it work." She leaned into him, resting her forehead against his chest, trying to calm her panic. "I can't stop thinking about Jackson. About what would have happened if you hadn't–"

"Don't think about it, just…" He fell back on the bed, his eyes closed and his breathing shallow.

Full-blown panic gripped her as she moved over him, shaking him gently. "Wake up!" He wasn't responding. Her hands shook, and she gulped back a sob as it tore from her throat. "Shane!" Get a grip, she frantically told herself. She looked at the blood soaking the white sheet. She had to heal this wound, or he was going to die. She placed her hands on his chest and felt the warmth of his skin and the ripple of muscle beneath. She forced her mind to think of how she felt in the car, snuggled against him. Her happy place, where the peace and calm that he brings her, is like slipping into the warm sun after being cold. When the thoughts steadied her racing heart, she closed her eyes and imagined the wound closing. She whispered, "I'll heal you," willing it with all her strength. Relief washed over her as she suddenly felt the heat in her body rising. The current flowing through her veins was rushing and building. The now-familiar feeling was taking over, and she embraced it, forcing it to keep flowing.

The heat wasn't enough to burn him, but it made him feel like he was standing too close to a fire. He opened his eyes and saw the blue light glowing from her hands. The pain in his side was gone. He saw the wound was healed. "I'm good now, Cass." He cleared his voice. "You can stop. Open your eyes." She wasn't stopping. He felt better than ever—a renewed feeling of fortitude.

Startled by his sudden words, she opened her eyes. He was gazing at her with a concerned look. She tipped her head down to stare at her hands. How had she possessed this incredible power all her life and never known? Only days had passed since she'd left the orphanage, and already she'd been forced to use it three times. All because she was being sought after and needed protection. He'd killed Jackson, and while she felt no genuine remorse, what she did feel was panic. She needed this feeling, the energy and knowledge of what she held, and she didn't feel like she could make it stop. The blue light continued to radiate, her body heating to an uncomfortable temperature. Her throat and mouth were parched.

"Try and pull it back now, Cass." His voice remained calm, but he felt a twinge of alarm at how hot the room had become, and the light was still emanating. She was breathing heavily as if exerting a lot of energy. "I'm okay. You need to stop."

Panic flooded her—not just from not being able to control the flow rushing through her body, but fear at this new life she was living and the reality of extreme danger they seemed to be constantly in. "I can't!" Her voice strained as she felt tingling and enormous heat.

He held her face as her body trembled. "Look at me." Her face was mere inches from his. He leaned in and gently kissed her cheek. "Take a deep breath through your nose, hold it for a second, and breathe out through your mouth." He gently rubbed her shoulders. "That's it, just breathe deeply." The heat was dissipating; the blue halo was gone.

She allowed her eyes to roam over his bare chest. His body was simply magnificent. "Shane, I'm extremely thirsty." Her throat ached for water. Her tongue was so dry, she was surprised she could speak.

Grabbing his pack off the floor, he unzipped the top and pulled out a bottle. She quickly unscrewed the cap and gulped it down.

She handed him the empty bottle. "I need more." Her thirst was torment.

He shook his head in concern. "It's not a good idea. We need to ration it. Too much water at once could make you sick."

"You don't understand. I *need* it, Shane." She didn't understand it either, but the thirst was horrible. She felt like she'd never get enough water to satisfy.

164

Reluctantly, he handed her another bottle, watching as she gulped it down. "We've only got two more. We'd better save them." He reached for a blanket in the corner of the bed and pulled it over the blood-stained sheet. Then he grabbed a clean T-shirt from his pack.

Disappointment had Cassie frowning. She was fine with Shane being shirtless. As far as she was concerned, it was entirely unnecessary for him to ever wear a shirt again.

"Hey, if you really need more water, I'll give you another one." He'd run back to the house and look for more bottles if he had to. He hated to see her unhappy.

"I'll be okay." Though she wasn't sure if she believed that.

"I'm so sorry so much has happened to you." He felt responsible. Before he came into her life, she'd been a normal orphan, living a simple life, and no one knew who she was. However, Mr. Jamerson had known her identity and planned to sell her, so he couldn't be too hard on himself. "But I'll never regret finding you." He lay beside her on the bed and smiled when she did the same, facing him. "Do you want to tell me how you're feeling?" Moments ago, he knew she was having a panic attack. The stress had to be affecting her.

"I miss my friends. I hate not knowing what's going to happen." She swallowed, trying to block out the image of Jackson that kept creeping into her mind. "I hate feeling scared. I can't stop thinking about what..." She closed her eyes and let out a long, slow breath. "This is my life now." She was trying to accept it. She wanted to be strong. She wanted to face things with strength and determination.

"No." He placed his hand behind her knee, pulling her closer, bringing her leg to his. He kissed her forehead, promising himself he wouldn't cross the line. "This isn't how your life will be. You haven't met many good people yet, but you will. You'll love the ranch. Your parents and PJ have been safe there for years now. You might have to travel someday, but you'll have your family. You'll have joy and laughter, because your family is wonderful. I promise you'll be happy."

She felt drained, her eyes heavy, but she couldn't draw her gaze away from Shane's. She loved talking to him, hearing the hope he gave her, and feeling the warmth of his body. "The world is a scary place."

"It can be, but you wouldn't believe how far the world has come." Every nerve in his body was alive with want and need. His body was wired and revved up. He could probably do two hundred push-ups and still run a marathon, because whatever healing ability she possessed also came with a handy turbo boost to the system. He smiled at her, knowing she was about to fall asleep. She needed the rest. She'd had a traumatizing day, on top of all the other over-whelming events. Maybe he could put some happy thoughts in her mind. "One day, I'll take you hiking to a waterfall. There are tons of them in the United States. You will love the sound they make, it's deep and endless, like the earth itself is breathing. The silver water crashing down makes you feel wonderful and alive. The spring is my favorite, when the wildflowers are most potent, and..." He could see she was sound asleep. He kissed the top of her head. "Good night, sweet Cassie."

Chapter 25

"You'll never know how happy I am to see you, Dad." Shane greeted his father in the driveway of the dilapidated farmhouse with a hug. The sun was just up, and already the temperature was near eighty. A fly buzzed around his head as a soft, humid breeze rustled the trees.

Ian looked at his son. "You look like you've been through a lot." He knew that look in his son's eyes. They held the quiet of someone who had survived the worst parts of life without ever falling apart. His cargo pants were covered in dirt and blood stains, and his shirt was clean but wrinkled. His hair looked like it hadn't seen a comb in days, and his facial hair was thicker and rough, giving him a more worn, restless look. He turned to face the dilapidated house. "Danny told me you guys ran into trouble." He sniffed the air. There was still no word on Alex, which was troubling.

"Yeah, it stinks. There's a rotting corpse in the house. Psycho Jackson didn't feel like burying his mother when she died, so he left her where she was. His body is out back."

"Show me." Ian stepped around his son and walked toward the side of the house. Glancing over his shoulder, he asked, "Where's Faith?"

"It's Cassie, Dad." He pointed toward the barn. "There's a boat back there. She was still sleeping, and I didn't want to wake her." When his father called to say he was almost there, Shane was too relieved and happy to fall back asleep. "I had no choice with Jackson, Dad. The man was deranged, and big as a damn bear."

"No one is blaming you, son." Ian was more concerned about evidence that could link Shane to the killing. He stopped short when he reached the back yard and saw the massive, obese man covered in blood with flies swarming him. "I'm sorry you were forced to do this." The body and the house would need to be burned to protect him.

Cassie gasped from behind them, seeing the mangled body.

"Damn it." Shane instantly blocked her view. "I didn't want you to see this." He pressed her face against his chest, covering her eyes.

It wasn't at all what she imagined. She hadn't asked him how he killed Jackson, because she didn't want to know. She didn't want any more horrible images swimming in her head. How would she ever get this picture out of her mind now? No wonder Shane had a giant cut on his side last night. He had wrestled with an ax, and that ax ultimately split Jackson's head open. Bile was coming up her throat. If she didn't get fresh air, she was going to hurl. She pushed him away and ran toward the small blue car parked in the gravel driveway.

Ian shook his head, covering his nose. "Go sit with her. I'll take care of this and be there in a minute."

There were no clouds to shade the sun's rays that poured down like a heavy and relentless weight, baking the compact car. Shane rolled the windows down and sat in the back with Cassie. Her wavy hair, once braided, was now tangled and covering her face. She covered her eyes with her hands, but it didn't seem like she was crying. She was far from the clean, sheltered, simple girl he'd met at the orphanage. Shane desperately wondered what she was thinking. Seeing Jackson's body must have shocked her. He shouldn't have left her to wake on her own and wander out to find him. Would she think him a brutal murderer? Jackson had swung the ax first, slicing him badly before Shane wrestled it away. Severing Jackson's hand was unavoidable because he'd been reaching for a butcher's knife, which he could have easily thrown at Shane. He'd give anything to go back and prevent her from seeing the horrific scene. But there was nothing he could do now. He watched his father pour gasoline through the house and along the outside walls. Then he emptied the container over Jackson's body and lit a match. There would be no one to mourn Jackson or to care. Cassie looked up at the sound of the flames rising and engulfing the house.

Ian opened the driver's door, glancing at his son's stoic face. "You riding back there?"

He liked sitting beside her, especially when she used him as a pillow. But she was staring out the window. He doubted she'd want to snuggle after what she'd seen. "I'll come up front." He moved to the front seat. "Have you heard from Alex?" He was starting to think Alex hadn't escaped the Twin Seekers.

Ian backed out of the driveway. "No one has spoken to him, but Danny got an email from a stranger, claiming he's alive."

Shane raised a brow, glancing at his father. "An email?"

"I know. It's all very odd. But you know Danny... he's on top of it."

The conversation continued, as Cassie stared out the window at the black smoke billowing over the trees, until they were far enough that the fire and Jackson's grotesque body could only be seen in her mind. She listened to Ian explain that Amy and Andrew were settled in their new apartment. After the mall, Ian had no problems getting them safely to Colorado. It gave Cassie comfort to know that Amy was at least spared any of the frightening experiences she had endured. Ian described their apartment, how their jobs were perfect for them, and they were safe.

"Both Amy and Andrew were pleased when I left." Ian glanced at Cassie in the rearview mirror. She hadn't spoken and looked like a distraught wreck. He turned with concern to his son, deciding he wouldn't ask for details about what they'd experienced. Danny had already filled him in enough. "We need to find a place where Cassie can clean up." He didn't want to introduce Lily to a mentally absent girl, who looked like she'd been through hell.

"You know, Dad, it's been a long, hard journey. Let's just get her to the damn ranch as soon as possible, before anything else goes wrong." Shane glanced at the car's battery meter, hoping it was

169

enough to get them there. He felt Cassie had reached her limit regarding the shock, stress and fear she could handle. She was already having nightmares, constantly on edge, and after seeing Jackson's body, she'd probably never view him the same. And yet, he'd never apologize for doing whatever was necessary to keep her safe.

After a few hours, she cleared her throat. "I need a bathroom."

Ian nodded, keeping his eyes on the road. "We won't be able to go anywhere public. Even if you brush your hair and clean your face, your dress alone will have people staring."

"Dad." His father's comment was insensitive. He didn't want Cassie to feel even worse.

Catching the look on Shane's face, Ian sighed. "Sorry, sweetheart. I know this is hard for you. Unfortunately, the world has become obsessed with the idea that Lily's a healing alien, and that there's more like her." Maybe it was time Cassie learned some important history. He knew the orphanage kept all social media and current events from the kids.

"I met your mom before you were born." He turned down the air conditioning so she could hear him. He told her his entire story.

Ian saw that she was listening. "That was a long time ago, Cassie. Over the years, we've learned that when faced with disaster, people need hope."

He noted the sign that indicated the next exit had a gas station and a few places where they could find a bathroom for her to use. "The silver lining is that your mom unified people with a common interest. Rich, poor, white, minorities…everyone believed Lily could heal, and that she was the nation's hope. These groups—the Twin Seekers and the Alien Surveillance Association—were born from the desire to learn about and utilize Lily. Your mom and Dad faked their deaths, but that didn't last long. People found out she was still alive, and it's been a challenge keeping her safe."

"Dad," Shane sighed again. He didn't want Cassie to hear more negative things. He leaned back over the seat and rested his hand on her knee. Glancing at her somber face, he offered her a

170

reassuring smile.

Ian wasn't going to sugarcoat what Cassie's life would be like. Perhaps if her picture hadn't been posted all over social media and the news, she could live a more normal life, still being able to venture out freely. But now, she'd live the same way Lily and Kate did. It wasn't horrible, but it wasn't easy. "You'll have to wear better disguises, and your security will need to be increased somewhat. Lily and Kate mostly stay at the ranch."

Everything he said felt like it didn't apply to her. She stared at Shane's compassionate eyes. "I lived my childhood under a dome that prevented me from going anywhere. I always imagined that when I was grown, I'd get to travel, see the world, experience things." Her voice was sad, despair evident on her face.

"You will." Shane knew what she was thinking. She was going from one cage to another. Losing the freedom she desperately desired and fearing her life would always be like the past few days. "I'll take you to see the waterfalls in Hawaii. We can hike on your parents' property. They own several acres of land, and the forest is beautiful. You can ride horses and soak up the sun every day." He felt relieved when she offered a small, closed-lip smile.

Cassie couldn't imagine what her family had experienced, and Shane and Ian had shared it all. It had been a rough few days, but she believed there was hope for a happy future. She'd have to make the best of her life. She'd have to grow a backbone and become strong and confident like Shane. She couldn't remain the scared, fragile girl she'd been. Life wasn't exactly what she had planned, but she was starting to believe she was, in fact, special. She glanced down at her hands, remembering the heat that poured from them. Then, an image of Jackson flashed into her mind, and she felt her stomach turn.

Chapter 26

The helicopter ride was fascinating. It felt surreal to be inside a flying machine. Few people had the luxury of flying in planes or helicopters, but the pilot was a friend of her father's. He worked for the news and had access to airspace that other flying crafts didn't have. From how it was explained, Cassie understood this was another person doing a kindness for her mother. Peering down at the trees and fields, she felt small—a tiny dot in an enormous world.

Shane offered her a granola bar, but she shook her head. She was too nervous to eat. The sun was still high in the sky, and Ian promised she'd meet her parents before nightfall. They'd driven eight hours, and now they'd fly the rest of the way.

The helicopter dipped and turned. She glanced up front at Ian and the pilot. They were both smiling and talking. She wished she could stay in the air and continue flying over the land, the horses grazing in fields, the buildings and homes below, and the people so far away.

"We are almost there," Ian shouted from the front. "Remember that when we land, we have to walk. Are you up for it?"

"We're ready!" Shane clasped her hand, excited at finally reaching the acres of property that hid Lily and Patrick's ranch. Fortunately, they had reached this point with no further scares. He regretted that she would meet her parents looking like a stranded kid in the wilderness, going weeks without a shower. But that didn't matter. What mattered was they had arrived safely, and it was a beautiful, warm, sunny day.

"Are you nervous to meet your family?" Ian smiled at Cassie, while grabbing his backpack off the floor. "I'm just going to send a quick text to Danny letting them know we've landed. We have a ten-minute walk, then we'll be there."

She nodded. "I'm a little nervous, but I'm mostly excited…I think."

Shane laughed, placing his hand on the small of her back, as they exited the chopper. "Come on. There's no road leading to their house. You follow a hidden path through the woods until you reach their electric fence."

"This is part of the Pineywoods of East Texas." Ian stepped behind her, tossing his pack over his shoulder. "Your brother loves living here."

"It smells wonderful."

"It's mostly pine." Shane couldn't catch a distinct scent.

There were a variety of wildflowers Cassie could not identify. It would be wonderful to learn all the many plants and their scents, the way she had at the orphanage. Her heart skipped a beat as they continued their walk. Her life was drastically changed from her orphanage days, and anticipation made her jittery.

***

Lily, Patrick, PJ, Kate and Danny stood on the long, narrow driveway as Ian, Shane, and Cassie walked toward them from the woods. Lily squeezed Patrick's arm, trying to calm the pounding of her heart. "She's beautiful." Her throat ached as she tried to hold back tears. "I don't think I can keep it together." She glanced at her sister and brother-in-law to see their reactions.

Patrick leaned over and kissed Lily on the head. "I can't believe how nervous I feel. I didn't think I'd feel this way." They had been preparing for this for weeks. Ian had called them hours ago to say they were finally safely on their way. He'd had time to imagine what it would be like, and by God, he wouldn't cry. "She walks like you."

Kate brushed tears from her cheeks. One look at her sister's face, and Lily knew she wouldn't bother trying to control her emotions. She glanced at PJ, who was the only one not teary-eyed. "Patrick Junior, you'll probably have to do all the talking for us, because we'll all be too busy sobbing to get a word out."

PJ glanced from his Aunt Kate to his parents. He knew this was the most important day of their lives, yet he wasn't feeling emotional like they were. Being nervous, weary, and extremely apprehensive wasn't bringing tears to his eyes the way it did everyone else. For so long, he had convinced himself Faith would never be found. Even now, he didn't believe she was real. Although the closer she got, the more he couldn't deny she looked like his father: same straight nose, same long, slightly arched brows, and almost identical lips.

"Why are they walking so slowly?" Kate felt nervous impatience and let out a long sigh.

For a brief moment, Lily closed her eyes, recalling the plane crash. She'd held her newborn baby in her arms, sending all her healing energy into the small infant, whom Patrick had protected with his body. She'd memorized every feature of the baby she loved with all her heart. The tiny fingers, her puckered little lips, and her reddish-brown hair that was unusually long for a baby. She'd kissed and cried over her sweet baby girl before she'd passed out from the exertion of using all her strength to heal both Patrick and her baby. When she came to—no longer cradling her baby, lying in Patrick's arms, the anguish that someone had stolen her baby had been excruciating. She never let go of the memory of her baby's face. The love never faded. Now that minor miracle was slowly walking toward her. Her biological child was created with her unique DNA and Patrick's, the man she loved with all her heart. This beautiful young girl she never gave up hope of finding.

Taking a deep breath, Cassie appreciated that Shane had offered her the support and comfort she needed. He'd put his arm around her, holding her close to him. His reassurance and strength helped her keep moving. He'd felt her body shaking and had begun rubbing his hand down her arm, helping to soothe her.

She stared at the five people standing before her and instantly knew who everyone was. Although her mother and Kate were identical, she knew her mother stood between her brother and father. One look at Patrick's smile, and she knew he was her father. She had the same hair color as her brother, and sure enough, she had her mother's eyes. Her mother's hair was now black, cut just above her shoulders. Her aunt Kate had blond hair that framed her face in a choppy cut to her chin. It was a totally different look, yet her face was completely identical to Lily's.

"Oh gosh." Lily took a hesitant step forward. She wiped tears from her eyes, knowing without a doubt that the young woman standing before her was her long-lost daughter. Lily didn't know if Cassie would welcome a hug from her, but she had to embrace her child. She hugged her, feeling how thin and petite she was. She smelled sweat and earth. "I…I'm your mom," she whispered. "I've been searching for you since the day you were born."

Cassie wrapped her arms around the woman whose body was similar to hers. Thin, petite, and almost the same height. She smelled citrus. "Hi." It was all she could get out because her throat was so tight. Next, she was pulled into her father's arms. Something about his strong embrace and gently placing his hand on her head made her heart ache even more. So, this was what it felt like to feel a father's embrace. This was what she'd never had growing up. The feeling was new and astounding.

"This is your brother, PJ." Lily's voice sounded strained with emotion.

"Hi." PJ gave her a quick, awkward hug. She was much shorter and barely reached his shoulder.

"We have the same hair color." Cassie stared directly into his brown eyes. They didn't have the deep red or specks of gold that hers had. They were more of a normal brown, with perhaps a little green in them, and she thought he was a good mix of both her parents. He had a longer face than her father, but his eyebrows were the same. She determined that one day, he'd be quite handsome when he

175

loses the boyish look and gains more weight.

"I'm your Aunt Kate, and this is my husband, Danny." Kate reached for Cassie's hands and held them as she examined her. "This is the happiest day of our lives." Her smile was wide and beautiful. "You're a knockout. Absolutely stunning! Obviously, you get all your beauty from me."

A warm blush rose to Cassie's cheeks as her family laughed at Kate's remark. Cassie glanced down self-consciously at her tattered, dirty dress, figuring it didn't matter what a mess she was.

The reunion was terrific, and Cassie could practically feel the love pouring from her family. She was suddenly aware that her stomach was no longer in knots, and the flutters had stopped. Her family was instantly likable. They each had a genuine, easy way about them. Kate had an aura of spunky energy that made her smile.

"Come see the house, Cassie." Patrick had been practicing her name all morning. He was used to thinking of her as Faith, but now, looking at her, he felt Cassie was a more fitting name. He turned to shake Ian's hand, patting his back. He did the same with Shane. They knew how grateful he was without him saying a word.

The house was enormous, with tall cathedral ceilings, arched doorways, crown molding, beautiful, stained hardwood floors, and bold, colorful furniture. Giant canvases of horses hung on the pale-yellow walls. A broad curved staircase led up to five bedrooms and below was a master suite bedroom off the kitchen. Everything was tastefully decorated, and Cassie was in awe.

As they climbed the stairs, Lily explained that the home was just a loan, but they would live in it as long as possible. "This is the first place we've found large enough for all of us to live comfortably." Lily glanced out the window, which offered a spectacular view of rolling hills and a red barn. "The man who owned this house was extremely wealthy. Both his daughter and wife were very sick. Wealth meant nothing to him if he lost his family. I healed them, and the man was so grateful that he gave us his home. He has another house on the ocean, so it's not like we put him out." She chuckled as she watched her daughter observing everything. "He knew this home was secure and would provide us protection."

Each wing of the orphanage was painted cheerfully, and Cassie thought about the digital moving pictures on the walls and the enormous dining room where she'd lived for years. The orphanage had been nice, but it had never felt like home. It couldn't compare to this.

"Here's your room." Lily opened the door. "I hope you like it."

It momentarily stole her breath away. "I love it." An enormous crystal chandelier hung over the king-sized bed. The comforter was beautiful, and Cassie had never seen such pretty pink and white satin throw pillows with lavish ribbons. The curtains were white with pink stripes that arched around the oval window. It was the prettiest, most cheerful room she could ever imagine. "I never dreamed a room could look like this." She ran her hand along the wildflowers painting on the wall next to the closet. A pink, life-size stuffed panda bear sat in the corner. She touched the soft fur. "We were never allowed to decorate our room at the orphanage." She wished Amy could see the room and the house. "My best friend is an artist. She would love all these paintings."

Lily clasped her fingers together to hide the jittery feeling she felt. She was alone with Cassie, knowing everyone had purposely given them privacy. "I have to ask you something." Lily felt the emotion once again rising up in her throat. Patrick had warned her not to get too personal right away and not to ask too many questions because he thought Cassie would need time to feel comfortable. But the question had weighed on Lily's mind for years. She had to know the answer. She moved over, sitting on the pink bench next to the bed. A few footsteps sounded in the hall, and then it was quiet.

"You can ask me anything."

"You weren't ever hurt, were you? It's the one thing that has haunted me since the day I lost you." The greatest fear Lily had was the thought of someone experimenting on her child. Lily had experienced what scientists do in the name of study and research. For 19 years, she'd prayed her child never had to endure such a thing.

177

Staring into Lily's tear-filled eyes, Cassie felt overcome with emotion. Here was her birth mother, a stranger to her, yet she felt a bond. Both of them had been robbed of her childhood, yet there was sincere love and hope in the question. "I was never harmed. I believe whoever stole me from you wanted to keep me safe. I was not unhappy living at the orphanage. I was well cared for." She felt differently about it now that she was out, but she would not resent her years there. She would only regret she had not been found sooner. "I was very sheltered and never knew what I was missing. I had friends, jobs I enjoyed, and I liked school very much." Seeing the relief wash over her mother's face, she added, "Many times my friends made me laugh, and I felt happy."

Lily leaned forward and hugged her daughter again. "All the years of your life, I've missed. I've never stopped wondering if you were safe and okay. It's all I wanted for you." She moved her hands down Cassie's slim arms and squeezed her hands. "We never stopped looking for you." A weight was being lifted. "Your dad and I never gave up hope. It's why we named you Faith… I had faith that we'd find you."

"All the time I lived at Saving Souls, I never knew I could heal people. I never knew about you or what the world was like. I'm thankful you found me."

"Ian told us you have the ability." He'd told them how she'd used it to heal his extensive wounds and the gunshot that Shane would have died from. "Your brother doesn't have the ability. I didn't think the gene, or whatever it is, would be passed down. The idea that my child could possibly carry that same genetic structure was always the best hope for the human race. Part of me was glad your brother didn't have it, because it comes with an enormous responsibility." She stared into her daughter's eyes. "It's a miracle that you have the ability. You can choose to look at it as either a blessing or curse. I'm choosing to believe it's a blessing, and our finding you is the greatest blessing of all."

"My best friend Amy and Shane would have died if I didn't
178

have the ability." She pictured Ian's beaten face, Amy's bloody body lying on the floor, and Shane's bullet hole and the deep gash down his side from Jackson. She thought about all the pain and deaths she'd seen, and how she could make a difference. "It's a gift."

"Oh sweetheart." Lily held her daughter tightly. Knowing her unique trait would not die with her was a surreal moment. Lily had three miscarriages after she gave birth to Cassie, before finally having PJ. She was disappointed she hadn't been able to carry more children, but now it didn't matter. Cassie had the ability. She did in fact pass it on, and one day Cassie could pass it to her children, and their children's children—henceforth the beginning of a new race of humans—Evolution. Doctor Price was right. He was the scientist who created the genetic building block that somehow nature allowed to survive inside a human body. Perhaps it was nature's way of ensuring the survival of the human species on a planet where radiation and disease could one day kill every living being. She never liked Dr. Price for what he'd done to her mother, but she wished he were alive to know that Cassie had the ability. "I'm so glad you feel it's a gift."

Pulling away slightly, Cassie studied her mother's face. She did not look old, as she had imagined her. She had only a few light lines around her eyes, and her skin was pure and firm. If Cassie could guess, she would think her mother was still in her late twenties or early thirties. But Lily gave birth to Cassie when she was 26, which would make her 45 now. "I have so many questions for you."

"I'm sure you do. But first, you should take a shower and change into clean clothes. You're probably hungry." Lily walked over to the armoire and pulled out a set of clean undergarments. Then she opened the closet doors, revealing an incredible walk-in closet.

"Oh wow!" A small pink chandelier lit the room. Cassie walked into the closet, staring at the rows of clothing. She felt the material of a silky dress.

"As soon as we found out your size, Kate and Danny went shopping. Kate loves to shop."

"I thought you couldn't go out in public."

Lily caught the surprised expression, followed by the hopeful look on her face. "We have to wear very clever disguises. Danny has gotten quite good at making us look like an entirely different person. But it takes time and work. Kate doesn't mind it, so she gets out more. But yes, Cassie, we try to live normal lives. We just don't take too many chances." She picked out a pair of khaki shorts and a pretty brown tank top with white lace around the collar and straps. "This looks like it'll fit well and will go beautifully with your hair. Everything you need is in the bathroom. Take a nice, long, hot shower and make yourself at home." She handed her the clothes.

The idea of a shower and clean clothes was very appealing. "I'd like that, thank you."

Chapter 27

The kitchen was the heart of the home. It was the size of three normal rooms combined. A long wooden table with eight comfy chairs was adjacent to a square island with four wrought-iron barstools. The traditional design had black and beige swirled granite counters forming a large L, which complemented the dark wooden built-in cabinets and stainless appliances.

Shane stood at the island with one leg perched against a barstool and watched as Kate, Danny, Lily, and Patrick took seats at the kitchen table. PJ closed the refrigerator and walked to sit beside his aunt, handing her a glass of iced tea.

"Tell them what you've learned," Ian said, entering the room and leaning against the doorframe. He smiled at Lily, his heart filled with joy for her. Shane could tell her far more about her daughter than he could.

"Her ability is much stronger than yours." Shane crossed his arms. "She's not able to control it very well yet. It seems like it's hard for her to stop once it gets going." He pulled the stool out, deciding to sit down. He realized he had a lot to say about Cassie.

"Go on." Lily wrapped her arm around Patrick's.

"She gets extremely thirsty when she's done healing. It's like she needs to drink gallons of water. I think the healing must completely dehydrate her." He watched PJ draw circles around the top of his glass with his finger and realized everyone was patiently waiting for him to continue. "I don't think she sleeps well. She has nightmares, tosses and turns a lot. Sometimes she talks in her sleep. She has dreams that she thinks might be memories, but they're vague."

He recalled what she'd told him about her dreams, but decided he wouldn't share that with her family. If she wanted them to know her nightmares, he'd let her tell them. "I can tell you she's brave as hell." He'd been impressed with how well she held herself together at Jackson's house. She could've become hysterical, and a traumatic event like that could have made her shut down completely. But she not only held it together, she also healed a wound that might have otherwise killed him. "She handled herself well in every situation we faced, and unfortunately, we hit a lot of trouble getting here."

Lily wanted to know everything possible about her daughter. "I'm happy to hear she's been coping." She wondered what else Shane had learned about her. They'd been together quite a while. He spent weeks in the orphanage with her, and then days on the road. It made her sick to hear about what happened in Mississippi, when some deranged man had tied them up. She felt Ian had been holding back a lot of details. "Cassie needs to be strong because her life will never be the same now. She's all over the news and social media, and it makes my heart ache that everyone knows she's my daughter. Everyone will be looking and…" She didn't need to finish her sentence because everyone in the room fully understood what that implied.

"Can she tell when people are sick?" Patrick was absently caressing Lily's hand. His wife could simply touch a person and know if they had cancer, or what parts of their bodies were infected by disease.

"No." Shane sighed. "If she has that ability, she hasn't figured it out yet. Her school Administrator knew about her. He'd asked her over the years if she could touch someone and heal them. She never understood what he was asking, and didn't know she had the ability until her friend got shot. This is all new to her." He surveyed everyone sitting at the table. "There's something else about her healing. She's healed me twice now, and both times she left me feeling *more* than healed. It's like she gives you an extra burst of energy. A physical boost that makes you stronger, more…alive." He didn't know how to explain it.

"Shane's right." Ian glanced from Shane to Lily. "After she healed me, I swear I felt like I was 19 again. I even think I look younger. Not only did she heal all my cuts and bruises, but I think she healed my arthritis. I've had no pain in my knees or back since. I'm starting to think she healed every ailment I had." He couldn't believe how young and exuberant he felt.

"Wow!" Danny leaned back in his chair. "I'm going to have her heal me then. I've got major issues with my shoulder." Arthritis and an old bullet wound. He could certainly use an added energy boost as well.

Patrick recognized Lily's look. He knew exactly what she was thinking, and Kate did also. If anyone else ever found out how powerful her ability is, she'd be in even more danger.

"She also has an enhanced sense of smell. She can detect scents from great distances, even small traces others can't discern." Shane recalled how she'd smelled Jamerson's cologne at the house before he appeared. "She can't stand the sight or smell of blood. Both make her weak and lightheaded, which is kind of ironic to me." He grinned a little. "Most people don't find the scent of blood strong, but she does." Shane thought about how she offered to jeopardize her safety to save his dad, and her selfless concern for her friends. "She's a lot like you, Lily. She thinks of everyone else before herself. She's sensitive and caring." There was a lot he could say about her. "She's pretty great."

"You've gotten to know her quite well." Kate tried to keep the humor from her voice. She wondered if everyone else could see what she did.

"You sound like you're in love with her," PJ said, using his typical teen sarcasm.

Bingo! Kate smiled and gently pushed PJ's head. Leave it to an oblivious teen to point out the obvious.

Shane turned a heated glare toward PJ. "I'm her friend. My job was to befriend her and keep her safe. Which I have."

Patrick held his hand out and frowned at PJ. "No one is accusing you of anything, Shane. You've done an exceptional job, and we're forever in your debt."

"Cassie seems like a lovely young lady, and it's obvious that all our risks and hard work in finding her were well worth it," Ian said. "Kate's worried that I won't know what to do with myself now that we've found her."

"We still have to find Alex," Kate and Lily said simultaneously.

Everyone in the room fell silent at the mention of Alex. They all believed and hoped he was okay, since he'd managed to send an email. But until they heard from him directly, they couldn't stop worrying. Danny was on standby as always, in case Alex should need anything.

"Alex deserved to be here." Lily felt her heart squeeze, and she feared for her brother. She wished he could have witnessed the reunion.

"He should be here," Kate agreed. "The longer we go without hearing from him, the more worried I get. His email that said, 'I'm alive and will be in touch,' isn't enough to ease my mind."

Danny looked at both Shane and Ian. "I've got a plan I need to run by you. We need to help him."

Cassie stood unseen in the hallway, listening to the conversation. She had stopped before rounding the corner upon hearing Shane say, "Her ability's much stronger than yours." She hadn't meant to eavesdrop, but she couldn't believe all the things Shane said about her. He was expressing thoughts she hadn't even realized herself. His deep understanding of her was astounding.

The hot shower was wonderful, but she'd been too anxious to linger. She hurried to dress and brushed her teeth because she was eager to be with her family. She hadn't expected Shane to be discussing her. She rounded the corner and offered a small smile when Ian turned to her. "Hi." Her nerves returned as she wasn't sure where to sit.

"Hi!" Everyone at the table beamed at her. "Sit here." Patrick stood and pulled a chair out.

"Are you hungry?" Kate walked to the refrigerator. "You must be. I made lasagna."

Cassie didn't know what that was, but she would eat anything, and perhaps food would ease the queasiness in her belly. "Yes, thank you." She glanced nervously at Shane. Her hair was still wet, and she had braided it to the side. The outfit her mom had given her fit snugly, and she felt self-conscious about the way the top scooped low enough to reveal a hint of her cleavage. But it was beautiful, soft and clean. Shane had showered. He wore clean tan pants with many pockets and a black t-shirt. His hair was still slightly wet and lay nicely parted to the left. He looked perfect, she thought.

"We'll talk about finding Alex later," Patrick told Ian. He leaned over and kissed Lily on the forehead. "Don't worry."

Glancing around the room, Cassie realized they didn't want to discuss things in front of her. "If you're going to search for Alex, I'd like to hear your plan." She didn't want to be shut out just because they may think she's fragile.

Patrick set his hand on Cassie's shoulder. "Why don't you have dinner, then join us in the family room? We can all talk more after you've eaten." He turned to PJ. "You should tell Cassie about the birth of your foal last week. I'm sure she'd enjoy hearing about the horses." He wanted his son to bond with his sister. And this way, he'd have a few moments alone with Ian and Shane.

Kate pulled Cassie's dinner from the microwave and set it on the island next to PJ. It made her feel good to offer food. She understood Lily was a bundle of nerves, but looking at her beautiful niece, she couldn't stop smiling. "Come sit over here, sweetheart."

PJ watched as his long-lost sister pulled out the stool beside him. He wondered if she'd care about his horses. What kind of relationship would they have? Would they have anything in common besides hair color? Part of him was thrilled she'd been found. He'd always known what it meant to his parents. He'd always wondered about her himself. What kind of life did she have? He figured it must have sucked to be stuck in an orphanage for so long.

185

As he watched her try the Lasagna, he wondered how his life would change. Having her there was a significant risk. His family managed to stay hidden for years, but now the entire world was looking for her. She was the new focus of both the Twin Seekers and the Alien Surveillance Association. Both groups had thousands of members. Substantial rewards were offered. Some people knew their location, friends who pledged their lives to help. But that didn't mean the lure of large rewards wouldn't win out over friendship and honor. The fact Uncle Alex was still missing also made him anxious. If Alex were caught and forced to disclose their location, all the peace and happiness they had here would be gone. He'd lose his horses.

"Probably Jason, what's got your tongue? Tell Cassie about your horses," Kate urged.

PJ rolled his eyes at his aunt. She had lots of silly nicknames for him. Probably Jason was the name she used when she teased him. He knew he was in trouble if she called him Patrick. Usually, she just called him Junior. "Do you like horses?" He had a slight weariness in his voice.

"I've never seen a horse before…in person." She stared at her plate, as images of her dream appeared. She'd been placed on a horse with a woman who sat behind her. She was going somewhere, but didn't know where. There'd been fire and smoke, and she felt like she was falling from the horse. She'd felt terrified and remembered holding on for dear life. She was barely paying attention as PJ described his three horses.

Kate smiled at her nephew. "Tell her the name of your new foal."

"His name is Healed. I named him that because when he was born, he wouldn't eat. He had something wrong with him, and I thought he was going to die. But my mom healed him." It'd been a sacrifice for his mother, because it made her unconscious for two days. His mother could no longer expend healing energy without becoming weak or passing out. Whatever was wrong with the horse had required a lot of strength to cure.

186

"That's nice." She missed some of what he said. Her focus was off. While the Lasagna was delicious, she had eaten fast because she was eager to get back to Shane and Ian. She didn't want to miss hearing their plan and whether they were going to leave.

It was evident to PJ that Cassie was uninterested. He shared a glance with his Aunt and knew she thought the same. But unlike her, he'd voice it. "It's obvious this conversation is boring you." He hopped off his stool and turned to walk out the room.

"Junior." Kate frowned at her nephew. She hoped he wasn't feeling bad about Cassie's presence. It would be an adjustment for everyone, and she could understand if PJ was feeling a little jealous.

"I'm going to feed the horses," PJ replied over his shoulder as he left the room.

"Don't worry about him. He's just…."

"It's my fault." Cassie carried her dish to the sink and began to wash it. "I'm sorry I didn't seem more interested in what he was saying. I have a lot on my mind. I didn't mean to hurt his feelings."

"I'll do that, honey. Just leave it in the sink." Kate took the plate from her, noticing the weariness in her eyes. "Go sit down with your parents." She'd have a chat with Junior and make sure he was okay. Junior had always been like a son to her. He'd been the light, joy and focus of everyone's lives. Now he'd have to share the spotlight, which would not be easy. As she watched Cassie leave, she shook her head with a smile. Now that Cassie was in their lives, everything would change. But hopefully for the better.

Chapter 28

The sun was setting, turning the sky a magnificent purple. Lily watched as her son led Healed out of the barn. He'd brush and feed him, then rake up manure and hay for another hour. He'd lay fresh straw down and spend more time talking to the horses.

"How was your dinner?" Patrick asked as Cassie stepped into the room.

Lily turned from the window and walked to the sofa where Patrick sat. "Come sit with us, Cassie." It was still hard to think of her daughter as Cassie. Her birth name was Faith, and for 19 years, that's how Lily thought of her.

Shane and Ian sat across from them in easy chairs that faced the sofa. A glass oval coffee table separated the sitting area. Cassie took a seat beside her mother and across from Shane. "The food was great. It's unlike anything I've ever tasted before."

"I can imagine." Lily knew the orphanage offered limited food choices. Shane had said the food was very healthy, but it was not meant to be eaten for enjoyment, but rather for health.

Ian stood from his chair. "Shane and I will go pack some gear. We'll give you some time to talk." He tipped his head to Shane, indicating it was time to leave.

Cassie felt that Shane had barely looked at her. His eyes quickly left hers after he offered a brief smile. In a panic, she reached for his arm. "Wait!" She stood up. You're not leaving, are you?"

Shane's brows drew together as he faced Cassie. "We've got a lead on where Alex might be." He gazed at Lily. "Is it okay if I tell her?" He didn't want to keep secrets from her, and he didn't want her to be worried and upset. When Lily nodded, he explained. "Our history teacher, Mrs. Reynolds, was taken by the A.S.A. We think Alex discovered she was taken and was trying to rescue her. She was taken because Jamerson told the leader of A.S.A. she tried to help us escape. Alex doesn't want anything to happen to her because she's the reason we found you. She's the one who left the email on our website, telling us where to find you."

"We know where he is, and Shane and Ian will get him." Patrick stood and walked to a small minibar to pour himself a drink.

"No." Cassie took Shane's hand. "I don't want you to go."

"He's trained for this." Ian's tone sounded sharper than he intended. He was suddenly uncomfortable with the attachment that Cassie seemed to have to Shane.

"I don't care." She didn't like how Ian was willing to place his son in dangerous situations. "I've had to heal you twice. Two times you could have died if I hadn't been there. Why would you risk putting your life in danger again, when I won't be there to heal you?" She cast a glare at Ian. "Don't you care that Shane could be hurt?"

Ian went to speak, but Cassie cut him off. "It's my fault Alex was taken. It's my fault people keep getting hurt. If you're going for Alex, I want to come with you."

"No!" Lily shot from her seat in panic, placing her hand over her heart. "We just found you. There's no way I'm letting you go!"

For a moment, Ian felt like he had stepped back in time. "I'll keep Shane safe." Cassie sounded exactly like Lily at her age. Always wanting to help and always feeling responsible. "We have a solid plan that shouldn't involve too much risk."

Patrick walked to Lily's side to offer her comfort. "I'll go. I'll find Alex and bring him home. Shane, you can stay here with Cassie."

Shane let go of Cassie's hand and stepped away from her. "No, I'm going." He glanced from his father to Cassie. "I'll be fine." His father had warned him not to get too attached. He'd told him, 'Feelings only get you in trouble. You lose focus and strength, and love will only cloud your judgment.' Shane had assured his father he didn't have more than 'friendship' feelings for her, and now was his chance to prove it. His father would be disappointed if he allowed her to call the shots. "You'll spend time getting to know your parents, and I'll be back before you know it." There. He told her.

With the tone in his voice, Cassie felt Shane's abrupt distance. There were two sides to him: soft-sweet-affectionate-Shane, and the strong-stubborn-take-charge-Shane. From the tick in his jaw, she was seeing the side she only liked to see when he was saving her life. He was making it clear he didn't want to be with her. Perhaps she was foolish to care so much for his well-being. "Then go, Shane! It won't matter if I'm not there to heal you. After all, I'm just a job!" She pushed past him and ran up the stairs. She wouldn't let him see her cry.

Lily signed, looking sadly at Shane. "She cares for you. If you leave, she'll be hurt. I don't want that." She'd do everything in her power to make her children happy.

What good would it do to stick around? Shane glanced at his father. He'd made it very clear that he was never to cross the friend-ship line. How many times had he resisted the pressing urge to kiss her? He'd done everything he could to keep her safe, earn her trust, and not fall in love. His father was right. It was time to focus on his future and the rest of his life. They'd get Alex back, and then he and his father would be free to live their own lives. His life didn't include living on the ranch with her and her family. "I'm not staying. I'll be ready to leave in an hour. Tell Cassie I said goodbye."

The window in her bedroom was cracked. Cassie moved the curtain aside to stare out it. She took a deep breath, smelling wild-flowers and horses. She forced her tears away. She didn't care that she'd just made a fool of herself. Why should she feel embarrassed about her outburst? Maybe it was childish, but she was entitled to feel angry. Or was she? It's not like Shane was anything but a friend. PJ had said it sounded like Shane loved her, but he made it clear that he didn't. They were friends, and she was simply a job he had com-pleted. A knock sounded, and she turned to see her mother peek her head into the room.

"May I come in?"

Cassie nodded, moving over to the bench to take a seat.

Lily crossed the room and sat on the end of the bed. "The last thing I want is for you to be upset. I know how you must feel about Shane."

"I don't feel anything for Shane. I think it's dumb that he enjoys getting shot at and sliced up. I guess maybe I wasn't ready to lose another friend. I already lost Amy and Andrew."

"I'm sorry." Lily felt she was looking at herself in a mirror. Cassie was so much like her at that age. She could still remember how she'd felt about Patrick, and how hard in love she'd fallen. "I met your Dad when I was 24. I'd never been in a relationship before." She smiled when Cassie looked at her with interest. "I was on the run from the government. Actually, I was on the run from the entire world. Everyone wanted me. Your dad kept me safe. He was kind and gentle without ever losing his fierceness. Do you know what I mean?"

Cassie nodded. She knew exactly what her mother meant. Shane could be sweet and loving in one moment and powerful and protective in the next. She didn't like that he was forced to kill men, but even as she pictured Jackson's mangled body, she wouldn't have wanted him any other way. She needed protection, and he had proved himself capable of the job. He made her feel safe and secure. He replaced her worry with peace she'd grown to appreciate. In fact, she relied on it.

"It's easy to fall in love with strong men who protect and make us feel special. And of course, it doesn't hurt when they're extremely handsome." Lily offered a small smile, knowing that girls found Shane Webster quite drool-worthy.

"My father is very handsome," Cassie agreed.

Lily playfully bumped Cassie's shoulder. Yes, her daughter was just as naïve as Lily had been at her age. She assumed that Shane and Cassie would work things out in their own way and in their own time.

She wouldn't push the issue. "I'm sorry Shane's leaving. He asked me to tell you goodbye. You know, these strong, competent men like to play the hero when they can. Shane likes to feel useful, and he knows that his father counts on him."

"I don't like his father," Cassie said softly, immediately regretting it. "I just think it's wrong for a parent to willingly risk their child's safety."

In a way, Lily agreed. She had never even once considered putting PJ at risk. If anything, she spent her entire life doing everything she could to keep him safe. She'd managed to keep the world from knowing he existed. He didn't have her ability to heal, but that wouldn't stop people from wanting to capture him and test him for themselves. Now that she had Cassie back, she'd go to the ends of the earth to protect her.

"Shane had a different kind of upbringing," Lily explained. "I feel responsible for most of it. I wasn't exactly thrilled he was constantly working with Ian to help find you. But the truth is, Shane ended up the one to find you. He was young enough to go under-cover inside the orphanage. He was young enough to relate to you and earn your trust, so he could get you out. Ian made sure he had plenty of necessary training. In most situations, Shane can easily take care of himself. Everything that happened in our lives has led to this moment, and I wouldn't change that for anything."

It made Cassie's heart ache thinking of Shane leaving, but she could do nothing about it. She had her family now, and it was wonderful to be with them. "I think I may have hurt PJ's feelings earlier. He was telling me about the horses, and I didn't appear very interested. I'd like to go out and see them and perhaps apologize." Cassie rose from the bench and crossed her arms over her chest. "I don't want to talk about Shane anymore."

Lily nodded, standing up. "I'll walk down to the barn with you." She had been so overwhelmed by having Cassie home that she hadn't paid enough attention to PJ. He was her baby boy, and until now the center of their lives. They had used Alex, Ian, and Shane to search for Faith continuously so she and Patrick could give PJ a happy, normal life without the focus constantly on their long-lost daughter. She hoped with all her heart that her son and daughter would like each other and only add to each other's lives.

Chapter 29

The rain beat down so hard that it was like someone dumping a giant bucket of water from the sky. The drops splashed the blades of grass, and a shallow stream formed on the gravel driveway. Cassie sat on the porch in a comfortable rocking chair, feeling comforted by the soothing rain. She studied the green rolling hills, the horses under the barn awning, and the pine trees swaying against the barn.

"You're up early." Lily stepped onto the porch, checking her watch, which read 6:10 a.m. Cassie had been there ten days, and Lily knew she wasn't sleeping well. She handed her a mug of black coffee, just the way she liked it. "Did you get any sleep?"

"Yes. Thank you. I slept okay." She lied. She didn't sleep much at all. She had difficulty pushing Shane from her thoughts all night. She missed him like crazy. All she could think about was how he'd held her in the car, how he looked at her, and the sound of his voice. She wanted to go back in time and have him all to herself again, even if it meant more danger. She thought about their night on the boat, when she had fallen asleep in his warm arms. His voice soothed her when she was in a state of panic. There was something about him that just calmed her nerves. She'd never gotten to kiss him, and she didn't even say goodbye. Regret was eating away at her.

"Mind if I join you?" Lily paused until Cassie nodded, then sat in the rocking chair beside her. "I love a good downpour."

"It's wonderful to smell the grass, the rain, even the horses." Cassie inhaled long and slow. "We never got to leave the dome, so I never had the chance to smell rain before. I missed feeling the wind on my face."

"You didn't get to go outside? Ever?" Lily had seen pictures of the orphanage and knew it was a glass cage, but she hadn't given much thought to being cooped up. Over the past few days, she'd had a chance to learn more about the life Cassie lived there and felt relieved it wasn't as bad as she feared. But never having gone outside… that sounded awful.

Cassie caught concern in her mom's tone. "The courtyard was beautiful, and we could get plenty of sun there. I guess that was close to being outdoors. The greenhouses were humid, had plenty of vegetation, and smelled like earth. There was grass, and the glass ceiling was so clear that you could see the stars at night. There were some special days when they allowed the kids to camp on the grass and spend the night looking up at the starry sky. I was younger then, maybe eight or nine, but I'll never forget how exciting it was."

Lily was happy to hear that Cassie had a happy memory, since there weren't many she shared. "You said the greenhouse was your favorite job. Do you miss it?"

"Not yet. But maybe I will. I've been thinking of my life there." She took a sip of her coffee. "The greenhouse had a pleasant smell. It was hot and humid, which made many students hate it. But I loved how we could dig in the earth, plant new seeds, and watch them grow. I loved the smell and the way the sun's rays shone down."

A warm smile spread across Lily's face. She sensed that her daughter loved nature, just like her. "I suppose you get that from me. You're welcome to help me in the garden after the sun dries the grass. This storm is supposed to end soon."

After living on the ranch for ten days, Cassie was familiar with everyone's daily routine. Junior liked to get up early and tend the horses in the barn, and Patrick would often help him. Kate preferred to do all the cooking and seemed to really enjoy it. Cassie had gotten used to finding her in the kitchen. There was always some new and exciting dish to try. Lily enjoyed working in her garden but would spend most of her time with family members, chatting with them and enjoying their company. She'd fool around in the kitchen with

Kate, teasing her about adding too much sugar or killing everyone with salt. She'd help PJ brush the horses and find ways to ruffle his hair or kiss him on the cheek. And then there were times when Patrick and Lily would disappear to their bedroom for hours, and sometimes she'd hear laughter from down the hall. Danny had an impressive office with five computer screens, laptops of various sizes, and other technical gadgets she had no clue about. The library was Cassie's favorite room in the house. She'd spent some of her time reading. Most of all, she liked reading the magazines. They told her about current events, and she felt empowered learning about the world. She'd read hundreds of articles about her mother, conspiracy theories, and what A.S.A. and Twin Seekers were doing. They were constantly in trouble with the law. The government seemed to frown on the groups, yet they never did much to stop them. Cassie loved sitting on the wide porch, enjoying the breeze and fresh air.

"Do you plan to do more reading?" Lily asked when Cassie didn't respond. "I know how much you're enjoying all the books and magazines. I hope it's not getting you depressed, though. Your Aunt Kate doesn't like to follow the news because it only makes her sad. She'd rather not know about all the problems and turmoil in the world."

"I'm fascinated by it. Maybe because I never had access to it growing up, but I find it interesting to hear the voices of authors who talk about world events." She'd often come across articles that mentioned her mother, and the testimonies of people she'd healed. "It's interesting hearing about the radiation."

"Radiation is still slowly killing people. It never really goes away. Over time, people develop diseases from it. But clearing the land, air purifying, and sand have greatly helped. I'm glad you weren't exposed to radioactive air growing up." Although Lily suspected it wouldn't have harmed Cassie at all. Her body would have healed itself.

Patrick stepped out onto the porch and gave Lily a quick kiss on the lips before glancing at Cassie. "Hey there, kiddo," he smiled.

"You're up early this morning. How did you sleep?"

Cassie laughed. Her parents were a lot alike and often said the same things. She figured when you spend all your time with someone, you start to act like them. Julie used to say to her, "Now that's just what Amy would say. Gosh, you guys are the same."

Now she wondered if Amy would become more like Andrew. Would Amy suddenly become a fast eater and love Kale chips? The thought of her friends made her heart ache. She missed them almost as much as she missed Shane. Danny told her that perhaps next week she would be able to call them. It was still too soon to make contact, and he didn't want to risk anyone's safety, especially now that the world knew who she was. People could be watching Amy and Andrew, thinking they might contact her. Danny felt he could keep them safe as long as her friends had nothing to do with her.

"Are you okay?" Lily asked.

Her parents had been talking, but Cassie was distracted by her thoughts. She'd been thinking about Amy and her mind was racing with memories. "I'm fine." She looked up and saw that the rain had stopped. PJ was walking over the grass toward them. "I think I'll take a shower and get dressed."

"PJ's coming to get his favorite apple-cinnamon pancakes. Kate's whipping up a batch right now," Patrick told her.

"It's like he has ESP and knows whenever she's making his favorite dishes," Lily laughed.

"I'm sure he can smell them. They smell amazing." Cassie rose from her chair.

Lily and Patrick shared a look. They couldn't smell anything from the kitchen.

"Shane said you have an incredible sense of smell," Patrick replied, moving aside as Cassie walked to the door.

"I guess." At the mention of Shane's name, Cassie frowned at the ground. She wished the ache in her chest would go away.

Lily stood as Cassie walked by. "Eat some pancakes before you shower. We'll join you soon." She automatically leaned into Patrick as Cassie left.

Patrick folded his arms around her, kissing her cheek. "I think she's adjusting well. She seems to like it here. I wish she weren't having trouble sleeping."

"She misses him," Lily sighed. "I wish we hadn't let him leave."

"It's good we've had her all to ourselves. I like not having to share her yet."

Lily smiled. "Remember when we wanted to be alone, and Alex was always around?"

"Of course." The memory made Patrick chuckle. "His timing was always terrible, and I could never get you alone."

"You managed just fine."

"Want to be alone right now?" He playfully ran his hand up her side.

"You two are gross," PJ said, climbing the porch steps. "I haven't even eaten yet, and already I've lost my appetite," he teased. He was used to seeing his parents be affectionate. Aunt Kate would always say, "Get a room." He didn't know what that meant, but it always made everyone laugh.

Kate was flipping pancakes on a griddle when Cassie entered the kitchen. Danny sat at the table, staring at his laptop, sipping coffee.

"What would you like to drink, sweet pea? I've got milk, orange juice, coffee, or…" Kate saw Cassie holding a mug. "Oh, you've already got coffee. Good." She tipped her head to the pot. "Help yourself to more." She tossed a pancake in the air, watched it land on the spatula, then flipped it onto a plate. PJ walked into the room with his parents, and she handed him the plate. "Just in time, Probably Jason."

Lily rolled her eyes. Kate would never stop calling Junior that. It had been her joke for many years, and she loved it. "We'll be upstairs if you need us," Lily announced, then laughed when Patrick took her shoulder and pulled her away.

"Ugh, those two are sickening," Kate laughed, winking at PJ as he shoved a huge bite of pancakes into his mouth. "Easy there, kid. You're going to choke if you keep shoveling food in like that."

"They're so good," PJ mumbled with his mouth full.

Being around her family made it hard for Cassie to feel down. Kate always lifted her spirits. She was fun, spunky, and always smiling, teasing someone. Her entire family was amazing. She couldn't help but think about how much she missed out on being in the orphanage. But the past was the past, and she didn't want to dwell on it. Knowing she had family for life made her heart soar. Over the past few days, Cassie couldn't help but wonder why Kate and Danny didn't have children of their own. Kate was a second mother to PJ and was great with kids.

"Kate, how come you don't have any children of your own?" Cassie realized she spoke the question aloud and instantly regretted it when Danny and PJ dropped their smiles.

The sudden question took Kate aback. "Oh, uh, well…."

"I'm sorry, I shouldn't have said anything. It's none of my business." Cassie felt her cheeks warm.

"Oh, honey, don't apologize. And it *is* your business. We're family, and you can ask us anything." Kate leaned against the counter and clasped her hands in front of her.

Danny smiled sadly at Cassie. "Kate's had four miscarriages. She hasn't been able to carry past the first trimester. It's been hard on us, but the doctor says we shouldn't stop trying. It hasn't hurt Kate's health, so we keep letting nature take its course. Whatever's meant to be will be."

Kate blew a kiss to Danny, mouthing the words "I love you." Then she looked at Cassie. "It's okay, because I don't need my own kids. I've had to parent this little stinker for years, and he's quite the handful." She playfully rubbed PJ's hair, then tipped his head back so she could plant a loud, sloppy kiss on his forehead.

"Right," PJ replied good-naturedly.

"And now I have you," Kate added, with a loving smile to Cassie.

"There's still time." Danny had not given up hope. "You never know. Heck, I'm in my prime, and your Aunt Kate is barely aging."

Always the optimist, Kate thought. That's one of the things she loved most about her husband, and he had been the most supportive, loving man she could ever ask for. "Considering your mom is the most famous woman on earth, and her ability has made our lives a tad… difficult, I'd say I'm the most blessed woman on earth. Life has been good, considering what it's thrown at us."

"I'm glad." Cassie felt her throat grow tight at the love filling the room. Kate and Danny were the sweetest, most positive people she'd ever met. Despite all their hardship and pain, they still felt blessed and always smiled. They inspired Cassie to want to be that way.

"So," Danny said, sensing it was time to change the subject. "I got word from Ian this morning."

PJ had woken early and heard his father and Danny talking before heading to the barn. He didn't need to listen to it again, so he got up and carried his dish to the sink. Then he kissed his aunt on the cheek before leaving. He was getting used to Cassie being around, but he still wasn't sure how to talk to her, so he mumbled, "See ya," as he walked past her.

Cassie nodded and gave him a smile before facing Danny. "Are they okay? Did they find Uncle Alex?"

Danny nodded. "They're on their way back here as we speak." He glanced down at his watch. "They should be here within two hours."

"I'm sure Shane will be glad to see you," Kate added. *And then someone can stop moping around,* she thought.

Cassie shrugged her shoulders. "I'm just happy Alex is okay."

Kate looked at Danny knowingly. Cassie's dismissal of Shane didn't fool them. "Alex found your teacher, Laura Reynolds, and they're all headed back here. I think he'll have quite a story to share with all of us." Her eyes widened as she thought about dinner. "I'd better start cooking, in case everyone is starving. I don't think there's enough leftover pancakes." She reached for her cookbook. "Maybe I'll make Alex's favorite Panko Crusted Chicken Piccata."

Danny laughed. Kate had just finished making breakfast and was already preparing dinner. "You're going to have a lot of people to feed, Love. Pasta might be better." Kate loved to cook. He appreciated that she was good at it; it always gave her something to do. It made her happy, and that made him happy. He also enjoyed watching her. He'd been her childhood friend and neighbor and had loved her for as long as he could remember. They'd been together for over thirty years, and he still couldn't believe how beautiful she was.

"You're right," she told him, and pulled out her pasta.

"Thanks for breakfast," Cassie said before leaving. Her heart raced at the thought of seeing Shane again, and she was excited to see her teacher. Relief washed over her, knowing Mrs. Renolds was safe and on her way, but she had to force the image of Ian's tortured face from her mind. With time to shower and find a cute outfit, she marveled at how she'd never thought much about clothes until she had access to so many. Her mother told her part of being a teen was dressing up and experimenting with makeup. Lily had given her something called mascara, which Cassie thought made her eyes look amazing. She'd never used makeup before and barely knew what it was. Over the past week, Lily had been sharing many new things with her. Cassie wondered if Shane would notice the dramatic difference.

The storm passed by breakfast, and now the sun shone on the green grass. Peering out her bedroom window, Cassie saw her mom and PJ heading toward the barn. Lily was likely to work in her garden, and PJ probably planned to ride his horses. Aunt Kate might appreciate her help in the kitchen, but cooking wasn't one of Cassie's favorite activities. She'd rather be outside in the sun, surrounded by the smell of summer. She turned to see herself in the full-length mirror. She'd taken her time getting ready, blow-drying her hair and keeping it down, the strands shiny and straight below her shoulders. She'd outlined her eyes like her mother had shown her and admired her pink lip gloss. She still wore the necklace Amy made for her, but she also wore a long silver necklace from Aunt Kate. The young woman staring back at her was far from the plain, basic, unadorned orphan from weeks ago.

Chapter 30

Lily watched PJ gallop around the yard on his horse, his smile brightening the beautiful day. It warmed her heart to see him so happy and carefree. She felt a deep sense of contentment knowing both her children were safe in her care. Her heart swelled as she saw Cassie walking toward her across the grass, carrying a basket that likely held muffins or biscuits from Kate. It was a wonder they weren't all overweight with such delicious treats always around.

"Thank you, sweetheart." Lily took the basket from Cassie and examined the assortment of muffins. "Did you eat some?"

"Yes. The Blueberry is my favorite."

There was no question that Cassie had been upset over Shane's departure. They had both refused to say goodbye, which Lily suspected was the reason for Cassie's melancholy. Although the last ten days were filled with joy in getting to know each other, there was also a shadow of sadness due to Shane's absence. "Shane should be back any moment. I can't wait to see Alex." She wanted her brother to witness the complete happiness she felt having both her children together.

"I know."

"You look beautiful this morning. I love earth-tone colors on you. They really complement your hair."

"Thank you." Cassie gazed down at her burnt-orange blouse and brown shorts. The clothes in her closet were amazing, and she'd never get used to choosing from such a lovely assortment each day. She noticed her mother tended to dress similarly, also choosing browns, khakis, greens, and reds. Today she wore a red tank top with khaki-colored shorts and brown ankle boots. Cassie loved all the cute tennis shoes. They were much more comfortable than the black rubber shoes she wore for years in the orphanage.

"Would you like to ride one of the horses?" Lily smiled and then glanced over at PJ. "I'm sure your brother would love to ride with you."

"No, thank you."

This was the fourth time Cassie had turned down the offer. Lily was starting to think there was a specific reason for her refusal. "Are you afraid? It's okay if you are."

"When I was little, maybe five, I remember being on a horse," Cassie said, settling onto the blanket Lily had laid on the damp grass. "A couple was fighting over me. I think the man wanted to hurt me, and the woman was trying to protect me. She put me on a horse, and we galloped away fast." Cassie closed her eyes as the memory resurfaced. "I was terrified. I kept slipping off because I couldn't hold on."

Lily placed her hand over her suddenly racing heart. Cassie hadn't yet mentioned any childhood memories, and Lily was almost afraid to hear what she'd have to say.

Glancing across the field at PJ riding his horse, Cassie continued. "The woman rode behind me, and I think there was a fire. I can't remember it clearly." It bothered her that the memory only came to her in a vague, fuzzy dream.

"Go on."

"That's all I remember. The memory comes in my dreams. It scares me. In my dream, I remember how I felt on the horse and how badly I wanted to get off it."

"I see." Lily hated not knowing what had happened to her child. "You don't remember what they looked like?" It didn't matter who had taken her, as long as they hadn't hurt her. Whoever placed her in the orphanage may have saved Cassie's life. Lily would never have all the answers, but she could live with that. Her daughter was here now and safe.

"No. But I don't think I was ever hurt. I think the woman

204

protected me and was kind." She wanted to ease the pain she saw in Lily's eyes. She knew what her parents had gone through over the years, agonizing over their missing child. They'd told her how Lily had given birth to her on an airplane. Right as Cassie came into the world, the plane crash-landed. Lily had healed Cassie and Patrick at the same time because they were both about to die from their injuries. Then Lily passed out, and Patrick hadn't regained consciousness until Cassie was already gone. They knew a nearby family had found the plane and taken her. The family claimed they sold Cassie to a man who offered a large sum of money. Her parents followed all possible leads but never found her. Someone had gone to great lengths to hide her away.

Lily dug her hands into the dirt. "It must have been the woman who put you in the orphanage." She loved the feel of the earth between her fingers. Today, she was planting wildflowers to grow alongside the barn. The cool, damp soil helped calm her nerves. "I suppose it was good she put you there because it kept you safe." Her voice was tinged with a mixture of resignation and hope. She had to believe it had all been for the best; otherwise, the pain would be too unbearable.

Cassie picked up a packet of seeds and handed them to her mother. It reminded her of the greenhouse at the orphanage. She'd been thinking about it a lot the past few days. She'd been thrilled to learn that Julie and Caleb had made it safely to Colorado and were now living near Amy and Andrew. She had Shane and Alex to thank for that. Both made sure her friends were safe. She looked up at Junior as he galloped around them and hopped off his horse. "I'm sorry I can't ride the horse. I don't want to be on one."

"It's completely okay, Cassie. Thank you for sharing that memory with me. We'll never pressure you to do anything you're uncomfortable with." She placed her hand over hers reassuringly. "I didn't know what you'd be like. I imagined a million different daughters. I didn't know if you'd be damaged, difficult, scared, timid... crazy," she chuckled. "But you're perfect, Cassie. Your dad says he sees a lot of me in you. I think you're better. Stronger," tears welled in her eyes. "I loved you before I lost you, and now that I've gotten to know you, I can honestly say I love you more than I ever thought possible," she glanced up at PJ, who was listening with a pleased look on his face. "Both of you have my heart."

There was still much to learn and share, but Cassie felt the same. She leaned into the hug her mother offered, appreciating the bond they'd formed.

"Are those muffins?" Junior asked, approaching them. He bent over, picking up the basket. "Don't let me interrupt your huggy session." He was now used to seeing his mother hug Cassie and noticed she'd also been overly affectionate with him lately. He couldn't begrudge her.

Rolling her eyes, Lily pulled on Junior's arm. "I could use a hug from you too, my sarcastic boy."

Junior laughed, allowing his mom to pull him down into a hug. "Okay, okay, don't crush the muffins. The blueberry's my favorite."

Suddenly, a loud alarm pierced the air.

"Oh God," Lily's heart sank. She quickly stood, pulling Cassie with her. She looked toward the house and saw Patrick running out the sliding glass door onto the deck. He waved at them to go and yelled something to her, but she couldn't hear. She could see he was wearing his emergency backpack. "What did he say?" she asked PJ.

Cassie's heart raced. She'd heard most of what he said. "They've been followed, get to the fort, and I heard the word horse."

"Mom!" PJ pointed over Lily's shoulder toward the fence. "They're cutting the gate!"

Lily understood immediately. Alex must have been followed by the A.S.A., who were already in the house. Patrick was probably headed back to help Danny and Kate, whom she prayed were safely in the tunnel. The house was unsafe, so they would have to escape another way. She turned to PJ. "We have to take the horses, jump the fence, and get to the fort." She knew PJ understood the protocol, but Cassie looked terrified and confused.

"I can't leave the foal!" PJ's heart sank.

"You know you have to, son." Lily handed the reins to him and then ran inside the barn. She quickly pulled Pepper from her stall and tossed a saddle on her back. Then she ran back to where Cassie and PJ stood arguing.

PJ's eyes were wide and scared. "She won't get on the horse!" He looked past his mother to see Shane running toward them. "Cassie won't get on the horse!" He repeated, this time to Shane. He prayed Shane would tell them they didn't have to leave. Perhaps his dad and Ian had already eliminated the intruders.

Lily reached for her son's arm to stop him. "Don't do this to me! Get your butt on that horse and get Cassie to the fort!" She glanced at the three men nearly done cutting through the fence. In mere seconds, they would be inside.

With a bloody lip and sweat dripping from his face, Shane reached the two horses. "Get on!" he yelled at the three of them, watching Cassie shake her head. There was no time to argue. "It's get on the damn horse or get captured!" He knew Lily wouldn't hesitate at those words. He picked Cassie up and tossed her on the stallion, then he mounted it behind her. "I've got her!" He could see Patrick running toward them from the house. There wasn't enough time to prepare another horse. "Lily, get up here with us!" He reached his hand out for her. She was petite enough to share the horse with him and Cassie. "PJ, you ride with your dad!"

When Lily was on the horse, Shane kicked his heels into the stallion and galloped forward. He headed away from where the three men were squeezing through the fence. Toward the back of the lot was a low dip in the ground, the one spot where the fence was short enough to jump. He didn't need to look back to know Patrick and PJ were behind him on the mare. Gunshots sounded, but Shane kept his eyes on the fence ahead. He'd jumped it many times with PJ, but never with two other people on the horse. Cassie was leaning too far over the horse's neck, and he could feel Lily gripping his waist, her fist filled with his shirt that uncomfortably tugged on his neck. He pulled Cassie toward his chest. "Hang on, Cass, I've got you." The jump was coming up. "We're going to jump the fence."

Panic ripped through her chest. "What? No!" She saw the fence ahead, and it seemed impossible. "Shane!"

"I can do this!" He felt Cassie's bottom on his lap. He held the reins on either side of her, caging her in. "Hang on, Lil!" He let the horse take over. The stallion was an excellent jumper, and Shane was able to guide him over. As soon as they hit the ground, Cassie's head whipped back and cracked Shane in his already cut lip. Tasting blood, he slowed the horse and glanced over his shoulder at Lily. "You okay?"

Lily nodded, focused on PJ and Patrick, who had also cleared the fence. Of course, PJ knew what he was doing. She was relieved they were safe and not far from the fort.

"We lost them for now, but they'll be on us any second." Shane saw the narrow dirt path that led to the underground fort. They couldn't take the horses into the thick forest. "We have to run from here." He waited until Patrick helped Lily down before he swung his leg around and hopped off. He reached for Cassie and breathed a sigh of relief when she wrapped her arms around him.

"Let's go!" Patrick told his family. "Run!"

PJ kissed his horses, rubbing their foreheads. "Home," he told them. He knew they would end up at the front of the house. They wouldn't be able to get to the stables unless someone opened the gate, but there was nowhere else he could send them. It broke his heart to say goodbye, knowing he might never be able to return to the ranch.

Low branches and thick brush covered what had once been an obvious path but was now heavily overgrown. It was hard to run on the uneven path, but they soon stopped at a large pine that had fallen over in a storm. The enormous roots were sticking straight up, covered with dirt. Patrick moved a few branches over until a wide wooden plank was revealed.

"I've got it." Shane stepped around Cassie and helped Patrick

208

lift the board.

"Get in."

Lily looked at Patrick and then down at the pit. "It'll be wet. Did you…" Her eyes landed on Patrick's side, and she noticed the growing bloodstain. "Are you hurt?" Alarm made her voice louder than she intended.

"Shh," Patrick hushed her and turned her around. "I'm okay, just get in." They needed to hide. Patrick could already hear dogs barking. He knew the A.S.A would cover every square inch of their property. "We've got supplies inside," he told PJ, as his son followed Lily into the pit. He appreciated the way Shane helped Cassie in. Once everyone was in, he placed the plank almost all the way over the top and arranged the branches to cover the wood. Then he unzipped his pack and pulled out a can of skunk spray. He began to spray the path and the branches covering the pit. The skunk smell would throw off the dogs and disguise all their scents. Patrick placed his hand over the stitch in his side and cursed at the blood covering his hand. He felt the ground shift below his feet and quickly climbed into the narrow opening of the pit. Pulling branches over the opening sent a searing pain down his side, and he stumbled back inside the dark pit.

"Dad!" PJ, grabbed his father, and helped lower him down to the ground. Lily had spread a blanket over the tarp that covered the wet, muddy floor.

Shane switched on his flashlight, but when he heard the dogs approaching, he dimmed the light against the fabric of his shirt. Then he moved over to Patrick. "How bad is it?"

"It's a knife wound." He grabbed Lily's hand when she gasped and went to touch him. "No, Lil. You can't heal this. We can't afford to have you unconscious."

"I can do it." Cassie moved over to her father and set her hand on his arm. Her heart was pounding, but her voice was steady and calm. She closed her eyes, focusing on her father's shallow breathing. She could smell the horrible skunk odor and resisted the urge to cover her nose. Instead, she breathed through her mouth, concentrating on healing her father. Finally, after a long moment, she felt the heat rising inside her. Knowing that she was improving her ability to conjure it when needed was a relief. The blue light slowly began to emanate from her hands. She could feel the currents pushing through her fingers.

The black pit was filled with the glow of her blue light. The heat made everyone wipe their foreheads. Lily lifted the back of her hair off her neck. Shane's lip throbbed, and he'd taken a few good punches in the ribs. One might be broken. He turned the flashlight off and handed it to PJ, since there was enough light to see. He slipped his hand under Cassie's free hand, feeling the heat against his skin. "Mind if I borrow a little of this?" he whispered.

Dogs were barking, and a twig snapped. Feet crunched the earth nearby. Cassie lost focus as her heart raced. She pulled back, and the blue light disappeared. No one said a word, and everyone looked at the entrance covered with a board and branches.

"Skunk was here!" Someone yelled.

"They probably backtracked to the house. We've got the others!" The voice was clear, and they could hear the dogs panting. "It stinks here. Let's go," the man said.

Lily leaned against Patrick in relief.

"Not a word yet," Patrick whispered. He wasn't taking any chances. They would sit quietly for at least a few more minutes.

Finally, after long minutes of silence and the dogs getting almost too distant to hear, PJ exhaled a long sigh and turned the flashlight on. "This is all her fault. I knew her coming here would bring trouble." The thought of never seeing his horses again made his heart ache. "They caught everyone else."

"Patrick Jason," Lily's voice held a warning and disappointment. "None of this is Cassie's fault. If you need to blame someone, place the blame on the factions. A.S.A. and Twin Seekers are the ones who followed Alex."

"This is my fault." Shane's voice sounded calm, but a slow

burn had him clenching his teeth. Junior's words were hurtful, and he knew Cassie would take it to heart. He pulled water from his backpack and handed it to her. "Here, I know you're thirsty." He leaned over when she took the bottle, staring intently into her eyes. "None of this is your fault. We should have checked Laura Reynolds for chips. We should have known they'd put a tracker on her."

Patrick watched Cassie down the water and wipe her mouth with her hand. "Thank you, Cass. Your ability is incredibly strong." He glanced at Lily. "Ian was right. She gives some extra boost. I felt whipped before, and now I'm pretty sure I can take on the world."

"You can always take on the world, and you have since the day I met you." Lily leaned over to kiss him.

PJ leaned against the dirt wall, not caring if worms or spiders were in it. "I knew this was going to happen." His voice had a bitter edge. "I knew once she was found, our lives would never be peaceful again. We'll never be able to return to the ranch. My horses won't be cared for, Aunt Kate could..." His voice broke, and he couldn't continue.

"Oh, honey." Lily moved over to comfort her son, wrapping her arms around his neck.

"We're all together, and alive." Patrick's voice held a stern roughness as he gripped Junior's ankle and squeezed. "Enough with placing blame. We will get Kate back. We'll get them all back."

"We always do," Lily whispered.

The day they got the ranch, Patrick worried Junior would get too attached. The ranch was only a temporary reprieve. He tried to warn his family that nothing could ever be permanent. His family fell in love with the house, the barn, and the land. The gift of the house was a double-edged sword. The pain and disappointment from leaving it might equal the happiness it brought. Patrick heard the pain in his son's voice, and his heart ached. Aunt Kate was like a second mother to him, and not only would he be devastated over losing his horses, but he'd be worried sick over her, and everyone else.

"Look. We've faced tough times before," Patrick said, rally-

211

ing his family. "Junior, you were very young when we last ran from A.S.A. You don't remember Uncle Alex being hospitalized. We hid in a jungle with many natives until we finally saw your uncle." That's also when Sarah died. They lost not only their homes and belongings, but also a very special person. "We got through that horrible time and found happiness again. We always make it through. This time, we've got Cassie, so our family is complete. As long as we have each other and are safe, that's all that matters."

"We don't have all our family, Dad," Junior responded.

"We will."

Shane moved over to Cassie and pulled her onto his lap. He couldn't take seeing her beautiful, sad face and not touching her. He'd missed her terribly and had been thinking of her way too much. She felt lighter than usual, and he wondered if she'd lost weight. Was he responsible for that? He wrapped his arms around her and tucked her head under his chin. For a moment, he wanted to punch PJ for putting the sheen in her eyes. Cassie cared how people felt, and she was absorbing everyone's pain. "I learned a lot about the A.S.A. when we were finding Alex. I know where their base is, who their leader is, and even some of the members."

"We'll need to get our hands on a computer to access Kate and Danny's GPS."

"All Danny's equipment is back at the house," Lily replied to Patrick. Fear of A.S.A. having access to Danny's information made her palms sweaty.

Shane caressed Cassie's arm as she took a deep breath. He smiled, knowing she was purposely smelling him to avoid the skunk odor her powerful senses were picking up. "When we reached the house, my Dad shouted a warning to Kate and Danny to get to the tunnel. Danny was upstairs, so of course Kate went flying up the stairs after him. My dad and I were fighting A.S.A. members in the kitchen."

"I shot two of the men coming in the side door. Someone came up behind me," Patrick added. He'd taken a few good punches

212

in the gut and a deep slash from a knife before taking the guy down. Now, thanks to Cassie's healing, he didn't feel anything. "I went out the back door to warn you." He looked at Lily and PJ. "But more men came around the side, and I wanted to give Kate and Danny a chance to get to the tunnel." That's when he shouted to Lily to mount the horses and make it to the fort. When he reached the door, gunshots were going off. He could see he was too outnumbered to reach Kate and Danny. So, he headed out the back.

"My dad yelled at me to leave the house and find you." Shane looked at Lily and wrapped his arms tighter around Cassie, as she snuggled closer to him on his lap. "He knew you, Junior, and Cass had no protection." He hadn't wanted to leave his father but followed the order. Cassie and Lily's safety had to come first.

Lily was too upset to force a genuine smile, but she set her hand on Shane's arm. "You handled that horse well, Shane. I was impressed you could jump the fence with both of us."

"Yeah, you're such a hero, Shane," Junior alluded. "Maybe you could rescue my horses, while my dad takes on the world."

Patrick sighed. He knew his son was not only hurting but was also jealous. Perhaps he'd always been envious of Shane, but Patrick could do nothing about that. "Nobody handles a horse like you do, son. We're very proud of you, too." He always tried to build his son up. PJ was a good kid and had many special qualities. He had Kate's sense of humor, Uncle Alex's walk and attitude, and his mother's heart.

Lily's heart ached for the pain she knew her son felt. "We have contacts. We'll find someone to get your horses. They'll be cared for, I promise." Lily rubbed her thumb along her son's cheek. "You'll have them again someday." She glanced at Cassie, noticing how she fit perfectly in Shane's lap. Seeing the two of them together, observing their obvious affection, helped ease the ache in her heart. She had always loved Shane like a son. He was a terrific young man, and she couldn't ask for anyone better to love her daughter. She stretched out her legs beside PJ's and leaned into Patrick. She closed her eyes and prayed when his comforting arm wrapped around her. She prayed that her brother and sister were safe and would soon be reunited.

Chapter 31

Hungry, bloodthirsty mosquitoes swarmed around Cassie's face. She kept swatting at them. Her nostrils were filled with the smell of Lemon-Eucalyptus bug spray, which happened to be working, because she wasn't actually being bit. The only one with a problem was Junior, who kept slapping his skin and grunting.

They waited in the pit until dark, when it was safer to travel. The clouds kept blocking the moon, casting the forest into darkness. Cassie tried to keep her gaze on the bouncing beam from the flashlight PJ was carelessly swinging, but her eyes kept drifting to the darkness around her.

She glanced at Shane walking beside her. He walked with ease, straight, and confident in the darkness. She didn't know what she was stepping on, and it startled her every time she broke a twig or crunched leaves. She'd never walked on a forest floor at night. She wanted to walk like Shane. She was thankful she was at least wearing comfortable tennis shoes.

"The roads about fifty feet away," Patrick pointed to the West. His watch was a cell phone and a computer with GPS. He'd called an emergency contact. If everything went well, Shane's grandfather, Marty Webster, would pick them up. The man was 82 and still in excellent health. He and his wife had moved to Texas to be closer to Lily, because their son and grandson weren't far away from wherever Lily was. Patrick grinned at the thought. Ian had become part of the family years ago. He might have once had a crush on Lily, but Patrick knew it was harmless. Ian was more caught up in Lily being the key to evolution. Patrick glanced at his wife, feeling a soft tug on his heart. She belonged to him, and he belonged to her. They were soulmates in every possible way.

"What are you thinking about?" Lily stepped closer to her husband as she carefully stepped over a branch.

"This reminds me of Virginia."

"Except it wasn't dark, and we fortunately aren't being chased at the moment."

"Oh, no doubt they're searching for us. They've probably squared off the entire property." He knew their only advantage was traveling through the forest at night. Hopefully, most A.S.A. volunteers would be sleeping, or at least unwilling to search a dark forest. "Okay, everyone, stop a moment and get down." They were almost to the forest's edge, where the road was. Men might be stationed along the intersections. "I'll scope it out and make sure it's safe. Then I'll come get you."

"No need," Shane replied. He pointed to the road. "I see the light over there."

Everyone turned, and Patrick spotted the outline of a car parked on the road's shoulder. The signal was for Marty to use a red light inside his car if it was all clear.

"Yup, that's him." Patrick grabbed Cassie's arm to stop her. "Hang on a sec, sweetheart. Shane, let's do a quick perimeter check first, just to be sure."

Shane nodded. They had learned years ago always to take extra precautions. It was how they lived and why they were still alive and free. His father would have said the same thing. Shane could always hear his father's wisdom running through his mind. "Never trust anything or anyone. Always go with your gut. Don't get too attached to anyone. Love can make you weak, lose focus, and distract you." That was the motto Ian lived by. Shane didn't necessarily agree with the last part. Lily and Kate had loving relationships that few are fortunate enough to find, and he wanted what they had. He'd never find it if he didn't trust or open his heart.

He headed opposite Patrick, keeping his body low as he

climbed the small hill beside the road. He glanced over at the long, narrow street, hearing only the chirping of crickets and the occasional rustle of leaves, likely from nocturnal animals. When Patrick nodded to signal the all-clear, Shane did the same. He then returned to where Lily, Junior, and Cassie were crouched in the tall grass and weeds.

Everyone piled into the luxury Ecoshell. There were three rows of seats, and all five could sit comfortably. Lily greeted Marty with a kiss on the cheek before climbing over the seat to the very back. Headlights beamed down the road, and Shane quickly shut the car door. "Go!"

It was just after midnight, so they expected very little traffic. Most of the surrounding land was a national forest, but there was a campground a few miles away. Shane figured the other car might be headed there and luckily turned off before heading in their direction. "How's it going, gramps?" He asked, after the vehicle was moving and he was seated beside Cassie.

"It's good to see you, boy," Marty replied. He wasn't exactly thrilled, knowing the A.S.A. captured his son. But it wouldn't do well to sound worried, and only further upset his grandson and Lily's family. He turned his head quickly over his shoulder to glimpse at Cassie, before setting his eyes back on the road. "It's a pleasure to meet you, young lady. I've got to tell you, you look just like your daddy, but a hel'va lot prettier. I can see your Momma's eyes." He extended his greeting to PJ as well.

"Thank you." Cassie blushed at the praise. He had a raspy voice and short, solid white hair that reminded her of the Q-tips she'd seen in the bathroom at the ranch. She hadn't known what they were for until PJ told her he used them to clean his ears.

"Still no word from Ian or anyone?" Patrick was hopeful that perhaps Ian had been able to make contact.

"No. Nothing on the news yet either."

Patrick peered at Shane from the front seat. "The safe house will have computers we can use. It'll be a good place to stay until we get our family back."

"You mean it'll be a good place to sit and hide, until something else bad happens."

Lily frowned at Junior. "I know how hard this is for you. But you need to trust us and have a little more faith." She and Patrick would not risk running. Hiding was always the safest plan, and they managed to keep Patrick Junior safe for 15 years.

"That's enough, son," Patrick warned. Knowing his pain, he was willing to cut Junior some slack, but the negative talk upset Cassie, and he didn't like seeing the worry in her eyes.

"My horses are probably thirsty," PJ mumbled sadly.

Not as thirsty as I am, Cassie thought to herself.

Patrick turned to where Lily and Junior sat in the car's rear. "The moment I can access my connections, I'll have someone retrieve the horses." The horses probably already had tracking devices implanted, and anyone attempting to care for them would be taken and questioned. Neither the government nor the police would ever be helpful. Too many people believed that aliens appearing as humans were living on Earth. The factions were comprised of government officials and law enforcement. Luckily, Lily had her own special-interest group, full of men and women who secretly pledged their devotion to keeping her and her loved ones safe.

Marty glanced in the rearview mirror. "I've got a friend who owns a cattle ranch. He's got a big barn and can take care of your horses. I'll find a way to get them, and in time, I'll let you know how they're doing."

"Thanks, Marty." Lily looked at PJ encouragingly, hoping he felt a little hope.

"I hate to say it, Lil, but it's like the past is repeating. Except this time, it's not just you all over the news. Cassie's picture is on almost every TV station, and the orphanage is also getting media coverage. They are doing investigations now. Some of the factions claimed Saving Souls might be harboring other aliens. They're investigating the kids. And did you know the Twin Seekers say you and

Kate have at least ten children? Apparently, there are a lot of little alien redheads running around."

"Oh no!" Cassie felt her heart sink. "My friends. They'll... what about Amy and Andrew?" Her mind was racing.

"Grandpa," Shane groaned. He wished his grandfather had kept that information to himself. It was the last thing Cassie needed to worry about.

"Sorry." Marty felt bad when he noticed everyone in the car was fretting. "I just thought you should know it's more important than ever for you all to stay hidden."

Patrick turned in his seat, setting his hand on Cassie's knee. "Your friends are safe. We've got an entire group in Colorado watching out for them. No one from the orphanage knows where they are, and their identities have been changed."

"Their pictures are on the news."

Patrick wished Marty would stop talking. "You don't need to worry about them. Our good friend Connie will know what to do if they're in danger. She has two sons trained in combat who have started their own 'Save Lily' coalition. They know our friends are important to us, so trust me...they'll be kept safe." He watched Cassie move closer to Shane. He was glad she felt close enough to Shane to seek his comfort. She was upset, and he was grateful if Shane could ease her fear.

He tried to picture his long-lost daughter as a child in pigtails. Did she laugh often? Was she scared or sad, and if so, was anyone there to comfort her the way Shane was now? Her eyes reminded him so much of Lily, and how she looked when she was young and vulnerable. Lily's emotions were always present in her eyes. He never had to guess what she was thinking or feeling. She'd been a girl against the world, with nobody but her brother to watch out for her. That part of history wasn't going to repeat. Patrick vowed that Cassie would never be alone. He looked at his wife, and his heart was filled with so much love he wondered how it didn't explode. He would ensure his children had as much love and support as possible. It would not be just a young girl and boy against the world. Cassie could have anyone who made her happy, and anyone who could protect and love her. By God, Shane was doing a hell of a good job so far.

"We're here," Marty said, turning into a dirt driveway. "This house belongs to my neighbor's brother-in-law. He uses it during the winter. Since it's August, it's vacant. Since Lily cured my neighbor, that entire family has been dying to help her."

"Kill the lights." Patrick checked the chamber of his gun. "Stop the car and wait here. I'll check it out."

When the house was cleared and Patrick felt safe to enter, he waved them in. After everyone was safely inside, he ensured all the doors and windows were locked before explaining their emergency exit strategy, should they need one. The house was old, probably built in the 1980s, on a three-acre lot. The woods were close enough to the backyard to have excellent cover, should they need to escape. In the morning, Patrick would dig another hideout pit in the ground. It certainly came in handy last time. Their lives always required exit strategies and contingency plans. A mile down the road was a newly developed subdivision and party store, so they weren't too far from civilization. The grass outside the home hadn't been mowed all summer. It appeared to be abandoned, which wasn't necessarily good. Abandoned homes invited break-ins.

PJ headed straight to the kitchen and opened the refrigerator. "Great. This isn't even turned on, and I'm starving."

Lily rubbed PJ on the back. "Mr. Webster has some groceries in the car. Shane is bringing them in."

On cue, Shane stepped into the kitchen holding three large grocery bags. "There are Ding Dongs in here." He placed the bag on the counter. The kitchen was small, but clean. It had a four-person wooden table and yellow cabinets with white counters. The floor was well-worn white tile, and a rustic wooden door led out the back. Shane had already determined where all the doors were located and where they led. He reached inside the bag and pulled out a white box with the words Hostess written across the top. "Here." He tossed the box to PJ.

PJ tore the box open. "These are mine." He declared.

"What's yours?" Cassie entered the kitchen.

"The Ding Dongs," PJ mumbled with a full mouth.

"Ding Dongs?"

"They aren't just *your* Ding Dongs." Shane walked over to take a wrapped cupcake from the box.

PJ turned his back on Shane, holding the box close to his chest. He quickly shoved another bite of the chocolate cupcake into his mouth, laughing when Shane tried to take the other half from his hand. "No..." he chortled again with food half falling out of his mouth. "One man should never touch another man's Ding Dong."

Lily chuckled. It was nice to see her son laughing and playing around with Shane. "There are potato chips and Oreos, too." She pulled more items from the bag. She handed bottled water to Cassie. "All the garbage and junk food a growing boy could want."

Cassie stared at the food on the counter. "I thought the world didn't have garbage food anymore, because people are on health kicks." She smiled when Shane handed her a Ding Dong and took a bite. "Wow, this is good."

"It's total garbage," Lily said. "Full of sugar and chemicals. But no, the world won't do away with all the unhealthy food, because there will always be people who want this stuff." She rolled her eyes at her son.

Shane held up the cupcake. "The good thing about these is that they have a hundred-year shelf life! They can survive whatever apocalypse comes our way."

"Your kids like the unhealthy stuff." Marty took a seat at the kitchen table. He had been listening to the conversation just outside the entrance to the kitchen.

"You mean all ten of my redheaded kids?" Patrick smiled as he entered the kitchen and took a juice from Lily's hand.

"Yup, all ten. Kate's ten children probably like junk food too." Lily leaned into her husband as he casually laid his arm across her

221

back.

Marty accidentally bumped into a picture frame on the wall when he leaned back in his chair. It fell to the floor and loudly crashed as the glass frame shattered. Patrick quickly turned around, pulling his gun from his back. Shane pressed Cassie against the counter, shielding her with his body.

"Oops." Marty bent over. "Sorry, kids."

Patrick let out a long, slow breath, then looked at Shane. "Glad I'm not the only one who's jumpy." It was nice to see how Shane's immediate instinct was to protect Cassie. "Let's get to work now. We need to focus on finding our family."

"Yup." Shane turned to Cassie. "I want to talk to you later." Before she could reply, he brushed a soft kiss along her cheek and then followed Patrick out.

Lily sighed. The moment of normalcy was over. One minute her kids could laugh and joke, and the next they feared for their lives. On the one hand, they could enjoy the simple pleasure of cupcakes, and on the other, they would focus on forming a plan to rescue Alex, Kate, and Danny. This was her life. Lily turned to Cassie. "Why don't you take a shower? I'll fix some dinner."

PJ followed his dad and Shane. If they were going to discuss finding Aunt Kate, he wanted to be a part of it.

The house was fully furnished. Unlike the ranch, it was far from lavish, and smelled musty, but Cassie was too concerned for Kate, Danny and Ian to pay attention. The furniture was old and showed more wear, but there were four bedrooms and five beds. A large seventy-inch flat screen TV hung on the wall just above the fireplace. There were towels in the bathroom, shampoo and conditioner on the bathtub. The curtain had small mildew spots, but the tub appeared clean. She hopped in for a relaxing shower.

As Cassie was drying off, a knock sounded on the door. She wrapped the towel around her and opened the door a crack.

"Found some clean clothes for you. These will be big, but I think they will work." Lily handed her a pile of clothes. "The woman who owns the house left clothes in the closet. She's a size 6. Here's a belt. Your dad added another hole for you."

"Thanks."

"Are you okay, sweetheart?"

"Yeah. I was just thinking what a shame it is all those beautiful clothes were left in my room." She had begun to think of the ranch as her home. She had cherished her bedroom. "I wanted Amy to see everything."

"I know exactly how you feel." Lily mourned having to leave the ranch. "But we'll find another great place to live. There are many beautiful places in the world, and adventures to be had."

PJ walked past the door. "This place is a dump," he grumbled. "Which bedroom is mine?"

"Whichever one you want. We won't be here long, PJ. You just got spoiled being at the ranch but try to remember it could always be worse." She turned back to Cassie. "Come on out when you're dressed. I can braid your hair if you'd like."

Cassie nodded.

Chapter 32

The television was muted, but Patrick lay on the couch flipping through stations. He had a gun resting on his upper thigh, his arm bent behind his head for a pillow, and he'd changed his clothes to clean jeans and a gray short-sleeved shirt with the word "Corona" and palm trees. Cassie observed him for a moment while taking the chair across from him. Even after being in his company for ten days, she still wasn't used to the idea that he was her father. She had once called him "Dad," which felt strange and awkward. His face had lit up, and he'd taken much pleasure from the simple word, so she decided to say it more often. She didn't know why it was harder to say that word than "mom." She referred to Lily as Mom several times, perhaps because Lily had greeted her saying, "I'm your mom." Kate referred to Lily as her mom all the time. She'd say, "Go tell your mom dinner is ready," or "Let your mom know Patrick is heading out."

Across the screen, a weather report was issuing a severe thunderstorm warning. A brunette newscaster stood in front of a brick building, speaking into a microphone. Cassie had no idea what the woman was saying. She turned to Shane, who was standing by the window. The long blue curtain was pulled across the window, but Shane spied out through a crack. He had also changed his clothes, and his hair was still damp. She caught the faint scent of lemon. He'd replaced his muddy pants with clean black ones, and his blood-stained, sweaty shirt was replaced with a clean white t-shirt that fit his muscular torso like a glove. Every ripple, every curve stood out. His left arm was folded across his waist, with his hand resting on the butt of his gun tucked in his waistband.

Lily walked into the room. "I'm pretty tired." She had showered after Cassie and wore jeans and a blue button-down blouse. "I'm going to bed. PJ took the corner-right room. Cassie, you can have the one on the left."

"I'm coming with you." Patrick stood up. "You also look tired, sweetheart." He looked at Cassie as she hugged her mom goodnight. The jeans she wore were too baggy on her small frame. He could see where they bunched up with the belt pulled tight. The shirt, a simple navy-blue V-neck, fit fine. Her hair was wet and braided down her back. "Everyone needs to get some rest." Emotions had been running high. Worrying over their family would only cause further stress, so the little sleep they could catch was important. He wrapped his arm around Lily's waist. "Don't stay up too late, kids."

Shane crossed his arms over his chest, nodding goodnight to Lily and Patrick. "I'm just going to chat with Cassie for a few minutes." Finally, they would have a moment alone together.

Patrick returned Shane's nod with a slight one of his own and a silent look of agreement. He'd allow them some privacy. Cassie was nineteen. She was more mature than most adults twice her age, and he trusted Shane completely. He'd vowed years ago, before he had children, that he'd never behave like Lily's brother Alex did. Alex was forever trying to keep men away from his sisters. Lily had been in her twenties when he'd met her, and from how Alex behaved like an overprotective father with a shotgun, he'd found it challenging to enjoy alone time with her. He vowed he wouldn't do that to his own kids. However, glancing at his daughter's beautiful face, he finally understood Alex's behavior. He trusted Shane but decided to keep an eye on the situation. "Goodnight, guys," he and Lily said simultaneously, while leaving the room.

An old red-yellow swirled rug covered the scuffed, worn hardwood floors. A small wooden coffee table with a big missing corner chunk was in front of the brown couch. Cassie moved over to where her father had been, and when she sat down, the heat from his body was still there. She and Shane were finally alone. They had spent a few hours in the pit, but they were quiet, and the conversation mostly centered on what Shane and Ian had gone through during their search for Alex. Now she was alone with him, and her stomach was in knots. Her palms felt sweaty, and her mouth was dry.

Shane studied her a moment before sitting down beside her. Lord, he'd missed her. Every day that he'd been gone, he imagined her beautiful face and those incredible gold and red eyes—eyes that always captivated him the way they did now. "You smell nice."

"Lily had some perfume she offered me. I've never smelled perfume before."

"I like it." He felt a lump in his throat. She finally glanced away from him, settling back against the couch. He noticed how her small hands clutched the bottom of her shirt, wringing the material. What could he say to her? *It was ridiculous how much I missed you. I wish I hadn't left the way I did. I can't get you out of my head.* "Looks like you had a nice week with your family."

"I did. You were right. They're very likeable people. Easy to talk with, and easy to...love." She whispered the last word.

"Will you look at me?"

She swallowed and set her eyes on his.

"I'm sorry. I never wanted to hurt you." He took her hands and felt her tremble. Or perhaps it was him. "I'm sorry for the way I left. I should have said goodbye."

Shaking her head, she felt the tension drain away. "I'm not upset with you anymore. I was at first, but it's gone now." It was the truth. The very moment he had pulled her onto his lap in the pit and held her close when she needed it, all her anger and hurt feelings toward him disintegrated. He had a way of replacing her fear and anguish with contentment. "I'm just relieved that you're okay. I'm glad you threw me on the horse because I wasn't going to, which could have hurt someone."

Shane's lips curved slightly. "You did fine."

"I was terrified."

"I know you were." He'd seen her look and how she'd shaken

226

her head at PJ and backed away. He'd felt her shaking and remembered when she'd told him about her dream. "You're very brave, Cass."

She couldn't draw her eyes away from his. "I don't feel brave. I'm scared for Kate, Danny, Mrs. Reynolds, your dad, Alex…. I keep thinking about the way your father was hurt. I can't bear the thought."

"Don't think about it." He leaned in closer, resting his forehead against hers. "We know right where they are. Your dad has already contacted people who'll be here in the morning. We'll get them back."

She leaned back with a sigh. "That doesn't make me feel better. I'm terrified you'll both get captured too. Or hurt."

He was uncertain of how to ease her concern. "We won't. They're still at the ranch, Cass. The fact they haven't been moved is a good sign. It means A.S.A. is still searching the grounds, hoping to find us. We figure they probably know about the tunnel that runs under the house. They're expecting us to use it. My grandpa's getting us bulletproof vests. We'll also wear neck and arm bands to protect against darts."

"Shane…"

"I know it's still scary, but we've done this before. I'm trained for this, Cass. We are dealing with a small group of men who belong to A.S.A. More than likely, they have no military training. They may belong because they believe there are aliens and want to make a difference. Many A.S.A. members want to capture Lily to have her heal their loved ones. We have the advantage."

"I thought the A.S.A. was really dangerous. You and Alex made it sound like they're out for blood."

"They are worse than Twin Seekers and can be dangerous, but a specific group captured Laura Reynolds. We think the leader and the men who tortured my father are dangerous, but the rest of them were kind to Mrs. Reynolds and seemed to disagree with the leader. Mrs. Reynolds explained that the group is mostly interested in learning if you're real. Everyone wants to know if Lily's children will have her ability to heal." He brushed his fingers down Cassie's cheek.

"People need something to believe in. If they have a focus, it makes getting through the hard times easier. In a way, Lily helped the country come together. She helped to end the petty fighting and disagreements because everyone could agree on one thing. There was a woman out there who may or may not be an alien, but she can heal. And knowing that one person has that extraordinary gift makes everyone intrigued. It makes people want to know if there are others like her, or if her children will have the same ability. Lily has been the mystery and magic of our nation." He reflected on how the government also played a role in using Lily as a beacon of hope. "It's hard to explain, Cass." He knew that her sheltered life made all this seem not easy to comprehend.

His breath was warm, and his lips looked soft. "You're doing a good job explaining." Her voice was a soft whisper, and trembled a little.

A few moments of silence followed as he became lost in her eyes, forgetting what he was talking about. "You'll never know how much I missed you, Cass."

"I missed you."

He couldn't resist her anymore and slowly kissed her. He could have sworn her lips were made only for him. They seemed to melt into each other with a pleasure he'd never felt before. Whatever weight had been on his shoulders and whatever nerves had been bundled flowed away like melting ice. "Wow," he whispered against her lips.

"Dude," PJ said, entering the room. "Don't get her knocked up, man. We've got enough problems." There was humor in his voice, and a slight smile curved his lips. "Sorry to interrupt. I've got to get some water." He walked past them, into the kitchen.

Cassie felt her cheeks warm, but part of her didn't care. When PJ was out of sight, she leaned into Shane for more.

It took Shane a moment for the brain fog to clear and his heart rate to slow down. He heard PJ opening kitchen cabinets and the

228

glass clinking on the counter. It was probably good that PJ would be walking by again; otherwise, they'd both get too carried away. Shane was sure that all his composure was gone. With significant reluctance, he pulled away, focusing on her soft lips. What was he going to do about her now? He crossed the line, and now there was no way he'd ever be able to resist her again. He was done for.

PJ stepped back into the room, holding a glass of water. "I know my dad is against me going with you tomorrow, Shane, but you didn't seem as opposed. I'd appreciate it if you'd try talking to him."

Shane shook his head. "You know he won't go against your mom, and there's no way she'll allow you to go."

"Yeah, well like I said…I won't just sit here like always, while you two risk your necks to save my Aunt."

"PJ, don't do anything stupid." He didn't like the look in his eyes or the conviction in his voice. He watched as PJ stormed out of the room.

"What was he talking about?" Cassie asked.

"PJ wants to come with us. He feels his father treats him like a child. He has something to prove, and I'm afraid he will soon rebel. He won't keep doing what your parents tell him to do."

"He hates me." Her mom told her that PJ didn't mean what he said in the pit, but she didn't believe her. "I think he blames me, but Lily said it's not my fault."

"Do you believe her?" He rubbed her cheek with his thumb. "Do you think all this is your fault?"

A part of her felt responsible, but it wasn't her fault she turned out to be the daughter of a famous healing woman. She had no control over anything that was happening. "No. It's not my fault. Perhaps it's the fault of our gift, but I can't help that." Her voice held a note of melancholy as she looked down at her hands. "I get why the world would want us. Amy, you, my dad…you were all going to die." She glanced up at him, her heart in her eyes. "I'm grateful I have this power to heal. I see why it's the most valuable thing on earth. It's not my mom's fault that she has it, nor mine. It's not right to blame anyone when it's just the circumstances of life. PJ is hurting, and I feel for him. I'd do anything to help change the situation. But it is what it is and blaming me for it doesn't seem right. I lived in that orphanage, never knowing who I was. I had this gift all along and never knew it." She lost the point of her conversation. "I'm just thinking out loud. I don't even know what I'm saying."

He kissed her gently on the cheek, moving slowly to her lips as he spoke. "You're just putting things in perspective." She was level-headed and intelligent, and he was relieved she didn't blame herself. Blame was a heavy burden, and he would never want her to carry that. He kissed her again, aware of feelings that actually terrified him. How could he keep her safe when he'd been so lost in her that he hadn't heard PJ walking down the hall? Perhaps his father was right. With great reluctance and self-control, he slowly pulled away from her. "It's late, and you need to get some rest."

"I don't want to be alone."

There was one bedroom that had two twin beds in it. He assumed he'd be sleeping in the same room as her, simply because Patrick and Lily had the master bedroom with the king-sized bed, and PJ had already taken the bedroom with the single twin. "I'm going to do another quick perimeter check, then I'll be in."

"I don't want morning to come."

"I know." He'd have to leave her again.

Chapter 33

Four men sat at the kitchen table. Each looked like someone's grand-father. Their clothes even fit the stereotype. Shane shook his head as his own grandfather adjusted his gray wool cardigan. It was August, and Texas was experiencing a heat wave, yet Marty Webster and his cronies were dressed for winter. "No way." Shane crossed his arms over his chest and knew from Patrick's nod that he was in complete agreement.

"I agree." Lily nodded, catching the unspoken message be-tween Shane and Patrick. No way could they pull off a rescue mis-sion with these gentle grandpas. "We don't have a choice now, Pat-rick. We have to call him."

"No." Patrick ran his hand through his hair in frustration. "You know that will only open Pandora's box."

Cassie walked into the kitchen just as her father spoke. One look at her parents and Shane, and she knew something was wrong. She glanced at the four white haired men at the table. One of them was squinting up at her through a pair of thick bifocals. "What will open Pandora's box?"

Lily pulled Cassie into a hug. "Good morning." She swept her arm out for an introduction. "Cassie, you met Shane's grandfather last night, and these are his four friends, Roger, Allen, Jerry, and Tom." She smiled as the men greeted Cassie in turn. They were all pleased to meet the long-lost daughter. "They came to help us res-cue Kate, Danny, Ian, and Alex."

"And Mrs. Reynolds." Shane wanted them to remember his teacher. He knew how fond Cassie was of her, and she was important.

"Yes." Lily turned to her husband, "But this won't work, and I know how you feel about him, but I'm afraid it's our only option."

Marty leaned against the window and folded his arms. He glanced around the room, feeling the weight of the situation. He was old, but he didn't feel it. He still knew how to shoot a gun, and his aim with dart guns was even better. His buddies, all in their upper seventies, were still in reasonably good shape. It was a fine group of men, and unfortunately, all he could come up with on short notice. His buddies were ready to risk their lives to help Lily's family and save Ian. Ian was Marty's only son, and the A.S.A. probably didn't care about him. They'd find out he wasn't an alien, so who knows what they might do? He understood Patrick and Shane's refusal for their help, but he was worried about his son and wanted to ensure he could help in any way needed. He knew who the "him" was that Lily kept referring to. He sensed there was going to be an argument. "We'll go sit in the family room while you figure this out. I've got some good news to share with Junior. Any idea where I'll find him?"

"He's still in bed," Lily replied. "I'm sure he'll be up soon." It was seven in the morning, and PJ didn't have horses to feed or barn responsibilities now. He'd probably never get out of bed again.

Once the men left the room, Lily took a seat at the kitchen table. Shane pulled Cassie to his side and showed no modesty when he kissed her on the cheek and greeted her good morning. She caught the pursed lips on her dad's face before he leaned against the counter and stared directly at Lily.

"I have to say, I agree with Lily." Shane set serious eyes on Patrick and moved to sit next to Lily. "I think it's our only option. Pulling together another team will take too long. If they move from the ranch, we'll lose the upper hand of knowing layout of the property. Distracting the men at the tunnel, while we go in through the back, is our best shot. We need a good-sized team and trained men for this."

"We've never been in this predicament. We can't screw this up." Lily smiled when Cassie sat beside her, spreading a napkin on the table for her muffin.

Patrick glanced at Cassie's confused look. "There's a lot of history you don't know, Cassie. I suppose this is an important part of our past; we should explain." He nodded at his wife to continue.

"You know how Kate and I were formed with modified DNA and implanted in my mother's womb?" Lily waited until Cassie nodded. "Well, the doctor who created that fluke genetic coding watched over Kate and me since we were born. When I was twenty-four, we found ourselves in a situation where everyone I loved would have died. But Dr. Price saved us. We met him for the first time that day, and he explained that he'd been trying to keep me safe all my life."

Without thinking, Cassie rose from her seat and went to sit on Shane's lap. He automatically wrapped his arms around her waist. Lily leaned back in her chair, watching the ease they shared. "Dr. Price was a very wealthy man. He saved us all from being killed." She could recall the day like it was yesterday. "He then faked our deaths so the world would stop searching for us." She had already told Cassie how their faked deaths had allowed them to live peacefully in Australia for a year. "Dr. Price promised us that if we were ever in danger, he would help us. He had a team working for him, whose sole job was to keep us safe. They were like guardian angels. They left us alone, but were always there watching from the shadows, ready to protect."

"That sounds nice." Cassie felt the warmth of Shane's arms and was absentmindedly caressing them.

"It was." Patrick agreed, walking over to lean against the kitchen table beside Lily. "It was great until Price died, and his son, Hugh, took over."

Lily's shoulders slumped as she looked at Cassie with troubled eyes. "Our arrangement was fine until we had PJ." She hated talking about this because it brought back painful memories. "To make a long story short, Hugh Price is also a doctor. He was fascinated by his father's creation of genetically altered DNA. He wanted to continue to research." She pushed a lock of hair behind her ear. "When

233

PJ was born, Hugh wanted to study him. He claimed that he only needed PJ's blood to determine if he had the same DNA as me." Lily wanted to know if her baby was normal and trusted the doctor. She'd been told he wouldn't be hurt. That a simple blood draw was all he'd feel.

Cassie braced herself because she felt the story was about to turn ugly.

"He hurt PJ." Patrick rested his hand on Lily's shoulder. "PJ was just a baby, so thankfully, he has no memory. But we had to rescue him from an underground lab."

Lily closed her eyes at the painful memory. She didn't know what they did exactly, but she knew they did more than blood samples. And she knew Hugh was more interested in replicating his father's work than he was in her child's safety. "Patrick and I agreed we would never again ask for his help. We severed all ties with him and insisted he leave us alone." Patrick had almost killed Hugh Price, and they had gone through hell to remove him from their life.

"And now you want to call him?" Cassie asked.

"Yes." Lily glanced at Patrick with a plea in her eyes. "Because his last words to us were if we ever truly needed him, he'd be there. He was torn between wanting to honor his father's wishes to keep us safe and his own desire to create a new superhuman race. But I believe he wasn't entirely bad, and right now he's the only one who can truly help us."

"But at what cost?" Patrick felt torn with frustration. He could never trust Price. He took a deep breath as Lily's eyes filled with tears. He gently caressed her cheek, hating to see her cry. He knew she felt the same way about Price, but perhaps she was right. Maybe Price was the best way to save their family. "I'll do this because it's what you want. I'll ask for his help because the organization his father started is strong enough and big enough to help us take on the A.S.A."

"It's the best option we have right now." Shane knew time was not on their side.

"What did I miss?" PJ entered the kitchen and stared at the group sitting with solemn expressions on their faces. "What's going on?" He glanced at the box of muffins next to the sink. If his aunt Kate were there, they'd have fresh pancakes or black bean omelets. There would be homemade blueberry muffins and fresh sliced fruit.

"Just filling Cassie in on a little family history." Lily rose to greet her son by simply placing her hand on his shoulder. "Did you talk to Marty?"

"Yeah. He's got someone to take my horses, if and when we clear the ranch."

"We will soon." Patrick walked over to the muffins and picked one out of the box. Junior had a large appetite, so they'd be gone fast if he didn't have one. He set a reassuring hand on his son's back. He'd call Hugh Price for help and get his family back together. They'd find another place to hide, hopefully one that accommodated horses. Hugh Price could help with that as well. But Patrick had to consider whether he wanted Hugh to know where they lived. He had a feeling Alex would be just as opposed.

Chapter 34

Alex observed Kate as she slept. His wrists still stung from the swollen, raw skin caused by his attempts to free himself from the rope. His arms were tightly bound behind his back, pulled against the metal bar on the garage door. Ian and Danny were in similar positions, but he was grateful that Kate and Laura were only tied to a leg of the workbench. Kate had squirmed close enough to the cement floor to find some rest.

He'd stayed up all night trying to twist and work the knots on the stiff rope. His fingers were raw and bloody, and no progress had been made. The man who tied them must have been a damn good boy scout.

Dawn was breaking. Alex could see sunlight filtering through the crack in the door. He heard the horses neighing from the yard, thankful the men had brought them inside the gate. At least Junior's horses could get water. He kept replaying yesterday's events in his mind. Call it OCD, but he'd never been able to stop dwelling on mistakes, constantly analyzing the wrong moves and replaying the should-haves in his mind.

He glanced at Laura, who stirred in her sleep. Funny how he no longer thought of her as Mrs. Reynolds, Cassie's teacher. She was still legally married, but she said her husband left her over a year ago. He'd found a younger blonde woman with inherited money who didn't have to work six days a week. When Alex had first met her, she had a matronly teacher/librarian appearance, but not now. Her hair cascaded down in a tangle of messy curls, and in the dim light, he could see her soft olive skin had a sheen of perspiration. The garage was stiflingly hot. He could hear her soft breathing and was glad she'd been able to sleep. She'd been nothing but a pain in the ass since he'd met her. If she hadn't gotten knocked out, Ian wouldn't have stopped to grab her off the ground. If Ian hadn't stopped, he wouldn't have been shot in the shoulder with a dart. And of course, once Alex went to aid Ian, Kate and Danny felt they needed to help, and now here they all were, losing circulation in their wrists and arms. His head was pounding, and he'd kill for water.

Damn, how he hated tranquilizer guns. They could render a person unconscious in a matter of seconds. He'd been shot with several darts, so unfortunately, the serum left him feeling weaker and nauseous than usual. At least he hadn't gotten sick like Kate, when she woke in the middle of the night. She'd also been terrified and a little shocked to see all five of them bound and captured.

The door from the house opened, and Alex could see the outline of Ass Number One. He'd given the men numbers because there were six of them. But Number One was the worst, which is how he earned the label. The guy was at least six feet tall and had the face of a young boy. He reminded Alex of Alvin from the Chipmunks. That friendly face made it easy to fool people into thinking he was a nice guy. What a mask, he thought. He was pure evil. He'd enjoyed being rough with Kate and Laura. And for that, Alex was going to enjoy hurting him.

"Rise and shine," Ass One sneered, switching on a light. "It's time for you to tell me where your precious alien is hiding."

"You can start with me." Ian's voice cracked a little, since his throat was dry. "I'm the most talkative of the bunch."

Alex shook his head. Of course, Ian would volunteer to be tortured before he'd let anything happen to the others. "I'm a pretty good talker myself." He felt he could take Alvin the Chipmunk on and was eager to be cut free from the restraints.

"Actually, I'm the brains of this entire family." Danny was wiggling against the wall to scratch an itch.

Ass One bent over and cut Kate's rope. Then he forcefully

237

yanked her up by the back of her hair till her toes dangled close to the ground. "I think I'll start with the alien's sister. I have a feeling I'd waste my time with you three."

"Don't you touch her!" A surge of fear tore through Danny. "I'll tell you what you want but leave her alone!" He couldn't let anything happen to the love of his life. A deep rage simmered at his need to break free and pummel the man hurting his wife. Helpless and desperate to make him release her, he yanked hard at the rope, digging into his flesh. "I know right where they are, and I will show. Let her go!"

Kate tried not to moan. She knew it would kill Danny if she showed she was in pain when he yanked her head back and put his mouth near her ear.

"Do you remember when you were pretending to heal people in The Square?" Ass One, tightened his grip on Kate's hair, his anger toward her evident in his cruel grip.

"The government forced her to do that!" Alex shouted. "Let her go!"

"My father had radiation poisoning and stood in that line for four hours to be healed. He came home that day thinking you cured him." Ass One pushed Kate to the ground. "My father died two weeks later. All you did was lie and give my family false hope. I was ten years old and watched my father suffer as his immune system slowly shut down, and he lost the will to live."

The government had fooled the world into believing she was dead. For an entire year, Kate was held captive in Northern Michigan. She'd been confined to a small room and hidden away while her family grieved. Then, after a year of solitude, she'd been forced to impersonate her sister. With their identical looks, the world believed she was Lily, alive and well and offering to heal people. The government used her to give hope to the radiation victims.

"She was forced to do that! She was a victim, same as you!" Danny glanced at Kate with all the love in his eyes.

"Cut him loose," Ass One, told Ass Two. "And tie that alien

back up." He figured a man in love would give up any information.

Danny was relieved they'd take him. His mouth was filled with the leaden fear that they'd hurt Kate. She was tied roughly to the table, but at least he didn't hurt her again. As soon as he was cut free, he was yanked up by ass two. His hands were still bound behind his back, but he was free from the metal bar of the garage door. He moved toward Ass One and quickly kicked him in the groin. The satisfying blow was worth the gut jab the other man gave him.

"Danny, No!" Kate held back a sob as the evil man punched Danny hard across the face. "Please, don't hurt him!"

"I'm okay, baby." He glanced up at the Asshole. "I'll tell you whatever you need to know. Just don't hurt anyone."

"You can't, Danny. Please." Tears dripped down Kate's cheek as she stared at him with pleading eyes.

Alex knew Danny didn't have the training and skill to take on two men. If Alex were freed, he was sure that between his incredible rage and skill, those men wouldn't stand a chance. "Take me! I know where they are and will take you to them."

Ass One stared at Danny. "Where are they? Tell me now, or I'm taking the Alien, and I promise you there will be no mercy."

"There's a safe house about five miles from the ranch. It's on a few acres just east of a quiet neighborhood. I'll need my computer to get you the exact address."

Ass One, cut Danny's ropes, freeing his wrists, and deliberately cut his skin in the process. "Try anything again, and I'll cut off her ear. Understand?"

Danny nodded. Full of love and sorrow, his eyes rested on Kate momentarily. He mouthed, "I love you," before being shoved through the door. As it shut, he could hear Alex's soothing words of comfort.

"Kate, Laura, listen to me." Alex kept his voice low. "You were both too drugged to do anything yesterday." They hadn't even woken till the middle of the night. "But you can both push up on the table and try to pull the rope out from under it."

239

Both women turned to examine the table. "It's attached to the wall, Alex. It's not going to move." Kate's rope was tied even tighter this time.

Ian coughed and hushed them. When the footsteps disappeared outside, he nodded to Alex.

"The table's only attached by two worn, rusty brackets. If you push up on it with your legs, you should be able to raise it just enough. You only need a tiny space to slip the rope under."

Willing to try anything, Kate looked at Laura and then rolled to her side, swinging her legs around so she could lift the table. Laura wore a skirt, and when she did the same, Alex got a view of her toned legs and white cotton panties. He had no idea that under that frumpy knee-length skirt and plain ruffled blouse, there was a fit body.

"That's it, ladies, use your leg muscles. Push."

Laura grunted, trying to pull the rope down to the floor. "It's not working."

"Kick it," Ian encouraged. "It'll bust loose."

Kate pulled on the leg and pushed up on the table. She used all her strength, but it wasn't working. The workbench was solid wood. Although it lifted slightly, it wasn't enough to fit the rope under.

"Okay, it's not working." Alex glanced around the garage. He hadn't been able to see last night when it was dark, but now he could study their surroundings. Patrick was a neat-freak and always kept the garage organized. All the tools were in a red box far from Laura and Kate's reach. There were other boxes stacked by the door, but those were also out of reach. His eyes went back to Laura's legs and rested on her strappy sandals. They were ugly. Why would an attractive woman choose to wear leather sandals with all those metal buckles? Thin metal buckles! "Laura, see if you can pull that buckle off your sandal. It's probably sharp enough to fray the rope if you can get it off. If you work at it…."

Kate glanced at the buckles. They were thin and sharp. "That'll work! Why didn't you think of that sooner?!"

"It's soon enough." Ian knew that once Danny disclosed the

240

safe house location, Shane, Cassie, and Lily would be in danger. Patrick was there, and he'd be ready for an attack, but that didn't put his mind at ease. He wanted to be free to ensure his son and Lily were safe. And now that Cassie could heal, nothing was more important than keeping her safe. He breathed a sigh of relief when Laura pulled the buckle off. "Good job! Try to hurry!"

Chapter 35

Patrick had asked Marty and his friends to patrol the house. They might not be able to help with the rescue, but they could keep watch while Patrick and Shane discuss the rescue details. In Patrick's opinion, the call to Price was risky, but it would improve their odds. Price wasn't the kind of man who hesitated or messed around. He seemed ready for battle at any given moment. He was sending men, and Patrick wanted a solid plan to discuss when they arrived. They were still a few hours away, giving Patrick more time to secure another safe house location. He glanced up from Marty's laptop, leaned back in his chair, and caught a glimpse of the TV in the other room.

The television was on mute; nobody was watching it. The A.S.A. had sent the news stations a photo of Cassie from Saving Souls. They had also circulated a conspiracy theory video claiming that Cassie was the alien offspring of Lily, with supposedly at least eight more children running around with healing powers. Some were even rumored to have telepathic abilities and telekinesis. Patrick felt a twist in his gut. The danger with such nonsense is that now any child who appears different or unique will end up missing.

A.S.A. members will be conducting illegal experiments on any misfit kids. The media loved to dramatize the A.S.A. It was great entertainment to make the faction sound mysterious and powerful. The world had changed over time. All those 'doomsday preppers' who believed the world would end or become like "Mad Max" when a few plants were bombed hadn't considered Lily McCallister. Who knew one person's ability to heal could change the focus of an entire nation?

"They've played that video ten times this morning," Shane commented as he leaned over to see what Patrick was looking at. "I think our plan is pretty solid. I want to go over the controls for the drone bug again. It's been a while since I've used one." Shane knew the tiny bee drone with a spy camera was crucial for scoping out how many men were patrolling the ranch. If he crashed the drone, it would ruin their chances of having eyes on the ranch before going in. He needed to brush up on his remote flying skills.

"Yes, let's go outside and practice."

Cassie was reading in the bedroom. She was thankful for a decent selection of novels in the house. The orphanage never had enough books to satisfy her insatiable joy of reading. The owner of the house had a lot of romance novels, lined neatly on a shelf. Cassie had never read one before and found it fascinating. It was interesting to hear how women thought of men. She realized how naive she was in the art of romance. According to the book she was reading, open affection meant something.

She heard arguing outside of her room and went to the door to listen. It sounded like Lily and PJ.

"I forbid it. You will stay here while your father and Shane go after them. He knows what to do. We've got some good help coming."

"I'm not staying here. I'm not a little kid anymore. I might not have taken a million training classes like the almighty Shane, but I know how to fight. Dad's taught me enough moves." PJ lifted his chin. "I can help. I'm fifteen!"

As the arguing continued, Cassie bowed her head wearily against the door. So she wasn't the only one wanting to help. Listening to PJ's argument made her think of her conversation with Shane last night. She felt the need to intervene in case anyone got hurt. Unlike PJ, she could at least save lives. Hearing the passion in Lily's voice, she knew PJ would not get his way. She had come to understand her parents well enough to know they would never stop protecting them.

243

A knock sounded on the door, startling her. She opened it slightly and smiled at her mom.

"Are you hungry? I'm cooking lunch." Lily had the urge to spend time with Cassie. "You're welcome to join me. I'd love the company."

Torn between wanting to read her book and not wanting to cook, Cassie glanced at the floor. "I'm going to nap, if you don't mind. I didn't sleep well last night." It was the truth. Shane had slept in the other bed beside hers, and she hadn't stopped thinking of him.

"Cassie?"

"What?" Her head sprang up, meeting her mother's concerned eyes. "I'm sorry, what did you say?" She had completely tuned her mother out with thoughts of Shane and that darn romance novel.

Lily figured Cassie was probably physically and mentally exhausted. It wasn't easy to act normal and feel fine when nothing was. It was a constant battle not to dwell on what horrible things could happen to her siblings. Lily was trying to be strong for her kids. She was trying to hold herself together and function like a normal person, because otherwise she'd completely fall apart. She couldn't imagine a world without Kate, Danny, and Alex. And Ian was her dear friend. Nothing could happen to any of them because she couldn't survive it. "I know you're worried. So is PJ. We must stay here and trust that Shane and Patrick will succeed. I've been in this position before when Kate was held captive. Patrick and Alex got her back, and everything worked out." She reached her hand up to touch Cassie's face. "Have faith that it'll be okay." She needed to say the reassuring words not just for Cassie, but for herself.

"It will." Cassie hugged her mom.

"Take a nap, then come in the kitchen to eat when you wake."

A few moments after Cassie settled down with her book, another knock sounded at the door. She rose to find PJ standing with his hands on his hips, wearing all-black clothes and a backpack slung over his shoulder.

"Do you want to help?" His voice was laced with resentment

as he stepped into the room.

"Of course." She shut the door.

"My Dad and Shane are outside playing with the drone."

"The drone?"

"It's a flying camera in the shape of a bee." PJ waved his hand in dismissal of the subject. "Anyway, my dad recruited a bunch of guys to help with the rescue, and they'll use the drone to scout the property. And while they do that, I've got this." He pulled his backpack off, unzipping the top. He pulled out an orange monarch butterfly. Cassie had seen them flying around the greenhouses, but PJ hit a button, and this one flapped mechanical wings, rose off his hand to circle the bedroom. PJ snatched it back and returned it to his pack. "When Dad and his team go inside the house, we stay outside and create a diversion. There's a box of old fireworks on the side of the barn. Uncle Danny got them one year for the Fourth of July, but I was worried the noise would scare the horses. So I hid the box on the side of the barn. We can take the fireworks and set them off in the woods. I think a lot of the men will come running. You and I can hide in the underground fort until Dad can rescue everyone. We won't be in the mix of the action, but our diversion can help them."

Cassie felt her pulse quicken. PJ seemed pleased with and confident of his idea. "How will we get the fireworks or even get on the property? Isn't there a fence?"

"With the drone." PJ pointed to the butterfly inside his backpack. "We'll be able to see everything without putting ourselves at risk. Those men have already cut the fence, so we'll slip in when no one is watching."

It sounded like a simple plan, with minimal risk, but she didn't like the idea of going against her father and Shane. "What if our interference messes up Dad's plan?"

"I heard their plan. I know what they're doing, and we won't be interfering. We'll be helping." He read the reluctance on her face, knowing what she needed to hear. "We can at least be close enough that if someone gets hurt, you can heal them. We'll be able to monitor what's happening with the drone." His father would finally see he could come up with good ideas and offer solid assistance.

"Yes, but..." Cassie felt like PJ didn't like her. She was surprised he was willing to take her with him.

"If I get hurt or Aunt Kate or anyone else is hurt, you are the only hope." He wondered if she was about to protest the way she crossed her arms over her chest. He could see she was debating it. "Look, my mom can't heal people anymore. It makes her weak, and she passes out. If Aunt Kate is hurt..."

"I'll heal her, or anyone else who's hurt. I'll go." She figured PJ would go with or without her and didn't want him to be alone.

"They're leaving tonight just after dinner. We are only five miles from the ranch. I figure it'll take us at least an hour to walk five miles to the ranch." He glanced down at her shoes, which he hoped would be comfortable. "We might have to run a little. I know the forest, and I know how to stay hidden. We need to tell everyone we're going to bed early. We sneak out the back in a couple of hours."

Cassie nodded.

***

The book wasn't helping take Cassie's mind off her nerves. She read the same sentence three times before putting it down. Her body hummed with nervous anticipation. In a couple of hours, she was going to sneak out with PJ and risk her life or, at the very least, upset her family.

A knock sounded. She felt too nervous to get up and open it. "Come in!"

Shane opened the door. "Are you awake?"

"Yes." She sat up, leaning against the headboard of the bed. He had changed his clothes to all-black. Cassie was beginning to think all rescue missions required solid black clothing. She glanced down at her baggy jeans and white blouse and pursed her lips.

Entering the room, Shane quietly shut the door. He noticed the

246

hole in the bottom of the door, where perhaps someone had kicked it. The paint was a light faded yellow, and the carpet was brown. Not a very attractive room, but it was clean. He imagined it was better than the small white rooms at the orphanage. "Hi." He felt his pulse rise at the sight of her.

"Hi."

"We're leaving tonight." He dropped down on the bed beside her. The yellow comforter felt soft as he picked up the book she was reading. "My White Knight." His lips curled. "Is this a romance?"

She laughed. "It's excellent. We didn't have books like this at the orphanage."

"I'm sure." He dropped his smile and stared at her lovely face. "I wanted to say goodbye this time."

"It's not goodbye. It's see you soon."

He stared into her eyes and took her hand. "I'll get them back, Cass. We've got a solid plan. There's like twenty men here. Your dad's preparing them and is confident we'll outnumber the A.S.A. at the ranch."

She didn't say anything. Part of her wanted to tell him what she and PJ planned, but she knew he would only stop her. He would tell her parents, and then PJ would really hate her. This was a chance to help make things right between her and PJ. He resented her being there. He blamed her for having to leave the ranch. Perhaps if she could help him, he'd forgive her. He'd see she wasn't so bad. If the intruders left the ranch, PJ could get his horses to safety, making him happy. She wanted to help him. She wanted her brother's approval.

"What's wrong, Cass? Are you worried? Tell me what you're thinking." He moved closer.

Of course she was worried. She was concerned about everyone and everything but didn't want to talk about it. She glanced down at the book she'd been reading. It had given her other things to think about. It made her wonder more about Shane. She wondered about their relationship. Was he going to be her boyfriend? Did he intend to tell his father about his feelings for her? She was curious about his past relationships. He'd told her he hadn't had the opportunity to date many girls, but she now had more questions. He was much more experienced than her, and Cassie wanted to know what he thought of her. Was she still just a job? When he kissed her last night, things had changed between them, but she didn't know what it meant.

He was waiting for an answer, and as always, she couldn't pull her eyes away from his. "What am I to you?"

He glanced down at the novel, shaking his head with a tender smile. "So this book has you thinking?" He was reminded of how sheltered she'd been. She'd never been exposed to the internet, television, or romance books. She was naïve and extremely inexperienced. For a nineteen-year-old, she was smart and mature in many ways, but she'd be completely out of her realm with relationships. "You mean a lot to me. I'm…" He didn't know what to do about her. He couldn't hide his feelings, and it was obvious her parents already knew. His father figured it out two days after he'd left her at the ranch. "I wasn't supposed to feel like this for you. The moment I met you, you were annoyed with me." He chuckled. "You didn't want to show me around and barely spoke to me. I was so excited because I'd finally found you. I was drawn to you, Cass. Maybe it's because I had all these ideas of what you'd be like, and you turned out to be nothing like I imagined."

"Is that good?"

"It's good." He pulled her to his chest. "You know that things are complicated for us, right?"

Not really. She didn't see why or how things had to be complicated. "Why?" Her stomach fluttered. She couldn't lie beside him, feel his warmth, and smell his scent, without getting butterflies and lightheaded.

"Cassie, you'll have to live with your family forever. It's just the way it is. You will always need protection. You'll never be able to come and go as you please." He watched the worry lines form between her eyes and set his lips on her brow. "It's not a bad life. There's nothing wrong with living with family. I know PJ loves having Aunt Kate and Uncle Danny around all the time. But the fact is, you'll be moving around a lot. You'll never stay in one place too long. I don't know what kind of life I'm going to live. After we find my Dad and your family, I don't know what direction I'll be headed in. I don't think my father approves of my feelings for you."

"Does it matter what your dad thinks?" She didn't care much for Shane's father. He seemed stern and opinionated. Ian raised his son for a specific mission. Even though she was happy that the mission found her, she wasn't sure it was worth Shane missing out on a normal childhood. "I don't care what your father thinks."

Shane thought about her question. His first instinct was to say it didn't matter, but deep down, he knew that wasn't true. There had always been a part of him that sought his father's approval. His father was passionate about helping Lily and her family. Ian held strong beliefs and views. Shane didn't want to disappoint him by not sharing those passions. "I know it shouldn't matter. He used to tell me that once feelings get in the way, it makes it difficult to stay focused on what's important. You must avoid love to avoid heartbreak. You have to care, but not so much that you won't see the enemy coming."

"What are you supposed to stay focused on?" She felt confused. Why would a father encourage his son not to fall in love? Or was he just not allowed to fall in love with her?

Shane swallowed as he took a deep breath, staring into her eyes. "You were always the focus, Cassie. Finding you and keeping you safe. I don't know anything past that."

Guilt was building up, weighing on her chest. She would sneak out with PJ, which could put them in harm's way. Shane, her parents, and Uncle Alex seemed obsessed with keeping her safe. "Shane…" she wanted to tell him, to ease her burden. But then he moved his lips to hers, and she was lost.

***

Kate's legs itched from the sticky sweat rolling behind her knees.

She wiggled against the restraint and used her ankle to scratch a few spots. She looked at her brother and Ian. "He's been gone a long time." The knot in her stomach wouldn't subside till she knew he was safe. "God, please don't let them be hurting him."

"Danny will be okay, sis." Alex couldn't stop watching Laura, praying she'd fray the rope any moment. It was taking forever.

The door opened, and the leader of A.S.A. walked in. Ian smirked at Alex. "Do you think he's pissed that he got shot and I got away?" He referred to the safe house when Jamerson tried turning Cassie in. He tried to sound casual to mask his trepidation in seeing the leader again—the sick bastard who'd enjoyed beating his face to a bloody pulp. If Cassie hadn't healed him, he'd still be black and blue with broken bones.

"Well, you may have escaped then, but you certainly can't escape now, can you?"

Ian smiled inwardly. Laura had been working on the ropes for over an hour. She had them half-frayed, and the sharp edge of the metal buckle was working.

The man glanced at Kate. "We haven't been formally introduced. I'm Trevor."

"Asshole Number One," Alex muttered, deciding this guy was definitely worse than Alvin Chipmunk. He deserved the number-one slot.

"Where's Danny? Are you hurting him?" Kate's voice trembled. She glanced at the man wearing black jeans and a red button-down short-sleeve shirt. He was average height and carried all his extra weight in his protruding belly.

Trevor walked over to Laura, and she froze. "You seem a bit wiggly." He was getting ready to glance at her restraints.

"I have to pee, and some insect bit my behind."

Her comment made him laugh, and he tossed his head back with a gap-toothed smile. "I guess you'll have to pee your pants. I'm almost done getting what I need. I'm certainly not going to have any use for you."

The blood drained from Laura's face. She'd been working the rope so long, she had a blister on her thumb, and her skin was broken open and raw on her finger. She held the buckle in her hand, desperate to ignore her pain and continue sawing at the rope.

"If this next house is empty, I'll be forced to hurt you, Kate. My patience with your husband is wearing thin. I understand your sister has many safe houses to hide in, but I think Danny purposely gives me the spots he knows they aren't in." Trevor walked over to Ian and sneered. "I see the alien healed you." He couldn't wait to get his hands on Lily's daughter. He knew she could heal, even though Jamerson had claimed otherwise. "The alien offspring will be mine." He wanted Cassie to bear his children. Superhuman babies, with the ability to heal. He turned back to Kate. "I'm not the kind of man who enjoys hurting a woman, but you're not one hundred percent human, are you?" He walked over to Kate and knelt beside her. "Your father was an alien who raped your mother. Guess that makes you only half-human. And isn't it a shame that you didn't inherit the healing power?"

"That's what the government wants the world to believe, but that's not the truth." Kate felt ice in her veins. "I'm nothing but human."

He slid his hand down her cheek, tightening his hold on her chin. "You haven't aged much at all. Your face is still very young." He studied her with cold eyes. "Is that part of your alien DNA?" He wondered if her lack of wrinkles and youthful skin was something that could be studied. Perhaps she held the key to the fountain of youth. "When I find your sister and finish what the government couldn't, I'll find a way to duplicate her powers and find out why you still look the same after all these years."

"They aren't aliens, you dumbass," Alex spit. "They were created by a doctor experimenting with the first genetically modified human DNA. Lily is a fluke of nature, and what she has can't be duplicated. There are no aliens… just a person created by another person with a genius breakthrough in genetic engineering." He was

251

sick of all the lies, the conspiracy theories and the lack of knowledge by all Americans.

Abruptly, Trevor whirled on Alex, slamming his fist across Alex's face. He yanked his head back by his hair and gritted his teeth. "You think I'm dumb enough to believe some doctor created a super-being? I happen to know for a fact that aliens exist and have been living among us for centuries."

"Don't touch him!" Kate stared at her brother through a blur of tears. She couldn't handle any more of her loved ones being hurt. It was the most helpless and heartbreaking experience. Like watching someone drown and being just out of reach to save them. It tore at her heart.

Trevor turned to Kate. "You better hope your sister and her offspring are at this next location, or I'll come back to prove how non-human you are to me." He turned and stormed out of the garage.

"He's crazy! We have to get out of here!" Kate choked.

"I'm working on it." Laura felt a surge of adrenaline when she frayed more of the rope. She was pressing down as hard as she could, rubbing back and forth as fast as her numb, sore fingers would allow. She was almost there.

Ian had been trying to break the metal pole, but it was too securely attached to the door. Alex was thinking the same thing, but their position severely limited their ability to do anything.

"Yes!" Laura yanked her hands apart.

"Laura, I'm going to kiss you." Alex's heart soared, as relief washed over him. "Get the clippers from the toolbox."

Ian's eyes stayed on the door. "Hurry!" He was praying it wouldn't open.

The big metal clippers were razor-sharp. As soon as she cut Alex's ropes, he cupped her face and quickly kissed her lips. Then he took the scissors from her and cut Ian's rope.

Ian went straight to the toolbox and pulled out a hammer. It wasn't exactly a weapon of choice, but it would do. "Okay, now comes the hard part." Ian glanced at Alex. They had to figure out how

252

to get the women out safely and find Danny. Alex was already in attack mode by the door, with Kate beside him. If anyone entered, he'd be ready. No way were they going to lose their chance to escape now.

Chapter 36

"I've changed my mind," Cassie told her brother when he returned to her room. Shane and Patrick were in the kitchen with the rest of the team. It appeared they had many strong, capable men, and she believed Shane was right. They would outnumber the A.S.A. men. The rescue mission should prove successful.

PJ narrowed his eyes. "You're the reason we're in this mess. I should have known you wouldn't help me."

"It's not that I don't want to help. It's that we can't put our lives at risk. Shane said he and dad have a good plan. I don't want to mess it up. We need to trust them, PJ."

This was PJ's chance to show his parents that he wasn't just some helpless kid anymore. He was strong and smart. He could prove to them he could be useful, and he was sure his diversion would help. "I'm going without you. I don't need you anyway. You keep being the good little girl they think you are. Stay here and do nothing while the family I love risks their necks for you." He threw the words at her in anger before opening the door.

"Wait!" She reached for his arm. She couldn't let him go alone. "I'll come."

PJ opened his backpack. "Put this hat on and keep your hair covered." He handed her the cap and a pair of black-rimmed glasses with plain, clear lenses. "You need a disguise. People know your face now."

"I thought you said we'd be in the woods, where no one would see us."

"We will, but you should have a disguise, just in case." He'd learned from his father always to take the necessary precautions. He eased his head out the door, peering down the hall. His mother was in the kitchen, believing her kids had gone to bed early. It hadn't been difficult to act fatigued at dinner. Patrick and Shane would be leaving shortly, and he hoped to beat them to the ranch. Once he saw the hallway was clear, he walked to his bedroom window, which opened onto the backyard. "Grandpa's guys are patrolling the house. I just took them some of Mom's brownies."

"So?" She didn't see the relevance. "It's not like a treat will distract them."

PJ smiled. "I laced the brownies with tranquilizer serum." He'd taken it from his father's darts.

Cassie frowned. "Junior, that wasn't wise. They're old men, which could be dangerous if they fall or ingest too much. They could get hurt. Shane's grandfather will be angry."

PJ shrugged off her concern by opening the window and glancing at the yard. "They'll be fine." He could see one man already lying in the grass. "I didn't offer any to Marty. He was with Dad and Shane out front." It was now or never, he thought. No one was around, and he could hear voices on the side of the house. "Follow me and do what I do."

They ran across the tall grass to the edge of the forest. PJ pulled her down behind a tree as he stared back at the house. When he saw no one had spotted them, he took her arm. "Let's go. We have to run for a while." He was leaving later than planned. He suspected his father and the others would be leaving soon.

"I can't run anymore." Cassie stopped beside a tree to catch her breath. They'd run a long way. It hadn't been easy jumping over roots and rocks. The ground was uneven, and the trees grew close in spots. She felt sweat trickle down her temples and wiped her forehead. "This is dumb." It was dusk, and she was swatting at mosquitoes swarming for blood. They had sprayed bug repellent, but her sweat had worn it off. Soon, there wouldn't be enough light to see inside the forest.

"We're almost to the ranch." PJ checked his watch. The GPS indicated there was less than a mile to go. He glanced around, looking for the path they should have come across already. The trees all looked the same, and he realized he might have gone the wrong way. A branch snapped, and he quickly pulled her down behind a shrub. It was probably a deer, but they were close enough to the ranch that men could be patrolling the forest.

They were running out of time. He wanted to create a diversion before Shane and his father appeared. He wasn't sure why he hadn't reached the trail, which would make it much easier to run. His worry and frustration had him glaring at Cassie.

"I'm sorry you hate me so much," she told him quietly, breathing heavily and resting on her knees. "I'm sorry I put everyone in danger and made you lose the ranch."

He stared at the sincerity in his sister's eyes. Eyes that reminded him of his mother and Aunt Kate. "I don't hate you."

"You act like you do."

"I'm mad at the world, Cassie. I'm mad mom and dad still treat me like a child. I'm mad the world thinks my mom is an alien, and it's ruined our lives."

She slapped a bug that landed on her arm. "Well, at least you got to have them all your life. I've heard enough family stories to know it hasn't all been bad."

The forest was quiet, other than the crickets chirping. As he looked around, he saw nothing but trees and brush. Mosquitoes buzzed around his ears. Thirst tempted him to reach for the water in his pack. He turned back to Cassie. Her words made him feel guilty. She was right. Now that he thought about the note he'd left on his pillow, telling his mother not to follow him, he realized that, of course, she'd come after him. Weariness was creeping in as his muscles began to tighten. He pulled out the water, offering her the first sip. Perhaps his idea, as good as it was, wouldn't work. "Don't drink it all. I didn't bring much."

She took small sips, resisting the urge to drain it. "Thanks."

She handed it back to him.

"I know I've been a complete jerk. I'm sorry." He took a sip of water before putting it away.

"Did you hear that?" She raised her head, inhaling the air. "I smell cologne."

Another twig snapped nearby. PJ turned and saw the man walking toward them. "Stay here," he whispered to her before standing up.

"No!" She tried to yank his arm down, but he broke free and walked away. Her legs suddenly felt wobbly. She heard the rustle of leaves, the crunch of earth, and bit down hard on her lower lip. She wished she'd tried harder to talk him into staying inside. Instead, he'd made her feel guilty; she hadn't wanted him to be alone.

A bug flew into her eye, and she quickly wiped at her blurry eyes. When her vision cleared, she'd lost sight of him. The forest had gotten much darker. Panic welled up inside her. A gunshot sounded, and she quickly scanned the trees. Then she saw a large man in black pick-up PJ and tossed him over his shoulder. Panic coursed through her, knowing she had to do something. She couldn't allow shock and fear to paralyze her the way it had in the past.

As she moved, she tripped over PJ's pack. She quickly opened it up, checking inside. Her hand shook as she pulled out the dart gun. She had no idea how to use it, but she'd seen Shane and Alex handle their weapons, and aimed the barrel away from her body with her finger on the trigger. She was careful with her steps, so she could get close to the man without him hearing her.

The man stopped walking and set PJ on the ground. He pulled out a phone, placing it to his ear. "Yeah, it's me. I've got some kid—a boy, maybe in his teens. I don't see anyone else. No, I shot him."

Cassie aimed the dart gun at the man's back. *Please work.* She pulled the trigger, then dropped low to the ground.

When the man fell to the ground with a loud thump and lay still, she quickly ran to PJ. His eyes were closed, his lips were drawn. "PJ," Cassie shook her brother. When he didn't move, she searched his clothes for a wound. Her hand felt something wet just above his waist, and when she turned it over, she saw blood. The scent suddenly reached up like a claw, making her head spin.

"Run." He whispered in a strained, low voice. "Leave me, Cass." He felt his body fading as his eyes pleaded with her.

She ignored him, knowing if she didn't act fast, he was going to die. She breathed through her mouth, trying to ignore the smell and exhaustion. She closed her eyes from the darkness surrounding her and tuned out the crickets, the soft rustle of wind, and the buzzing of blood-thirsty insects. She felt the energy inside rush through her like a tidal wave. The heat was instant, the current strong. Every time she used her gift, she got better at it. Pride and relief calmed the slamming of her heart. She was squeezing his arm, knowing the healing was working. She'd never get used to the incredible feeling.

Suddenly, she felt a hard tug on her hair and cried out. Her hands instinctively reached up to the man's hand that was tugging on her hair.

"I hate air-tranks!" The man's voice was angry and hard as he yanked her. "Not enough to put you out for long, but they leave a hole in your skin that hurts like hell." The man hated the new popular weapon. That's why he stuck with his good old-fashioned revolver.

"Let me go!" She tried to kick him.

PJ opened his eyes, bolting upright. It only took a heartbeat for his eyes to adjust and assess what was happening. He felt a surge of energy as he got to his feet. He quickly moved around the side of Cassie and kicked the man in his leg just at the kneecap.

"Ugh," the man groaned, letting go of Cassie. He had a bad knee and the little shit just damaged it further. He bent over in pain, trying to reach for the gun behind his back.

Cassie fell forward, landing on a heavy branch. She picked it up and swung at the man, connecting with his shoulder. PJ then punched him in the gut. The man was about a foot taller and a lot heavier. The punch didn't penetrate, so PJ kicked him squarely in

258

the groin. That worked. The man doubled over as Cassie brought the branch down on his head. She didn't know if she hit him hard enough, so she whacked him again.

"Easy there, sis. Dang." PJ put his arm out to stop her. "You got him. He's not getting up from that."

She was shaking and dropped the stick. "He shot you."

"I know." He stared down at the man. "First life lesson… always finish the job, otherwise they just get up and come after you again." He pulled the man's gun out from his waistline and aimed it at his head.

"You said he's not getting up. Don't shoot him!"

"He's A.S.A!"

She was taken aback by her brother's look of hatred. "It's murder." She didn't like his cold eyes, and he suddenly didn't look fifteen anymore.

"It's survival. It's us or them."

She smelled the blood flowing from the man's temple. It suddenly reminded her of Jackson and the gruesome way he'd been killed. "I'm done. I'm going back. If you continue this fool's errand, I won't be there to heal you again. If it's us or them, my choice is to run and hide." She understood now why her family lived the way they did. Why her parents would never want PJ to participate in rescue missions. They wanted him shielded from these exact situations. She stared at her brother's face as she backed away. "Please come with me."

A man shouted in the distance, and PJ felt his heart race. It was probably too late for his plan now. He realized he'd just been dying from a bullet wound. Perhaps he wasn't ready to fill Shane's shoes. He pulled his little LED flashlight from his pocket, aiming it toward the way they came. "Run!"

The amount of energy PJ felt was overwhelming. They ran as fast as they could until Cassie tripped and fell over a branch. He helped her up, knowing he needed to keep her safe. If anything happened to her, his parents would be devastated. He'd wanted to help, but now he could see how foolish his idea had been. There was a reason his father waited for all those men. There was a reason they called the one man his parents swore they would never contact. He brushed Cassie's hair from her face. "Can you keep running?"

"I'm so thirsty, I feel drained. I need water." She shook her head. "I won't make it without water." They had left the backpack with the water in the woods. She had been too busy running scared to think about returning for it until it was too late.

"Come on, I'll help you."

She stumbled as her vision began to blur. "I can't walk." Her tongue was as dry and stiff as cardboard. All she could think about was water.

"I'll give you a piggyback ride." He turned around and reached for her legs, placing his hands under her knees. When she jumped on his back, she thought of Julie and remembered when Caleb had offered her a piggyback ride to class. They weren't allowed to do that, so watching them break the rule had caused an exciting thrill. She wondered what it would be like to have someone carry her, but she never imagined it would be her brother, and they'd be running from danger. She'd never felt exhaustion like this. The feeling of dehydration was consuming her, draining her.

"Hold on, sis." He remembered what Shane had said about her need for water after healing. Panic set in, making him quicken his steps. The energy boost she'd given him was finally wearing off. Running through the woods at night was difficult, and he had to be careful with his steps. Suddenly, he heard dogs barking. They sounded close. Without his backpack, he had nothing. No weapons, water, or skunk-spray to throw dogs off their scent. He stopped to check his watch. They hadn't run far enough, leaving too much distance to reach the safe house. The barking was getting louder. He couldn't outrun dogs. Not with Cassie on his back, and she was too weak to run.

He pivoted to the left, heading toward the road. If he could make it to the road, Shane's grandpa, Marty, could come pick them up. Although he realized Marty and his friends had been included in the rescue mission and might not be at the house. He tried to hit the watch call button while holding her. The dogs were getting closer. He feared they wouldn't make it to the road in time. His legs were starting to burn; he could feel her slipping. Was she even conscious? "Cassie?"

"PJ, I'm so thirsty, I can't take it."

What a fool he'd been thinking he could help his family. Danny's words suddenly popped into his mind. *It takes a team of professionals to get a job done. A team.* "Please stay with me, Cass. Try to hang on. We should be on the road in a minute."

As soon as PJ's feet hit the pavement, he lost his balance. His knees crashed to the cement. He felt the sharp sting as blood instantly pooled from the torn skin. The dogs were close enough now that when he aimed his flashlight, he could see three men pulling against the dogs' leashes.

"Stop!" A man called out.

PJ re-adjusted Cassie on his back and stood up. He began to run down the street with her, praying a car would come by. He should have called Marty sooner. It was too late now. There was only forest on either side of the road. He knew there was nowhere to go. "Cassie, I'm sorry." Remorse tore at his tight throat. He'd been cruel to her. He'd acted like an idiot kid, putting her in harm's way. Wouldn't his father be so proud now?

A dog running free suddenly bit deep into his ankle. He cried out in pain and fell to the side, pulling Cassie down with him. Another dog clamped onto his arm as he tried to roll over her to protect her. If he was going to be mauled, at least his beautiful sister wouldn't be. He tried to kick the dog off, but the pain tore through his leg. Another dog bit into his pant leg, tearing the material before its jaws slammed down, puncturing his flesh. The dog on his arm was bearing down so fiercely that he started to black out from the pain.

He suddenly heard the sound of screeching tires, and a woman's bloodcurdling scream, followed by a dog's pained yelp. PJ turned to see his mother shooting dogs and men. His vision blurred, and immediately she was beside him, pulling him off the ground and dragging him into the car. "I'm sorry, Mom." His words were only a whisper as pain clouded his mind.

Lily pulled Cassie to her feet and dragged her to the front seat. She pushed back tears, checking the rear-view mirror while speeding down the street. No one followed, so she slowed to the forty-mph speed limit. PJ moaned from the back, and Cassie leaned against the door. Her eyes were closed, and her face flushed red.

The night was quiet at midnight, and no cars were on the road. Lily pulled into the garage of the safe house and quickly got out to examine PJ. His black pants were soaked with blood. She could see from the torn material that his wounds were horrific. Blood oozed from the deep puncture wounds on his arm, pooling on the seat and dripping down the floor. "Please, God." She pulled his pant leg up and stared at the mangled, torn flesh peeled back from the bone. More blood was pooled inside his shoe.

She'd need every ounce of strength she had to heal her son's extensive wounds.

"Cassie…" PJ said faintly, half-opening his eyes. "She needs water."

"What?" Lily couldn't hear the barely audible words.

"Water… she needs water."

Lily glanced at her daughter and understood what he was saying. She ran inside the house and quickly grabbed three bottled waters from the refrigerator. Then she carefully held the water to Cassie's lips. "Drink this, sweetheart." She held the water while checking for wounds on her daughter. PJ was losing too much blood. She needed to start healing him.

Once the cold water filled Cassie's mouth, she took the bottle and began guzzling it. Her stiff tongue and dry throat felt instantly soothed. She took the cap off another bottle and continued chugging the water, feeling her body re-energizing. It felt as if the water was bringing her back to life. She turned her head and watched her mother's face turn red as she healed PJ.

"Mom, don't…" PJ said. "You can't do this." He turned to Cassie, staring at her through glazed eyes.

"Hush." Lily continued to pour all her energy and healing strength into him. She focused on his arm, watching as the flesh continued to close. He'd have scars, and the skin on his legs might be jagged where the flesh was torn, but at least his blood was clotting around the wounds, and he wouldn't bleed out anymore.

"I'm sorry, Mom. I screwed up. I'm so sorry."

"I love you, son. You're safe now, that's all that matters." She looked at Cassie. "You're both safe, and I love you both so much." She felt the energy draining from her body. The currents she poured into her son were starting to diminish. She feared she wouldn't have the strength to finish. Ever since the doctors had done their horrible experiments on her, her healing ability had been weakened, causing too much strain for her metabolic energy. "Promise me you'll stay here. Wait for your father to return. Promise me you'll take care of Cassie and never put yourself in danger again." Her voice was desperate, knowing soon she'd be unconscious.

"I promise." PJ squeezed his mom's hand, his voice sounding stronger with conviction. The pain was gone. His wounds were almost healed. He began to stand and caught his mom around the waist as she collapsed.

Cassie got out of the car and followed them inside. "Will she be okay?"

PJ laid his mom down on the sofa. "Yes. She could be under for days, though. I don't think we should stay here. Those men could track us."

"You just promised you'd stay here and wait for Dad." Cassie, still thirsty, sat down wearily on the chair across from her mother. "Do you have a way to reach them?"

"Dad has a pager. I can call it and he'll know something's wrong. It's used only for emergencies, but we can't call him yet. We could blow their mission. I've already caused enough damage. We

263

should at least put Mom in the car and be ready to leave."

"And go where?"

"I don't know. We'll drive until we can meet up with Dad."

"The A.S.A. is everywhere. Call Dad, PJ. He has to come help us."

"He'll be furious with me. He'll never trust me again."

She stared at her mother's closed eyes and red face. "Will you get me some more water, please? I'm still very thirsty."

When he nodded and left the room, Cassie moved to her mother and rested her hands on her arm. Before the water, she'd felt too weak to do anything, but now her healing energy came immediately. She barely had to will it, and it was there. A smile formed on her lips as she appreciated that she was now the master of her ability. She could command it at will, bringing it in seconds. She watched as the blue light radiated over her mother's skin.

When PJ entered the room and saw the light, he knew what Cassie was doing. Perhaps it was a good idea. He hated when his mother was unconscious or too weak to move. He set the water on the table and knelt beside Cassie. She took her hand and put it on his wrist while keeping her other hand on Lily.

"It's working." PJ watched as his mother slowly opened her eyes and smiled. He felt his body tingling, and a renewed sense of energy filled his limbs. The puncture wounds on his arm miraculously disappeared. His mother hadn't been able to heal his extensive bite wounds fully, but Cassie was. "You're amazing."

Lily stared at the blue glow, feeling incredible warmth radiating from Cassie's hand. Something extraordinary was happening to her, and she'd never be able to explain it to Patrick or anyone unless they experienced it for themselves. She imagined it was close to what an addict feels when they shoot drugs into their veins. Instead of feeling light and high, she felt exuberant and energetic. A hyper feeling that made her want to stand up and run. "Okay, Cassie, you can stop now."

The front door suddenly opened, and Danny called Lily's

name. He held Kate in his arms; her head was draped back with her eyes closed. Lily saw the blood-soaked shirt and immediately fear gripped her chest. Danny knelt beside her, cradling Kate to his chest. "Everyone has made it back safely, but Kate's lost a lot of blood." His voice trembled.

Lilly took Cassie's hand and set it on Kate's arm. "You've got this, sweetheart."

Cassie felt relieved hearing that everyone had made it back. It meant Shane was safe. But seeing Kate passed out with her yellow shirt soaked in blood reminded her of Amy, and the familiar panic was beginning to set in. Danny's face was a torrent of pain. Her need for water triggered even more panic.

"Sweetheart, look at me." Lily sensed Cassie was inwardly freaking out, and having been in her shoes many times, she understood how hard it was to concentrate, when fear and panic were setting in. She set her hand on top of hers. With encouraging eyes, she smiled. "You can do this."

Staring at her mom's beautiful face, eyes full of understanding and love, Cassie felt the energy flowing through her again. She was able to reel in her anxiety and find her calm. Her strength in these situations was improving. This was her life now, but she wasn't alone. She had her mom, who understood and would love her no matter what. Cassie felt it deep inside every time her parents spoke to her.

"That's it, sweetie, don't stop." Lily could feel the magnetic currents coming from Cassie's hand. The same currents that once ran strong through her body, but never to the point where they seeped from her pores. It was beyond a miracle that her daughter possessed a healing ability stronger than hers ever was.

Bloody cuts marred Danny's face. She was used to seeing and smelling blood, so it didn't make her stomach revolt immediately. So much energy was pouring from her; she'd never felt so powerful. The raging current was stronger than all the other times she'd healed, because feeling the love for her family and wanting to save them was the strongest emotion she'd ever felt. She placed her other hand on

265

Danny's wrist and watched as the cuts on his cheek began to close. This was the longest she'd gone, pouring out her energy. She knew she could make it stop now if she wanted, but Kate wasn't moving.

"She's not coming back!" Danny couldn't live in a world without his wife. He stared at her with desperate eyes, fear coursing through him. "She can't be gone!"

PJ knelt beside his mom. He set 4 bottles of water on the floor beside his sister. He knew she'd need it. "Bring her back. Please, Cassie, bring her back!" Tears streamed down his face. He silently vowed that if she could heal Kate, he'd love his sister forever and become the best brother he could be. "Don't stop!" Why wasn't she opening her eyes? Why was it taking so long?

Moments ticked by as Cassie continued pouring her energy into Kate. The heat was becoming unbearable, making it challenging to keep the force moving through her veins. The thirst almost crippled her. She glanced at the water, need and yearning stronger than ever. She would have to pick it up.

"No!" It had never taken this long for a person to recover. Lily felt her heart tearing apart and shook her head in denial. Patrick had quietly wrapped his arms around her, holding her tightly. They both stared at their daughter, praying she could heal Kate. Lily remembered years ago when she held little Eric, her friends' child, in her arms. He'd been shot and was near death when she'd poured every ounce of her energy into him. She'd thought they'd lost him, and the sorrow was unbearable. She considered it a miracle that his extensive wounds hadn't killed him. Now she begged God for another miracle.

Cassie fell back, her hands falling limp at her side. She couldn't keep it up. "I just need to rest for a second. I need water." The anguish on everyone's faces brought tears to her eyes. She felt like she had let them all down. Seeing Danny kissing Kate and whispering endearments crushed her heart. She swallowed hard, trying to ignore the parched dryness of her throat, and placed her hands back on Kate's arm, willing the power to return. She needed to keep trying.

Everyone loved Kate, and so did she. Nothing was happening, and even as she closed her eyes to concentrate, she couldn't feel anything but the heaviness of her limbs, the ache in her heart, and torturous, unbearable thirst.

Lily grabbed Kate's hand, panic coursing through her, as she willed her healing to begin. Cassie had given her the extra boost she needed to pour all her strength into her sister. The room was silent as everyone prayed in anguish for Kate to wake.

Slowly, Kate's eyes fluttered, and Danny let out a ragged breath. "Oh, thank God!"

It only took Kate a matter of seconds to register what was happening. She'd been shot. She remembered Danny lifting her and running to a car. "Did we all make it?" She was suddenly swamped with kisses, smothered by Danny. She grasped that she'd almost died and how that pain would affect her family.

After everyone took a few moments to recover from the near-loss, Lily wondered where Alex was. Glancing behind, she saw him standing in the corner, wearing an expression she knew well: love and tension, and his half-cracked smile showed relief.

"I never doubted you two." Alex approached his sister and Cassie to hug them. After everything he'd been through, his mind and body begged for a break. "We're all going to need a deserted island in the tropics, and maybe some therapy." He couldn't wait to relax and ease his bone-deep exhaustion that no night's sleep seemed to fix. Although with his entire family, including Laura, all safe under one roof, he finally felt some of the stress strapped to him like a belt melt away. He'd been standing beside Laura Reynolds, and her arm was looped around his elbow. She'd formed a bit of an attachment to him, and he couldn't blame her, given what they'd been through.

When it was Kate's turn to hug her brother, she gave him a teasing, light push. "How come I'm always the one who has to get shot?"

Lily stretched her arms to embrace both her siblings. "No more, okay? My heart can't take it."

Danny leaned over and joined the circle. "Mine either." He turned Kate's face and kissed her hard.

"Where's Shane and Ian?" Lily glanced at Patrick.

"They're outside keeping watch, making sure we weren't followed." Patrick leaned over and kissed her softly. "Are you okay?"

Knowing everyone was together and safe, she was better than okay. "She's incredible." She glanced from her husband to Cassie. "Thanks to our daughter, I'm feeling excellent. I just used my healing strength on Kate, and I'm not exhausted. I'm wonderful." She laughed.

Shane walked in and glanced around the room. "What did I miss?" Kate was healed, and the heat in the house felt like a sauna. He approached Cassie as she finished drinking the last bottle of water. She felt touched that PJ had thought of her and brought her more water. It made her feel there was hope for them to have a caring relationship. Shane was genuinely happy to see her and relieved she could heal Kate in time. He gently took her face between his hands and softly pressed his lips to hers. His hands moved to the back of her neck, and he couldn't stop holding her closer.

"Umm…" Lily laughed.

"Wow, they kiss better than we do." Kate was thrilled to see them openly expressing what she already knew from the moment they'd arrived.

Hearing the comments, Shane slowly drew his mouth away but kept hold of her. He glanced at Patrick. "Sorry." He wasn't really. "I'm sorry, but I just had to do that."

Patrick shook his head and gazed at Lily with a half grin. "Believe me, I understand." It didn't feel that long ago that he'd been in the same position as Shane. He was crazy in love with Lily and couldn't resist kissing her every moment that he could. And he still felt that way. "Not sure your dad's going to, though." Patrick turned to Ian, standing in the doorway with a clenched jaw.

"Are you okay with this?" Ian crossed his arms and glanced from Patrick to Lily, with too much ice in his voice.

"Ian, I couldn't have picked a better man for my daughter." There wasn't anything more to say. Patrick figured he'd need to have a pep talk with his buddy sometime soon.

Danny reached out to Laura and pulled her into a hug. "It's nice to meet you, finally." He was grateful she had given them Cassie's location.

Laura took the opportunity to introduce herself to everyone with hugs and nervous hellos. She finally embraced Shane and Cassie. "I'm so happy you kids are safe." She'd been worried about them, and when A.S.A. took her, she'd prayed for their safety.

Lily glanced at her son, who had moved to stand at a distance, watching with a smile, but his eyes held torment. He had distanced himself from the reunion. He didn't participate in the rush of emotions. All the smiles stretched wide in relief, and voices raised in excitement. The air was filled with laughter, disbelief, and the unbreakable bond that always brought them together. But Lily's heart ached because she understood what her son was feeling.

PJ watched each family member with nervous jealousy, which cut through him. He'd never seen his mother look at him the way she'd looked at Cassie. Everyone was in awe of her. Everyone had their uses: Mom and Cassie with their healing, Dad and Uncle Alex with their protective skills, Danny with his computer skills and endless resources, Aunt Kate with her cooking and positive attitude that kept everyone happy, and Shane and Ian, who found his long-lost sister. What could he offer? He tried to help but only succeeded in getting himself hurt, almost killed. He knew his parents loved him, but he'd never seen his father look at him with such admiration and wonder as he did at Cassie. His heart was a bag of mixed emotions. Though relieved and thrilled to see Aunt Kate alive, Cassie saved her. He wanted to hug all of them, tell them how much he loved and needed them, but he felt unworthy. Inferior and useless. Unable to bear hearing his mother tell everyone what he'd done, he silently left the room and retreated to his bedroom.

Everyone noticed him leave. They were having a family moment, appreciating the victory of another successful mission. They were grateful that Kate was alive, and everyone was happy to meet Laura.

Patrick pulled Lily aside. "What's wrong with Junior? What happened while we were gone?" He'd noticed PJ's blood-soaked clothing and torn pants. He knew the practiced smile that hid his son's quiet ache. He knew his teenage boy wanted to be more. He'd begged to be part of the rescue mission. Patrick was torn between wanting to help his son feel more useful and wanting to protect him. He knew Lily would never agree with him facing danger.

Lily glanced at Cassie, who was still secured to Shane's side. She would never lie to her husband, but didn't want to share all the details. She knew precisely how PJ was feeling. Jealous and ashamed. "Cassie and PJ wanted to help…they felt left out. Ultimately, all that matters is both are home safe, and I couldn't be more proud of them." That was the truth. She'd leave it at that for now. "I'm going to go speak to him."

Patrick sensed more for her to share, but he'd let it go. There was still a tremendous amount of work to do. They needed to leave the house as soon as possible. Find another more secure place to stay. Ian had killed the leader of A.S.A., and between Alex and Danny, the rest of the men were also dead. The plan had gone relatively well, except for Kate being shot. Something would always go wrong, but luckily, Lily and Cassie were priceless saviors. The majority of the evil A.S.A. men were dead. No doubt, the leader had been the one who kept that smaller group of the faction going. Without him, Patrick hoped the others would return to their everyday lives and give up trying to find them. Of course, now that Dr. Price was back involved with the safety of their lives, they'd have more protection. And possibly more trouble. Price would know about Cassie now, leaving Patrick with a shadow of fear that will never leave him.

Patrick regarded Alex and Laura for a moment. Whatever experience they'd shared had pulled them together. Cassie had said Laura was her favorite teacher. Perhaps it was a good thing that Alex appeared interested in her. He'd never got over the loss of Sara, which continued to break Lily's heart, knowing her brother was lonely. Still, they'd need to decide if Laura would stay or need a safe place of her own. As always, they would solve one issue at a time.

"I need more water."

Everyone turned to Cassie, and her confession broke the chatter in the room.

Shane kissed her forehead. "I'm on it."

Chapter 37

The new secluded safehouse had a wonderful wrap-around porch facing the setting sun. Lily sat on the deck; her face tipped toward the sun as the rays wrapped around her like a blanket. The yard was surrounded by a tall, wooden privacy fence, ensuring no one would see if she raised her tank top to tan her midriff. She wore white shorts and a mint-green tank top, relishing the fabulous Texas heat.

Ian cleared his throat as he stepped onto the deck. "Mind if I talk with you?"

"Hello." She pulled her shirt back down and sat up a little straighter. "Pull up a chair. The sky is crystal-clear."

He wasn't a fan of the heat. He preferred mild temperatures and clouds to cover the burning sun. There was no rain in the forecast, just continuous days of stifling heat. That's why the grass was a burnt wheat, and the flowers beside Lily were wilting. "Laura and Alex went on a supply run. Patrick and PJ are doing something on the computer with Danny, and Kate is cooking."

"Where are Cassie and Shane?"

Ian pursed his lips. "That's actually what I want to talk to you about." He sat down in the chair beside her, folding his arms. "They went for a walk in the woods."

They were surrounded by forest, an hour north of the ranch. The house belonged to Ian's cousin's friend, who was spending time with their daughter in Canada. Lily liked it much better than the other safe house they left two days ago. PJ liked it because it was more modern and had room for everyone. In-laws' quarters had been built on the side of the house. "I'm all ears." She and Patrick had been waiting for this conversation. It was only the third day since the rescue, and she figured she'd hear from Ian once everyone had time to rest.

"First, I'd like to ask if you're okay."

Lily offered a faint smile to her dear friend. She'd always been incredibly fond of Ian, and even more grateful. When she'd first met him, he'd been a young computer geek, working for various news stations. He lived in Canada with his parents, and he'd put her on National TV, so she could ask the world for help rescuing Kate. She'd already been crazy in love with Patrick, so as Ian grew into a handsome man, she didn't notice. One day, Patrick gently pointed out that Ian was in love with her. It dawned on her that Ian was no longer the dorky, skinny guy she'd first met. He'd taken martial arts classes, weapons training, and developed himself physically. Anything and everything that would make him the kind of man who could protect a woman. He had wanted to be like Alex and Patrick. But she hadn't realized that he'd done it all for her. Even now, he could look at her, but she wouldn't know what he was thinking. He hid his feelings well, but his actions spoke louder than words. He was always concerned for her, always there for her. "I'm the best I've ever been. You know how happy I am when my family is together and safe." She set her hand on his arm. "That includes you and Shane. You're family too."

"I know." He tipped his head down at her hand. He'd loved her since the moment he met her. He'd always known that he would never be anything but a friend to her. And he was okay with that. Patrick was like a brother to him, and so was Alex. When Lily and Patrick lost their daughter, her pain tore him apart. He vowed he'd find their lost child. "Nineteen years ago, when I promised I'd find Faith, I never dreamed it would take so long. Time has flown, though, hasn't it?"

"It has."

"Shane is in love with her."

"I know." Finally, he introduced the subject that needed discussion.

"Watching the two of them together is like history repeating itself." Lily allowed Ian a moment for her words to sink in. "It's like Patrick and me all over again." She stared into her friend's eyes. "You need to be happy for them, Ian. You need to let Shane know you're okay with it." He'd been moody and angry with him, affecting Shane.

"I'm not okay with it." He had to be honest with her. He couldn't explain why it bothered him so much. He leaned back in the chair and stared at the faded wood planks. He valued her thoughts and opinions. "They're both young. Shane doesn't need to have his heart broken when he's barely had a chance to live."

And there it was, Lily thought. Ian had been in love with her, and he'd suffered being unable to have her. He didn't want his son to be hurt the way he'd been.

"He's got his entire life ahead of him," Ian continued. "I know I kept him from having a normal childhood, but now the mission's complete. Your family's together and safe, and there's nothing left for us to do. Shane can go to college. He can get a job. He doesn't have to spend his life keeping her safe. She has her entire family for that."

Lily leaned forward with sad eyes filled with sympathy. "I'm sorry you wasted your life for me. I never wanted you to give up a life of your own. I wanted you to have love and happiness. You should not have spent all those years searching for my child." Tears welled in her eyes. "Although without you, we never would have found her. Without Shane..." She'd tried to tell him years ago, when his marriage was falling apart, that he needed to focus on his life and family. Perhaps he couldn't love his wife because he wanted what she and Patrick had, which was simply unattainable. Her marriage to Patrick was a rare and precious bond most people are never fortunate enough to find.

His eyes shot up to hers. "I have no regrets, Lily. I didn't waste my life on you. If I could go back, there's nothing I would change. Searching for Faith...Cassie...the future of mankind was never a waste of my time. It's not just that I love you, Lily. I also love the idea of you. I wanted to find Cassie because I had to know if your

274

daughter could do it. I prayed that your gift of healing would be passed on." He sounded excited as he smiled. "She's amazing, Lily. Her children will be amazing."

"Her children could be *your* grandchildren."

He looked at her as if the thought had never crossed his mind. Then his smile faded. "Only if she loves him the way he loves her." He didn't want his son to follow in his footsteps. To love a woman he could never have.

"I understand why you wanted and needed to help me. You've spent years of your life devoted to keeping us safe. You're Patrick and Alex's best friend, and you've helped us all in ways we'll never be able to repay. But in the process, you sacrificed a lot. I'm sorry for that. Part of you must notice what you've given up and lived without." She would never be his lover, because her heart and soul belonged to Patrick. But she would always be his friend, and she would always love him dearly. "But Ian," she implored him with her eyes. "Shane isn't going to end up making those same sacrifices. Cassie is in love with him." She emphasized the words in love.

It clicked. The idea, the truth, and the reality he hadn't recognized. His lips curled up. "You're right. History *is* repeating." But this time, Shane could end up with the woman he loved. "I've been so hard on him. He must resent how overbearing, disapproving, and tough I've been on him."

Lily leaned forward and took his hands in hers. "You know that I've lost nineteen years with my daughter. It's never too late to fix things. Even if something can't be fixed or changed, the act of trying is often the reward."

Ian stared into the eyes he'd always loved. When he met Alex and Patrick, he knew he wanted to be like them. He wanted to be tough, strong, and worthy. He turned his son into that kind of a man. He would not regret how he raised Shane, because now Shane could protect the most incredible young woman on earth. Ian was proud he found Cassie; now his son would get to keep her. "Cassie *is you*, Lily. She has your kindness, your eyes, and your spectacular DNA."

"And you raised your son to be strong and smart. He has your unwavering loyalty with a gentleness to balance it all out. I'm grateful he's deserving of my daughter's heart."

"And don't forget he's way better looking than me. He's Patrick."

Lily bent over to hug him. She cupped his face and lovingly smiled, "He's *you*, Ian."

"Am I interrupting?" Patrick opened the door to the deck. He crossed his arms and raised a brow.

"Yes, you are. We were getting ready to make out."

Lily laughed. She and Patrick knew Ian was entirely joking with his dry humor. That's why his comment was so funny. He would never in a million years do anything remotely inappropriate. He wasn't the type to even so much as flirt. It took her years to discover he had a crush on her because he was a master at hiding his thoughts and feelings. But they'd had a good talk. She hoped he'd offer Shane his blessing.

"It's time for dinner." Patrick knew he had nothing to worry about. He knew his buddy no longer held romantic feelings. He suspected that the crush had always been based more on the idea of what Lily represented, rather than the woman herself. Ian, like many, had been in awe of her ability. "Danny thinks he has found us a more permanent place to live, and he'd like to discuss it over dinner."

✳✳✳

The kitchen table was too small for all ten of them, so Kate decided to use the attached guest house, which had an enormous rec room. Two tan sofas faced each other, with two chairs on either side. Windows covered one side of the room, allowing plenty of light to illuminate the light gray walls. Black and white portraits were scattered on the walls, each framed with impressive mats and frames.

Shane sat on the couch beside Cassie, Lily on the end, across from Patrick and Ian, Junior slouched in a chair, holding his plate over his lap, Alex and Laura in the opposite two chairs, and Kate and Danny pulled up extra chairs near the window. It was a cozy gathering, and the sunshine pouring in helped brighten the mood.

"Well, don't keep us in suspense." PJ broke the silence. "Where are we moving to?" He figured it didn't matter where they ended up, because nothing would beat the ranch he missed more than he'd admit.

Danny cleared his throat. "You're going to love it, PJ. My goal was to find us another ranch with property. This place is two thousand square feet bigger. Normally, it'd be too expensive, but Price is willing to foot the bill for any house we find."

Patrick felt his gut clench. He didn't like having the doctor's son back in their lives, and he hated that Price would know where they lived. But he couldn't deny they never could've taken on the A.S.A. without his help. Then again, maybe they would have, since Danny, Ian, and Alex had managed to free themselves. They might have escaped on their own, but more of them could have been shot. Having the extra manpower to take out the A.S.A. team had proved invaluable.

"It has a horse stable, Probably Jason!" Kate couldn't wait to share the exciting news with him. And whenever she was happy, she would use her pet name for him.

"Really?" PJ's eyes lit in excitement.

"Yes." Kate's heart swelled at the joy on his face. "And Dr. Price is already handling the safe care of your horses."

"But it will be a while before you see them," Patrick warned. He didn't want his son getting his hopes up. "We have to make sure there are no tracking devices in them, and we can't move them too soon." Everything had to be handled with extreme caution.

Cassie couldn't see or talk to her friends because people could monitor them, waiting to see if they'd reach out to her. If they did, it could put them in danger. Cassie understood that the same would go for Junior's horses.

"The ranch is surrounded by ten acres of private land, nestled between the mountains. There's only one access road, but plenty of places to hide in the mountains. A small town about ten miles away has a population under a thousand. There's no radiation, and the water's clean."

Alex had left it up to Danny to find a place. He hadn't had the chance to find out what State he was looking in. "Okay, that sounds great. So, where is it located?"

"Well, before I mention that, I'd just like to add that there's also a lake on the property with excellent fish."

"Huh. Where's it located?"

"And the best part is there's an underground tunnel that wasn't completed, but allows for a secret exit."

"Great, because that came in so handy at the ranch," PJ said sarcastically. He wasn't a fan of tunnels.

"Where is it located?" Alex was losing his patience.

"And the kitchen is wonderful!" Kate chimed in with her typical exuberance. "It's got enough room for a twenty-person table, and the stove is a solar-tech."

Danny appreciated Kate's enthusiasm and reached out to touch her shoulder. "And don't forget the extra-large butler's pantry."

"Where's it located?" Alex, PJ and Patrick asked loudly at the same time.

Danny sighed. "Keep in mind it's perfect." He flinched when he noticed the impatient expressions on everyone's faces. "It's in Scotland."

Chapter 38

The room went silent. Cassie had read a book about the Scottish Highlands and knew waterfalls were there. The book described the country as a magical place full of green rolling hills and spectacular mountains. She had dreamed what it would be like to see such grandeur. Her excitement was already high just from hearing Danny's description of the house, but her heart sank, realizing it'd be harder to see her friends.

Shane rose to his feet abruptly. "I need a drink." He left the room.

Cassie got the feeling he wasn't happy. She looked at her smiling parents, which made her feel a little better. PJ was busy shoveling large bites of pasta in his mouth, so she couldn't tell what he was thinking. Ian, Alex and Mrs. Reynolds did not look pleased. In fact, Mrs. Reynolds appeared anxious. Alex's mouth turned down, and his eyes fixed on the floor. "Is there something wrong with Scotland?" She felt wary just asking the question.

"It's fine." Lily crossed her legs and sighed. "It's probably for the best. We lived in Australia for a while. The U.S. feels like home, but we aren't safe here." She glanced from Cassie back at Danny. "We've never been safe here." And what no one wanted to say was that they'd probably never be able to return to America. Her mother was buried in a small cemetery in Virginia. She'd probably never revisit her grave.

Alex stood up, glancing at Laura. "Want to go for a walk?"

"Sure." She offered Cassie a small smile. "I'm glad to know that wherever you go, Cassie, you'll be in good hands." Her voice sounded optimistic, but her eyes held a sadness that didn't match her tone.

Cassie hadn't spoken to her teacher much since she was rescued. They hadn't had many opportunities. But Cassie heard Shane and Ian say that Laura had no job, home, or husband. Cassie wondered what she would do. What would become of her? She wanted to ask, but Alex took her hand and was already leading her from the room.

Ian rose without a word and left the room as well. Cassie looked over her shoulder to see if Shane was coming back. How long did it take to grab water? She assumed she was missing something. "Will everyone go to live in Scotland?"

"Everyone is welcome." Kate smiled. "I hope they will." She loved having lots of people around and cooking for everyone.

PJ stood up with his empty plate and looked at Danny with apprehension. "You sure know how to clear a room. When do we leave?"

"Not sure. You know it takes time to develop the strategy for getting out. Price is trying to secure a private jet for us. We'll need new identities and disguises. Especially you, Cass."

"I'll cut your hair for you." Kate offered her a hopeful look. "I love to cut hair." She ran a hand through her own short, choppy hair as if that was proof.

Aside from Kate, Cassie could feel a current of tension in the air. She took another bite of her pasta, but her appetite was gone. Shane didn't appear to be returning, so she decided to search for him. She found him in the backyard sitting on the railing of the deck. She paused before opening the door, just to appreciate the view of his broad shoulders and muscular arms. Sometimes staring at his body would make her head light. She opened the door, and he glanced over his shoulder at her.

"Hi."

"Hi." She stepped beside him, staring at the dead grass and the weeds growing along the fence. "What are you thinking?"

He lifted his legs back over the railing to face her. "Come here." He took her hand and led her down to the bottom step, shaded by a Maple tree. He angled his body toward her, staring into her red, golden eyes.

"What?" She knew from his expression he was searching for the right words. She had a sick feeling he was going to tell her he wasn't going to go with her. She moved to lean against the tree, her heart racing, and preparing for the worst.

"You have to go to Scotland."

"I know." She felt her stomach twist. "I wish I could talk to Amy. See her before we leave."

One corner of his mouth lifted as if he wanted to smile, but couldn't quite complete it. "You'll see her soon. My dad's already working on relocating them. With the world searching for you, they will be a target." He read the concern on her face and went to reassure her. "They're safe for now. We've got people protecting them."

"Okay." She had faith in her family. "Tell me what you're thinking, Shane."

"I don't really know how you feel about me." When her eyes lit in surprise, he laughed. "Well, maybe I kinda know how you feel about me, but…" He wondered how deep the feelings ran. Were they deep enough that she'd want him around forever?

She reached for his hand. "Shane, I…"

He interrupted her, needing to say quickly what he was thinking. "I have to go with you to Scotland. I honestly don't know how to be away from you."

"What?" Joy and utter relief filled her heart. She wasn't sure she'd heard him correctly. She'd been bracing for the day when he'd leave. She assumed he and his dad would go their separate ways now that she's safe in the care of her family.

He placed his hands on either side of her arms and stared into her eyes. "I'm in love with you, Cass. The week I left was the worst week of my life. I felt sick to my stomach. I couldn't wait to get back here and see you again. When trouble followed us to the ranch, all I could think about was getting to you. And after we rescued everyone and saw you were safe at the house, it was like I could finally breathe again."

Relief washed over her. "I thought you would tell me you didn't want to go with me."

He pulled her into a hug. "I don't ever want to be away from you. Not for a minute."

"Why did you seem mad when you left the room? Are you unhappy about moving to Scotland?" She leaned back to see his face.

"I knew once your identity was public, leaving the country was your only option. I thought I'd stay and perhaps try finding a job, a place to live, and possibly attend college. I was prepared to tell you that I wouldn't join you. I know your parents and Alex can keep you safe. My dad's not going to go, and I don't like the idea of leaving him. But then I came out here, and all I could think about was how miserable I was before. I thought about how I want... no need... to be there when you see your first waterfall. I need to be with you, because I can't see my life without you."

It was her turn to open up. He'd said he didn't know how she really felt. Of course, he wouldn't know, because she'd never said anything. "When you were gone, I had my family; getting to know them was important. Each day, I had things to do—books to read. I tried to keep my mind off you, but I couldn't. I had things to be happy about. My family is wonderful, and I already love them dearly. But there was a hole in my heart, Shane. There was a sadness I couldn't shake. It's because you left, and I didn't know if you were safe. I missed you, because I'm in love with you."

A weight lifted when she finally said the words, and he felt at peace. "Then it's settled. We both go to Scotland, and you're stuck with me." He leaned his forehead against hers before gently kissing her.

"Mind if I interrupt?" Patrick stepped out on the deck, glancing at their spot under the tree. He couldn't help but grin as he interrupted his daughter and Shane, who were sharing an intimate moment. Only a fool couldn't tell how much in love they were, and he was no fool. "Shane, you're the one I need a word with. Cassie, would you mind giving us a moment?"

"Sure." She climbed the steps and glanced at the doorwall, catching a look of satisfaction from her mother. She felt her cheeks flush, knowing she and Shane had an audience while kissing. She was glad that's all they'd done.

When Cassie shut the door, Shane leaned against the railing. "What's up?" He asked Patrick.

"Danny needs to know right now who's going. He's already making plans."

"I'm going."

"Good." Patrick stepped closer to him. "You're in love with her." It wasn't a question, so much as a statement.

Shane nodded. "So much so it scares me."

"I know exactly how you feel." He glanced up at the clear sky, the white cloud in the distance that was a simple stretched line. "I was in your shoes once. Lily, Kate and Alex had to move to Australia. I knew from the moment I met Lily that I'd never leave her. The way I loved her… I didn't have a choice."

"My dad's not going to be happy about me leaving."

"You might be surprised. Lily had a good talk with him."

Shane studied Patrick a moment. "I hope that's true. I don't want to leave him with hard feelings, but I can't follow his views on relationships any more. I don't care if I wasn't supposed to fall for her." He ran his hands through his hair in frustration. "Tell me how anyone could resist her? Tell me how I wasn't supposed to care for her?"

Patrick laughed. "She's a terrific kid, and so are you, Shane. I couldn't ask for a better man to love my daughter." He held his hand out and smiled when Shane shook it. "We've got to start training her."

Shane agreed. It was important for Cassie to learn how to fight and shoot a gun. Lily and Kate had both learned the skills years ago.

It had helped them on many occasions. "I'll train her."

"PJ needs more training, too. After what happened, he will be more inclined to learn."

"What exactly *did* happen while we were at the ranch?" Shane had heard that Cassie and PJ wanted to try to help and had made it to the woods before Lily found them. He hadn't been told all the specifics.

"Let's just say a valuable lesson was learned." Patrick patted Shane on the back before heading inside.

Chapter 39

September seemed to be flying by as fast as the falling leaves. In the first four weeks, they stayed at three different safe houses, each with unique appeal. What Cassie found interesting was the way every home had different decor and colors. Someone had placed a green sofa angled beside a glass table, or chosen long white curtains with blue polka dots to hang from a window. Someone had to decide how to arrange those pieces and what color to paint the rooms. Tiny holes in the wall once held a painting or photograph. Cassie would often wonder what had been there. Who had lived there? There was a story behind each house, and she enjoyed hearing it.

Always, it involved someone who'd been healed and was grateful to Lily. The stories of what happened to the owners of the houses were fascinating. She loved hearing how other people lived, learning about the real world that she had suddenly become a part of. While each home held a story, she knew none were large enough to accommodate all ten people. Laura Reynolds stayed with the family until Alex could decide what to do with her. He didn't seem to mind having her around. Cassie suspected there was more to their relationship.

Ian had left a week ago to run a secret mission for her parents. It all seemed very hush-hush, and Shane wouldn't tell her anything. But Cassie didn't care about what Ian chose to do with his time, as long as it didn't involve Shane. They were currently in a new safe house. Cassie assumed that they'd be moving again soon. They seemed to return feeling compromised whenever Alex or Ian went on a supply run. Perhaps it was an innate feeling that someone might recognize them, or possibly they were followed. Whatever that instinctive feeling, they wouldn't ignore it. They wouldn't chance anything.

They'd only been in the current house for four days. PJ would say it was by far the most spacious and 'upscale'. Apparently, the previous owner, a man Lily healed two years ago from a deadly brain tumor, had spent ample time and money on a high-tech security system; one that seemed to please all the men of the house. With five bedrooms and three bathrooms, it allowed for more privacy. It had a kitchen that Kate could enjoy cooking in. Cassie had learned that her aunt could feel at home in any kitchen with non-stick pans and a dishwasher. But she was happiest in a kitchen with lots of counter space and dual ovens.

Kate seemed different the past few days. She'd been quieter and less chipper. Cassie wondered if Danny was finalizing the move to Scotland. He'd been doing a lot of planning, making new arrangements. After Cassie talked with Danny, she learned there was always a tremendous amount involved with safely relocating. Danny seemed eager to leave the U.S., as did everyone else, including Kate, so she wasn't sure what was weighing on her aunt's mind.

***

Blocking PJ's punch, Cassie stepped forward, kicking him in the leg. It was not a hard kick but enough to send PJ off-balance. Her mind was wandering too much. She wasn't staying focused on the fight. PJ quickly regained his footing, trying to sweep her legs. She jumped back, kicking her leg again but added a quick uppercut this time.

PJ noticed how much quicker and stronger she'd become in four weeks. She was petite but had strong legs and knew how to use them. Shane had told her that if she strengthened her core, the power of her kicks could take down a giant. "Bet I can hold a plank longer than you." PJ enjoyed challenges with his sister. He liked that she was as competitive by nature as he was. He wanted to strengthen his core as well. He'd been practicing the plank since she'd held hers for two minutes longer.

Cassie laughed. "You can still do way more push-ups than me. Can't you be satisfied with that?" She dropped into the plank position beside her brother. She reached one arm out and playfully pushed him over. Their training together had given them an unspoken connection, and their friendship had become comforting. She was learning that she had more similarities with her brother than just her hair.

Shane approached them, shaking his head. "You'll never beat her, PJ." He handed each of them a bottle of water. "I think Cassie holds some national record or something."

Completely out of breath, PJ collapsed. Cassie gulped down the water. "The plank is easy." She loved rubbing that in, as she glanced at PJ lying face down on the grass. Shane laughed, then grabbed her around the waist.

"Kate and Danny have something they want to share with us. They told me to tell you and PJ to come inside."

"Is everything okay?" She wondered if Danny had finally finished the plans to move safely to Scotland. "Are we moving to another safe house?" She watched as PJ stood, stretching out his arms. She glanced around the yard and realized Lily may have planted the hydrangeas for nothing. Of course, the gardening she'd done was for her enjoyment, but still it seemed a shame to grow something without having the opportunity to enjoy it.

Shane took her hand. "Let's go inside and see what's up."

The moment Cassie opened the French doors, she gasped. Joy and immense surprise immediately overwhelmed her. "Amy!" She darted around the kitchen chairs and flew into her friend's arms. "I can't believe you're here!"

"We missed you so much." Amy felt tears welling in her eyes. She'd been so worried about her friend.

Andrew lifted Cassie off her feet in a tight hug. He smelled like tomato sauce, which delighted her even more. "I can't believe you're really here." She kissed his cheek, feeling a slight patch of stubble.

"We're sorry we didn't tell you they were coming, but we've

learned that until people arrive safely, it's better not to know anything." Lily had been on pins and needles, knowing that if anything had happened to them on the way, Cassie would be devastated. She was feeling emotional at the happiness on her daughter's face. "Amy and Andrew will be moving to Scotland too, but they can't come with us at the same time. They're going to stay here until we arrive in Scotland first. Then Alex will bring them over." The house's security system would make it easier to keep Cassie's friends safe, and Ian was choosing to stay behind, remaining in the house until he could decide his next move.

Shane hugged Amy and Andrew. He had been in contact with his dad during their trip, so he knew that luckily things had gone smoothly.

Cassie turned to him, folding her arms across her chest. "When your dad left last week, you wouldn't tell me where he was going. But you knew, didn't you?" It was Ian who went to retrieve her friends.

"Yes." Shane put up his hands in surrender. "But don't be mad, we wanted it to be a surprise, and—"

"I don't like to announce things before they happen, because I've learned that can jinx it." Ian learned from many past missions that getting the job done first is best. He was relieved he'd been able to retrieve Amy and Andrew without any complications.

"Julie and Caleb didn't want to come." Amy suspected they might change their minds in the future, and she was pleased that Ian had told them they had the option at any time.

"It's okay," Ian added quickly. "They're being looked after. I think if A.S.A. or Twin Seekers were going to pose a problem, they already would have. But just in case, we'll keep an eye on them."

Andrew glanced at the big bowl of pasta Kate had placed on the counter. "They're good, though. Julie's gaining weight."

Everyone laughed. "She eats all the time." Amy elbowed Andrew. "Like someone else I know."

Being reunited with her friends was a dream come true. A weight was lifted, knowing she wouldn't have to worry about their safety. Cassie examined Amy, noticing that she'd also put on a few pounds and cut her hair much shorter. She wore mascara, which made her brown eyes wider, and her lip gloss was pretty. Her red shorts fit snug around her waist. She wore a loose-fitting gray T-shirt that matched the color of her sandals. Andrew's face was fuller, though his body didn't look much different.

"I've got lunch ready." Kate was pleased to feed everyone. She had prepared sinfully high-calorie cheesy bacon pasta for everyone. She knew Amy and Andrew would be arriving at noon, and they'd be hungry.

"Wait!" Amy shouted excitedly, placing her hand on Cassie's arm. "I've got a gift I can't wait to give you!" She glanced at Ian as he nodded his head. He walked to the hallway, where the gift was leaning against the stairwell.

After a moment, Ian returned to the room holding a large canvas. The front of the canvas faced his body. Amy quickly ran over to take it from him. "Close your eyes, Cass," she said. Her tone was thrilling, which made Cassie laugh.

Amy turned the painting around to face everyone in the room. "Okay, open your eyes!"

Orange, brilliant lavender and perfect gray and yellow clouds filled the sky painting. Below was the road lined with trees painted so well they appeared almost real. "Oh, Amy." Cassie's eyes filled with tears. It was the most beautiful painting she'd ever seen. "Your talent is incredible."

"It's our sky." The sky she and Cassie had both admired before they were separated.

"She only painted it about twenty times until she got it exactly how she wanted it." Andrew felt proud of his girl. "Sometimes I couldn't pull her away from the paint."

Amy nudged him playfully. "It had to be right. It was like our first real day in the real world. The first sunset we got to see together without the dome."

Cassie pulled Amy into another hug. "I love it. I'll cherish it forever."

Lily saw Patrick and knew he also felt the joy of Amy and Andrew's presence. Cassie's happiness was important to them. They met Amy and Andrew and spoke with them while Cassie was training with PJ. Lily was impressed with them and the mature way they spoke. They were handling their situation well. Perhaps years of living in the orphanage helped them be agreeable. If they'd chosen not to come with Ian or resisted going to Scotland, Cassie wouldn't have the peace of mind knowing that her friends could be part of her life. It also made keeping them safe a lot easier. Lily learned long ago that it was never a good idea to stay in one place too long. It was probably just a matter of time before someone discovered the kids in Colorado.

Leaning back, Amy spotted Cassie's tiny beaded necklace. "You're still wearing this?" She felt a lump in her throat. She had missed her more than she thought possible. She had liked the apartment and the greenhouse work in Colorado, but she'd wanted to be with Cassie. She wanted more from life than their daily routine. When Ian arrived and presented the details of his plan, the opportunity to see and do more made her feel giddy with anticipation.

"I'll never take it off." Cassie glanced back at the painting in awe. "And now I'll never go anywhere without my painting. It looks so real." She noticed PJ was staring at Amy. "Oh, Amy, have you met everyone? This is my brother, Patrick Jason. Or you can call him PJ, or—"

"Probably Jason." Kate laughed, setting napkins on the counter.

"We all met when you were outside," Lily said, as PJ shook hands with Amy and Andrew. "Alex and Laura will be here shortly." Alex was always doing perimeter checks. "Let's all grab some food. We can visit in the family room."

Ian told Amy and Andrew about Laura Reynolds and how she was staying with the family. Amy looked forward to seeing her again. She followed Shane to the counter to get food, while Cassie leaned her painting against the wall. "We've got so much to catch up on. I've been reading about A.S.A. and the Twin Seekers. It's hard to believe I'm best friends with the daughter of the most famous woman on earth." Her eyes landed on Lily, who appeared to be a beautiful woman.

"Cassie, you're just as famous now. Your photo is always on the news." Andrew dug right into his plate of food.

Shane lifted his brow, wanting to remind everyone. "That's not a good thing."

"We—"

"Breach!" Alex called out urgently as he and Laura quickly flung open the front door. "Been spotted!" He told Ian as Laura ran toward the kitchen. He quickly deadbolted the door.

Ian and Shane both pulled their guns out from behind their backs. Patrick opened the pantry door, revealing a secret entrance that led under the house and out to the backyard. It would open in the vacant lot behind the house—land that the previous owner purchased for his underground bunker. The road was nearby, where Alex and Ian had parked a Windmobile two days ago. Protocol was followed.

Shane took Cassie's hand and began to lead her. "Wait, my painting!"

"I've got it, sweetheart," her father called out. "Just get going."

"A painting is easier to move than horses," PJ muttered, as Lily set her hand on his shoulder when he began to descend the stairs.

"Wow, less than an hour in your company and we're already on the run." Amy followed behind her friend. "Guess nothing has changed with you guys."

Andrew glanced at his plate of food longingly before following everyone through the secret door. "That pasta was delicious." He didn't get to finish it.

No one outside knew the house had a secret escape tunnel. Many homes had underground bunkers because, after the terrorist attacks, people didn't want to breathe the air. The tunnel led to a bunker, which had a storm door to the outside.

Shane climbed a set of stairs. "Wait here." He pushed open the door. He surveyed the quiet lot. Just a few trees lined the yard. The road was visible. The house they'd left was a few yards away, blocked by thick pine trees. "It looks safe."

"Send the drone out." Alex gently moved past his family to hand Shane a small bumblebee. He used the remote control to scan the area.

The bunker was dark, except for the flashlights Ian and Patrick held. Lily rested her hand on Cassie's shoulder. "It's going to be okay. You know that, right?" This was never the life she wanted for her children. But soon they'd be in Scotland. She knew there was always hope for a more secure life. She'd had years of security at the ranch. Danny was ready to move them, so this was only a minor setback.

Cassie turned slightly to look at her mom and everyone else. "I know." She wasn't feeling her usual panic. She was concerned, but she wasn't overcome with fear or anxiety. Everyone she loved was beside her, including Amy and Andrew. That was all that mattered.

After Shane and Alex gave the okay to leave the shelter, they all piled into the wind mobile, slightly out of breath from the run. The wind mobile was round and meant to seat no more than ten, but Amy and Andrew sat on the floor in the middle. Andrew pulled his legs up to his chest so he wouldn't hit the central computer. Alex squatted beside him, punching coordinates into the GPS. All twelve scrunched together, elbow to elbow.

Laura squeezed beside Danny and took the moment to say hello to Amy and Andrew. She set her hand on Amy's knee. "Glad you guys could join the team." That's how she'd come to think of Alex's family.

"We're happy to see you, Mrs. Reynolds." Amy thought her teacher looked different but great. She wore black pants with many pockets and a form-fitting white blouse. It was feminine and pretty. Her chestnut-colored hair was down, with spiral curls just below her shoulders.

"Call me Laura. I'm no longer Mrs. Reynolds." She was divorcing her husband, and no longer their teacher. She glanced at Alex with a small smile.

"Next safe house is twenty minutes away." Alex moved to sit closer to Laura and took her hand. "We're good, everyone. No need to worry now." He felt confident they weren't being tracked. Only two men who'd been snooping around the property had seen him. He wasn't sure who they were, but they'd got a good look at him, and one had reached for his phone. Alex had felt it was time to leave that house anyway. He glanced at the canvas on Patrick's lap. "Nice painting."

"Thanks." Amy observed Cassie's family. She noticed that Alex held Laura's hand. Cassie's parents had their arms linked, and Kate had her hand resting softly on PJ's knee. Danny stared at his small tablet, but his other hand rested over Kate's leg. Ian wore the same serious look she always saw on his face, but he appeared comfortable beside his son. She turned her head to stare at Cassie as Shane kissed her cheek. There was a lot of love and affection in the crammed Windmobile. These were all good people; anyone could see they were, in fact, a team.

Ian and Alex discussed their next move. Patrick suggested that Ian and Danny secure the house first because they were unknown on social media or among the factions.

"You all seem pretty at ease." Amy felt safe now. She had no family of her own, except for Cassie and Andrew. She was happy for her friend. What a new life this was for her.

"We're used to this, honey." Kate set warm, understanding eyes on the kids. "I just wish we'd gotten to eat first."

"Me too!" Andrew blurted out.

Everyone laughed.

Chapter 40

October in Scotland brought fantastic autumn colors, but wet and cool temperatures came with it. As the wind whipped leaves from the swaying branches, Cassie tucked her hands in her pockets, feeling a shiver. She watched the leaves whirling in the air, trying to stay together. The larger leaves seemed like parents, while the smaller ones landed on or beside them. Even as they danced on the ground, they remained close together. Cassie wondered if anyone else noticed how leaves piled up, resembling a family. She leaned back, breathing deeply. Shane came up behind her and wrapped his arms around her waist.

"What are you thinking about?"

"It's silly." She would have laughed, but she was feeling nostalgic. Not so much missing life in the United States, but thinking about it. She remembered how the warm August sun felt on her skin the day she and Shane walked to Jackson's horrible shack in Mississippi. She remembered the night she and PJ foolishly tried to help. The smell of the dogs as they bit into PJ's flesh, and how weak she'd felt from dehydration. She recalled the underground tunnels, the Windmobile, and the fear of running from the men chasing her. She remembered how the forest surrounding the ranch smelled. The air here had a clean, potent aroma. She'd never want to breathe anything else ever again. Oak trees lined the rolling hills as far as her eyes could see, with mountains appearing like a blurry painting in the far distance.

"Nothing you think is silly." He spun her around so he could see her eyes. The eyes he absolutely loved. "Tell me."

"I was just remembering all the things we've been through.

How different this country is, and how much I love the smell of the air."

"No radiation here."

She nodded. "It's only been a week, and I'm already in love with it."

"More than the other places? The ranch?"

"More than anyplace." She glanced toward the house. She saw PJ wearing his red jacket, heading to the barn that would eventually hold his horses as soon as Price could arrange their transport.

Shane sighed, frowned a little as he touched her face. "You can't get attached, Cass. PJ learned the hard way that you can't love a place too much. You might have to leave here someday."

"I know. I'm more in love with my family, and the idea that each day is a new possibility. My mom continues to warn us that peace of mind and security can change anytime. I know she's right. I'm happy right now. I'm happy with this." She leaned in and kissed Shane softly on the lips. "Aunt Kate is going to keep this baby. I can feel it."

"She's glowing. She's feeling pretty confident about it now."

"She was scared." Kate hadn't seemed like herself before they left for Scotland, and now Cassie knew why. She was pregnant and terrified to hope. "They lost all the other ones. But I think she's right, Shane. When I healed her, it healed whatever caused her body to miscarry. She said she has felt different ever since."

"My dad's knee pain is gone, and Danny and your father haven't had an ounce of arthritis. You do heal people in many ways, Cass."

"I want her to experience the joy of motherhood. They deserve it so much. Kate's already proven to be a great mom and Danny..." Cassie's voice caught in her throat as she struggled to express her feelings, her eyes glistening with emotion. "I've missed out on so much, Shane. Every day with my family feels like a gift."

He gently caressed her face. "You've got me, too."

She leaned in to kiss him. "I've got it all." Her heart was overflowing with gratitude and love.

295

www.ingramcontent.com/pod-product-compliance
Lightning Source LLC
Chambersburg PA
CBHW020234260626
47156CB00002B/672